PRAISE

"Bardsley launches her Harper Landing series with a touching, chaste romance that sees two struggling people find solace in each other . . . Their shared path from heartache to happiness is sure to inspire."
—*Publishers Weekly*

"Once I started reading it, I could not put it down."
—*Harlequin Junkie*

"Authentic, emotional, and heartwarming, *Sweet Bliss* is the kind of read that you'll want to savor like dessert. With characters you'll cheer for and a romance that will make you swoon, Harper Landing will quickly feel like home."
—Laurie Elizabeth Flynn, bestselling author of
The Girls Are All So Nice Here

"This sweet, heartwarming love story feels like a breath of fresh air, transporting the reader to a small-town haven where people band together, the bad guy never wins, and you can count on happy endings. A feel-good beach read."
—Kathleen Basi, author of *A Song for the Road*

"As sweet as the title suggests but packing an emotional punch, *Sweet Bliss* is a heartwarming, swoony romance that will sweep you away and stay with you long after you turn the last page. You'll fall in love with Aaron, Julia, baby Jack, and all of Harper Landing, a cozy community where everybody knows your name. Julia and Aaron each have their own challenges and past heartaches to overcome, and watching them not only fall for each other but also bring out the best in each other makes for a beautiful story. Bardsley has written a sweet page-turner, and I can't wait for her next novel, *Good Catch*!"

—Elissa Grossell Dickey, author of *The Speed of Light: A Novel*

"The chemistry between Julia and Aaron is palpable. Their hearts are big and broken and bursting with attraction to each other. I loved watching the two fall in love."

—Casey Dembowski, author of *When We're Thirty*

PRAISE FOR *GOOD CATCH*

"Bardsley returns to small-town Harper Landing (after *Sweet Bliss*) with a charming, uproarious romance . . . As Marlo and Ben navigate knee-slappingly disastrous dates, their walls break down and they discover what they've been searching for. Their humorous transformation from enemies to lovers is a delight."

—*Publishers Weekly*

"A charming small-town romance . . . fantastic and hilarious."

—*Harlequin Junkie*, Top Pick

"Bardsley is a talented writer with a gift for conveying all the foibles and charms of small-town life. Perfect for those who enjoyed her charming debut, *Sweet Bliss*, Bardsley's standout sophomore effort is a wonderful romance with equal parts humor and heart."

—Elizabeth Everett, author of *A Lady's Formula for Love*

"Finally a novel captures the complex ways that dyslexia continues to inform an adult life."

—Kyle Redford, teacher and education writer at the Yale Center for Dyslexia and Creativity

"With sharp writing and well-defined characters, Jennifer Bardsley takes readers back to the world of Harper Landing. *Good Catch*, the second book in the series, is a sweet enemies-to-lovers romance that is equal parts heartwarming and hilarious."

—Kate Pembrooke, author of *Not the Kind of Earl You Marry*

the
history
of us

ALSO BY JENNIFER BARDSLEY

The Harper Landing Series

Sweet Bliss
Good Catch

Other Titles

Genesis Girl
Damaged Goods

Writing as Louise Cypress

Shifter's Wish
Shifter's Kiss
Shifter's Desire
Bite Me
Hunt Me
Slay Me
Slayer Academy: Secret Shifter
Mermaid Aboard
The Gift of Goodbye
Books, Boys, and Revenge
Narcosis Room
Quick Fix

the
history
of us

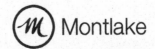

JENNIFER BARDSLEY

 Montlake

Text copyright © 2022 by Jennifer Bardsley
All rights reserved.

Published by Montlake, Seattle

www.apub.com

Amazon, the Amazon logo, and Montlake are trademarks of Amazon.com, Inc., or its affiliates.

ISBN-13: 9781662500954
ISBN-10: 1662500955

Cover design by Letitia Hasser

Printed in the United States of America

To my mom, for the incredible care and attention she showered upon my grandma.

CHAPTER ONE

The Owl's Nest smelled like lasagna and disinfectant. Andrea Wint didn't think it was a bad combination necessarily. It was four thirty in the afternoon, after all, and the residents would eat dinner in thirty minutes. Her father was fed comfort food and lived in a spotless environment. The caregivers were constantly wiping down high-traffic areas and tidying up after residents so they wouldn't trip. Wellness counselors scheduled games, exercise, and field trips. This was one of the best memory-care facilities in the greater Seattle area.

To Andrea, it was worth every penny, and she was grateful that they could afford it, knowing that not every family was so lucky. But she wished that her father could be anywhere but here, in a facility locked up tighter than Fort Knox, waiting for his body to fade away like his brain.

For a while, Tom Wint's Alzheimer's had progressed slowly enough that she and her mom had been able to care for him at home, but those days were gone.

"How was game time?" she asked him. They sat on a comfy couch by the window in the dayroom. An aquarium full of tropical fish hummed quietly next to them. "I saw on the schedule that you played chair volleyball this morning."

"Oh yeah, that. It was something." Tom looked down at his leather slippers. "Where are my shoes?"

"Back in your room. Do you want me to get them for you?"

"No. These slippers are nice. Lydia gave them to me for Christmas."

"I gave them to you last week. Not Mom." It didn't matter who had given him the slippers—not really—but Andrea felt like clarifying. Lydia Wint had moved on with her life. She still paid her husband's medical bills and kept in contact with his doctors, but she hadn't visited Tom in months, not since moving in with Roger, her boyfriend.

Andrea's stomach clenched when she thought about her mom and Roger. She could barely bring herself to text Lydia, let alone accept her invitation to dinner in Roger's penthouse overlooking Lake Washington. Yes, Tom's early-onset Alzheimer's disease was difficult on everyone, but it didn't mean you abandoned the person you loved and shacked up with your podiatrist.

"I love these slippers." Tom wiggled his feet. "They're so companionable."

"I'm glad they're *comfortable*," Andrea replied, gently correcting his error. Sometimes she didn't bother and let the word goofs slip past her, like dandelion fluff on a summer breeze. But usually, she did offer the correct word. Her father had once had a masterful vocabulary, and he would have wanted her to say something. At least, that was what Andrea thought he would have wanted.

"Look at that." She pointed at the heel of each slipper. "Your name is on those slippers, so you can always find them."

"Well, what do you know?" He peered down at his ankles. "*Tom Wint*. That's me."

"If you see someone else wearing slippers with your name on them, you can ask for them back." Andrea slipped a lock of golden-brown hair behind her ear.

"You're so smart." Tom squeezed her hand. "I'm glad you came. I haven't seen you in a while."

"I was here last night, Dad. And the night before." Her smile faded. "I come every afternoon to visit you before dinner." Andrea reached into her giant purse and pulled out a brochure. "I booked a new client today. My graphic design business is booming. This is the mock-up I did that landed me the job." Andrea pointed to pictures of teens in braces. "It's a chain of orthodontists. I'm designing their brochures and website update."

"That's great. Did you have braces?"

"I sure did. For two and a half years." Andrea pointed to her bottom incisor. "But now this one has become crooked again because I stopped wearing my retainer."

Tom peered into her mouth. "They look pretty straight to me."

"Thanks." Andrea put the trifold away since Tom didn't seem interested in reading it. "Have you been brushing your teeth?"

"I think so."

She'd need to double-check that with the floor manager.

Tom stared at her, his gaze unfocused, but he still wore a smile. Four-day-old stubble poked from his chin. "I better visit the john," he said.

"Okay. I'll be right here when you get back."

Tom stood and looked to the left and right. "Which way is it? I'm turned around."

"Your room's that way." Andrea pointed down the hall. "Find the door with your picture next to it." She didn't mention that there were multiple pictures of Tom in the shadow box next to his door—images of him at every age so that he'd be sure to recognize himself.

"Good idea." Tom took off at a brisk pace.

As soon as she saw her father safely enter his bedroom, Andrea hopped up from the couch and hurried over to the nurses' station in the corner of the room. Tom was supposed to receive an assisted shower and shave every other day, and she wanted to know why that hadn't happened. Not shaving was one thing, but if they were lying about her father bathing or brushing his teeth, she'd call the National Guard. Luckily, Huan was on duty. He was the head nurse, and Andrea had built a positive rapport with him.

"Hi, Huan," she said in what she hoped was a friendly manner. "What are your boys up to?"

"Keeping me busy, that's what." Huan grinned and put down the tablet he was reading. "Both of them are in Little League, and I have a game to get to as soon as I clock out tonight."

"Good thing it stopped raining." Andrea rested her elbow on the counter. "Question for you—I noticed my dad's beard was growing out. Could you please look in the records and find out when was the last time he had a shower and a shave?"

"Sure." Huan typed on the tablet. "Let's see. Today's Thursday, and it looks like he showered two days ago on Tuesday. Tom's on the schedule for another shower tonight. There's also a note saying the shave didn't happen because the sound of the electric razor bothered him."

"Oh. That's odd. Dad always loved a clean shave."

Huan looked up from the tablet. "I know it's scary when you're used to seeing your parent look a certain way and they change. But you have to pick your battles."

Andrea sighed. "I understand that. It just seems like I don't win any of them now."

"There's a caregiver support group Wednesday night that—"

"No, thank you."

"Are you sure?" Huan raised his eyebrows.

"I have all the support I need." Andrea walked away from the desk, her conscience prickling. Had she fibbed? No, she decided. She hadn't. Her best friend, Heidi Karlsson, was always there for her. That counted.

"Help!" someone shouted. "It hurts!"

At first her brain didn't register that it was Tom crying out, but when he called for help again, Andrea ran full speed toward his room.

"Resident in need of assistance," Huan's voice blared over the intercom. "Room Two."

She found Tom in the bathroom standing in front of the sink. His fingers were stuck inside the metal paper towel dispenser, and blood trickled down his wrist. "Oh no!" Andrea yelped, feeling the pain like it was her own injured knuckles. "Dad, what happened?"

"Get them out," he cried. "Please."

"I will. It'll be okay. I promise." She took a closer look at his injury right as Huan entered the room too.

"Hi, Tom," said Huan. "What's the matter?"

"The edge of the dispenser is slicing into his skin," said Andrea. "If we move his fingers, the cut will get worse."

"It looks like you accidentally put your fingers up where the towels go, huh?" Huan asked.

"This isn't right," said Tom. "It hurts."

"I'll get our handyman," said Huan. "Cade will get you out of this jam in no time." He hurried away.

"Hear that, Dad? Help is on the way." Andrea patted his back and smiled bravely, even though her heart was fracturing into a million pieces. How had her father, the smartest man she knew, forgotten how to use paper towels?

"I'm scared," Tom whimpered. "Why did this happen to me?"

"I don't know. But I'm right here with you. Dad, look at me. It's going to be okay."

She could do this. She wouldn't cry. Tom needed her to be strong. Andrea would call upon every ounce of creativity in her bones to calm her father's fear. She would make small talk and keep his mind off his predicament.

"It rained hard this morning," she said. "Did you go into the courtyard when the sun came out?"

"Huh?" Tom looked back at her blankly. "There's a courtyard?"

"Yes. It's full of flowers. Well, daffodils at least. That's the only thing blooming right now." The lump that had formed in Andrea's throat threatened to bring forth a torrent of tears. She blinked them back and smiled harder. "I love daffodils. Don't you? They're so yellow and cheerful."

"It hurts. It hurts like hell."

"I know, Dad. I'm sorry. Help is coming, and I'm right here with you. Did you watch television today?"

"No." Tom shook his head. "I don't like TV."

"Books are always better than TV," Andrea said. "That's what you used to tell me when I was little. You've given me great advice my entire life."

Except for now, when she needed it most.

"Hello there, Mr. Tom," drawled a friendly voice.

Andrea looked over her shoulder and saw a handsome man with blond hair and a million-watt smile. "You must be Cade," she said. "I've seen you before but didn't know your name."

"Yup. That's me."

"My fingers!" Tom wept.

"Easy there now. It'll be all right." Cade set his toolbox on the ground before inspecting the towel dispenser. "Don't you worry one bit. A Phillips screwdriver ought to do the trick. Four screws and *pop*. You'll be free."

"I'm sorry," said Tom. "I'm so sorry to bother you."

"You're not bothering me," said Cade. "In fact, you saved me from unclogging a toilet over in assisted living. I owe you one."

"See, Dad? Cade's here. It's going to be okay."

"It sure is," said Cade as he selected a screwdriver. "Hey, aren't you the coin lady?"

"I am." Relief flooded her soul as Andrea remembered what was in her purse. She still had two tricks up her sleeve—or rather, her pocket and handbag. "Look what I brought," she said, pulling out the steel penny. "I thought you might like to see this." It was a 1943 steel cent, rusted so badly that the wheat on the back was barely visible.

"A steelie!" Tom's eyes lit up, and his tears stopped. "Can I hold it?" He held out his free hand.

"You sure can." Andrea dropped the coin into the palm of his untrapped hand.

"Do you know what this is?" Tom asked.

"I have no idea." Cade snuck in beside them and began unscrewing the dispenser from the wall.

"Dad, why don't you tell us about it?" Andrea moved to the other side of the sink so Cade would have more room to work.

"It's a 1943 penny made with steel and a thin layer of zinc." Tom stared down at it. "See that letter *D*? This one was minted in Denver. It was World War II, you see, and copper was needed for the war effort, so they used steel instead."

"I didn't know they used steel to make coins." Cade dropped a screw onto the counter.

"War impacts everything," said Tom. "Even numismatics."

"Numis what?" Cade asked as another screw came loose. "Hey, Tom's daughter, would you mind holding the dispenser for me while I unscrew the last ones?"

"Sure." Andrea climbed up on the counter, put her foot in the sink, and held the metal box in place. "My name's Andrea, by the way. Thanks so much for helping us."

"My pleasure," said Cade.

Tom still gazed at the penny. "Numismatics is the study of coins. I have a steelie just like this that I keep in my pocket, only it's in better shape. Sometimes coin collectors do that; they keep an inexpensive coin in their pocket just for kicks." He put the coin onto the counter, patted the elastic waistband of his pants, and tried to stuff his fingers in a nonexistent pocket. "That's odd. I don't know where mine is at the moment."

It's right in front of you, Andrea wanted to say. *I show this penny to you every day.* It was too dangerous for her father to keep a choking hazard with him. Even if he knew better than to eat it, another resident might not. "You know a lot about coins," Andrea said, prompting him to keep talking.

"Sure do." Tom nodded. "I've collected them my whole life."

"Darn," said Cade. "These last two screws don't want to cooperate. I'll get my electric screwdriver."

If the electric razor had bothered Tom, how would her father react next to the drill? Andrea said a quick prayer.

Tom gave the penny back to her. "I'd keep this someplace safe if I were you. It's not worth much, but it does have history."

"I bet it does." Using one hand to hold up the box, Andrea quickly pocketed the coin and then put both hands back on the dispenser.

"You can let it go for a sec." Cade fiddled with his electric screwdriver. "I'm still setting up."

"Great." Andrea rolled her shoulders back and rested against the mirror. The tension that had crept into her neck eased slightly.

"Do you have any other coins you want to know about?" Tom asked.

"I do." Andrea climbed down from the counter and unzipped her purse. Tom's cognitive skills were crumbling, but at least he could still talk about his favorite hobby. Numismatics was his only hobby, actually. Between work and family life, her father had never had much free time until now. "I have this gold coin I was hoping you would look at," she said.

"Real gold?" Cade asked.

"That's right."

Tom straightened. "Let's see it."

Andrea dug into her purse until her fingertips brushed against the plastic flip coin holder. It made her nervous carrying a coin worth $2,000, which was why the rest of Tom's collection was back home.

Before she'd moved into the blue house on the bay, she'd hired Karlsson Construction to hide a safe behind a wall in her living room. Heidi was the designer, and Dustin, Andrea's high school boyfriend, was the contractor. As awkward as it was asking Dustin to do anything on her behalf, Andrea had to admit that he did fine work. Nobody sitting in the living room would ever know there was $100,000 worth of double eagles behind a family portrait.

Now, opening the plastic flip and seeing the double eagle sparkle in the fluorescent light, Andrea knew that the most precious thing about this piece of precious metal was that Tom still recognized it.

"What type of coin is this?" she asked, waiting for his thrill of happiness.

Tom whistled. "Wow." He wiped the fingers of his free hand on his pants before picking the coin up carefully by the edges. "This right here is a Saint-Gaudens double eagle, named after the designer."

"That sounds fancy," said Cade. "Okay, Andrea. I'm ready for you to hold the box again."

"On it." Andrea climbed into position and felt glad that Tom was so engrossed in the double eagle that he was no longer upset about his trapped fingers. "What type of condition do you think that coin's in?" she asked.

Tom squinted at it. "Hard to say, but considering it's from 1909, I'd say pretty good. This one here appears to be almost uncirculated."

Cade buzzed the drill, and another screw popped out. "How much is that pretty thing worth?" he asked.

Tom looked up. "Now? Or face value?" He was so engrossed in the double eagle that he didn't complain about the electric drill.

"What's the difference?" Cade asked.

Andrea grinned. As Tom launched into his explanation of the gold standard, bullion, and obsolete coin denominations, she focused on the cadence of his voice and how he spoke with such authority on a subject he knew so much about. This was the father she had grown up with, wise and knowledgeable, kind but also loving. This was why she held on to his collection of double eagles instead of selling them to pay off her mortgage. She didn't have siblings or a mother who still cared, but she had thirty-seven gold coins that could make her father act almost like the man who raised her, at least for a little while.

"There," said Cade as he pulled off the towel dispenser. "I might not have followed that stuff about toning impacting value, but you're free."

"Thank you, sir," said Tom.

"Yes! Thank you so much." Andrea scrambled off the counter and grabbed toilet paper to press against Tom's bleeding knuckles. She flashed Cade a grateful smile. "You're officially my hero."

"That's what I'm here for." Cade put his tools away. "I better scoot, though. I still have that toilet in assisted living to unclog, and my wife and girls will be here soon to have dinner with my parents."

"You're married?" Andrea asked, annoyed at the squeak in her voice. Of course Cade was married. Nobody that handsome and charming would be single.

"Sure am." Cade clicked his toolbox shut. "My parents moved into the assisted living wing after my dad broke his hip. They've been there a couple of years now—that's actually how I got this job. It's perfect for me because I used to be a locksmith, and the assisted living wing needs new keys every time a resident moves in."

"How long have you worked here?" Andrea asked.

"Nine months." Cade stood. "My jerkwad brother-in-law fired me from my old job because he couldn't handle that homeowners liked me better than him."

"That's awful. He sounds like an egomaniac."

"Egomaniac is right." Cade shook his head. "But now I'm here at the Owl's Nest and get to hang out with cool people like your father." He flashed a thumbs-up. "Take it easy, Mr. Tom. I love chatting with you, but next time let's do it over a slice of apple pie."

"There's pie?" Tom asked. He gave the double eagle back to Andrea. "You should keep this locked in a safe. I have one in my house hidden behind a picture."

"That's right!" Andrea hugged him, thrilled that he remembered that detail from her childhood home. "I have one in my house too."

"I'll tell Huan that you'll need the first aid kit," said Cade as he left.

"Good idea," said Andrea. "Thank you again."

Later, after Tom's wound was cleaned up, Andrea escorted him to the dining room. Dinner was already in progress, but Tom still had plenty of time to eat. She kissed him on his cheek and walked away. The paper towel rescue meant that she'd missed her usual ferry, and she decided to use the restroom before she walked to the ferry terminal and waited for the next one.

The Owl's Nest preferred that guests used a public restroom in the assisted living wing, for hygiene reasons. The two sides were connected by a locked door with a keypad and cryptic riddle. *"How many months are in a year? How many days are in a week? How many letters are in Jitterbug?"* Andrea felt peace as soon as she entered the assisted living area, which was akin to a posh hotel. After she used the restroom, she came into the lobby to help herself to piping hot tea and cookies.

"Daddy!" a young voice called.

Biting into a snickerdoodle, Andrea turned her head and saw a small girl with short blonde hair run into Cade's arms. What cute kids he had. The older daughter stood next to them, wearing rain boots and a pink coat. Cade swooped both girls into his arms and lifted them in the air. But when Andrea recognized Cade's wife, she almost choked on her bite of cookie.

A short coughing fit later, Andrea sipped her tea and burned her tongue. Could this evening get any weirder? A few minutes ago, she'd been ogling Cade and calling him her hero, only to discover that he was married to Heidi and Dustin's little sister. Andrea hadn't seen Leanne in ages, but she'd recognize her anywhere.

"Do I know you?" Leanne asked. "You look familiar. Didn't you babysit me or something?"

Andrea gave a nod. "Hi, Leanne," she said. "That's right. I'm friends with Heidi."

"That's it!" Leanne palmed her forehead. "And Dustin, too, right?"

"Well . . ." Andrea winced. Even now, eighteen years later, the thought of Dustin hurt like a gut punch. One minute they'd been spinning around the dance floor together at the Seattle Tennis Club on prom night; the next Dustin was dumping her and arranging for a classmate to drive her home.

"Your brother, the jerkwad?" Cade raised his eyebrows.

"Uncle Dusty says you shouldn't call people names," the older girl said.

"In this case it's warranted," said Leanne.

"I *did* babysit you when you were little," said Andrea. "We played with Lincoln Logs together."

"I love those things." Leanne smiled. Her light hair coloring reminded Andrea of the oldest Karlsson sibling, Nathan, who owned a pizzeria in Port Inez. "Heidi mentioned that you'd moved to Port Inez but didn't say why."

"It's so I can visit my dad easier. Now I can walk on the ferry to Harper Landing each afternoon, visit my dad, and sail home in less time than it took me to battle Seattle work traffic."

"Traffic is the worst," said Leanne. "I'd stay and chat, but my mother-in-law freaks out if we're late. It was good seeing you."

"You too. But before you go, I have to tell you that your husband did a really good deed tonight. He rescued my father."

"Really?" Leanne hugged Cade and rested her head on his shoulder. "Aww, I'm not surprised. He's my personal superman."

"What'd you do, Daddy?" asked the littlest girl.

"I'll tell you all about it at dinner," said Cade. "I promise."

"It's quite the story." Andrea checked her watch. "I better go, too, or I'll miss the ferry."

"Thanks for the Lincoln Log fun," said Leanne.

"Anytime," Andrea said with a wave and left the building via the revolving front doors. Exiting the assisted living wing was easy, unlike the memory-care side with its locks, riddles, and key codes. The crisp March weather made Andrea shiver, but she welcomed fresh air. She zipped up her raincoat and pulled gloves out of her pocket. With each step away from the facility, she felt freer, like a bird escaping a cage. But guilt washed over her next—and shame at her relief that the visit was over.

CHAPTER TWO

"Slow down, Leanne, and start from the beginning." Dustin leaned against a doorframe and concentrated on what his younger sister was telling him over the phone.

"Cade's missing," Leanne said in a hysterical tone that was not like her. No, Leanne was as steady as they came. The wildest thing she'd ever done was marry Cade three months and two days after she met him—and six months before giving birth to their older daughter, Kendal. "Cade was supposed to pick the girls up from school this afternoon while I worked at the pizzeria, like I do every Friday afternoon, but he didn't show up. The school secretary called me in a huff."

Dustin bit back the words he wanted to say. The thought of Kendal and little Jane waiting in the freezing-cold rain for their irresponsible father brought forth every curse word in Dustin's considerable vocabulary, but he chose not to speak them aloud. "Are the girls okay?" he asked instead.

"They're fine. Nathan's feeding them pizza by the fire. But what about Cade? He hasn't called or texted, and I don't know where he is." Leanne took a deep breath before her words came out in a rush. "What if he's bleeding in a ditch somewhere?"

Goofing off is more like it, Dustin thought, but he didn't want to upset her. Leanne was the baby of the family, eleven years his junior, and he'd do anything to spare her feelings.

"Cade probably lost track of time and forgot to charge his phone," he said. "What time was he supposed to come home from work today?"

"Fridays are his day off."

Dustin looked through the unfinished great room to the skeletal kitchen he was remodeling. Karlsson Construction was the best in the business this side of Puget Sound. For a while, Cade had worked for them, too, until Dustin had caught him stealing copper pipes from a jobsite. That combined with Heidi's hunch that Cade had been skimming money from the communal coffee-and-donuts fund they kept in a box next to the snack station meant that Cade was too untrustworthy to wear the Karlsson Construction logo.

"When did you last see him?" Dustin asked.

"This morning. But now it's past six, and he's still not home."

"Maybe he picked up an extra shift at the Owl's Nest and forgot to tell you?"

"Nope. I checked. I called my in-laws too. We were just over there last night. They haven't seen him either. I was hoping you would know something."

"Me?"

"There must be something you could do."

"I wish there was."

"Okay." Leanne drew the word out. "Maybe he's stuck running errands and wasn't able to call. Sorry I bothered you."

But the way she said that troubled Dustin immensely. Leanne never sought out help or asked for favors. She clung to her pride like moss on pavement, especially after Dustin and Heidi had fired Cade thirteen months ago. It didn't make sense that she would think something was terribly wrong simply because Cade forgot to pick the girls up, no matter how egregious that was. It's not like it was the first time Cade had left his children in the lurch. Something was up; Dustin could smell it. Dread pooled in his stomach. Suddenly, as if driven by a sixth sense, he knew exactly what was bothering him about this conversation.

"Did you put your settlement money into a separate account like I told you to?" he asked.

"What's that got to do with anything?"

"Did you?" Dustin rolled his shoulders back and stared through the front window into the trees. This property had a forest view on one side and a panorama of Puget Sound on the other. "Are you positive Cade's not at the Clearwater Casino right now pissing away your money?"

"Of course he's not," Leanne snapped. "Cade wouldn't do that to me."

Except that he had—many times, in fact—and each time Leanne had to pick up extra shifts at Port Pizza, the pizzeria their older brother, Nathan, owned in town.

"You turned twenty-five last month," said Dustin.

"Thanks, Captain Obvious. I didn't know how old I was."

"That means—"

"I know what it means. Thanks for nothing." She hung up without another word.

"Crap." Dustin pulled the phone away from his ear. He knew he had handled that poorly. But now that Leanne was old enough to access her trust fund from the lawsuit over their parents' deaths, he worried that Cade's fingers would itch for that money.

Nineteen years ago, their parents had driven to Seattle to attend a Seahawks game. The tickets had been expensive, but Crystal and Josh had been huge fans who were celebrating their twenty-fifth wedding anniversary. On the way to the stadium, their old Ford truck had broken down along the waterfront, right in front of a building under construction. There, by where the Seattle Great Wheel was now, they had waited for a tow truck to come. But before help could arrive, tragedy had struck. In one fatal blow, a construction crane had collapsed and killed Crystal, Josh, and a family of three from Ohio parked next to them.

"What's going on?" Heidi asked as she came downstairs. A strip of ancient wallpaper stuck to her flannel shirt, and her jeans were covered in dust.

"That was Leanne. Cade neglected to pick the girls up from school. Have you heard from him?"

"No, but it's payday Friday. He's probably celebrating by gambling their rent money at the blackjack table."

"That's what I was thinking."

"I'm sure he'll turn up. He always does." Heidi glided into the kitchen and floated her hands out as she spun around. "Let's talk about this kitchen. I told you Shaker cabinets would look amazing, and I was right. Now all we need to do is install the quartz and slide in the new appliances."

"And hook up the gas, finish the backsplash, hang the chandeliers, and finish the edge work," Dustin grumbled. "And what's this *we* business? You don't do any of that labor."

Heidi grinned. "I'll tell you where to hang the lights. That's something. And they're not chandeliers; they're pendant lights. This is our twenty-first flip. You should know the terminology by now."

Dustin did know the difference, but he wouldn't say so. Riling up Heidi was his defense against her being so demanding. Heidi was only a year and a half older, but she had used that as an excuse to tell him what to do for thirty-six years.

"Besides," Heidi said, "I know you hate the all-white kitchen trend but—" Her phone rang, interrupting her. "Karlsson Construction," she answered. "That's right; this is she." Heidi wandered away into the back bedroom.

Dustin's phone rang, too, and he answered it without looking, figuring it was Leanne calling to either apologize or rip him a new one. "Hey," said Dustin. "What's up?"

"You tell me," said a familiar voice. It was Mack, his fishing buddy. "Huh?"

"I'm here on Cedar Road investigating an abandoned vehicle," said Mack. In addition to knowing the best places in the sound to drop crab pots, Mack was also the county sheriff. "I didn't need to run the plates to know this van belonged to Cade. It has his handyman logo on the side."

"Wait a sec." Dustin paced across the room. "What do you mean, *abandoned vehicle*? Is Cade there?"

"Nope," said Mack. "If you can get here fast, I won't tow it. I tried calling Leanne, but it went straight to voice mail."

"Try her at Port Pizza," said Dustin. "She and the girls are there with Nathan."

Five minutes later, Dustin was behind the wheel of his truck with Heidi in the passenger seat, driving toward Cedar Road, racking his brain for what might have happened to Cade. Of all the idiotic things his dumbass brother-in-law had done over the years, everything from selling illegal fireworks to letting his septic tank overflow because he was too cheap to drain it, Cade had never abandoned a vehicle by the side of the road.

Heidi, however, was more concerned about the call she'd received from the appliance store in Everett. "The stove's ready for pickup, but the dishwasher and refrigerator are on back order for three weeks," she said as she picked wallpaper debris off her shirt. "He was calling because he wanted to keep our business and hoped I didn't buy elsewhere."

"*Can* we buy elsewhere?" Dustin slowed the truck down to a crawl as they crossed Main Street and navigated traffic. The Harper Landing–Port Inez ferry had just unloaded, flooding the town with people passing through.

"Yes, but the shop in Seattle would be a wee bit more expensive."

"How much is a *wee bit*?"

"Ten percent." Heidi blew a fluff of brown bangs out of her eyes. "But if we don't get the appliances soon, it'll push back our completion date and totally mess with our schedule."

Dustin groaned. "Have you called the Seattle store yet to place the order?"

"Not yet." Heidi rolled wallpaper debris into a little ball and put it in the trash bag Dustin kept in the center console.

"Maybe we should buy the simpler models like I wanted in the first place."

"And let the kitchen look junky? I told you the stainless were more expensive than the baseline model, but at the price point we're aiming to list this house for, buyers expect—"

"Save it." Dustin held up his hand. "I don't care. Just have your way like you always do."

"When you say it that way, you make me sound like a controlling older sister instead of your business partner."

Dustin raised his eyebrows. "Your point?"

"I don't give you a hard time about decisions you know more about, like what type of hardware to use when you frame a wall or how thick the insulation needs to be in the attic."

He was about to concede she made sense. "That's—" he started to say, right as she interrupted him.

"I let you make whatever decision you want."

"Let me make?" He arched one eyebrow. "You let me make decisions you know nothing about?" Dustin smirked. "Boy, wait till I tell Mack about this."

"What's Mack got to do with it?" Heidi's cheeks turned pink.

"We're going to see him in two minutes," said Dustin.

"We are?" Heidi whacked his shoulder. "And you didn't tell me?" She flipped down the visor and examined her reflection in the mirror with a shriek. "I have wallpaper paste in my hair." Heidi glared at him accusingly. "In my *hair*, Dustin," she said through gritted teeth. "And you knew it."

"I got a ball cap in the back you could slip on," he said, trying not to laugh.

Heidi and Mack's on-again, off-again relationship had unfolded from the first day Mack had moved to town five years ago. Dustin tried to keep track of whether they were together or broken up, but it was difficult, bordering on impossible. In fact, the only good thing he had to say about Andrea moving back to town—aside from the impressive profit Karlsson Construction made on the flip—was now Heidi went to Andrea's house to cry her eyes out when she and Mack broke up instead of coming to him. Dustin's stash of Ben & Jerry's ice cream was finally safe from his sister's tears.

"Just because you're a heartless bachelor," Heidi was saying as she brushed her hair into loose brown waves, "doesn't give you the right to set me up for humiliation."

"I wasn't trying to embarrass you," said Dustin. "It's just Mack."

"Just Mack?"

"And I'm not heartless," said Dustin, feeling wounded. "Why would you say that?"

"Hmm . . ." Heidi uncapped a tube of lipstick. "Maybe because you've never been in love and don't seem to care about trying."

"Of course I care, and of course I've been in love."

Heidi finished applying her lipstick and dropped the tube in her purse. "Really?" She raised her eyebrows. "With whom?"

Andrea Wint. His heart felt like it was squeezing at the mere thought of her name. Her father had walked the Karlssons through the darkest times of their lives. Andrea and Heidi had been best friends for decades. But to Dustin, Andrea would always be the woman who broke his heart. Crushed it to pieces was more accurate, under the glittery spike of her high-heeled shoe.

"Who what?" he asked.

"Who were you in love with?"

"I dated Samantha Leroy for two years," he said, naming the woman he'd seen after college. "Doesn't that count for anything?"

"It counts," said Heidi, "but not for being in love."

"That's ridiculous."

"It's the truth." Heidi folded her arms. "If you were truly in love with Samantha, you would have followed her to Miami."

"And leave Karlsson Construction? Just pack up and move?" Dustin scoffed. "No way. If she truly loved me, she wouldn't have moved away."

Heidi jabbed him in the shoulder. "And if you truly loved her, you would have followed her wherever she went, even to Antarctica."

"Sometimes loving people means letting them go because that's what's best for everyone." Dustin's fists clenched over the steering wheel. "I'm not heartless," he reiterated.

"I know you're not," Heidi said in a soft voice. "You love me, Leanne, and Nathan like it's your full-time job. Plus, you're the best uncle any kid could ever wish for."

"Thanks." He rubbed his chin, and his thoughts drifted to a blue house in Port Inez Bay that Karlsson Construction had remodeled. The two-story craftsman with a wraparound deck had been just another flip as far as Dustin had been concerned, until Andrea had visited Port Inez last summer and bought it on sight. Dustin had thought he was over her until he'd taken one look into her blue eyes and felt the turmoil churn up again.

The fact was, Dustin *had* been in love, but he didn't want to tell Heidi about it. How could he explain to his sister how stupid he had been in high school? Not only had he fallen for her best friend, but he had let Andrea stomp on his heart. "Sometimes loving people means letting them go because that's what's best for everyone." Tom Wint had said those exact words to him in high school. No, it was better to avoid that conversation—and the blue house—altogether. Especially when there was important business to deal with at hand.

"Go ahead and call the shop in Seattle, and see if you can get the appliances," he said. "Even if they are a 'wee bit' more expensive."

"Yes! I knew you'd realize I was right all along." She eagerly tapped her phone.

Dustin zoned out while she made the call, still thinking about Andrea. He found himself wondering, like he so often did, what she was doing at this very moment and if she ever curled up in the dining room window seat he had built that overlooked the view. Was Andrea there right now reading a book and staring across the water? Maybe she had her laptop computer and was completing a project for her graphic design business. There were electrical outlets next to the window seat where she could charge her computer or plug in a lamp. He was glad he'd had the foresight to install them.

"What?" Heidi exclaimed into the phone. "That's not possible!"

Dustin snapped his attention back to the present and was alarmed to see Heidi's horrified expression.

"But Cade doesn't work for us anymore," she said. "We fired him over a year ago, and he was never on our line of credit to begin with."

Dustin's jaw clenched. He didn't like the sound of this.

"He's bought *how* many appliances? Seven thousand two hundred dollars' worth? Um . . . no, we do not. I don't care if he was wearing a Karlsson Construction hat. I already told you. Cade doesn't work for us, and he's not on our line of credit. We never gave you permission to send home refrigerators with anyone but Dustin or me."

Dustin fumed. Great. Just great. Cade must have moved from donuts, to copper pipes, to refrigerators. He was probably selling them for cash on Craigslist. His shifty brother-in-law had a gambling problem. Cade was always bragging about the lucky rabbit-foot that he kept on his key chain. He claimed he had found it the day he had won $3,000 at the Clearwater Casino—the same day that Jane was born. Dustin still hadn't forgiven Cade for missing Jane's birth, even though Leanne hadn't seemed to mind.

"Yes," Heidi said. "Call the police. This is fraud, and we don't owe you a penny." She hung up the phone and looked at Dustin. "Bad news."

"I gathered that."

"I better call all our vendors and double-check that Cade hasn't tried the same thing elsewhere."

"And what about the appliances?"

Heidi wrinkled her nose. "I'll call back the first store and beg. Maybe they can rush the back order or something."

"That'll have to wait." Dustin pointed across the dash. "There's Cade's van."

"And Mack's car." Heidi's shoulders slumped.

"You look great. Nobody would know you were covered in old wallpaper and paste an hour ago."

"Thanks." She took a deep breath and sighed. "Mack said . . . never mind what he said. Let's get this over with."

"Sounds like a plan. At least it's stopped raining." Dustin parked his truck behind Mack's car and walked up to Cade's van.

"You're here," said Mack, only he wasn't speaking to Dustin. The sheriff's dark-brown eyes locked with Heidi's green ones in a way that made Dustin feel like a third wheel.

"Of course I'm here," said Dustin, deliberately misunderstanding. "You said to come quick or you'd tow Cade's van. Has Leanne arrived yet?"

"No, but she's on her way." Mack shuffled a step back and held out his hand, indicating the driver's-side door. "There's been a development since I called you."

Heidi rubbed her hands up and down her arms to stay warm. "What sort of development?"

"Are you cold?" Mack asked. "I've got an extra jacket in the car."

"I'm fine," Heidi snapped. "We're here for the van."

"That's right," said Dustin. He zipped off his fleece and threw it over his sister's shoulders. "I'm also here to find out what Cade's up to."

Mack shrugged. "That's the development." He opened the van door.

"Cade left it unlocked?" Dustin cursed under his breath. "Of course he did. I wouldn't expect him to be responsible."

"Don't go blaming Cade just yet," said Mack. "It might not be his fault."

"What's that supposed to mean?" Heidi rolled up the sleeves of Dustin's fleece since they were too long for her.

"Cade's wallet is inside, along with the keys. But the wallet's empty," said Mack. "I already took all the pictures I need for my report, so the vehicle is Leanne's to drive home."

"Huh?" Dustin poked his head in the van so he could see for himself. There was Cade's wallet on the front seat, his Owl's Nest ID, and a punch card from Hunter's Fuel, the espresso stand, tossed to the side, like the wallet had been rifled through. The van key was still in the ignition, and Cade's personal key ring was on the floor.

"It seems like a robbery," said Mack. "Did he have a bunch of cash on him or something valuable in the back of the van?"

"I have no idea," said Heidi. "It's possible. We just learned that he's been swindling an appliance store in Seattle we buy from."

"I hope they report that to the local PD," said Mack.

"That's what we should have done a year ago," said Dustin ruefully.

"What do you mean?" Mack asked.

Heidi shivered in Dustin's fleece. "We caught Cade stealing copper pipe on a jobsite. But instead of turning him in for theft, we only fired him so it wouldn't mess up Leanne's life."

"It was Nathan's idea," said Dustin, not that it made a difference now.

"I didn't even tell my best friend," said Heidi.

"Hey, look." Dustin leaned down and picked up Cade's key chain from where it lay next to the gas pedal. "Something's missing." He rattled it.

"What?" Mack asked.

"Cade's lucky rabbit's foot." Dustin frowned. "He doesn't go anywhere without it. Which means . . . that bastard tried to stage this scene to make it look like he was robbed or kidnapped or both."

24

"Damn it," said Heidi. "I bet you're right."

"Yeah," said Dustin. "Cade's probably feeding a slot machine right now. What should we say to Leanne when she gets here?"

"I don't know," said Heidi. "She never listens to reason about Cade because she loves him so much."

"That makes her a fool two times over," Dustin grumbled. "First for trusting Cade, and second for believing in happily ever afters."

Heidi put her hand on his shoulder. "Don't say that."

"It's the truth." He shrugged away from her touch. "Leanne needs to toughen up and face facts—if not for herself, then for Kendal and Jane. Her husband's a scumbag."

"I'm not arguing with you there," said Heidi. She whirled around and faced Mack. "What are you going to do about this?"

Mack shrugged. "Not much I can do at this point. If Leanne files a missing person's report, things will be different."

"But the rabbit's foot." Heidi lifted her chin. "Doesn't it bother you that it's missing?"

"I'm not saying it does or it doesn't," said Mack. "But a missing rabbit's foot is far from a smoking gun. For all we know, Cade could be in the woods somewhere bleeding from a head wound."

Wouldn't that be nice? Dustin thought to himself but then felt guilty. He didn't wish bodily harm to come to Cade, but he did want his brother-in-law out of Leanne's life, far away, where he could never disappoint her again. But for that to happen, Cade would have to be charged with a crime. "How much jail time would Cade get for stealing from the appliance store?" he asked Mack.

"How much did he take?"

"Seven thousand two hundred dollars' worth of merchandise," said Heidi.

"That would be a class B felony. Cade could get ten years or be let off easy with a fine and restitution." Mack's radio beeped. "Hold on," he said. "I need to take this." Mack wandered away.

"I'm going to find him," Dustin told Heidi. "I'm going to track down Cade and haul his sorry ass back to town and throw him behind bars, where he belongs. With the help of that appliance store, that is. Can you call them back right now?"

"Deep breaths." Heidi grabbed his elbows and held him steady. "This isn't about vengeance; it's about Leanne."

"Of course it's about Leanne." Dustin spoke louder than he intended. "But what if it's not only about copper pipes and refrigerators? What if he also has access to Leanne's trust?"

Heidi blanched, her rosy cheeks losing their color in a heartbeat. "Leanne told me she kept those funds in a separate account."

"Funds? Call it what it is—blood money. If Cade gets his hands on it, he'll spend every last dime."

"Leanne's too smart for that," said Heidi. "She'll keep it in a separate account like we told her to."

"Will she? Who do you think she loves more, her family or her husband?"

"Cade *is* her family."

"Thanks for making my point for me. Cade's a thief. And it's time the whole world knew that."

Headlights flashed into their eyes, and a Subaru Forester screeched to a halt behind them. Leanne flew out of the car and raced forward without turning off the engine. "Where is he?" she cried. "Where's Cade?" Even in the dark, Dustin could see the fear in her eyes.

Mack held up his hands. "We don't have any definitive answers yet, so try not to panic."

"Panic?" Leanne hugged her arms. "Should I be panicking right now?"

"No," said Dustin in a firm tone. "It's going to be okay because Heidi, Nathan, and I won't let anything bad happen to you or the girls."

"I'll go turn off your car," said Heidi. "And park it properly."

Leanne raced to the van, poked her head inside, and shrieked. "Cade!" she called. "Cade? Are you there?"

"Leanne . . ." Dustin held out his arms but didn't know what to say.

Leanne stepped back from the van. "Where is he?" She grabbed Dustin by the shirt and shook his six-foot-three frame. "Where's my husband?"

"I don't know," said Dustin, wishing he could make her anguish disappear. "But I'm going to find him for you."

"Promise?" she cried.

Dustin nodded. "I promise."

Leanne threw herself into his arms and sobbed against his shoulder. "What am I going to do without him?" she gasped. "I can't let my girls grow up without their dad."

"Shh," he whispered, his heart hurting. Leanne had grown up without her father too. "It'll be okay. You can count on me." He looked over at the abandoned van. His scumbag brother-in-law was out there somewhere, and Dustin would do whatever it took to find him.

CHAPTER THREE

"Fabulous news!" Lydia gushed over the phone. "I heard a rumor that a two bedroom was being prepped for listing in Roger's building, and I tracked down the owner this morning, and she said yes, they'd already moved out and are staging it next week, hoping for a quick sale."

"How is that good news?" Andrea asked. It was Friday night, and she was walking away from the Owl's Nest. The short trip to Main Street was Andrea's favorite part of her journey home because she passed not one but two Little Free Libraries. The only problem was her mother knew her schedule and frequently called her on her walk to the ferry.

"The apartment would be perfect for you."

"What?"

"I know what you're thinking," said Lydia. "Roger's building is way over your budget. But this two bedroom is on the third floor by the elevator, which makes it cheaper—plus it doesn't have a view." Lydia spoke in a rush, which prevented Andrea from interrupting her. "I Zillowed it, and I think it'll go for a couple hundred over your house."

"Two hundred dollars?" Andrea paused in front of the first Little Free Library. It was stocked with kid titles that didn't interest her, although she had contributed a picture book about hedgehogs. This conversation with her mom made no sense whatsoever.

"Two hundred *thousand* dollars. You know how desirable the location is. But you could sell your father's coins, and I'll loan you the money to cover the difference."

Andrea spun away on her heel and marched down the sidewalk. "Mom, I don't understand why you're telling me this. I just moved a year ago. I love my house, and no way would I sell Dad's coins." Stopping in front of the second Little Free Library, which included a wide range of genres, Andrea took a paperback out of her purse and returned the book she had borrowed.

"Well, maybe you could rent your house out for the next year. Or turn it into an Airbnb. Those are popular, right? It's true that it's better to hold on to a property for two years before you sell it. But this two bedroom won't wait. We need to act now."

Andrea shook her head. "I'm not moving into Roger's building. That's ludicrous."

"No, it's not. This is a safe neighborhood. There's a storage unit in the basement, and every owner gets two guaranteed parking spaces. We could go for walks together in the morning after Roger left for work."

Andrea let out an exasperated puff of air. "I'm not saying this to be mean, but don't you think that's an awful lot of time for a thirty-six-year-old woman to spend with her mother?"

"You visit your father every day. How is this different? At least I would know who you were."

"Dad knows who I am," Andrea said, burning with indignation. "How could you say that?"

"Because it's the truth." Lydia's voice broke. "And I worry about you turning your life inside out over him. He wouldn't want that for you."

"I don't want to have this argument again." Andrea stared at the books in the wooden box in front of her without reading any of the titles.

"Move back to Seattle. There's nothing for you in Port Inez."

"My best friend lives in Port Inez. I go for walks with Heidi almost every day."

"So you'll walk with Heidi, but you won't walk with me? I see how it is."

"Mom, that's unfair."

"No, you're right. I'm sorry I said that. Of course you should have friends. But you have friends in the city too. Friends you can't see on a regular basis because you moved to the boondocks."

"I need to go or I'll miss the ferry."

"And how will you meet eligible men? You're still young enough that you could get married and have children. I want grandbabies."

"I don't need a husband to be happy."

"No, you don't. But you shouldn't rule out that possibility either. Who are you going to meet in a hick town like Port Inez?"

"Can we please not talk about my love life?"

"What love life? You haven't dated anyone since you moved. Unless you've rekindled things with Dustin and haven't told me about it?"

"Of course I haven't," Andrea snapped.

"I always liked Dustin," Lydia said wistfully. "He was the only boy you dated in high school who offered to help with the dishes. And he built you that beautiful house."

"He didn't build it for me. Heidi and Dustin remodel houses for a living. That's what they do."

"And it's a great house. It might have even appreciated in value enough to cover the cost of the apartment fully."

"I'm not moving!"

"Think about it," said Lydia. "I'd buy that place myself with savings if I could, but your father needs our assets. Dementia's expensive."

"Yeah. I get that."

"We should have bought long-term care insurance like I suggested, but he said it was a waste of money."

"Mom, I gotta go. Love you. Bye." Andrea hung up before Lydia could respond.

How could her mother be so awful? Andrea's whole body was tensed up like she was prepared to fight. Yes, the Owl's Nest was pricey, but it was worth every penny. Tom had been a lawyer, for crying out loud. He could afford it. And Lydia, of all people, shouldn't criticize Andrea for spending time with her dad. What happened to loving someone until death do us part? Lydia had abandoned Tom when he needed her the most.

Andrea's elevated pulse took multiple deep breaths to calm. Perusing the collection of books helped. The only title in the Little Free Library she hadn't read yet was a nonfiction book about a rowing team from the University of Washington. But sports bored her, and although she enjoyed history, the history of sports did not interest her at all. Andrea left *The Boys in the Boat*, by Daniel James Brown, where it was and walked away. Later this evening she could download a historical fiction book on her Kindle. It would take a bodice-ripping romance and a large glass of wine to recover from the conversation with her mother.

Steeling herself, Andrea picked up her pace and turned onto Main Street. Since it was Friday night, downtown Harper Landing was full of people. Each restaurant was packed, including the frozen yogurt shop, Sweet Bliss. Andrea thought about popping in and buying a cup, but she was too cold. Plus, she didn't want to miss the ferry. She could see it down on the water, approaching the dock. The boat would begin unloading momentarily, and as soon as all the vehicles had driven away, it would fill up again and sail off to the Kitsap Peninsula. Port Inez was the gateway to the Olympic Peninsula, Olympic National Park, and famous Pacific Northwest destinations like Forks, Washington, home of the sparkly vampires of *Twilight* fame.

Andrea reached the bottom of Main Street right as it began raining again and darted into the ferry terminal under a shower of drops. With a flick of her frequent-traveler card, she was through the turnstile. She

made a beeline for her favorite booth on the stern side, where there was
a communal puzzle spread out on the table. Her phone buzzed in her
pocket as she searched through the pieces for the golden orange of a
butterfly's wing.

Here's the link from Zillow in case you change your mind, said the
text from Lydia.

Not interested, Andrea typed back angrily.

What Zillow doesn't say is that the kitchen's been redone. Those
old pictures don't do it justice.

If you want to live near me so bad, you could move to Port Inez,
Andrea texted, trying to prove a point.

I would consider it, but Roger's practice is here.

Andrea cringed. Great. Now her mom thought she was serious
with that suggestion. The last thing she wanted was for her mom to be
her neighbor.

Have fun with Roger. Goodnight.

I don't want you to be lonely.

I'm not lonely! Talk to you later. Andrea turned off the notifications
on her phone and flipped it facedown on the table. No way was she
lonely. She had her thriving graphic design business and her daily trips
to see her father. Plus, there was Heidi, who had been her best friend
for almost two decades. Andrea and Heidi lived half a mile away from
each other and went on morning walks a few times a week.

Sometimes Andrea thought about getting a pet hedgehog for
company, like the one she had raised as a teenager. Spike the pygmy

hedgehog had been her constant companion throughout high school. Weighing sixteen ounces and capable of curling up on the palm of her hand, he'd kept her company studying late into the night and sometimes snuck to school with her in the pocket of her coat. Since Spike was nocturnal, he'd slept during the day, and her teachers had never known of his presence. But at the moment, she had enough to deal with without caring for a pet.

Now that Lydia had finally stopped bothering her, Andrea could focus on the puzzle without being distracted. By the time she had filled in a monarch's gold-and-black wing, the ferry had departed. When she finished an apple blossom, she was home in Port Inez.

Home . . . Andrea thought about that word as she walked off the ferry, onto the path that led to Port Inez Bay. Home to her was still the house in Magnolia where she had spent the first eighteen years of her life. She dreamed of it on occasion, when it was three o'clock in the morning and she was especially exhausted. After college at Central Washington University, Andrea had moved into a shared apartment in Northgate with friends until she had finally saved up enough money (with some help from her parents) to purchase a condo in Belltown. That's where she had lived for twelve years before moving to Port Inez last summer.

The blue house had been love at first sight. When she had seen that the listing price was only a little bit more than what her condo was worth, she'd swooned. Andrea still couldn't believe her luck and felt like the blue house was too good for her. It had three bedrooms and a formal dining room. Andrea didn't have kids to tuck in at night or guests to entertain. The two-car garage was wasted on her as well, since her Nissan Leaf took up so little space. As for the boating dock that attached to her private beach, Andrea didn't own a boat and was too cold blooded to swim in the water or attempt kayaking.

But Andrea had known she had to have the blue house from the moment she had seen the window seat. It framed the dining room and highlighted a view that stuck with you—water smooth as glass on a still day or choppy with conflict on a stormy evening like tonight.

The only drawback of her move to Port Inez was the possibility of running into Dustin. "Long-distance relationships never work," he had said, breaking her heart on prom night with a harshness she hadn't seen coming. "I don't want to be tied down in college." Even now, eighteen years later, his rejection stung, and she dreaded any possibility of running into him.

She pushed open the blue house's cedar door and flicked on the entryway light. After dropping her purse on the console table, Andrea unzipped her coat and hung it on the newel post by the stairs. Then she wandered into the kitchen and put leftovers from the night before into the microwave. While the chicken and veggies heated, she went back to her purse, took out the plastic flip, and walked to the living room to return the double eagle to the safe. Every evening she brought a different coin to show Tom.

It was dark, so she switched on the lamp next to the couch and then flicked the switch for the recessed lighting over the fireplace. The coziness of her house, the familiarity of her routine, and the steady patter of rain on the roof lulled her into a relaxed state that was the perfect way to begin the weekend. It wasn't until she swung back the family portrait hanging on the wall that she realized something was amiss. That painting of all three Wints smiling in front of the Space Needle twenty years ago was something that nobody but Andrea was supposed to know hid a secret safe. But tonight, when she unhitched the latch and swung it back on its hinges, Andrea gasped. There was no safe, only a gaping hole in the wall where the safe used to be.

"What?" Andrea exclaimed. She reached forward into the empty cavern and patted around, hoping that the safe had been knocked out of position. Maybe an earthquake? Perhaps it had fallen into the back of the stairwell, where Karlsson Construction had found the space for the ruse to begin with—but there was nothing.

"I need a flashlight," she said out loud, hurrying back to the kitchen for her phone. The microwave beeped as she searched in vain for the flashlight app, but she couldn't find it. "Damn it," she muttered as the microwave beeped again. Andrea opened and closed the microwave to keep it quiet and then raced upstairs to where she kept a flashlight underneath her bed for emergencies.

She tried not to panic. Her birthright wasn't gone; it had only fallen into the crevice behind the stairs. Andrea willed that to be true. The alternative—that she had lost her father's most treasured possessions—was too awful to contemplate.

Clicking the flashlight to full brightness, she sped back into the living room and aimed it into the drywall. She saw a thick layer of dust on the framing against the stairs but nothing else. Andrea blinked rapidly. For the second time that evening, her pulse raced like she was under attack.

"They're gone," she whispered, sinking to her knees. "All of Dad's coins are gone." The flashlight fell from her hand and rolled across the carpet. "We've been robbed."

Saying it aloud made it scarier. What if the thief was in the house right now? She'd been home alone this whole time and hadn't once questioned her safety.

Andrea grabbed her purse and phone, dashed to the front door, and flung it open. She stooped to pick up the decorative concrete hedgehog doorstop and clutched it firmly. If someone attacked her, she'd bash them in the face with it. Fingers trembling, she dialed 911.

CHAPTER FOUR

Dustin had no idea what he was doing. When Kendal had asked him to braid her hair, he had said yes because he hadn't wanted to disappoint her. He had googled instructions on his phone while she and Jane had brushed their teeth. But now that he had a hairbrush in one hand and a comb in another, he forgot everything that he'd seen on YouTube. There were three sections in a braid, right? Or were there four?

"Daddy never helps us get ready for bed," said Jane. She licked the mint flavoring off of her dental floss. "He plays video games after dinner."

Of course he does, Dustin thought to himself. Playing video games was fine, but leaving all the childcare to Leanne wasn't. Dustin fought to keep his disapproval from showing. Just because he thought Cade was an ass didn't mean he would disparage him to his daughters.

"You need to part it first," said Kendal.

"What?" Dustin asked.

"My hair. It'll stay neater overnight if you put it into two braids. Mom always does two braids."

"Oh. Right." Dustin used the comb to make a surprisingly straight part in the center of Kendal's blonde hair.

"I'll hold this half for you," said Kendal as she reached up and grabbed the left portion of her hair.

"Here goes nothing," Dustin muttered as he divided her remaining hair into three sections, hoping he remembered correctly.

"Uncle Dusty?" Kendal looked up at him. "You *have* braided hair before, right?"

"Not exactly," said Dustin. "Hold still." He slowly and carefully braided her hair into a long plait. "There," he said as he secured the end with elastic. "You'll be the prettiest girl in first grade."

"Thanks." Kendal let go of the chunk of hair she was holding. "Mom usually braids my hair so it'll be wavy in the morning, and my teacher, Ms. Nguyen, always notices."

"Braid my hair next," Jane pleaded.

"Your hair's too short," said Kendal.

"It is not." Jane pouted.

"We'll figure something out," said Dustin as he braided the second half of Kendal's hair. He spoke loudly to cover up the muffled sounds coming from down the hall. He couldn't tell if Leanne was shouting or sobbing, but he was relieved to know that Heidi was with her, trying to offer comfort.

"Why is Mommy crying?" Jane asked. "Daddy isn't even here."

"Does your mom cry a lot when your dad's home?" Dustin's eyebrows pinched together.

Kendal gave Jane a pointed look. "Nobody likes a blabbermouth."

"I'm not blabbing." Jane jutted out her chin but didn't say anything.

"It's not blabbing if you tell your uncle." Dustin finished off the braid. "I have every right to know if my little sister is unhappy. Wouldn't you want to know if Jane was crying?" he asked Kendal.

She frowned but nodded.

"Mommy cries whenever Daddy calls her names," said Jane.

Dustin felt like the wind had been knocked out of him. "What names?"

Jane's brown eyes darted to Kendal like she was seeking her big sister's approval. "Cow," Jane whispered. "*Fat* cow."

"Your mom is neither." Dustin could barely keep the edge from his voice.

"He also calls her lard—"

"That's enough, Jane!" Kendal said. "You know Dad wouldn't want you tattling, not even to Uncle Dusty."

"I don't care what your dad would want," said Dustin, unable to contain himself. "Your mom does not deserve to be called names like that. No woman does, and that includes you two as well."

"Sometimes Dad calls Mom his princess," said Kendal. "And last week he surprised us with donuts. He can be nice too."

"That's good to know, but it doesn't make up for hurting your mom's feelings." Dustin picked Jane up and set her on the bathroom counter next to the sink. "I think Kendal's right and your hair's too short to braid, but I bet we could brush it real nice. What do you say?"

Jane nodded. "Get out all the rats."

"It's a deal." Dustin brushed her curls section by section. "Kendal, why don't you go pick a book out that I can read to you before bedtime?"

"Okay. Ms. Nguyen says reading every night is important. You know she doesn't have a boyfriend, right?"

"You've mentioned that several times," said Dustin, who had no interest in his niece playing matchmaker for him. "Now scoot."

Twenty minutes later both girls were tucked into their twin beds, the night-light was on, the closet had been checked for monsters, and their bedroom door was left ajar. "Good night, girls," Dustin said as he blew them kisses. "Thanks for letting me be your uncle."

"Good night," Kendal whispered. Jane was already asleep.

Dustin walked down the hallway to the family room, where he found his sisters on the couch. Leanne was wrapped up in a blanket. Heidi offered her a box of tissues, and Leanne blew her nose so hard it squeaked.

"Any news from Cade?" Dustin asked.

Leanne shook her head, not making eye contact.

"I was just explaining to Leanne how it would be good to report Cade's credit cards as being stolen—that way fraudulent charges don't pop up on their account." Heidi spoke in a measured tone, as if she was struggling not to sound patronizing.

"That's a great idea." Dustin sat down in Cade's gaming chair. It was lower to the ground than he was used to but comfortable. "If Cade was robbed, you should definitely put a fraud alert on those cards. And if he's run off, then you can't let him ruin your credit."

"He didn't run off," said Leanne. "Cade wouldn't do that to me."

Wouldn't he? Dustin wanted to ask. It took all his restraint to hold that question in.

"Exactly." Heidi patted Leanne's shoulder. "That's why you should call your credit card company and your bank. You're saying that the most likely scenario is that Cade was robbed. Okay, so let's follow the procedures for when wallets are stolen." Heidi stood from the couch. "Where's your purse? I'll get your wallet so you can call the numbers on the back of each card."

"Great idea." Dustin nodded his approval. "What can I do to help?"

"Nothing," Leanne moaned. "Stop pretending like you can fix things when you can't. You don't even believe that Cade's innocent. You thought he stole from you on that jobsite, when that was a lie." She tossed the tissue box aside. "Cade would never steal pipes. He's not a thief!"

"It's not just the pipes," said Dustin. "Heidi told you about the refrigerators."

"I've never seen any refrigerators," said Leanne. "Don't you think I would notice if he was selling enormous stolen goods on Craigslist?"

"Let's all take a deep breath and focus on one thing at a time." Heidi set Leanne's purse on her lap. "Step one was filing the missing person's report, which you've already done. Step two is issuing the fraud alert."

"No!" Leanne pushed her purse away. "Cade might need those credit cards if he's lost somewhere and needs money to come home."

"But you think Cade's been robbed," Dustin countered. "Do you really want to give that robber a free pass?"

"No, but there's a chance Cade might need them," Leanne said in a tiny voice.

"Or there's an even better chance that he might max out your credit at the Elwha River Casino," Dustin said, losing what little patience he had left. "Or the Suquamish, or the Quinault." Those were just the casinos on this side of the water. Across Puget Sound there were even more to choose from.

"Cade doesn't gamble anymore." Leanne's tone turned snappish, and she wiped her nose with a tissue. "He promised he'd stop. That was his Valentine's Day gift to me. He's all done with gambling."

"So done that he threw away his lucky rabbit's foot?" Heidi asked.

Leanne's temporary resolve crumbled, and she blinked back tears. "His rabbit's foot has nothing to do with gambling."

"Bullshit," said Dustin.

"Dustin . . ." Heidi's voice bore a warning tone. "Be nice."

"No." He leaned forward in the gaming chair and almost rocked out of it. "I won't be nice. Cade is a husband and a father, and he has a responsibility to the people he loves." Dustin looked Leanne in the eye. "You deserve to be with someone who is honest and has a good character."

"Cade's full of character," Heidi said with a forced laugh, like she was trying to lighten the mood. When the joke fell flat, her tone became serious. "I agree with Dustin," she said. "Leanne, if you're worried about money or who will help with the girls, you don't need to be. Dustin, Nathan, and I—we're your family."

"Cade's my family." Leanne shrugged off the blanket. "I might have grown up without parents, but I don't need you here babysitting me anymore. I have the right to make my own decisions."

"Of course you do," said Heidi.

"We just want you to make wise ones," said Dustin. "Especially since Kendal and Jane are counting on you."

"I know they're counting on me." Leanne pushed up her sleeves. "You both are wrong about Cade, and if you don't believe me, ask your friend Andrea. Why, just last night she called Cade her hero."

Andrea . . . Dustin's muscles tensed. He tried to sit up straighter in the gaming chair but couldn't because the seat was concave. "How does Andrea know Cade?" he asked.

"Her dad lives at the Owl's Nest. He got his hand caught in a metal box yesterday, and nobody in the entire building knew what to do except for Cade." Leanne folded her arms across her chest. "If it weren't for Cade, the guy's arm might have needed to be amputated." Leanne shot Dustin a defiant look.

"Tom was hurt?" Heidi asked with concern.

Leanne nodded. "Blood gushed everywhere. And yet he was so out of it that the only thing he could talk about was coins. Gold coins this. Gold coins that. A hidden safe. Cade said he was totally bonkers."

"Don't talk about Tom like that." Dustin stood and walked to the fireplace. "We owe him everything, and he deserves to be spoken of with respect." He stared into the cold hearth.

"What do you mean?" Leanne asked.

Dustin whipped around to face her. "Don't you know? Tom was our lawyer when Mom and Dad were killed." Dustin would never forget how Tom Wint had walked them through the darkest time of their lives. The lawyer was their champion, savior, and knight in shining armor all rolled into one. "The settlement he won for us transformed our lives."

"Mom and Dad didn't have life insurance," Heidi explained. "And there were two mortgages on our house."

"If it weren't for Tom's help, we might have been out on the street," said Dustin. "I thought you knew that."

"How?" Leanne asked. "I was Kendal's age when they died, and only a little bit older when the lawsuit happened. I barely remember

Mom and Dad. That's why keeping my family together is so important. I fall asleep every night grateful that my daughters are growing up with both parents. Cade is—"

A phone rang, interrupting the conversation. At first it was unclear where the ringtone was coming from. Dustin, Heidi, and Leanne pulled out their phones at the same time.

"It's mine," said Heidi before she tapped the screen. "Hi, Andrea. Sorry, but this really isn't a good time."

"You barely remember Mom and Dad?" Dustin asked, his heart sinking into his chest.

Leanne's forehead wrinkled as she frowned. "Dad had a red plaid coat. I remember that. And I can picture Mom sewing something." She waved her hands around. "It was long and white, like a wedding dress."

"A tablecloth," Dustin murmured. "You're remembering the tablecloth she embroidered for the dining room to cover the ugly thrift shop table."

Heidi, who was still talking to Andrea on the phone, shrieked. "What? Your safe is missing? How's that possible?"

Dustin wasn't intentionally trying to eavesdrop, but Heidi's high-pitched squawk couldn't be ignored. The safe was gone? Dustin had installed it behind a family portrait in Andrea's living room. He'd spent far too long that day staring at that portrait, mesmerized by the gorgeous blue eyes that gazed out from it, mocking him.

Heidi spoke again. "Mack is there?" she asked. "Good. What did he say?"

Dustin also remembered the day that he had installed the safe, because it was the same day Cade had blown up a tree stump with a cherry bomb.

Cade . . . Dustin whirled around. "I never told Cade about the hidden safe, but he knew. Leanne, you just mentioned it."

Heidi's eyes opened wide. "That's right," she said, holding her hand over the phone to block the receiver. "You told us Tom talked about it last night when he was hurt and bleeding. So Cade knew about the hidden safe *and* the gold coins."

"What?" Leanne asked. "No, I didn't say anything."

Heidi removed her hand from the receiver and spoke clearly into the phone. "Andrea? Listen, is Mack still there? I need to tell you something."

"You have this all wrong," said Leanne with a cool glint in her eyes.

"Call the bank. Cancel your credit cards." Dustin spoke as calmly as possible, trying to make his little sister listen. "Protect your assets. Call a divorce lawyer."

"Divorce?" Leanne glared at him. "No way."

Dustin realized he'd gone too far with that last suggestion. He took a deep breath before he spoke. "Unless Andrea blabbed to a bunch of people about the hiding place for her safe, the only people who knew about its existence were Andrea, Heidi, me, and now your husband."

"You just want to believe Cade is a terrible person. You're ready to blame anything and everything on him," said Leanne. Her voice was ice cold. "But I've already told you. Cade's not a crook."

"I'll be right over," said Heidi into the phone. "Hang tight, and I'll be there in five minutes."

Dustin pulled the key to his truck out of his pocket, feeling frustrated that Leanne wouldn't listen to reason. "Call me," he told her. "If there's anything I can do, just call. Promise?"

Leanne sneered at him. "Trust me," she hissed. "You'll be the last person I call if I need help." Heidi leaned forward to hug her, but Leanne jerked back. "Get out of here," she said. "I don't want to see you either."

"You don't mean that." Heidi frowned.

Leanne squared her shoulders. "I do too." She wiped her cheeks with the back of her hand. "Cade will be here any minute, and he won't want to see you any more than I do."

Dustin cleared his throat. "Come on, Heidi. Let's go." He led the way out of the house and into the freezing-cold air. He was so furious with Cade that he didn't have room to be nervous about seeing Andrea. When he did think about her, he felt horrible that Cade's actions were causing her pain.

With a click of the key fob, Dustin unlocked the doors to his truck, and he and Heidi climbed into the cold cab. He cranked up the heater as soon as they'd driven off, his thoughts blazing like a furnace. "That asshole," he fumed. "First Cade stole from us, and now he's ripped off Andrea."

"Ripped off is right," said Heidi, who was still wearing Dustin's fleece. "It sounds like he literally ripped the safe out of the wall."

"I never should have introduced him to Leanne." Dustin banged his hand on the steering wheel. "This is my fault."

"Our fault," Heidi corrected. "I should have done a better job teaching Leanne to avoid scumbags like him."

Dustin turned on his headlights as he drove through the woods toward Andrea's house. "How many coins are we talking about? Do you know?" A second later he added: "Never mind. It's none of my business."

"It is our business, actually, now that our brother-in-law's a suspect." Heidi pushed a lock of brown hair out of her eyes. "I don't know how many coins there are or how much the collection is worth, but it's a lot. They were Tom's prized possessions." Heidi covered her face with her hands. "What has Cade done?"

"I don't know, but we're going to fix it."

The bay was in the distance, the blue house a tiny spot along the horizon—Andrea's house. Dustin knew every inch of the building from the inside out. He could feel the smoothness of the oak floorboards, golden with age but glowing. He'd built the wraparound deck with fragrant cedar. He'd climbed the roofline and replaced the shingles one by one. Andrea was there waiting for him, and he'd have to face her.

He had avoided seeing her since last summer when they'd done the walk-through and passed over the keys. The day of the closing, Dustin had barely spoken two words to her, even though it had been a happy day, full of celebration. Heidi had poured a bottle of champagne. But now there was only bitterness, and Cade was to blame. Cade and, by extension, Dustin himself.

"Shit." Dustin parked the truck on the street and turned off the lights. "I hope Tom doesn't find out about this." His anger smoldered now, coals of rage burning hot in his heart. He looked up at the front porch like it was the gate to hell. He would rather have been anywhere than about to face Andrea like this.

"Don't forget," said Heidi as she linked her arm through his. "You're heartless, remember?" She gave him a sly grin.

Words caught in his throat. Sentences strangled him. "That's right," he finally said. "Never been in love." Willing it to be true, he led them up the steps with a swagger fueled by justice. He *would* set things right. He would find Cade and make him answer to the law.

CHAPTER FIVE

Andrea swung her front door open before Heidi and Dustin reached the porch. She pushed back her tangled curls and wiped off the mascara that streaked down her cheeks with her sleeve. Hugging her arms across her chest like she could protect herself, Andrea wished that anyone in the world but Dustin was seeing her at such a vulnerable moment. At least Heidi was with him.

"I'm so sorry." Heidi held her hands out wide. "We came as fast as we could." She embraced Andrea in a firm hug.

"Thanks for getting here so quickly." Andrea held the door open for them. "Hi, Dustin." His eyes were the same emerald green that she remembered, but she'd forgotten how tall he was. He towered over her like a Douglas fir.

"Hi." Dustin nodded and waited for her to cross the threshold before entering the house.

Why did he have to look so good? The years had chiseled him in a way that wasn't fair. Equally unfair was how her heart betrayed her now, pounding harder than was normal just because Dustin was nearby. Andrea led them into the living room, where Mack stood in front of the jagged hole in the wall. Seeing the empty space made her feel robbed all over again.

"So?" Dustin asked. "What's the story?"

Mack's mouth gaped open, too, when he turned and saw Heidi. He cleared his throat before looking at his tablet. "No sign of forced entry. Nothing missing but the safe. Either the front door was left unlocked or someone knew what they were doing."

Andrea's pride stung. "The front door was *not* left unlocked. I always lock the handle and the dead bolt before I leave."

"Cade was trained as a locksmith." Dustin pushed back his thick brown hair, making it stand on end. "Locks wouldn't stop him."

Mack nodded. "That's been noted. But unless we catch him with stolen goods, it's unlikely we'll be able to pin this one on him. It's a rough average, but in general, only thirteen percent of home burglaries are solved each year."

"Oh no." Andrea squeezed her eyes shut. "This can't be happening."

"It's going to be okay, sweetie." Heidi threw her arm around Andrea's shoulders, giving her a hug. "We'll figure this out."

"You said the items were insured, right?" Mack asked.

Andrea nodded. "I have a special rider on my homeowner's insurance for the coins."

"Good." Mack turned off his tablet. "Call the insurance company first thing tomorrow. I'll handle things on my end, but I can't make any promises." He looked at the front door. "You should change the locks as soon as possible."

"I'll replace them myself," Dustin said with a grunt. "As soon as I return from finding Cade."

"Finding Cade?" Andrea wrinkled her forehead. "How are you going to do that?"

"It shouldn't be too hard." Dustin held up his hand and began counting off his fingers one by one. "First I'll start at the Clearwater," he said, naming the casino that was closest. "Then I'll check the Elwha, and if he's not there, I'll visit the Quinault."

"You really think he's at a casino?" Heidi asked.

Andrea gasped. "Spending my father's double eagles?"

"I don't know what those are, but yes," Dustin said. "Probably. Unless I can catch him first."

"Now, now." Mack put his hands up. "I don't encourage vigilantism."

"I'm not a vigilante; I'm a pissed-off brother-in-law." Dustin clenched his fists. "If Cade were truly a missing person or simply off on a hike somewhere, then why'd he take his lucky rabbit's foot with him and leave everything else behind?"

"I can't answer that," said Mack. "But I don't like the idea of citizens taking the law into their own hands."

"I'm not doing that." Dustin fished his key fob out of his pocket. "I'm finding my deadbeat brother-in-law and bringing him back to town."

"I've been robbed," said Andrea.

"Yeah." Heidi lifted her chin and looked at Mack defiantly. "And if you won't do anything to make things right, at least I have a brother who will."

"I *will* do something about it," Mack sputtered. "Would do something about it," he clarified. "But right now, I don't have enough evidence to charge him."

"If I find him with the coins, would that be enough?" Dustin asked.

"I couldn't say," Mack admitted. "That would be for the DA to decide."

"Circumstantial evidence!" Heidi appeared ready to pop, and Andrea knew enough to fear the explosion.

"I need to go," Dustin said. "I'm losing valuable time." He strode to the front door.

"Wait!" Andrea called. "I'm coming with you." She raced to the staircase and grabbed her jacket off the post.

"No, you're not," said Dustin. "I might drive all night. This could be dangerous."

She squared her shoulders. "Do you know the difference between a double eagle and a Walking Liberty?"

"Between a what?" he asked.

"Who was Saint-Gaudens?" Adrenaline rushed through her like an electrical current.

"I don't know," Dustin said, his voice rising. "Some Catholic dude? The patron saint of safes?"

"No," Andrea scoffed. "Augustus Saint-Gaudens was the New York artist from the Beaux-Arts generation who sculpted my father's coins. The twenty-dollar gold piece he designed is one of the most famous coins in American history." She jabbed her finger at his chest. "You need me," she declared. "You wouldn't be able to identify my father's collection without me."

"I could figure it out," he huffed. "I'm a fast learner."

She tossed her hair back and glared at him. "Ten seconds ago you didn't even know who Saint-Gaudens was."

Their eyes locked, and for a moment Andrea felt like she was eighteen years old again, at the Seattle Tennis Club, staring into a sea of prom dresses and realizing the horrifying truth. But she wasn't that naive teenager anymore, hungry for scraps of happiness. She was a grown woman with a vulnerable family member to protect. She would do anything to get her father's coins back. If that meant driving from one end of the Olympic Peninsula to another with the boy who broke her heart, so be it.

"Okay," Dustin relented. "You can come." He kept a firm grip on his key fob. "But I'm driving. The last time I let you behind the wheel of my—"

"I know what happened." Andrea yanked on her jacket. "That was a long time ago. I'm a perfectly fine driver, and you know it." Swinging her purse over her shoulder, she marched out of the house. Dustin followed a second later and unlocked the massive black truck parked in her driveway.

Emotions swirled inside her as Andrea climbed into the cab and clicked her seat belt. Being robbed had left her feeling angry and violated, but once Dustin slid into the driver's seat next to her, she felt jittery, too, like she was back in high school and he was picking her up for a date. The passage of time hadn't changed things; he was still the quintessential brooding hero. Teenage Dustin had been tall and lanky, with dark-green eyes that radiated sadness. He was even taller now, and his muscles showed definition everywhere she looked. Instead of sadness, his eyes flashed anger. Andrea wondered if the creases forming across his forehead would ever relax or if they were etched there permanently.

Dustin turned on the ignition, and a voice filled the cab. It was deep and resonant, with a familiarity that brought Andrea right back to high school. "That's Grandpa Gilmore," she said.

"What?" Dustin turned off the sound.

"The actor who played the grandfather on the *Gilmore Girls*." Andrea tried to remember his name. "Edward Herrmann, I think."

Dustin threw the truck into reverse and backed down the driveway. "He does a great job narrating this audiobook I'm listening to."

"I read audiobooks all the time. I listen to them while I cook or do laundry." She didn't add that audiobooks kept her from being lonely. When Dustin failed to respond, they fell into silence, and Andrea quietly seethed. So much for making polite conversation.

But it didn't matter to her if he spoke or not. She *didn't* care for him. There wasn't one piece of her soul that still loved him. Her body didn't notice every time Dustin shifted positions, moving his elbow to the right when he turned the steering wheel or reaching up to adjust the rearview mirror. Memories didn't bubble up, sucking her back to the past, like the time they'd visited Sol Duc Hot Springs, soaked in the mineral waters, and jumped in the snow. She didn't remember their first kiss, standing on the top deck of the ferry, icy winds swirling around them and Dustin's coat wrapped around her, body heat keeping them warm. When he'd kissed her so tenderly she'd thought her joy would be eternal.

Stop it, she told herself. Her breath quickened, and she forced herself to slow it down. True love was a fallacy that didn't exist. She'd spent her twenties searching for it only to be disappointed again and again. She'd been betrayed, exploited, belittled, and ignored. She'd watched her parents' marriage dissolve over an insurmountable diagnosis. This was her life now. She was a thirty-six-year-old realist. The man sitting next to her might look like he could step off the pages of a Gothic romance novel, but she had wised up and had quit searching for heroes.

The twenty-minute drive from Port Inez to the Clearwater Casino seemed to take forever. Despite the cold temperature outside, Andrea was warm. She perspired in her cashmere sweater and didn't remove her jacket until it was too late—she was cooked. Moisture pooled around her armpits. "How do you turn off the seats?" she asked, breaking the silence.

"The what?" he asked.

"The heated seats," said Andrea. "I'm roasting." The interior of Dustin's truck was luxurious and spacious, a far cry from the banged-up model he'd driven in high school with no air-conditioning and a tailgate that spelled *Yo* instead of *Toyota*. But this truck's fancy heated seats added to her discomfort.

"Oh. Sorry about that." He pointed to a button. "That's the control."

"Thanks." She punched it off.

Dustin cleared his throat and passed her an audiobook case. "This is what I've been listening to. It's nonfiction set in the Pacific Northwest. I know how much you love history."

Andrea turned on the map light so she could read the description. "*The Boys in the Boat*, by Daniel James Brown," she read out loud. "Huh. I just saw this in a Little Free Library near my dad's place." She turned off the light and returned the case to its compartment.

"You're welcome to borrow it when I'm done."

"Oh, I didn't mean . . . thanks." Andrea crossed and uncrossed her ankles, unsettled by how easily he offered to share. That easy relationship was gone.

"Looks like there's no traffic," said Dustin. "We should be at the Clearwater soon. Um . . . how is your father doing?"

Andrea pictured her father's bleeding fingertips from the night before. "As good as can be expected, considering he lives with Alzheimer's disease."

"He's at the memory-care place in Harper Landing, right?"

Andrea nodded. "He's been there over a year. The Owl's Nest is a beautiful facility. There's an enclosed courtyard so that residents can go outside whenever they want but not wander away."

"That's good, although I don't remember Tom being much of an outdoorsman."

"No." Andrea chuckled. "*Camping* to him meant staying in a Quality Inn instead of a Hilton."

"Your dad had such a strong work ethic I doubt he had much time to do either," said Dustin.

"True." Her tension melted now that the deafening silence had ended. It felt good talking with someone who had known Tom in his prime, back when his talent and determination had changed lives.

"Sometimes he'd send us emails about our case at eleven p.m."

Andrea nodded. "That sounds like my dad all right."

"How's your mom doing?"

"I figured Heidi had told you."

"Heidi's a lot of things, but a blabbermouth isn't one of them."

"Oh. True. Well, my mom moved in with her boyfriend three months ago, right before Christmas."

"Her boyfriend?" Dustin raised his eyebrows.

Andrea sighed. "My mom says that sixty-eight is too young to give up on living and that my dad would want her happy. But I think she's brushing over the 'in sickness and health' part of being married. I can't believe her. I mean, he's still her husband."

"That sounds complicated."

Andrea nodded. "Roger—the boyfriend—wants her to file for divorce so they can officially move on with their lives. But Mom hasn't because legally it would cause too many problems."

"That's tough."

"Yeah. She never visits him anymore either. That's why I make a point to check in on my dad every evening."

"I'm sure he appreciates that."

"Kind of." Andrea's voice squeaked. "He doesn't remember much, but he does remember his coins." A fresh pang of guilt lashed at her heart. She should have kept the double eagles in a safe-deposit box at the bank instead of thinking she could keep them secure at home. Taking a deep steadying breath, Andrea fought against tears.

"We'll get them back." Dustin patted her hand and then quickly pulled his arm away like she were poison. His rejection stung and made prom-night memories rush back at her like they had just happened yesterday.

"Don't do anything stupid," Tom had told her before she'd hopped in the Yo-Mobile with Dustin and driven off to prom. The Seattle Tennis Club had sparkled that night. Andrea had sparkled, too, in her satin dress with rhinestone earrings. She had felt like a princess the whole evening. But a few hours later she had become the fool.

"Do you feel better now?" Dustin asked.

"What?" Andrea flushed.

"The heat? Is it a good temperature?"

"It's fine. Thanks." Andrea did feel better. Dustin had adjusted the vents to blow cold air into the cab, which was a welcome relief despite the freezing-cold temperatures outside. But then Andrea noticed Dustin's thin T-shirt. Actually, she noticed his bulging triceps first and his lack of outerwear second. "You don't have a jacket on. I don't want you to get cold."

Dustin shrugged. "I'm fine."

"Of course you are."

"What's that supposed to mean?"

"You were always impervious to cold."

"Still am."

"You and your Nordic nature," said Andrea. As she recalled, being the descendent of loggers made Dustin tall, handsome, and weather-proof, but it also made him weird about money. Andrea's mother said it was because he was Swedish. "The Swedes are always too frugal for their own good," Lydia liked to say. There was even a Swedish word for it: *lagom*. Roughly translated, it meant "Enough is the right amount." Sitting in Dustin's tricked-out truck made Andrea wonder if he still epitomized that sentiment. It didn't appear so.

"This is a pretty truck," she said.

He snorted.

"What?"

"Nothing."

"It's not nothing," she protested. "Obviously I said something to cause that pissed-off noise. I deserve to know what it was."

"You called my truck *pretty*," he said. "It's not pretty; it's a Ford F-350."

Andrea ran her palms across the leather seats and batted her eye-lashes. "You don't think this is pretty? Especially compared to the Yo-Mobile?"

He looked at her sideways. "Form should follow function. Leather holds up better to dirt and debris, and unlike the Yo-Mobile, this truck has a back seat."

Andrea blushed. The Yo-Mobile's lack of a back seat was some-thing she vividly remembered, even though they had never gone beyond kissing. "How times have changed," she mused. "Now you have two car seats in the back."

"They're boosters," he clarified. "I took Kendal and Jane to the zoo last weekend."

Andrea was shocked. The Woodland Park Zoo was in Seattle. "I can't believe you drove there willingly," she said. "You used to hate Seattle."

"Still do." He nodded. "But there's a baby gorilla on exhibit that Kendal really wanted to see."

"Was it cute?"

He grinned. "Adorable."

A buzzing from Andrea's purse caught her attention. She retrieved her phone and saw a message. Here's a picture you can show people when you ask if they've seen Cade, Heidi had texted. In the photograph, Cade appeared relaxed. His blond hair was swept casually to the side, and he grinned like he knew the secret to happiness.

Thanks, Andrea texted back.

How are things going with my brother?

Fine.

Just fine? Heidi asked.

Andrea looked sideways at Dustin. Part of her wanted to kiss him. The other part wanted to burst into tears. It would have been easier if she had been the one to have dumped him all those years ago, but instead, it was the other way around. It's fine, she texted back. I can swallow my pride for one night if it means getting my coins back.

Thatta girl! I hope things aren't too awkward. Dustin stops talking when he's upset. He bottles up his emotions and never says a word.

We're talking a little bit, Andrea typed. I'll text you later. She stuffed her phone back into her purse, feeling slightly encouraged.

"Something important?" Dustin asked.

"Heidi texted a picture of Cade we can use to show around the casino."

"That was good thinking."

"Yes, it was." At least they could both agree that Heidi was smart.

Their conversation stalled again, and Heidi was right—the awkwardness was oppressive. Andrea struggled to come up with something to say. It occurred to her that maybe this was a good opportunity to finally clear the air. This might be a long night, and Andrea would rather go into it without their past history making things worse.

"You were right to break up," she said, thinking about prom night. "You were mature enough to realize that long-distance relationships are difficult and that college students should focus on their education." Andrea felt like an idiot as soon as she spoke. It was like she was parroting her father. That was the exact speech Tom had given her when she'd returned home in tears.

Dustin clenched his jaw before speaking. "Yeah, well, it seemed like the right thing to say, seeing as how you were only dating me out of pity."

"*What?*"

"You could have told me that you had your eye on another guy. I mean, yeah, I had been through a lot that year, but it wasn't like I would shatter." He kept his eyes focused on the road, not so much as glancing at her.

"I don't know what you're talking about. There was no other guy; there was only you."

"That's not true, and you know it."

"It *is* true." Andrea began to perspire again. Her cashmere sweater trapped in the heat. "You broke my heart when you dumped me, but I can see now that it was for the best."

"I didn't dump you. Well, okay, I did, because it was the wise thing to do. You were about to break up with me."

"That's ridiculous! I would never have done that."

"But I heard you," said Dustin, this time looking straight at her. His green eyes were so full of anguish that they pierced her heart. "When I was coming back from the restroom at the tennis club. I heard you tell your friends that you wanted to bring some other guy to prom but your mom wouldn't let you. I didn't catch the name, but I did know I was your pity date." He jerked his gaze away and stared back at the road. "Your second choice."

Andrea gasped. "This was because of Spike?"

"Spike? What did your hedgehog have to do with it?"

Andrea felt a thunk in her chest like an old rusty lock clicking into place. "I wanted to bring Spike to prom with me, but my mom wouldn't let me."

"No. That can't be true."

"It *is* true. I could have slipped him in my coat pocket, and the chaperones would never have known."

"But what would have happened when you took off your coat?" Dustin asked.

"You're taking my mom's side on this?" Andrea asked, her voice rising. "Eighteen years later?"

"Hold up, wait." Dustin shook his head. "I heard you tell your friend, 'He's the cutest, but Mom said I couldn't go with him, so now it's just Dustin and me.'"

"I was talking about Spike. No offense, but Spike *was* the cutest. He could have given that baby gorilla at the zoo a run for his money. And I'm sure I didn't say *just* Dustin. You were my dream date for prom."

"So," said Dustin, shaking his head like he was rattling his thoughts, "you mean I broke up with you because of your hedgehog?"

"Broke my heart is more like it." Andrea crossed her arms over her chest. "I cried for weeks over you dumping me." She wasn't ashamed to admit it. If anything, she wanted Dustin to know how much he had wounded her.

"Why didn't you say anything?"

"What do you mean, 'Why didn't I say anything'?" Andrea adjusted the vents so that cold air blew directly at her face. "You told me that long-distance relationships in college never worked and it was better to break up right away. I tried to talk you out of it, but you wouldn't listen."

"Because I thought—" Dustin's shoulders slumped, and he didn't finish his sentence. The Suquamish Clearwater Casino Resort loomed in front of them, brightly lit against the dark sky. He clicked on the blinker to turn into the parking lot. "Spike or no Spike, we weren't in the right emotional space for each other."

"It was a long time ago." Andrea stared out the window for a moment into the brightly lit parking lot, contemplating his half-assed apology. "You were probably right," she continued, looking back at him. "It might not have been good for us to have such an intense relationship when we were still young." Her word choice was spontaneous but truthful. Dustin was the first of many men who had broken her heart. She was too quick to fall in love; that was her problem. She could see that now with thirty-six years of wisdom behind her, but at eighteen she still believed in true love and happily ever afters.

"*Intense* was right." Dustin parked the truck and turned off the ignition. "That's how your dad described it too. You held me together that awful year. I don't know what I would have done without you or your father. I respected his advice a lot—to the point that I'd do anything he told me. *Almost* anything." When he turned his head and looked at her, Andrea felt her knees go weak, like they had back in high school every time he had been about to kiss her. Dustin took a deep breath, and for a moment Andrea's imagination ran wild, and she thought he *was* about to kiss her. But then he unclicked his seat belt. "Come on," he said as he opened his door. "Let's go get your dad's coins."

Andrea checked her watch so that Dustin couldn't see the disappointment on her face. It was 8:02 p.m. She should be home right now watching Netflix, but instead she was reliving painful high school memories and about to subject herself to the sound of slot machines. Plus, she missed Spike. The only thing that would make her feel better right now was reaching into her coat pocket and feeling his prickly presence. But he'd died years ago, when she had been a sophomore in college. Andrea climbed down from the truck.

"So what's the plan?" she asked, slinging her purse over her shoulder. "Do you really think we'll walk in there and spot him?"

"Yes, that's exactly what I think." Dustin's long strides were hard to keep up with. "Hopefully he's not feeding your triple eagles into the slots right now."

"Double eagles," Andrea clarified. "And don't joke about that. Whoever stole the coins must be clever enough not to spend them like quarters."

"Cade stole those coins, not whoever." Dustin folded his arms over his chest like he was trying to keep warm. "Look, I'm not sure if Heidi told you, but we fired Cade from Karlsson Construction because we caught him stealing copper pipe. He's definitely a crook."

"Damn. Okay then." She pulled up Cade's picture on her phone. Andrea didn't share Dustin's certainty that Cade would be easy to locate. "You check the slot machines, and I'll ask around at the table games to see if anyone recognizes his picture."

"All the employees will recognize him," Dustin grunted. "Cade's a regular."

They were approaching the entrance of the casino now, and although she wasn't a gambler, Andrea was impressed by what the Suquamish people had built. She had learned about the Suquamish and their famous leader, Chief Seattle, in school. The Suquamish Tribe had lived in the area for ten thousand years. The name *Suquamish* meant "people of the clear salt water," and their ancestors were expert canoe builders, fishermen, and basket weavers. The waters had once been an abundant source of salmon, cod, and clams, and the forest had teemed with game and berries.

Standing at the entrance to the casino was a burly-looking security guard. "Welcome to the Clearwater," he said. "May I see your ID?"

"ID?" Andrea felt flattered until she saw the sign next to him stating that all guests were required to have their IDs scanned to enter the property. "Sure," she said, unzipping her purse. "My driver's license is right here." She held it out and watched as he examined her picture.

"And here's mine," said Dustin.

Andrea stuffed her driver's license back into her wallet and swiped her phone screen to life, displaying Cade's photo. "Excuse me," she began, "but did you happen to see this man enter the casino earlier? We're looking for him."

The bouncer glanced at her phone and shrugged. "Can't say that I remember."

"Cade Tolbert," Dustin prompted. "He's here all the time. You must have seen him before."

The bouncer shook his head. "Lots of people come here. I check hundreds of IDs a night."

Andrea opened her wallet back up and removed a crisp twenty-dollar bill. "Now do you remember?" she asked as she offered it to him.

"Nope." He refused the money. "I don't accept bribes, and even if I did, twenty bucks wouldn't be worth me risking my job." He pointed at the cameras. "See those? We're on TV."

"Well, that's good to know." Andrea smiled at the camera. "Thanks for the tip."

"Thanks for what?" the guard asked. "I didn't do anything."

But Andrea didn't see it that way. Now she knew about the security cameras, which meant that a record of Cade might exist on film.

"Come on." Dustin touched her elbow and gently pulled her inside. "Let's start canvassing the place."

"Maybe we can ask the concierge or security desk to search the video and find Cade's face?" Andrea suggested.

"Sure. I'll do that while you check the tables and slots."

"Okay." Secretly, she was relieved that she didn't have to sweet-talk her way into getting the security footage. She would much rather chat with semisloshed gamblers.

When they walked through the double doors, Andrea expected to enter a cloud of cigarette smoke, like the last time she and an old boyfriend had gone to Vegas. Boy, had that trip been a mistake. After dating Jim for only three months postcollege, she had been sure he was the one. She had entered the MGM Grand with dreams of a Vegas elopement and departed with a headache, a failed relationship, and a strong aversion to peach-flavored champagne. But instead of smelling like Vegas, the Clearwater's air was fresh. Andrea saw NO SMOKING signs everywhere she looked.

"I'll go hunt down that video." Dustin took off without saying goodbye.

Abandoned again in a casino. This was familiar. There might not be any smoke, but the cacophonous sounds of the slot machines took Andrea straight back to her memories of Jim and the MGM Grand. On their second night in Vegas, Andrea had come back from her spa treatment early and discovered Jim tangled up with a cocktail waitress and her feather boa. The worst part had been coming home and telling her mother why she and Jim had broken up.

"I told you he was a loser," Lydia had scolded. "You're too old to believe in fairy tales."

Andrea had smartened up, all right. She now knew better than to trust anyone. Keeping her phone handy with Cade's picture on it, she walked up to the first blackjack table she saw. "Excuse me?" she asked the dealer, holding out the phone. "Have you seen this man?"

"Cade?" The dealer shook her head. "Not tonight, I haven't."

"Thanks anyway." Andrea showed Cade's picture to the players as well, but they all shook their heads.

She paused for a moment by the free soda fountain and helped herself to a small drink of Diet Coke. After she gulped back the liquid, she tossed the cup in the trash and fished the steel penny from her pocket. "Come on," she whispered to herself. "This can't be the next to last coin in my collection. Dad's counting on me." Replacing the steelie, she squared her shoulders and kept going.

Working from one table to the next, Andrea circumnavigated the room until she had asked every person she saw. Then she snaked through the slot machines. From the corner of her eye, she saw Dustin speaking to a woman wearing a pantsuit who looked like she was a manager.

"No luck?" Dustin asked her when they regrouped.

"No," Andrea admitted. "You?"

Dustin shook his head. "No. I'm going to ask the hotel reception if they have security tapes too. How about you ask over at the players' club desk?"

"Okay." Andrea nodded. "*Goodbye*," she said pointedly as he started to walk away again without saying anything.

"Oh. Yeah. Bye." Dustin stuffed his hands in his pockets and took off.

Andrea hurried over to talk to a woman who had glossy brown hair and a curvy figure. "Hi, Mary," she said, reading the clerk's name tag. "My name is Andrea Wint, and I'm really hoping you can help me."

"Are you already a club member, or would you like to sign up?" Mary smiled, flashing teeth so straight they would make an orthodontist proud. "It's free to join."

"That sounds fun, but I'm not here to gamble." Andrea held up her phone. "I'm looking for this man here. Have you seen him?"

"Cade Tolbert?" She blinked her thick eyelashes, and her smile turned icy. "What do you want with Cade?"

Andrea felt a shot of luck spike through her. Lots of the employees had recognized Cade's picture, but none of them had looked like they wanted to bite her for asking about him. "I'm friends with his wife," she said. "Leanne's worried he might have been assaulted." Some of that was the truth, at least, and Andrea felt no guilt for embellishing.

"Oh shit. Poor Cade!" Mary's annoyed look disappeared.

"Yeah," said Andrea, sensing genuine concern. "His van was abandoned by the side of the road, and he didn't show up to pick up his kids from school. Hopefully he's found soon because it's freezing tonight."

"I haven't seen Cade in a few days." Mary leaned on the counter and rested her chin on her hand. "He stops here for the buffet a few times a week and always says hi. I used to date his brother-in-law."

"You did?" Heat flushed up Andrea's neck.

"Uh-huh. For a couple of years. That's how I know Cade and Leanne so well." Mary analyzed her computer. "Hang on. I'm not supposed to do this, but I don't want Cade to freeze to death." Her long red fingernails clicked on the keyboard. "I'm looking up his players' club number. Yup. It says he hasn't used it since Tuesday afternoon." She tapped the mouse and clicked out of the screen. "Sorry I couldn't help you."

"You did help me actually. Thanks." Andrea knew she should turn around and walk away, but standing in front of Dustin's ex-girlfriend sparked her curiosity—and her jealousy. "Two years, huh? That sounds like it was serious." The longest any of Andrea's relationships had lasted was six months, and that was with Dustin.

"Yeah." Mary sighed. "We broke up three months ago. It still hurts to talk about."

Andrea fought to keep her face neutral. *Dustin broke up with a Clearwater employee three months ago and didn't think to mention that on our drive over here?* "Breakups can be hard," she said.

"Ain't that the truth. In the end our schedules were just too complicated."

"Working the night shift would be difficult," Andrea said as she privately wondered why Dustin didn't adjust his schedule accordingly. There was no law that said that homes had to be remodeled in the daytime instead of the middle of the night. Noise ordinances, maybe, but Dustin could have figured that out.

"Incredibly difficult," said Mary. "And with the restaurant business taking off like it has in Port Inez, he was busier than ever."

"Huh?"

"The fast foot ferry," Mary explained. "It's brought a huge uptick in his business."

Andrea knew what the fast foot ferry was, but she didn't understand what that had to do with Dustin and Mary's relationship. Six months ago, the local transit agency had begun a pedestrian-only ferry route from Seattle to Port Inez. What had once been an hour-and-a-half commute on the ferry from Port Inez through Harper Landing and down into Seattle could now be completed in twenty-two minutes. "So you're busier here at the resort, I take it?"

Mary nodded. "We have a courtesy shuttle that picks guests up at the ferry dock. But Nathan's the one who has really been affected by that ferry."

"Nathan?" Andrea felt a ridiculous sense of relief.

"Yeah." Mary nodded. "Port Pizza's business spikes every night when the fast ferry unloads. He had to hire extra waitstaff to keep up with the demand. We never saw each other."

"There you are," said a deep voice behind her. Andrea turned around and saw Dustin. The dejected look on his face melted away when he saw Mary. "Oh, hi, Mary," he said, taking his hands out of his pockets. "It's good to see you. It's been a while."

"Hi, Dustin. I was just telling your girlfriend here that I haven't seen Cade since Tuesday."

Andrea held up her hands. "We're not together."

"Oops." Mary grinned. "Well, maybe you should be. You'd make a cute couple."

"Um . . . thanks," said Andrea. She looked at Dustin from the corner of her eye and saw him smirking.

"Give us a call if Cade shows up," said Dustin.

"Will do. And tell Nathan I said hi." A pained look flashed across her face as Mary went back to her computer.

"So what's the plan now?" Andrea asked as she followed Dustin out through the lobby. "You were certain Cade would be here."

"I was sure he would be at a casino," Dustin clarified. "But I don't know which one." They walked through the doors and into the cold air. "I'm heading to the Elwha River Casino. That's the next closest place where Cade might be."

Andrea placed her hand on Dustin's broad shoulder. "If we're driving to Port Angeles, then I need to use the restroom before we go."

"We're not going to Port Angeles together," said Dustin. The skies opened, and raindrops fell. "I'm dropping you off in Port Inez."

"That's what you think." Andrea pulled up her hood. "It's my home that was robbed. I'm not giving up until we track your miserable brother-in-law down. I'm getting my father's coins back if I have to follow Cade all the way to Mars."

CHAPTER SIX

At least his truck complied. Dustin felt the engine roar with satisfaction as he picked up speed on the road to Port Angeles. The sky was inky black, and trees lined the horizon as far as the eye could see. Rain pounded against the windshield. Andrea had called his truck *pretty*, but that was the wrong label for a workhorse. This wasn't the Yo-Mobile, but chauffeuring Andrea made him feel like he was in high school again. Eighteen years later, and she attracted him as strongly as ever.

"I don't understand why we're driving to the Elwha River Casino and not to the Point," said Andrea. "That would be closer." Her wet raincoat was in the back seat, and she had turned the heaters on full blast.

"The Point banned Cade for stealing chips."

"Oh." Andrea warmed her hands in front of the vents. "What about Seven Cedars in Sequim?" she asked.

"He's banned there too."

"Wow."

The blue sweater Andrea wore was the same color as her eyes. Dustin could get lost in those eyes. He had, in fact, but he refused to let that happen to him again. It would be safer for everyone if Andrea went home to Port Inez and Dustin continued pursuing Cade on his own. That's what Tom would have wanted too. He'd made it very clear that Andrea and Dustin weren't right for each other. What Dustin had told Andrea about breaking up at prom was only half of the truth. But he didn't want to think about that now.

"It's either the Quinault or the Elwha," said Dustin, "and the Elwha's closer."

"The Quinault would be closer to Oregon if Cade decides to leave the state."

Dustin knew Andrea had a point. But choosing the Elwha over the Quinault took them past Port Inez. His heart clenched, protecting itself against the departure that was imminent. Hopefully he could convince Andrea to let him drop her off at home before he took the Hood Canal Bridge over to the Olympic Peninsula. She'd held him together like duct tape during his senior year. When they had parted, it was like his soul had ripped in half. Having her so close to him brought up emotions that he couldn't process right now or perhaps ever.

"The Elwha is one and a half hours away, but the Quinault is two and a half hours." Dustin adjusted the windshield wiper speed. "Cade's lazy. He probably picked the one that's nearer."

Andrea shook her head. "The Clearwater was closest, but Mary said Cade's players' club number hadn't been used since Tuesday."

"Which proves that Cade's lazy," said Dustin. "He usually goes to the closest casino."

"Or the nicest." Andrea shrugged. "No cigarette smoke means Leanne wouldn't be able to smell it on him and know he was gambling."

"I hadn't thought of that."

"That's because you don't think like a cheater."

"True." Dustin chuckled but wondered why she'd mentioned that. Had someone cheated on her? "Listen, it's almost ten p.m. Why don't you let me drop you off at home, and I'll text you when I reach Port Angeles? There's no need for both of us to drive all over the place in the middle of the night."

"Actually, there is a need for both of us." She settled back into her seat. "Do I really have to highlight your numismatic failings again?"

"Double eagles, not triple eagles. I get it. You can text me a picture of what they look like."

"I'm not going to entrust one hundred thousand dollars' worth of coins to a grainy picture I found on the internet."

"He's not going to unload them tonight."

"You don't know that. For all we know Cade has a buyer lined up and is mailing them at a twenty-four-hour shipping center right now." Andrea shuddered. "I need to find them, Dustin. They're my most valuable possessions—and not because of how much they're worth."

"Understood," he said in a low voice. "But I can find them without you."

"You don't know that. If you insist on ditching me, I'll hop into my car and drive to the Quinault myself. Maybe that would be a good idea, come to think of it. We could be in two places at once."

"You can't drive your Nissan Leaf all the way to Ocean Shores in the middle of the night."

"Sure I can. It has a one-hundred-fifty-mile range when it's fully charged." She typed into her phone. "Google says that the casino is one hundred twenty miles away."

"But it's the middle of the night," said Dustin, unable to keep the edge of concern from his voice. "It's dark outside."

"Yeah, that usually happens at night." She put her phone back into her purse.

"What if you need to recharge the battery?"

"I'll find a charging station along the way."

"How long does it take to charge?"

Andrea shrugged. "It depends on the charging option."

The turnoff for Port Inez was approaching. Dustin made a snap decision. He'd rather have Andrea nearby where he could see her than worry about her tiny car crapping out in the middle of the woods. Plus, he didn't like the idea of her confronting Cade alone. Andrea was one of the smartest women he knew, but Cade was a charmer. What if he tricked her, or worse? "It's better if we stick together," he said.

"You think?" She gave him a sly grin.

"Yes, given the options," said Dustin, realizing too late that he had been played. Shoot, here he'd been worried about Cade tricking Andrea, when it was really he who should watch out. Andrea was the master at getting what she wanted by making people think *her* idea was *their* idea.

In high school, their first date had been to a Halloween party at her friend's house in Seattle. Andrea had somehow convinced him not only to attend a party in the city but to wear matching costumes. Since it was too far to drive home that night, he'd crashed on her living room couch. The next morning when Tom and Lydia had walked into their living room, Dustin had had to explain why he was dressed like bacon. The costume didn't make much sense without Andrea there dressed like eggs.

"Maybe we should stop real quick in Port Inez," said Andrea. "So you can pick up a coat."

"What? I don't need a coat."

"You're wearing a T-shirt. What happens if the truck breaks down on the side of the road somewhere and—"

"My truck's not going to break down." He caressed the steering wheel. As far as Dustin was concerned, reliability was his truck's most important feature. "Besides, I've got a blanket in the back if something happens."

"Is it the same blanket you kept in the back of the Yo-Mobile?" The corners of her mouth turned up.

Dustin grinned. "Probably." The old Pendleton blanket had come in awful handy for impromptu makeout sessions on the beach, in the woods, and at the park. Those were some of the most memorable kisses of his life. The exit to Port Inez flashed past him, and Dustin felt nervous excitement for the road ahead.

"No coat, and you're cold already." Andrea pointed at the hair standing up on his arms.

Dustin ignored her statement. She didn't need to know why he had the chills.

"So the players' club clerk at the Clearwater," Andrea said, yanking Dustin back to the present. "It sounds like she and Nathan dated for a while?"

"Yeah." Dustin nodded. "It's a shame it didn't work out—I liked Mary."

"She seemed nice. She mentioned something that made me think about our situation."

Dustin tensed. What did that mean? Nathan wouldn't have told Mary anything about him and Andrea. As far as Dustin knew, Nathan hadn't even told Mary how much money each sibling had received in the settlement: $4.3 million. "What did Mary say exactly?"

"That there was a courtesy shuttle from the ferry dock to the casino, which would have been one way Cade could have gotten to the Clearwater without his van." She turned her head and looked at him. "He didn't stay, and he didn't gamble. In fact, we don't know if he was there at all. But he for sure didn't have his van. Did Cade own another vehicle?"

"Not that I know of. The Subaru was a gift to Leanne on her eighteenth birthday from me, Heidi, and Nathan. I don't know how she and Cade financed the van."

"So no third vehicle?"

"Not unless Leanne bought him something when she turned twenty-five last month."

Dustin didn't bother explaining the details of the trust funds to Andrea because she had been there the night Tom had taken the siblings out to the Old Spaghetti Factory and explained the rules. Nobody could touch their money until they turned twenty-five, but they did have access to college tuition and limited funds for daily expenses. Tom's goal had been to protect them from foolish choices, but the legalities had also caused problems. In order for Heidi and Dustin to have the capital to start Karlsson Construction right out of college, they'd had to borrow money from Nathan and pay him back later.

"Okay, so how is Cade traveling right now?" Andrea asked. "This seems like a basic question we should have examined earlier."

"You're right." Dustin kneaded the back of his neck. "I charged off to the Clearwater on instinct, positive that Cade would be there. I never stopped to examine the logistics."

"Don't blame yourself. I was right there with you." She leaned her arm on the console, making Dustin extra aware of her added closeness. "Let's think. How did Cade get from the abandoned van on Cedar Way to my house two miles away and then to wherever he is now?"

Dustin rubbed his chin. "Your house is within easy walking distance to the ferry, which means he could have traveled to Harper Landing."

"Or taken the fast foot ferry to Seattle."

Dustin shook his head. "The foot ferry is one way only in the evening. It sails to Seattle in the morning and comes back to Port Inez at night."

"Oh, I haven't ridden it yet, so I didn't know."

"I haven't either, but our real estate agent won't shut up about it."

"Why's that?"

"Because it's turned Port Inez into a bedroom community for Seattle, which is causing home values to skyrocket. You're lucky you bought here when you did."

"I love my house." Andrea beamed. "It's beautiful."

A warm rush of pride washed over Dustin when she said that. But he didn't have time to relish that feeling; he needed to focus on Cade. "The foot ferry won't run until tomorrow morning, but Cade could have walked onto the regular ferry going to Harper Landing and then taken a bus from there."

Andrea nodded. "Or he could have taken a courtesy shuttle from the ferry dock to the Clearwater Casino and then left with someone he knew from there."

"That's right. Or maybe he took a Lyft or Uber."

"Do we have Lyft and Ubers in Port Inez?"

"Sure we do," said Dustin. "My buddy Ryan from high school drives for Lyft, and Heidi knows a woman who drives for Uber. I forget her name."

"That sounds like a place to start." Andrea swiped her phone to life. "I'll text Heidi and ask her to find out." As she was typing on the phone, it rang. "Hello?" Andrea asked. "It's Heidi," she whispered to Dustin.

He could have guessed that already from the sound of his sister's voice over the phone. "No luck yet?" Heidi asked, her voice carrying.

"Not yet," said Andrea. "Although we do have more information." She explained about Mary looking up Cade's players' club account and then asked Heidi to text the Uber and Lyft drivers to see if they had seen him. "Now we're going to the Elwha," she said.

"Okay," said Heidi. "Tell Dustin I'm sorry I stole his fleece."

"I will," said Andrea, with the hint of a smile across her lips. She hung up the phone. "So that's why you aren't wearing a jacket."

"Yeah. It was thirty-eight degrees when I left the house this morning. I'm tough, but I'm not Canadian. Heidi, on the other hand, is just plain forgetful."

"Forgetful is right. That's why I always meet Heidi at her house when we go for our morning walks. Otherwise, she'll forget we're meeting up and leave me waiting in the cold."

Dustin chuckled. "If it were me she was meeting, she'd tell me I was the one who got the time and date wrong, instead of her."

"Yep." Andrea laughed. "I always loved how close you all were and how you'd get on each other's nerves and bicker."

Dustin arched his eyebrows at her. "Really? You thought it was fun when Heidi ordered me around?"

"Heidi was so good at it that it was hard not to be impressed."

"She's still good at it," he admitted, thinking of the new appliances they had purchased.

"Nathan was protective of you, and Leanne was the baby of the family but serious at the same time." Andrea sighed. "Too serious, now that I consider it."

"Really? What do you mean?"

"I don't know much about children, but she was much more well behaved than the other neighborhood kids I babysat."

"Huh. I suppose you're right." Looking back at it now, Dustin did see that Leanne had been more reserved than Kendal was at that age. Guarded, almost, like she had been afraid to make a mess or be too noisy. "Nathan did everything he could to give Leanne the most normal childhood possible," he said loyally.

"I'm not criticizing Nathan."

"Yeah, I know."

"That must have been so hard for him too. I can't imagine what it would have been like for him to be twenty-three and stuck with a seven-year-old to take care of."

"Nathan was twenty-one when you met him. Our parents had been gone for five months by that point. It must have been hard for Nathan to deal with a high school senior like me who thought he knew everything."

"Plus Heidi, who actually did know everything," Andrea said with a wink.

Dustin chuckled but sobered up a moment later. "At least Heidi, Nathan, and I remember our parents. We had lots of time with them."

"Not enough time with them, though."

"No." Dustin clenched his jaw. "Leanne told me tonight that she barely remembers anything about our parents. Nothing except my dad's coat and a stupid . . ." The words stuck in his throat.

"A stupid what?" Andrea asked softly.

"It doesn't matter."

"I think it does. Memories always matter."

Dustin rubbed his knuckles across his nose but said nothing. Andrea didn't press him to continue, but he knew she wanted him to. "A stupid tablecloth," he blurted out. "That we only used one time."

"Hmm . . ." Andrea rested her palm on his knee. "Well, now that one time lives forever."

"If only it could," said Dustin.

He didn't like examining the past. History, yes, but his personal history, no way. Looking forward was the only way to function. But now that Andrea was poking and prodding through his memories, his mind wouldn't stop chewing on them.

Andrea pulled her hand away. "How old was Leanne when she had her first daughter?"

"Nineteen," he said. "She dropped out of college right after Kendal was born. Cade convinced her that finishing her degree was a waste of time, even though I offered to pay for day care." He couldn't keep the bitterness from his tone. "She was studying to be a nurse. She would have been a great one."

"Leanne can still be a nurse—or a stay-at-home mom. She can be a pizza parlor waitress, or a pilot, or anything she wants," said Andrea.

"Not if Cade steals her money."

"We won't let that happen. Let's get back to the transportation issue. What's another way Cade could have left Port Inez?"

Relieved that she'd changed the subject, Dustin dove right in. "Bicycle? Motorbike?"

"With my safe in the basket?"

Dustin shook his head. "Maybe he cracked the safe, stole the contents, and dumped it behind your house. We didn't think to look."

"Mack inspected the perimeter before you arrived to look for signs of entry and didn't see anything."

"But Cade's a locksmith. I'm sorry, Andrea. It's my family's fault you're in this position."

"No, it's not. You didn't steal those coins."

"But it is. Cade's my brother-in-law. Heidi and I should have pressed charges when we caught him stealing from us, instead of just firing him. But we didn't want to make things worse for Leanne or the girls."

"You weren't stupid. You were taking care of your family like the Karlssons do. That's one of the things I loved about you guys. No matter how bad things got, you took care of one another."

"You make us sound like we were the perfect family, which we never were."

"Compared to my house, you were."

"Your house?" Dustin took his eyes off the road for a second to look at her. "But I loved being at your house. It was the first fully restored Pacific Northwest craftsman that I had ever been in. Plus your father was there, doling out wise advice." Even advice he didn't want to hear, like how Andrea and Dustin weren't right for each other and the sooner she and Dustin parted ways, the better. "You're a serious young man," Tom had said, "with a sober disposition. But my daughter is sparkly and effervescent. Her creativity draws her to people who aren't right for her." Dustin pushed that memory away and focused on the positives. "Your mom was great too. She took really good care of me."

"You sound like a labradoodle. You'll love anyone who feeds you."

"It wasn't just the casseroles," he protested. "She invited my whole family over for Christmas. Heidi still talks about the floral arrangement on the mantel."

Andrea groaned. "My mom and her flower club. That's how she met Roger, her new boyfriend. Mom was at a flower-arranging competition at the Tacoma Dome and wrecked her feet by wearing flats all day. Her doctor referred her to a podiatrist, and now Roger's taking care of her feet for life."

Dustin cringed. "I did *not* need that visual."

"Neither did I. Honestly, I try to ignore the fact that they're together. I figure if I decline enough dinner invitations from her, she'll finally stop asking."

"If my mom asked me over for dinner, I would say yes," said Dustin. "No matter who she was with."

"Really?" Andrea shot him a look. "You're going to pull the dead-parents card on me?"

"I'm just saying that there are worse things than having your mom shack up with a foot doctor."

"It's not just that."

"Isn't it? Because your mom is still alive, and you could see her if you wanted to. Unlike my mom or dad, who I haven't been able to see in nineteen years."

"You have no right to judge."

"Nineteen years," he said again, letting the words sink in. "The last time I ate dinner with my mother, I was a junior in high school."

"I said"—Andrea spoke with grit in her tone—"you have no right to judge."

"Don't I?"

"No," she said. "You don't. Tragedy isn't a competition, and if it were, there are worse things than dying in the prime of your life—like your body outliving your brain, for example." She turned away and stared through the passenger-side window.

"Andrea," he said. "Look—"

"No, you look." She whipped her head and faced him. "Last night my dad got his fingers stuck in the metal box that holds the paper towels in his bathroom. The week before, he was caught urinating in the wastebasket. My father, Dustin, who graduated from Yale." Her eyes misted with tears. "So don't tell me how I should feel about my mother abandoning him. Your life might have been harder than mine when we were in high school, but it's certainly not harder than mine now." She pulled a tissue out of her pocket and blew her nose before staring out the window and ignoring him.

Nausea pooled in his stomach even though he hadn't eaten since lunch. Every tendon in his back, neck, and shoulders felt tight enough to snap. This was exactly why he had wanted to drop Andrea off in Port Inez. He had made things worse between them, and that left him feeling gutted. "I'm sorry," he said. "I shouldn't have said anything."

When she didn't answer, his guilt turned to anger. She, of all people, knew what he had said was true. If Dustin had the opportunity to see his mom again, he would take it, no matter what douchebag she brought with her to dinner. He had spoken from the heart, and Andrea was throwing that back in his face.

"How about we listen to the radio?" he suggested, not expecting her to answer.

"Fine," she muttered.

"Okay." He turned on the media player. They still had a for-ty-five-minute drive ahead of them. Unfortunately, winding through the Olympic National Forest meant that their radio options were lim-ited, and Dustin had been too frugal to spring for satellite. It was either static, static, static, or country, which he knew Andrea hated.

"No music is fine too," she said.

"Or how about the audiobook?" Dustin offered.

"Sure."

"I'll give you a quick recap before I turn it on, since I'm in the middle of the book."

"Whatever." Andrea shrugged.

"*The Boys in the Boat* is about Joe Rantz, who rowed for the University of Washington and went on to compete at the 1936 Olympics—only I haven't gotten to that part yet. His mom died, his father abandoned him, and he was so poor he only owned one sweater. He grew up in Sequim," said Dustin, naming a small town they were about to drive past.

"One sweater?" Andrea looked at him like she was checking if he were serious or not.

"It was the Great Depression. Rowing saved his life." Dustin pushed the play button and let Grandpa Gilmore take it away. This was the first time he was listening to the story on audio but his third time reading the book.

It took all of two minutes before Andrea was hooked. Dustin could see the look of interest wash over her face like spring rain. Even after all these years she was shockingly predictable. He'd known she would love it. Andrea turned the volume up slightly to make it easier to hear over the windshield wipers. Then she settled back into the leather seat, completely engrossed in the story.

Her love of history was something that had attracted Dustin from the very beginning. The first time he had met her was when she had tagged along with Tom on his trip to Port Inez to discuss the Karlssons' case with Nathan, Heidi, and Dustin. Dustin had wondered why she had come, but then she had opened up a small suitcase of toys and invited Leanne to play. Tom had brought her along as a built-in babysitter. But it was the toys themselves that had caught his attention. They were vintage pieces like you might find at an antiques store in Port Orchard. She even had a tin of old Lincoln Logs.

Their first date had been to her friend's Halloween party, but their second had been to the MOHAI, the Museum of History and Industry in Seattle, after Dustin had mentioned he'd never been before. Andrea had insisted he would love it, and she'd been right.

Dustin had taught Andrea things about history, too, like the difference between old-growth and second-growth trees. He had taken her on hikes in the woods and pointed out the divots in stumps where loggers would stick planks to stand on as they sawed through the trunk. He'd driven her to Bainbridge Island to honor the spot where on March 30, 1942, Japanese Americans had been forced to leave for imprisonment.

He'd studied the tide charts and taken her to see the Haleets petroglyphs when they weren't submerged.

They had soaked up local history together, both the good and the bad, their shared fascination bringing them closer together. When Dustin had confided that his dream was to start a business one day restoring old homes, Andrea had whipped out her notebook and drawn him a logo to use for his website. He still had that scrap of paper tucked away in a book somewhere.

Listening to the audiobook made the drive pass quickly, and they reached Port Angeles ten minutes before eleven. The Elwha River Casino was tiny compared to the Clearwater, but the parking lot was packed. Dustin pulled into one of the last remaining spaces and was tempted to sit in the truck for a few minutes and let the chapter finish. But time was of the essence, so he turned off the ignition.

"Well?" he asked. "Are you ready?"

Andrea slowly unclicked her seat belt. "That book is amazing."

"I knew you'd like it," he said softly. The truth was he thought about Andrea every time he learned a new element of local history. Without her to share it, the experience felt incomplete.

"I'm sorry I snapped at you about my mom and Roger." She put her coat on and hitched the zipper.

"I'm sorry things are so hard with your dad."

Andrea zipped up her coat. "It is what it is." She opened her door, and the night air that rushed into the cab was shockingly cold.

Dustin felt the icy breeze but refused to let it bother him. The sting came from witnessing the sadness in Andrea's eyes and knowing that Tom Wint, his adolescent hero, was suffering.

CHAPTER SEVEN

Walking up to the casino and watching Dustin stoically shiver in his thin T-shirt made Andrea think about the rowers on Lake Washington from the audiobook. If she didn't get the opportunity to finish the story with Dustin in the car, she would pick it up from the Little Free Library next to the Owl's Nest.

"Are you ready?" Dustin asked.

"Sure." She fished her driver's license out of her purse and opened Cade's picture on her phone.

They spoke with the bouncer first to ask if he had seen Cade.

"That dude?" The man scratched behind his ear. He was one enormous block of muscle and bulk, like a brick walking around in a black shirt, black pants, and sneakers. "Yeah, I've seen him around, but I couldn't tell you when."

Andrea glanced up in the corner of the room and saw cameras. "Thanks anyway," she said, about to walk off.

"Yeah," said Dustin, shaking the guy's hand. "Thanks."

"Wait a sec." The bouncer made a fist and frowned. "Show me again?"

"Of course." Andrea held up her phone.

"That looks like Lisa's boyfriend."

"Lisa's boyfriend?" Andrea's eyebrows shot up.

"Lisa the cocktail waitress, not Lisa from payroll," the bouncer clarified, as if that settled it. "She has red hair and a tattoo of a vine on her wrist."

"Thanks." Dustin shook his hand one more time. "We appreciate it."

"Wow," Andrea whispered, once they were out of earshot. "He was really helpful. I didn't have to bribe him or anything."

Dustin flashed a tight grin. "Not that you would have been able to figure out how."

"What's that supposed to mean?"

"Back at the Clearwater, you waved that twenty-dollar bill around like it was a flag. Of course the poor guy couldn't take it."

"Oh . . ." Andrea bit her bottom lip.

"In this instance we got quite a bit of information for forty bucks."

"You—" Andrea blinked rapidly as she worked out what had just happened.

"Yes, me." Dustin grinned. "Come on. Let's find Lisa the waitress with a vine tattoo. If Cade really does have a girlfriend, I might need you to talk sense into me so I don't do something stupid." His smile faded, and his green eyes pooled with anger. "This could explain a lot of things."

"Like what?"

"Cade's girlfriend might have driven to Port Inez and picked him up in her car." Dustin led them up and down the aisles of the casino floor, through a sea of slot machines. "That would explain how he left town."

Andrea yawned. "You're right. That makes perfect sense." Unfortunately, this section of the casino wasn't smoke-free. The thick presence of smoke, combined with the late hour, was getting to her. Her mind wasn't as agile as it should be. Food would help, she realized. Her uneaten dinner languished in her microwave back at home. An advertisement for a Friday-night fry bread promotion beckoned to her. The casino was so small that they'd already finished a loop. "I haven't seen any waitresses with red hair. Let's split up and ask people."

"Good idea," said Dustin.

Compared to the massive Clearwater, the Elwha Casino was cozy. It was owned by the Lower Elwha Klallam Tribe, known as "the strong people." They had lived near the lower part of the Elwha River on the Olympic Peninsula since time immemorial. It took twenty minutes for Andrea to circle the floor three times and show Cade's picture to anyone who would speak to her. When they regrouped, Dustin told her that he had attempted to get the security team to review video footage but had been told to bug off unless he had a warrant.

"Well," Andrea said with a frown. "This was a waste of time."

"Not true," said Dustin. "At least we know Cade wasn't here."

"Good point. We also have the tip about his possible girlfriend." Her eyes drifted to the fry bread poster. "Let's get something to eat before we go. I'm famished."

"Okay," he said. "But we should eat fast. It's a long way to Ocean Shores."

Andrea unzipped her wallet and took out cash. "My treat since you're driving."

"That's not fair. It's my fault—"

Andrea held up her hands. "Stop. This is Cade's fault—nobody else's." She ordered two plates of fry bread, two sodas, and a package of huckleberry taffy.

"I'll grab a table," said Dustin as he collected the drinks.

"Great." Andrea nodded. She checked her phone while she waited for their bread to fry.

Any luck? Heidi had texted.

No, Andrea replied. He's not at the Elwha either.

How's my brother? Are things okay?

Andrea glanced over at Dustin, who was seated at a nearby table and also checking his phone. Something he read must have been funny because a smile drifted across his face. His jaw relaxed, and the lines disappeared from his forehead. For a moment, he looked like he had in high school, and Andrea could have sworn they were in the food court of the Seattle Center, about to ride up to the top of the Space Needle to celebrate his eighteenth birthday. That had been a great day.

Dustin's fine, she texted. Why didn't you tell me he broke up with me because he thought I wanted to take another guy to prom?

What?

You didn't know?

Of course not, Heidi answered. Dustin doesn't exactly pour his heart out to me.

Oh. Andrea sighed.

I don't think my brother pours his heart out to anyone.

That's not true, Andrea typed. But then she deleted it. Maybe Dustin didn't want Heidi to know what he was capable of. I'll text you when we get to the Quinault, she said instead. Their order was ready, and she put away her phone.

The need for calories trumped conversation as Andrea quickly ate the hot meal. It wasn't until she wiped her greasy fingers on a napkin that Andrea became aware of how quickly she had shoveled food into her face. "Hungry?" Dustin asked with a sly grin. He was only half-done with his bread.

"I told you I was famished." She reached for another napkin. "And you eat slow." She checked her watch. "It's past midnight. We have a three-and-a-half-hour drive ahead of us."

"True." Dustin shoved a bite of bread into his mouth.

"It's frustrating that Lisa was a dead end," Andrea mused. She scanned the restaurant area for any sign of the redheaded waitress. "I keep hoping we'll see her."

"Me too. Although I don't know what I'd say if we did."

"You'd say nothing. If we find her, let me do the talking. Wait a sec . . ." Andrea stood. "I just realized I didn't ask the cashier if she knew Lisa. I'll be right back." She darted to the counter, grateful there was no line. The cashier was a middle-aged woman with thick fluttery eyelashes and a name tag that said Suzy. "Excuse me," Andrea began. "But have you seen this man here tonight?" She held out her phone with the picture of Cade.

Suzy glanced at the picture and frowned. "That asshole? No, I haven't seen Cade in weeks."

"Lisa's boyfriend, right?"

Suzy nodded. "But Lisa doesn't work here anymore. She was fired for giving him free chips."

"Sounds like she hooked up with trouble." Andrea reached into her purse, opened her wallet, and plucked out a business card along with a twenty-dollar bill. It was all the cash she had left, or she would have added more. "Here's my card," she said as she passed it over with the cash concealed beneath. "Could you please text me if Cade turns up?"

"Sure." Suzy slipped the offering into her pocket. "But I don't think he will. The only way Lisa will get her job back is if she dumps him, and that's not going to happen."

"Fools in love, huh?"

Suzy shrugged. "Love or stolen chips."

Andrea fought to keep her stride normal as she walked away, even though she longed to rush to Dustin and tell him the news. "Cade's not here," she said as soon as she sat down. "But he's definitely cheating."

When Dustin heard the details, his face turned beet red. "That bastard," he snarled. "Let's go." He stuffed the last bite of bread into his mouth and collected their trash.

After a quick restroom break, they were back outside and headed to the truck. "Are you sure you don't want me to drive?" Andrea asked.

"Hell no." Dustin unlocked the truck, and they climbed in.

"I'm a great driver." Andrea clicked her seat belt. "I've never been in an accident."

"And how many speeding tickets have you gotten?"

Andrea fiddled with the heater vents but didn't answer.

Dustin drove out of the parking lot. "You're suspiciously quiet."

"Speeding tickets are a racket to make cities money." Andrea squared her shoulders. It wasn't her fault that there was a speed trap in Smokey Point. The last two times she had driven to Canada, she had gotten caught in it, but Dustin didn't need to know that. He also didn't need to know about that time she had blown through a blind inter-section in Port Inez a couple of months back. Hopefully Mack hadn't told him. She had told her father about the ticket, mainly because she had been so flustered about it, but Tom hadn't understood what she'd meant. He no longer knew what a speeding ticket was or why Andrea was ashamed to receive one. Small mercies.

"I'll never forget the look on your dad's face when you showed him the bill for the three speeding tickets from the intersection next to your high school," said Dustin. "I didn't know Tom could turn that shade of purple."

Andrea shuddered. The difference between her father's reaction to speeding tickets then and now made her heart ache. "Okay, first of all, the camera they installed in front of the student parking lot was brand-new technology, and second of all, they should have told us that they were installing it." She pulled a lock of hair out of her face. "And I wouldn't have been rushing to begin with if I hadn't been trying to get to Harper Landing before the ferry line became too long to reach Port

Inez." That was the truth of it. Since Dustin hated Seattle so much, Andrea had tried to visit him in Port Inez as often as possible so that the city wouldn't trigger sad memories for him.

"That's fair," said Dustin. "I'm glad to hear that speeding is no longer a problem for you."

He was giving her the benefit of the doubt, which she didn't deserve. But Andrea didn't correct him. Instead, she decided to put him on the defensive. "What about you? Do you still eat Red Vines for breakfast?"

"No," Dustin said a bit too quickly. "Never."

"Never? Not even for a midmorning snack?"

"Eggs and toast. That's my standard breakfast these days."

"You're saying if I reach into the glove compartment right now, I won't find licorice?"

"I didn't mean—" Dustin started to say, but before he could finish his sentence, Andrea had sprung open the glove compartment and discovered three boxes of Red Vines.

"Aha!" she exclaimed. "I knew it."

"You're one to judge. Are you going to share that huckleberry taffy or what?"

"I will absolutely share." Andrea ripped open the bag and peeled the wrapper off of a piece. She offered him the taffy, and his fingertips brushed against her palm.

"Thanks," said Dustin before he popped it in his mouth.

Andrea unwrapped a second piece for herself. "It's a good thing you're here to help me eat this because otherwise I might get sick."

"I'm familiar," he said a few seconds later after he had finished chewing. "I was surprised you bought it tonight. I always figured that afternoon in Harper Landing had ruined you for huckleberry taffy forever."

Andrea grimaced, knowing the exact afternoon Dustin meant. Back in high school, she and Dustin had met up in Harper Landing on a frosty day in January and visited the former candy store called the Sugar

Factory. The owner was a jerk, but the candy was cheap. After stocking up on candy, they had gone to the old-fashioned movie theater to watch a double feature. While Dustin had worked through a bucket of popcorn, Andrea had eaten a whole bag of huckleberry taffy by herself. Unlike Dustin, who could handle his popcorn no problem, Andrea had been groaning by the time they had left the theater. Dustin had walked her to where her car was parked next to his truck, but by then she had been experiencing too much nausea to drive home. Instead, she had lain on the blanket in the back of the Yo-Mobile for two hours, clutching her stomach until the nausea passed. Dustin had stroked her hair and offered her sips of water. He hadn't seemed to mind that she might puke in his truck bed at any moment.

"I've learned the value of moderation since then," said Andrea, even though she hadn't. The sugar was already messing with her brain. Eating two dozen pieces seemed like a safe number. She could handle that.

"Yeah." Dustin held out his hand for more taffy. "Right."

"Wow," said Andrea as she dropped another unwrapped piece of candy into his hand. "Lake Crescent sure is dark at night. I can barely see it."

"Yeah. Help me watch for deer."

"Will do. Think we'll see any elk?"

"It's possible."

They drove past Lake Crescent in silence. Dustin's truck managed the twists and turns in the road much better than her small car would have done, and she was grateful he was driving. Andrea scanned the forest for any sign of movement. Deer didn't worry her as much as Roosevelt elk did. They were particularly dangerous during calving season, and Andrea couldn't remember when that was. Spring probably. Andrea winced, imagining a 1,100-pound bull ready to charge. Olympic National Park was home to the largest herd in the Pacific Northwest. They were glorious creatures to see in the daylight but not something you'd want to run into in your car.

"There's a sign for Forks," she said a while later. "That means we're almost a third of the way there."

"Or will be once we reach Forks. And please do *not* start talking to me about vampires. Leanne would not shut up about them when she was in high school."

"How can we drive by Forks and not talk about the Cullen family?" Andrea dug into the bag for the last pieces of taffy. "Admit it—you loved the *Twilight* books. Everyone did."

"Never read them. Never intend to."

"How can you not read them or at least watch the movies?"

He raised his eyebrows. "Sparkly vampires? No thank you."

"There are also werewolves." Andrea smiled with pleasure at their easy banter. But then she frowned. "I'm not sure I'd like the series as much now if I reread them as an experienced adult. There's the whole 'Edward stalks Bella' part to deal with, but also the everlasting-love thing is hard to believe."

"Really? I'm surprised to hear you say that."

"I stopped believing in fairy tales when I saw my mom abandon my dad and move in with Roger." Andrea's personal history of failed relationships had also cautioned her against believing in happily ever afters, but she kept that to herself. What she had experienced with Dustin had been so good that she'd tried to recreate it with one guy after another to disastrous results.

"True love sells books and movie tickets, but the real world is more complicated," said Dustin.

"That's what my dad used to say. He also said that you can't count on people but you could depend upon your education."

"Yeah. I know."

"What?"

"I told you he used to dole out advice. Those bits were some of his favorites."

"Oh." Andrea leaned back into her seat, and they settled into a heavy silence. She thought of her father alone in his room in the memory-care center. Would she have to confess that his coins had been stolen? Maybe she could show him the remaining double eagle again and again and he wouldn't know the difference. Contemplating that subterfuge crushed her soul.

She watched the exit for Forks, Washington, go by without comment. Her teenage days seemed like a lifetime ago. Instead of Halloween parties, romantic dates, and pet hedgehogs, her days revolved around visits to an Alzheimer's home.

"I'm surprised you never married," said Dustin.

"Huh?" Andrea didn't know which startled her more—the break in silence or Dustin's direct statement.

"Whenever Heidi mentioned you over the years, you were always dating someone new. Plus, I know you wanted kids. You were great with Leanne when she was little."

"Oh." Andrea slumped forward. "Yeah. Kids would have been nice." She fought to keep sadness from creeping into her voice.

"You still have time. You're only thirty-six."

"I'm not sure any of that is in my future." Andrea rubbed the part of her neck that was cramping up. "I have all I can deal with right now; plus I have a knack for picking losers." Her hand slapped across her mouth, but it was too late. Fatigue must have made that information slip out. "Present company excluded, of course," she mumbled through her fingertips.

Dustin chuckled. "Losers, huh?" He leaned his arm on the center console. "The way your father described it to me, you were attracted to guys who weren't right for you."

"My dad said what?" She pulled down her hand.

"That you were bright and creative and—how did he describe it? 'Had a sparkly personality.' Or something like that."

"That makes me sound like a vampire."

"This was way before *Twilight*."

"Okay, but what does that have to do with me choosing guys that weren't right for me? And why did my dad tell you that in the first place?" Before Dustin could answer, the truth barreled into her like a Roosevelt elk. "Wait a second . . . did my dad say that *you* weren't right for me?"

Dustin didn't answer.

"He *did*, didn't he?"

Dustin scratched his neck. "He might have mentioned something like that."

The betrayal she felt was hard to process. How could her father have done that to her? "But that wasn't true," she protested. "I mean sure, my future boyfriends turned out to be losers; you were—"

"I was what?"

Perfect, she had been about to say. "Bright and creative too," she said instead. "Although I'd never describe you as sparkly."

Unless he took his shirt off.

Dustin sighed. "It wasn't that your dad didn't like me. He was really clear about that. He just thought that you had the propensity to be intense with people. And so did I. And that our intensity wasn't good for either one of us, especially since . . ."

"Go on," Andrea prodded.

"I didn't want to talk about this tonight."

"Tonight . . . or ever?"

Dustin frowned. "Our intensity might consume us. Your dad said that sometimes loving people means letting them go because that's what's best for everyone."

"And you listened to him? What a load of crap!"

"I wasn't *going* to listen to him. I told him that might be true, but it wasn't true for us. But then the very next day was prom and then . . . you and that damn hedgehog!"

"Spike is completely innocent! My father, on the other hand." Andrea folded her arms. "I can't believe he did that to me."

"He didn't do anything to you," said Dustin. "It was all my fault."

"Why are you so quick to take responsibility for things that weren't your fault?" Andrea twisted in her seat to look at him. "You were young and impressionable. He was practically your mentor. Of course you'd listen to what he said. My dad knew that and used it against you for reasons I can't understand."

"Is it really so hard to see? He was trying to protect you . . . and me, I guess. Your dad thought we would ruin our lives."

"*You* would never ruin my life. The guys I dated after you, on the other hand . . ."

"That doesn't sound good."

"It wasn't. But you probably don't want to hear about my old boyfriends."

"It's the middle of the night, and I need something to help me stay awake."

"I could drive," said Andrea.

"That's a hard pass."

Andrea rolled her eyes. "Fine. I'll tell you about my horrible love life, but you're going next."

"That's fair. You first, though." Dustin stretched out his arm over the back of the seat but kept it far enough away that his hand didn't brush her shoulders.

"Okay," she said, wishing he'd move his arm closer to her. "At Central I dated two guys—one who flunked out because he gamed all night and another guy who took a job teaching English in Tokyo and immediately fell in love with his landlady."

"Dude. That sucks."

"*Sucks* is right. After college I dated Jim, who worked in IT and gets points for liking sushi. But he also liked cheating, which I discovered when we went to Vegas and I caught him in our hotel room with another woman."

"That's awful," said Dustin. "I'm sorry that happened to you."

Andrea took a deep breath before she continued. "You'd think that would have taught me a lesson about being more careful with who I gave my heart to, but it didn't. My next boyfriend was Cam, who owned a car dealership and hired me to redesign their website and mailing campaigns. Cam seemed like a great guy at first because he loved to travel and ski. But then the check for my business services bounced. When I asked him about it, he said he was broke and asked to borrow twenty thousand dollars."

"Hell no," said Dustin. "Please tell me you didn't."

"I did." Her cheeks burned. "I felt bad because it turns out that all the fancy trips we took were on his maxed-out credit cards. He was basically a grown-up kid who didn't know how to budget. But then I found out that he had bought a new boat with money that belonged to his employees and couldn't make payroll."

"Did he ever pay you back the money you lent him?"

Andrea shook her head. "No. He didn't pay me for the work I did for his company either."

"I bet your dad blew a gasket when he found out."

"Dad would have wanted to sue, so I didn't tell him."

"But your money. He ripped you off."

"It was an expensive lesson. Which is why my next boyfriend—my last boyfriend—was an accountant. I hired Kyle to go over my books to make sure that I didn't have other clients who owed me money. Kyle was a CPA and completely reliable. He wasn't exciting, but he was dependable."

"What happened?"

Andrea frowned. "My dad got Alzheimer's is what happened. Kyle became jealous of all the time I spent with my dad. He thought I should toss him in the old folks' home and throw away the key. Every time

I visited my father, Kyle would sulk. It became this big thing, so I dumped him."

"Good call. You don't need people like that in your life."

"That's right." Andrea leaned her head against the window and rested her arm on the door. "I don't need anybody." *Except the employees at the Owl's Nest.* Without the memory-care staff, she'd be screwed.

"It's good to be independent," Dustin said in a quiet voice. "But everyone needs someone. I don't know what I would do without Heidi, Nathan, and Leanne."

"I always admired how your family supported one another." Andrea's heart pinched. Being an only child had often been lonely, but now it was ten times worse. A sibling would have helped shoulder the responsibility of her father's welfare. Even someone to take turns visiting him would be appreciated—or pitching in during an emergency. Like the time Tom had spent twelve hours in the emergency room with a urinary tract infection—Andrea had missed an important work deadline because of that. She'd hated to lose the client, but someone had had to be with Tom. Otherwise he had kept ripping out his IV because he hadn't known what it was. Every fifteen minutes when the blood pressure cuff had puffed up, he'd freaked out. Andrea couldn't have asked her mom to spell her because she'd gone with Roger to a podiatry conference in Florida.

Andrea perked up a moment later when she remembered that it was Dustin's turn to reveal secrets from his past. "So?" she asked. "Tell me about your old girlfriends."

"There's not much to tell."

"That can't be true." Andrea suspected that a guy as handsome as Dustin would have women clamoring for him. The jealous part of her didn't crave the details, but she couldn't help herself from wanting to know everything about him, including his past. "Start at the beginning, and don't leave anyone out."

"Okay. After college I dated a woman named Samantha for two years. She worked with children with special needs."

"She sounds like a keeper." How could she compete with an ex-girlfriend like that? Not that she wanted to. Still . . . two years? They must have been serious.

"Samantha was a good woman. But she hated it here in the Pacific Northwest. She thought the cost of living was too high. That's why she moved to Florida."

"And you didn't go with her?"

Dustin shook his head. "No, I didn't. I couldn't leave my brother and sisters like that. Plus, Heidi and I had just begun our business, and Karlsson Construction was starting to take off."

"So you just broke up? You didn't try the long-distance thing first like we had planned to before *we* broke up?"

"It didn't seem like a good idea." He looked at her sideways. "You have to be really intense about someone to even consider that option."

Andrea felt warmth wash over her, especially when Dustin's arm fell down a little and rested against the back of her neck. "Do you miss her?" she asked.

"Not really. Not how I . . ." His hand slipped down against the side of her right arm.

"Not how you what?" Andrea prompted.

Pop! The truck shuddered, and Andrea's seat belt tightened as Dustin applied the brakes.

"Damn," Dustin muttered. "I think we blew out a tire. Hang on." He turned on the hazard lights and pulled the truck to the side of the road.

"I'll call Triple-A." Andrea took out her phone and shook it. No bars.

"Don't bother. I can change it myself." Dustin reached into the back seat and handed her the Pendleton blanket. "Here. Try to stay warm."

"But you don't have a coat."

"I'll warm up putting on the spare. I have a full-size tire in the back." Dustin leaned forward and tucked the blanket around her like he was putting a small child to bed. For a moment, Andrea thought he might kiss her forehead, and her heart fluttered. But then he backed away, an anguished look upon his face. "Get some rest." He shut the door.

Andrea tried to stay awake, but fatigue overwhelmed her as soon as she was alone in the cab. Her senses whirred with images from that evening. The robbery. The casinos. The fry bread. The smell of sulfur in the air as Dustin pulled her from Sol Duc Hot Springs and dared her to make snow angels. No, that wasn't right. That was from before. Before prom and college. Before one man after another took advantage of her heart. Dustin never took advantage. Dustin held Spike in the palm of his hand like a snowflake, a tender caretaker, a steadfast friend. Only he wasn't her friend anymore. He hadn't been for eighteen years. Andrea burrowed under the blanket, shielding herself from the cold. She fought sleep. Raged against it. When she breathed deeply, she smelled the scent of wool and, beyond that, the faintest whiff of Dustin. Closing her eyes, she drifted off into one failed dream after another.

CHAPTER EIGHT

It was four o'clock in the morning, and Dustin couldn't stop yawning. The pitch-black sky didn't help matters. Sunrise was a couple of hours away. Andrea slept next to him, curled up with the blanket, and Dustin wished he could join her in peaceful slumber. His body cupped around hers would feel so natural. Sleeping next to her would be the ultimate privilege. Instead, he turned on the radio to the clearest channel he could find, an oldies station from Olympia. Humming along to Buddy Holly helped him stay awake as he drove the final leg to the Quinault Beach Resort and Casino in Ocean Shores.

As a kid, Dustin had thought of Ocean Shores, Grays Harbor, and Westport as the place to fly kites, drive on the beach, and wade into the freezing-cold Pacific Ocean. Some of his best memories were camping with his family at Ocean City State Park and roasting marshmallows over bonfires on the sand. Leanne wouldn't share any of those memories either, Dustin realized with regret. She was probably too young to remember their dad teaching them how to stake a tent and secure the rain fly or their mom cooking up chicken à la king on the Coleman stove. Leanne wouldn't know what it was like to burrow in a down sleeping bag, safe and warm in the tent, as wind whipped over the campsite.

"Will the rain fly hold?" Crystal had asked.

"It'll hold," Josh had answered. "Dustin and I staked it together." The area was so synonymous with camping in Dustin's memory that it seemed incongruous that there was a massive resort on the beach looming in front of him.

Dustin parked the truck and turned off the engine. He needed coffee, or bed, or both. Squeezing his eyes open and shut a few times, Dustin forced his brain to remain awake. Where was extra adrenaline when he needed it? Spent, a couple of hours ago on the side of the highway replacing the tire—that was where.

"Oh my gosh, I fell asleep." Andrea blinked her eyes open. "I'm so sorry."

"Don't be." Dustin grabbed his wallet and key fob. "At least one of us got some rest."

She unclicked her seat belt. "But I meant to keep you company so it would be easier for you to drive while you were tired."

"I'm fine," Dustin lied. "Let's go find Cade." He opened his door and climbed out of the cab.

"You don't think Cade's gambling right now, do you?" Andrea asked once she stood next to him. She checked her watch. "It's four fifteen."

Dustin shrugged. "Probably not. But maybe one of the servers or dealers saw him." He envisioned getting the info they needed, charging up the stairs, and pounding on Cade's hotel-room door. Dustin wasn't a violent person, but he'd pick Cade up by the scruff of the neck and drag him back to Port Inez by force, if necessary.

"Did you know that the Quinault Indian Nation is made up of seven different tribes?" Andrea asked as they walked up to the entrance.

"No, I did not." The corners of Dustin's mouth bent up. Leave it to Andrea to turn this into a history lesson.

"They lived in longhouses and built enormous cedar canoes. Even Lewis and Clark commented on their canoes. They could hold up to thirty people."

"That's amazing." Dustin's tired brain was having a hard time keeping up with her.

"They're also known for their basket-weaving artistry. If we had time, we could go visit the cultural center, but"—Andrea shrugged—"I guess that's for a different trip."

"Different trip," Dustin echoed—and one that he could envision himself taking with her. It surprised him, realizing that. Here he'd spent the last year avoiding Andrea and her blue house on the bay, and now he was itching to hold her hand. His fingertips twitched, so close to hers and yet so far. After he laced their fingers together, he would pull her toward him. Her heart beating against his. The feel of her shoulder blade under his hand. He wondered if she was still ticklish. So what if he was serious and Andrea was—how had Tom put it? Effervescent. Dustin would pursue that ticklish spot with an intensity that would make her laugh with delight.

The fatigue was getting to him—that was it. He wasn't thinking clearly. Exhaustion was making him delirious.

"Are you sure you're okay?" Andrea opened the door to the hotel. "You just yawned three times in a row." She held the handle and waited for him to walk through.

"Nothing a cup of coffee can't fix," he mumbled.

"Let's search for Cade and then get a room." Andrea blushed. "I mean, two rooms." Rosy cheeks looked good on her. Almost as good as the tight jeans she wore and that sweater that hugged every curve.

Dustin took out his phone, and for half a second he forgot he was doing and almost took her picture so he could keep it with him always. But then a slot machine rang out in the distance and rattled him awake. Dustin cleared his throat. "I better load up Cade's picture so we can find the jerk."

"Good idea."

The entrance to the casino floor was unmonitored, probably due to the wee morning hours. "I'll ask at the tables, and you survey the slots?" Dustin suggested.

"We're becoming pros at this." Andrea bumped her hip against his. "See you in a bit." She charged toward a blackjack dealer tending to a lonely customer.

The first gambler Dustin approached smelled like stale coffee. Her gray hair stuck out at funny angles, and her sweatshirt glittered with rhinestones. The woman tapped the slot machine screen on autopilot, hardly blinking.

"Pardon me, ma'am," Dustin said, holding out Cade's picture. "Have you seen my brother-in-law here tonight? He's missing."

Suddenly, the slot machine jangled. Lights flashed, and a peppy tune blared from the speakers. "That's more like it!" The woman clapped her hands. "Come to Mama!"

Dustin looked down and saw a row of kittens race around a basket on the screen. Dollar signs flashed. Thirty, thirty-one, thirty-two, thirty-three . . . the amount climbed higher and higher. "How much did you bet?" he asked as the numbers spun.

"Two bucks." She grabbed his sleeve. "You're my lucky charm."

"Oh, I don't know about that." He tried to step away, but she had a firm grip on his T-shirt.

"You're a hunky, tall glass of milk is what you are, baby," she said before kissing him on the cheek. "The kittens love you. Look at that. It's still going! I've been here all night, and this is the first time I've won over ten dollars."

"It's at a hundred and three dollars now." Dustin pointed at the screen. Even he was mesmerized by the spinning dollar signs. "Wow. It hasn't stopped yet."

The woman let go of his arm and rattled her cup. She belted out a Frank Sinatra song in an off-key way that attracted attention. Pretty soon, the whole area was staring at them. Halfway through her song, the kittens came to a stop, and a ticket for $184 spit out. "I'm queen of the world!" she cried.

"Uh . . . yeah. Congratulations," said Dustin. "About my missing brother-in-law." He held out his phone. "Have you seen him?"

She glanced down at the screen. "Nope. Sorry," she said before grabbing the ticket and rushing away.

Dustin moved to the next patron. He repeated the scenario dozens of times but without the winning kittens. The casino was larger than the Elwha, but there were fewer customers due to the hour. By the time he'd spoken to the last person, Dustin was furious with himself. He'd driven them on a wild-goose chase from the Kitsap to the Olympic Peninsula, and they still hadn't found Cade. There was no sign of the redheaded Lisa either. Dustin wished he knew more about Cade's girlfriend. Maybe Cade was with Lisa right now, wherever she lived. Or perhaps he was gambling at the casinos on the other side of the water. Hell, for all he knew, Cade could be on a plane to Mexico right now.

"I take it you didn't have any luck either?" Andrea asked when they reunited at the entrance.

He shook his head. "Not unless you count kittens."

"Huh?"

"Never mind. We should go home."

"Not until we've slept." Andrea held out two hotel key cards. "Come on. It'll be better in the morning."

"It *is* the morning," Dustin grumbled. "I can't believe how stupid I've been."

Andrea hooked her arm in the crook of his elbow and pulled him to the elevator. "We've both made unfortunate decisions, but that doesn't mean we're dumb." She squeezed his bicep and rested her head on his shoulder as they waited for the elevator to arrive. The intimacy of the gesture surprised him.

"What next?" he asked as they stepped into the elevator.

"Next, we sleep." She pushed the button for the third floor. "I'm exhausted."

"Me too," Dustin admitted. So that's why she was snuggled up onto his arm. She wasn't flirting; she was tired.

"Even after my power nap in the truck, I'm wrecked," said Andrea.

"Same." Dustin's head drifted closer to hers for a moment, and he breathed in the citrus scent of her hair. Unfortunately, it wasn't enough to mask the odor of cigarette smoke from the Elwha that clung to them like ivy. Still, Dustin didn't mind. He hadn't stood this close to her in decades. The way she fit beside him felt like a missing puzzle piece.

"Thanks for working so hard to find my father's coins," Andrea said in a quiet voice.

"Thanks for helping me search for Cade. Sorry it turned into a fiasco." His neck tilted down another inch, and their heads rested together for a few seconds before the elevator doors parted. Dustin stood straight, and they walked onto the floor.

"This trip hasn't been a fiasco," said Andrea as she led them down the hall. "We gained valuable information." She tightened her grip on his arm and yawned. When they reached their side-by-side rooms, she let go and handed him his key. "I don't know what will happen, but at least we tried."

"Yeah." He fingered the edge of the key card. "There's something to be said for trying."

"Not trying would have been the worst." She stared down at the tips of her shoes and then at him.

The blueness of her eyes dazzled him. He felt like he was eighteen again, standing at the top of the Space Needle and gazing into her lovely face. She'd worn that same color blue then too. He remembered that now. It was the day she had held up a giant poster that said HAPPY BIRTHDAY! on one side and WILL YOU GO TO PROM WITH ME? on the other.

"Not trying would have been awful," he echoed. As soon as he said it, he wondered, Had he tried with Andrea? Or had he given up the moment things became too intense? Tom had been right. Dustin and Andrea's relationship had burned like an ember that could set the Olympic Forest on fire. That type of power was frightening, especially when they were faced with a long-distance relationship during college. Well, he wasn't a teenager anymore. He was a grown man who made wiser decisions. Maybe this journey across the Olympic Peninsula hadn't been a failure after all. They hadn't found Cade, but they had reconnected with each other.

Dustin ran his hand down the side of her arm and hitched his palm under her elbow. "Thank you for your help," he said. For one crazy moment he thought about kissing her. It would be so easy to melt together, sink his lips against hers, and seal the night with a feeling that would make pain disappear. Because it would disappear; he knew it. Andrea had the power to make hurt go away. She had been a solace during the roughest time of his life. If he kissed her now, this failed mission would dissolve into something blissful. But they both would be too tired to fully appreciate it. Dustin didn't want to be mindless with Andrea. He couldn't risk screwing things up with her again.

"Good night," he said as he dropped his hand. "Or good morning," he added, considering the hour. Dustin unlocked the door to his room and crossed the threshold before he did anything dumb.

Ten steps later he crashed upon the queen-size bed, not bothering to pull back the covers. His eyes clamped shut, and he sank into darkness. He meant to sleep only a few hours. Catch a few Zs and get back on the road—that had been the plan. But sleep claimed him like a prisoner. It tossed him into the darkest part of his brain and threw away the key.

Trapped in his subconscious, Dustin dreamed of windswept beaches and raging campfires. A storm tore off his tent's rain fly and sucked the stakes out of the ground. Kendal and Jane shivered in their sleeping bags next to him.

"No!" Dustin shouted as rain pelted down. "I can fix this!" He struggled to unzip the tent and repair their shelter, but the zipper wouldn't budge. Outside the campfire burned hotter and hotter, the flames leaping out from their ring of rocks. If Dustin didn't act, they'd burn alive.

"Dustin?" a voice called, barely audible in the storm.

The fire was raging now. It had escaped the fire ring and attacked the picnic table. Dustin struggled to escape the tent and save Kendal and Jane, but his arms wouldn't move. "No," he called, a prisoner of his nightmare. "I'll protect you!"

Bang. Bang. Bang. A towering cedar threatened to pulverize them. Dustin thrust out his arms to shield the girls. "Dustin!" the wind cried.

His cell phone rang beside the bed, releasing him from the nightmare. It trilled an old-fashioned bell tone and jolted him awake. Dustin blinked a few times and wiped crust from his eyes. "Hello?" he mumbled without tapping the phone. It rang again. This time, he accepted the call. "Karlsson Construction," he answered.

"Hey, Dustin; it's me, Andrea. Where are you?"

Dustin looked to his left and right as he tried to figure that out. There was no campground engulfed in flames. He was in a hotel room with a cold fireplace and Quinault artwork on the wall. "I'm in here," he said. "In bed," he added.

"Really?" Andrea asked. "I've been knocking on the adjoining door for the past five minutes, and you didn't answer."

"Oh." His mouth tasted like sawdust, and his body reeked of sweat and axle grease. Dustin jumped to his feet. "Sorry about that."

"Are you hungry? I have food."

"Yeah. Hold on. I'll be right there."

"Great. I'm ending the call now because my phone's about to die again. See you in a few."

Dustin raked his fingers through his hair and stumbled to the door. It took him a minute to figure out how to unlock the latch, but as soon as he did, he saw Andrea standing beside the door next to a room service cart.

"I ordered breakfast. I thought you might be hungry."

The rich aroma of bacon and eggs made his stomach growl. "Thanks." He put his phone away.

Andrea peeked her head around his shoulder. "You made your bed already."

"No," he admitted. "I was too tired to pull back the covers."

"Exhaustion will do that to you. Well, let's eat in your room because mine's a mess." Without waiting for him to answer, she pushed the cart through the door and into his space. "I didn't know you were up yet or I would have brought this earlier."

"I was still asleep," Dustin admitted.

"Really?" She raised her eyebrows. "I thought I heard you talking to someone, but then when you didn't answer my knock, I thought maybe it was just the TV and that you were in the casino or something." She shifted her weight from one foot to the other and scratched the back of her head. "Sorry. I'm rambling."

"No, it's fine." He flicked on the lights.

"I mean, if you were with someone or talking on the phone to someone, it's no big deal. I don't need to know." She twisted the edge of her sweatshirt.

"I wasn't with someone," he said. "I was having a nightmare."

"A nightmare?"

"Yeah." Dustin shrugged. "I get them all the time. Heidi claims she knows when I didn't sleep well because I come to work grumpy." He pushed the cart next to a table and chairs by the window and pulled back the drapes.

Andrea walked across the room and stood beside him. "The sky's so gray you can barely tell where the ocean starts." She peered through the glass.

Dustin examined the view. Clouds blew across the sky, and waves rolled against the shore. Pale-green seagrass danced in the breeze. "Yeah," he said. "But it's peaceful."

She looked up at him sideways. "What was your nightmare about?"

"Nothing. It doesn't matter."

"You don't have to tell me if you don't want to." She stepped over to the table and fiddled with the coffeepot. "I should mind my own business."

"No, it's not that." He slumped into a chair. "It's just not important."

"Of course it's important. It was a nightmare. If you don't tell me, I hope you tell Heidi."

"Why would I do that?"

"Because if you don't process your nightmare with someone, it gains power, and you could dream it again." She lifted the carafe. "Coffee?"

"Yes, please." Dustin picked up a mug and held it steady as she poured. Was she right? Was ignoring his nightmares making them worse? He'd never had this one about a camping trip before, but he had endured a whole slew of nightmares that played on repeat in his mind's subconscious. Houses that fell apart . . . cars breaking down . . . loved ones sailing off on the ferry, never to return . . . They were nonsense, as far as he was concerned, but even nonsense could mess with your head.

"Cream?" Andrea offered. "I don't remember you drinking coffee in high school, so I don't know how you take yours."

"Black's fine. And no, I didn't develop a taste for coffee until college. I had a seven a.m. statistics class that almost killed me." Dustin sipped the liquid and let the caffeine revitalize him. "Where'd you get the idea that nightmares gain power?"

"My mom told me." Andrea added a generous helping of cream to her mug. "Things aren't so great between us right now, but I have to give her credit for this life skill; it really works. Whenever I would have a bad dream, I would tell her, and she would give me the script to make it stop."

"A script? You mean like a prescription?"

She shook her head. "No, a script to use if the nightmare happened again. Like, if I dreamed that I was at school, about to give a presentation, and all my teeth fell out, my mom would have me say: 'I am Andrea Wint, and I give great speeches. I can talk in front of anyone without being afraid.'"

"And you're saying this actually works?" Dustin drank more coffee.

Andrea nodded. "It does. Sometimes I'd feel the nightmares come on, and I'd use the script to talk my way out of them. Other times I'd wake up from a nightmare, say the mantra, and be able to quickly fall back asleep."

"You're lucky that you have a mom in your life who can still teach you life skills like that." As soon as he said it, he wished he could take the words back. Andrea might accuse him of playing the dead-parent card again, and he didn't want to begin the day with an argument. But she surprised him by ignoring his comment altogether.

"Have a bite of bacon while it's still hot." Andrea pushed his plate forward.

Dustin lifted the stainless steel lid off the plate. "Poached eggs. My favorite."

Andrea grinned. "They were all out of Red Vines, so I had to improvise." Her breakfast included toast, a fresh-fruit bowl, smoked salmon, and avocado.

Dustin bit into a crunchy piece of bacon and savored the salty taste. He was hungrier than he had realized. Last night he had teased Andrea slightly for wolfing down her fry bread, but if he wasn't careful, he'd eat so fast he would choke. Instead, he sipped coffee between bites and took his time. "I dreamed I was at the same campground that I used to go to with my parents," he said. "Ocean City State Park. Only this time Kendal and Jane were with me. The campground was on fire, and we were trapped." Goose bumps raced up his arms. "There was nothing I could do to save them."

"That sounds horrible." She blotted her mouth with a napkin. "Have you had that dream before?"

He shook his head. "Not at the campground."

"Hmm . . ." She pursed her lips. "Well, if it happens again, you could say: 'I am Dustin Karlsson. I keep Kendal and Jane safe. I am a wonderful uncle.'"

"Am I, though? Their dad left town, and I can't make it better."

"That's beyond your control. But you've got car seats in your back seat."

"Boosters."

"Boosters, whatever. You take them on fun adventures. No matter how mixed up their lives get, you'll always be there for them. That's keeping them safe, and that's being a wonderful uncle."

"Maybe." Dustin wasn't entirely convinced. Part of him wanted to get back on the road and find Cade immediately, but the other part wanted to linger over breakfast with Andrea. She was so easy to talk to that it felt like old times. The morning light played with the golden highlights of her brown hair and also revealed a few strands of gray. Her cheeks were as pink as they had been when she was a teen, but he saw faint lines on her forehead that hadn't been there before. Dustin felt like he straddled two time zones: then and now. "I see you're still a fan of avocado toast," he said, grinning at her over his coffee mug.

"Always." She mashed it with a fork before spreading it on the bread. "Me and avocados go back way before they became trendy."

Dustin smiled, thinking back. "So how did your mom learn about stopping nightmares?" He remembered Lydia keeping an impeccably clean home and colorful garden. But most of all, he remembered her sending him back to Port Inez with homemade frozen dinners in disposable aluminum pans. Lasagna, chicken-and-bacon casserole, swiss cheese croissant bakes—she had made it her personal mission to keep the Karlsson family fed.

Andrea put down her fork. "My mom studied psychology before she became a lawyer. Then she had me and quit her job."

"I didn't know your mom was a lawyer too. What type of law did she practice?"

"She was a public defender for King County. It meant long hours for little pay, so she quit."

"She just quit?"

"Well, not exactly. At first, they hired a nanny for me, but I guess nannies are so expensive in Seattle that she didn't break even. If she'd been in private practice, like my dad, it would have been fine, but public defenders don't earn much."

Dustin broke into one of the poached eggs. "That must have been a big sacrifice for her, especially after working so hard to become a lawyer."

"Says the labradoodle."

"I'm not making excuses for her," he said quickly. "I was trying to learn more about you."

"Oh. Well, yeah. I guess it might have been hard for her to quit working. If she really wanted to, she could have gone back after I was in school, but she didn't."

"Why not?"

Andrea shrugged. "I don't know. I never asked her."

"Was it your dad's idea?" Tom had definitive ideas about how other people should live.

"Maybe." Andrea looked doubtful. "But my dad was proud that she was a lawyer. He always joked that it was handy to have a defense attorney in the family and that he had her number on speed dial."

"Your mom is such a gentle person. Do you think she had nightmares about the people she was defending?"

"No." Andrea shook her head. "My mom always spoke respectfully of her clients. But she did sometimes talk about the horrible situations they were in. Poverty . . . domestic violence . . . drugs . . ." She looked away, and her eyes became unfocused.

"Maybe that's why she learned how to battle nightmares."

"Yeah, maybe." Andrea stirred her granola. "She also did some volunteer work when I was in middle school."

"What was it?" Dustin polished off his last bite of bacon.

"She advocated for kids in the juvenile justice system. Not as their lawyer but as an adult who stuck with them throughout the process."

"That sounds like a good use of her skills." Dustin wasn't surprised Lydia had done that. But watching how Andrea's countenance darkened when she talked about her mom made him want to change the subject. "These rooms are really nice. How'd you sleep?"

"Like a log. I turned my fireplace on and everything." Andrea pointed her fork at the cold hearth. "It switches on with a dial."

Dustin looked over his shoulder at the gas fireplace in his room. A fake fire was the perfect thing for easing the chill on a gray morning like today. Plus, it might help banish the remnants of his nightmare to be the one firmly in control of the fire. Dustin walked over to the hearth and turned it on. Flames sprang to life. "There we go," he said.

"Ambience." Andrea folded her legs and sat like a pretzel in her chair. "I like it." She wrapped both hands around her coffee, warming them.

"Might as well get what you paid for." Dustin sat down and ate his last bite of food.

"Might as well." Andrea grinned. "Remind me to collect the extra toiletries from your room too. I think Kendal and Jane might like them."

"That's a great idea. They'll love that."

"My dad always brought back little shampoos and soaps whenever he went on a business trip." Andrea set down her mug and speared a strawberry with her fork. She laughed.

"What's so funny?"

"Nothing. Just that my dad's worst fears have finally come true. I'm alone in a hotel room with Dustin Karlsson."

"Yeah, and . . ." Dustin stared at her. It wasn't until just now that he noticed her outfit. Instead of the blue sweater and jeans she'd worn the night before, she had on a red sweatshirt and tight-fitting yoga pants. "You're not wearing your clothes."

"Nope." She shook her head. Her hair was damp, and her face was freshly washed and makeup-free. He liked that, too, although it didn't matter to him what she chose to put on her face.

"Where did you get the new outfit?" Dustin asked.

"From the gift shop." Andrea turned to show him the screen-printed logo on the back of her sweatshirt. "Now I'm a walking advertisement for the Quinault Beach Resort and Casino." She poured herself a second mug of coffee. "I bought you one too." Andrea set the pot on the table. "I know how much you love matching outfits," she said, barely suppressing a giggle.

"Oh jeez." He'd complain, but she'd already plied him with bacon. "I should probably shower first." Dustin knew he reeked, and he didn't relish the idea of driving back to Port Inez with her while smelling like a garbage can. "I'll hurry so we can get on the road." Dustin set his coffee mug down and pushed away from the table. He stood at the same time as Andrea rose from her seat.

"I'll go get your sweatshirt," she said.

Dustin stepped right just as Andrea stepped left. Then he overcorrected by stepping left at the same time Andrea went to her right. The awkwardness was oppressive. "Shall we dance?" he asked, trying to lighten the mood.

"I wouldn't say no," she said with a laugh. Pale light from the gray sky illuminated one side of her face, and the flickering gas fire brightened the other.

Was that an invitation? Dustin raised his eyebrows. His shirt smelled like a monkey wrench, but maybe Andrea didn't care. He was just about to reach forward and cup her face in his hands for a kiss when she darted away. "I'll be right back," she said, hurrying to the other room. The door clicked shut behind her.

He felt like the wind had been knocked out of him. What an idiot! He had totally misread her signals, and now all he could do was curse his own stupidity. Dustin stomped away to the shower, not waiting for her to return.

CHAPTER NINE

Closing the door behind her, Andrea determined that she would rather be a coward than a fool. If there was one thing that her history of failed relationships had taught her, it was that she rushed into things too quickly. Had Dustin been about to kiss her? She balled her fists and pressed them hard into the top of her stomach. Probably not. That look in his eyes was most likely due to a bacon hangover, nothing else. Andrea was notorious for misreading signals, and she refused to embarrass herself.

Squaring her shoulders, she scooped up the bag with the sweatshirt and T-shirt inside, opened her interior door, and knocked on his. For the second time that morning, there was no answer. Pressing her ear against the wood, Andrea thought she heard the faint sound of the shower running. Leaving her door open, Andrea dropped the bag of clothes on her bed and walked up to the window. The sky was as gray as her mood, and the windswept beaches refused to calm. What if she had been wrong? What if Dustin *had* intended on kissing her? Did she want to kiss him back?

Absolutely, her heart murmured.

Dustin was the one man she had never stopped wanting, even though she'd spent the past eighteen years trying to forget him. It wasn't only the physical attraction that drew her to him like a magnet either. There was also the way he knew her better than she knew herself, even after all these years. Like how she wouldn't be able to resist an audio-book, no matter what the subject was about.

He knew other things about her, too, like how the back of her right ear was ticklish, but the left ear wasn't. He knew how her shoulders tensed up when she watched a scary movie and how to knead them in just the right spot to make her relax. Dustin knew that she loved cozy sweaters but couldn't wear merino wool because it made her itch. Even the Pendleton blanket in the back of his truck made her itch but never so much that she objected to snuggling underneath it while they watched the stars come out. If she got the chance to watch the stars come out again with Dustin, would she take it?

Yes, her heart whispered. *One hundred percent yes.*

Andrea sighed, uncertain how to proceed. Her baggy sweatshirt, air-dried hair, and lack of makeup didn't aid her self-confidence. When she was a teenager, it had been easy. Youthful optimism combined with a magic metabolism had made her feel invincible. She was the one who had invited him out on their first date. "Do you want to go to a Halloween party with me?" she had blurted out. It had been that simple.

But nothing was easy now. Not her age, or her life, or this messed-up situation they were both stuck in. Even her cell phone was dead. Andrea ran her fingers through her hair, and they caught in snarls. Fuming, she stomped across the room and unzipped her purse. All she had was a comb. Taking her purse with her, Andrea walked to the bathroom, where her phone was plugged into the wall. She had purchased a charger in the gift shop that morning, but it was off brand and slow.

Working in sections, she combed her hair to the best of her ability and slicked it back with a few drops of water. She found a tube of lipstick rolling around next to loose change at the bottom of her purse. After dotting it on her fingertips, she pinked up her cheeks and highlighted her eyelids. The overall effect was better than nothing, she decided. At least the yoga pants from the gift shop fit well and showed off her legs toned from lots of walking.

Andrea rested her palms on the counter and stared at her reflection in the mirror. Her golden-brown hair reminded her of her father, but her blue eyes were exactly like her mother's. Was Dustin right about Lydia? Had it been difficult for her mom to give up her career? Dustin had asked probing questions that Andrea had never thought about before. Andrea had grown up assuming that being a stay-at-home parent was all her mother had ever wanted. But was it? Lydia had never mentioned wanting to practice law again, at least not to her. Her father's job had provided all the money they had needed. As far as Andrea knew, Lydia had been happy taking care of both of them. Now, she didn't know what to think.

Looking back on it now, Andrea could see that she had felt closer to her father than her mother because her time with Tom was precious. His intense work schedule meant that the limited time he spent with her on the weekends usually centered on something fun like visiting the coin store in Greenlake. Tom had never reminded her to unload the dishwasher, like Lydia had, or taken her to the orthodontist to get her braces tightened. He hadn't scolded her for leaving wet towels on the bathroom floor or lectured her on the importance of hand-washing her angora sweater instead of tossing it into the washing machine. Tom loved to give advice but not about the mundane details of daily living. He wasn't a nag. If Lydia had been consumed by office work instead of household chores, would she have been the same way? Andrea had no way of knowing.

Her phone vibrated on the counter, rattling the soap dispenser and disrupting her train of thought. Startled, Andrea picked her phone up but left it plugged into the charger, since the battery was low. Looking at the screen, Andrea saw that the Owl's Nest was calling. "Hello," she said. "This is Andrea Wint speaking."

"Hi, Andrea. This is Huan. Don't panic—your father is safe, but I need to tell you what happened."

"Don't panic?" Andrea's pulse raced. "What's going on?"

"There was an incident this morning around five thirty a.m. We tried calling you earlier but couldn't get ahold of you. We called your mother as well but were unable to reach her either."

"My phone died. I'm sorry." Andrea tried to pace, but the charging cord yanked her back. "What sort of incident?"

"I can't share names because of confidentiality, but you'll be able to find out more information from the police report."

"Police report?" All the blood drained from Andrea's face, and she appeared ghostlike in the mirror.

"Another resident became confused and entered your father's room this morning. Thinking the gentleman was an intruder, Tom punched him. We had to call the police and issue a report, but the other family has decided not to press charges."

"Of course they shouldn't press charges! Their relative invaded my dad's private space."

"Yes, we understand that. But as you know, we can't have locks on any of the doors on the unit, for safety reasons. Residents wander in and out of each other's rooms all the time. Punching people, on the other hand, is less common, and we can't allow that."

"My father was defending himself."

Huan cleared his throat. "Be that as it may, we cater to a vulnerable community and can't keep residents who are violent."

"My dad's not violent." Hot tears sprang into her eyes.

"No, we have no reason to believe he is, other than this incident. We have a three-strikes policy at our center, and this is strike one."

Andrea could barely breathe. Her heart raced so fast she could feel it pound against her chest. If her father got kicked out of the memory-care unit, she didn't know what she'd do. "What's your responsibility in all of this?" she asked. "I hear you saying my dad has a strike against him, but where's your accountability for allowing this to happen? Why didn't someone on staff notice the other person entering my father's room?"

"That's, um . . . being looked into."

"I should hope so," Andrea said in a firm voice. "My father has never had a police record before in his entire life. Yet the one time it happens is under *your* care, when another person invades *his* space. My dad's not the culprit here."

"Nobody's the culprit. Alzheimer's is a cruel disease, but I know I don't have to tell you that."

"No." Andrea sniffed. "You certainly don't."

"Look, we will do our best to keep an eye on him and the other resident. Most likely one or both of them have already forgotten what happened. But please understand our three-strikes policy."

"You already explained that." Andrea squeezed her toes hard against the insoles of her shoes.

"Good. Well, I look forward to seeing you on your next visit. Have a nice weekend."

"Thanks," said Andrea, retreating into common courtesy. "You too." But as soon as she hung up the phone, her tears began to flow. After stumbling out of the bathroom and into the hotel room, she crumpled on the bed and covered her face with her hands. She sat there sobbing for several minutes. The food she had eaten for breakfast swirled around her stomach, and she felt physically ill. Andrea curled up into the fetal position and hugged her knees.

"Three strikes, and you're out." Andrea remembered Tom teaching her the rules of baseball when he had taken her to a Mariners game as a small child. A client had given him tickets to a skybox, and there was a complimentary buffet. Andrea had been only mildly interested in the game, but the unfettered access to Cracker Jacks had made a big impression. That, and the Mariner Moose, who had paid them a special visit between innings. "I used to collect baseball cards," Tom had told her, "but that was before I discovered coins." Then he had pulled out the steel penny and tossed it in the air like he so often did.

Andrea reached into her pocket to find the penny, but it wasn't there. The yoga pants had no pockets. She raced over to the dresser, where her clothes were folded into a neat pile, and searched her pockets, completely panicked until she felt the penny in her palm. Then she looked into her purse and saw the plastic flip with the double eagle in it. One hundred thousand dollars' worth of coins, and all she had left were these two. The odds of her finding the remaining coins were slim. She blew her nose again hard on a tissue.

For one second her thoughts were distracted by coins, but then the horrible truth crashed into her like a bullet train. Her father had punched someone. He now had a police record. How was this fair? It *wasn't*. How could she make it right? She *couldn't*. What was it Huan had said? "Alzheimer's is a cruel disease." She thought back to the free Alzheimer's Association workshop she and her mom had attended when Tom had first been diagnosed. "Sometimes patients with dementia are happy," the presenter had told them. "But anger and aggression can also be part of the disease." Up until now Tom had been happy in his senility. She had to do whatever it took to keep him that way. Andrea gripped the penny tighter. The tips of her fingernails pressed into her hand, causing pain. She put it in its plastic flip for safekeeping.

It wasn't until Dustin coughed that Andrea turned around and saw him standing between the two rooms, bare chested and wearing jeans.

"I knocked," he began, but after taking one look at her face, he closed the gap between them in three long steps.

"Andrea?" Dustin asked. "What's wrong?" Without waiting for an answer, he wrapped his arms around her in a hug.

Andrea squeezed her eyes shut and rested her cheek against his heart. Chest hair tickled her face, and she breathed in the scent of the hotel bodywash he had just used. She centered her thoughts on the smell and feeling of being encircled in Dustin's arms and willed herself to stop crying. But she couldn't. Her grief was a festering wound that had sat at the surface of her emotions ever since her father had been diagnosed. One tiny scratch, and the pain oozed out.

Dustin stroked her hair. "What happened?"

"My dad punched someone," Andrea said between gulps of air. "And they called the cops."

"Oh no. Is he all right?"

"He is, but he now has a police record." Andrea explained the details of her call with the facility.

"Crap." Dustin squeezed her tighter. "I am so sorry. I wish there was something I could say that would make it better, but there's not."

Andrea shook her head. "Nobody can make this better."

"Try to take some deep breaths at least."

"Okay." Andrea gasped for air and held her breath, forgetting to exhale.

"Breathe in for four seconds," Dustin said in a soothing tone, "and then out for five."

She tried again, following his cues. After several breath cycles, her pulse rate lowered, and she began to calm down. She heard Dustin's heartbeat underneath her ear, and it steadied her.

"Why don't you sit down, and I'll get you a fresh tissue?" Dustin guided her to the edge of the bed.

"Thanks." She sat while he walked to the bathroom and brought back the whole box of tissues. Andrea blew her nose while Dustin took the extra sweatshirt off the dresser and pulled it over his head.

He sat next to her and held her hand. Giving it a gentle squeeze, he used his other hand to brush hair back from her eyes. "Your dad wouldn't want you to be this upset."

Andrea's vision blurred with tears. "No," she agreed. "He wouldn't."

"He told me and Nathan and Heidi that the best way we could honor our parents would be to live our lives to the fullest. That meant finding something to be happy about every day for the rest of our lives."

"Have you? Been able to do that, I mean?"

Dustin squeezed her hand again. "Yes. Back in high school, that meant dating you. Saying yes to going to that Halloween party with you, yes to wearing a costume, yes to letting happiness come in alongside of the grief."

Andrea's breath sped up, but she forced it back to a slower rhythm. "What about after you broke up with me?"

"You mean after your dad interfered in our relationship?" Dustin sighed. "It was hard, but I still found ways to be happy. I'd throw rocks into the water from the beach. I'd watch the History Channel after school. I'd hike in the woods—anything to lift my mood. I wasn't always happy, but I tried to be because I knew that's what my parents would have wanted. At least your dad was right about that. They wouldn't have wanted any of us to be miserable."

"Okay, but what if my dad gets a second strike? What if someone wanders into his room again and—"

Dustin lifted his hand and cupped her face. "Stop. We can't predict the future. There's no use worrying about something that might never happen, is there? The question is," he continued, "What are you going to do today that will bring you joy?"

Missed opportunities flashed across her mind like lightning bolts. The necklace she hadn't purchased in the gift shop. The bacon she hadn't eaten. Walking away from that moment when Dustin might have been about to kiss her. He had that look in his eyes again, like he might want to. Was she misreading that? Could she risk making a fool of herself if she was wrong? There was only one way to find out.

"I'm going to spend the day with you," she murmured. "That will bring me joy no matter the reason for us being together."

Dustin smiled, and laugh lines peeked out around his eyes. "That'll bring me joy too," he said. He leaned forward and kissed her forehead.

Andrea slipped her hands behind his waist as he kissed the tears on her cheeks. She pushed her worries aside. Fears over her father's health. Anger over the lost coins. Concerns that reconnecting with Dustin might cause trouble. His lips hovered inches from hers until she lifted her face to meet him. When their lips touched, a warm glow burst from her soul. It radiated like a sunburst. She needed this escape, whatever it was. If it turned out to be a mistake, at least she had this moment of happiness.

Andrea tilted her head to the side, deepening the connection, and was thrilled when Dustin pulled her closer. Was this really happening? Was she kissing the boy of her teenage dreams? Her hands roamed up his back, and she marveled at the muscles she felt underneath her palms. Yes, this was the same Dustin Karlsson she'd fallen for in high school, but he was stronger. It wasn't just the ropy muscles that she was eagerly exploring; it was more than that. It was Dustin listening to her concerns, understanding them completely, and—unlike her last boyfriend—not running away when her father's illness made her dissolve. The softness of his lips didn't mask his strength.

She looped her arms around his neck and raked her fingers through his damp hair. Dustin's kiss tasted like minty mouthwash. Her tongue touched his, and she felt dizzy with glee. Her heart smiled when she realized they were making out like two teenagers. Dustin traced her jawline with his lips and continued exploring down her neck until he reached the sensitive spot behind her right ear, and she giggled.

"You're still ticklish back there, I see?" He kissed the spot again, throwing her into a fit of laughter.

"What about you?" Andrea asked as she walked her fingers up his arm. "Does this still give you goose bumps?"

He shivered. "Only when you do it." He leaned forward and kissed her again.

Andrea closed her eyes, savoring the contact. The rough stubble on his chin scratched her, but she didn't mind. She held on to his shoulders and pulled him closer. When her phone rang in the bathroom, she didn't hear it at first. It wasn't until the fourth ring that it breached her awareness. "My phone," she mumbled, dragging herself away.

"Yeah," Dustin murmured. "You better get that."

She stumbled away from the bed and into the bathroom. Looking at the screen, she saw that it was an unknown number. "Hello?" she asked, already prepared to hang up. If a spam call had interrupted her makeout session with Dustin, she would be peeved.

"Hi, um . . . is this the woman I spoke to about Cade?"

"Yes." Andrea's head cleared. "It is. I'm looking for him."

"This is Suzy from the Elwha. You gave me your number."

"That's right." Andrea stretched the phone-charger cord as far as it would go so she could stand at the doorway of the bathroom and see Dustin. "Thanks for calling me, Suzy. Do you have information about Cade?"

Dustin's eyes opened wide, and he crossed his fingers.

"Kind of," said Suzy. "Well, yeah, actually I do. One of the fry cooks told me that he saw Lisa in a sprinter van last night."

"The type of van that's also a camper?" Andrea asked.

"That's right," said Suzy. "They're crazy expensive. Anyhow, my friend said he saw the van parked behind the casino last night and that Cade was with her."

"And we missed him," Andrea said, letting out a whoosh of air. "Is the van still there?"

"I don't think so. I looked for it when I got off my shift this morning but didn't see it. That was at eight a.m."

"Did your friend get the license plate?"

"I doubt it. But I'll ask."

"Thanks for the information," said Andrea. "Can I Venmo you some money?"

"I wouldn't say no to that. I'll text you my username."

"Great. Please let me know if you hear anything else."

"Will do. Good luck finding him."

As soon as they hung up, Andrea raced into the bedroom. "Cade's in a sprinter van."

"How the hell did he afford that?" Dustin stood and clenched his fists.

"I don't know. Maybe he traded a hundred thousand dollars' worth of rare coins for it?" she asked in a pained voice.

Dustin's lips tightened to a thin line. "There are eighteen campgrounds in Olympic National Park," he said. "Plus all of the Olympic National Forest campgrounds. Hell, in a sprinter van, he could boondock anywhere. Cade could hide for years before we find him."

Andrea's phone buzzed with a text from Suzy with her Venmo information. She cut and pasted the handle and sent Suzy $150. Her phone's battery was halfway charged now, so she unplugged it from the wall. "Do you think he'll travel to Seattle? Or maybe leave the state?" she asked as she gathered her belongings.

"He's got to sell the coins, right? Where can he do that?"

"I don't know. My dad had coin shops in Seattle he frequented, but I'm not sure if there's one on the Olympic Peninsula."

"Let's look it up."

"On it." Andrea used her phone to google nearby coin shops. "There're two on the peninsula. One's also an antique store, which means they're less likely to specialize in high-end coins. Franklin's Coins and Guns in Port Angeles has potential, though."

"Coins and guns?"

"Yeah. I know that sounds like an odd combination, but in the coin world it's not. Sometimes people buy coins not because they care about numismatics but because they distrust banks and would rather invest their savings in gold."

"Oh."

"And sometimes those same people who distrust the financial system also distrust the government and have enough guns and ammunition on hand to take down a three-county area."

"Um . . ."

"Of course, my dad wasn't that type of collector," Andrea continued. "He's a coin nerd, pure and simple."

"As opposed to Rambo."

Andrea laughed. "Right." She looked at her phone. "This shop's open from twelve to four on Saturdays."

"Those seem like odd hours."

"Again, not for a coin shop. The most successful dealers often keep limited hours. They don't need to work retail unless they feel like it. A lot of their revenue comes from scooping up collections for a fraction of their worth and reselling those coins to collectors online." She sighed. Hopefully that wasn't happening to her father's double eagles right now.

"It's almost eleven thirty. Why don't you try calling them?"

"Okay." Andrea made the call, but all she got was an answering machine. "Hi," she said after the beep. "I'm looking for double eagles. Could you call me if you find some? Thanks." She hung up after giving her number and deposited the phone in her purse.

"That was rather sparse," Dustin commented. "You didn't leave your name."

"My dad told me you should never be too forthright with a coin dealer." Andrea put on her shoes. "They could rip you off."

"It sounds like we need to meet up with that dealer in person, then. Let's drive back to Port Angeles and see if they know something."

Andrea picked up her purse, secretly thrilled at the opportunity to spend more time with Dustin. "Good plan," she said, slinging it over her shoulder. "I'm ready when you are."

Dustin nodded and walked back to his room. His T-shirt, wallet, and phone were on the dresser. When he looked at his phone, he cursed.

"What's the matter?" Andrea asked.

Dustin's eyes sparked with rage. "A text from Heidi. Leanne told Heidi she's blocking her number, and now all Heidi's calls are going to her answering machine." Dustin stabbed at his phone screen, dialing Leanne. A few seconds later he turned the phone toward her with a miserable expression on his face. "Straight to voice mail. She blocked me too."

Andrea reached for his hand. "We're going to find Cade and fix this."

Dustin nodded and squeezed her hand. "Damn right we are."

CHAPTER TEN

Twenty minutes later they were on the road to Port Angeles, and Dustin's emotions were simmering like a double boiler melting chocolate. The memory of Andrea's kisses was sweet on his lips, and he was furious that family drama had interrupted them. If it weren't for his jerkwad brother-in-law, Dustin and Andrea would still be back in that hotel room, sharing kisses in front of the fire. Instead, they were driving the exact same route they had come along before, hoping to reach the coin store while it was still open. All to recover Tom's stolen property, even though Tom had been partially responsible for breaking them up in the first place. But Dustin couldn't be mad at Tom, because who got angry at someone with Alzheimer's? A monster, that was who. Plus, Tom was, and would always be, his legal champion. Without Tom picking up his family's case, Dustin might not have gone to college.

Dustin glanced to his right, where she sat next to him, texting a quick update to her mother. Had Andrea meant those kisses, or had they been an accident? His heart ached to find out, but he was terrified of knowing the answer. Her golden-brown hair was wound into a loose knot slowly unraveling at the nape of her neck. Dustin thought about throwing his arm around the back of the seat and resting his hand on her shoulder, but the road was slick from rain. It was safer to keep a firm hold on the steering wheel.

Normally wet weather didn't bother him, but today it compounded his anger. The dark clouds above matched the storm in his heart. Why did the universe hate him? Why did nothing ever go his way? Even the tag on his sweatshirt annoyed him. It scratched against his skin like a briar.

"Okay," Andrea said as she put down her phone. "I've communicated all pertinent details with my mother, including the stolen coins." She scrunched up her nose. "Thank goodness for texting so I didn't have to hear her say 'I told you so' over the phone."

"Did your mom really say that?"

"Not in those exact words, but she did suggest—for the hundredth time—that I rent a safety-deposit box at her bank."

"Yeah." Dustin narrowed his eyebrows and clenched his jaw. It was all he could do to hold back a torrent of curse words when he thought of the trouble Cade had caused.

"What's the matter?" Andrea asked. "You look like you're about to explode."

"Nothing," he mumbled, tightening his grip on the steering wheel.

"Is this about what happened in the hotel room? Was kissing me a mistake?"

"What?" He shot her a look. "No, of course not. I'm mad at Cade for interrupting it."

"Oh," she said, but her voice held a hint of doubt.

He reached for her hand. "Everything keeps getting ruined for us. We had a good thing going in high school, and I torpedoed it. Then after all these years we're together again, and *boom*, my dumbass brother-in-law screws things up."

"It's not screwed up." She squeezed his fingers. "*We're* not screwed up. I mean . . . I don't regret kissing you. Do you?"

"No." He groaned. "I just regret stopping."

Andrea grinned. "Well, maybe next time we won't have to. Until then, try relaxing a little. You look like Mount Saint Helens about to explode."

"Mount Saint Helens already exploded."

Andrea rolled her eyes. "Mount Rainier, then."

He let out a deep breath and tried to cool down his anger, but it was difficult. Every time he thought of Cade, he got worked up again. "It's my fault that Leanne met Cade," he confessed, withdrawing his hand.

"Huh?" Andrea's hair fell loose from the coil and spilled down her back in a shiny wave. Dustin wished he could run his fingers through it. "I met Cade in college," he said. "We were both in the same dorm. Cade was from Spokane, just an hour away from Washington State University, so sometimes we'd drive to his parents' house on the weekend, and Mrs. Tolbert would do our laundry." He looked at her sideways. "You know I'm a sucker for moms."

"Well, you are part labradoodle." Andrea clicked her tongue disapprovingly. "Did Mrs. Tolbert feed you dinner too?"

Dustin nodded. "Family dinners with napkins and everything. Cade may be a jackass, but his parents are all right. At least Leanne has decent in-laws."

"So how did Cade meet Leanne?"

"I was just getting to that. He wanted to be an actor."

Andrea tapped her chin. "He *does* look a bit like Matthew McConaughey."

"I'm going to pretend you didn't say that." Dustin glowered. "Anyhow," he said, continuing the story, "Cade moved to LA after college, with his parents supporting him because it was so expensive, and I didn't hear from him for nine years. But then, when I was twenty-nine, he texted me that he had moved back to Washington and was working as a locksmith."

"Where did he move to?"

"Federal Way, close to the airport. He'd taken an online training course and was working for a locksmith down there but also trying to audition for parts at a theater in the city."

"Seattle Rep? Fifth Avenue?" Andrea turned up the defroster since the windows were steaming up.

Dustin shrugged. "I don't remember, but both of those sound familiar. They kept turning him down, but he did get a minor role as an understudy in *Hamlet*. He offered me free tickets, and like a moron, I accepted. That's how Leanne and Cade met. She was eighteen at the time. Three months later she was married and pregnant."

"That must have been stressful for her."

"Yeah." Dustin nodded. "Heidi, Nathan, and I tried to be as supportive as possible. At first, Cade didn't want anything to do with her once she was pregnant. Then his parents threatened to cut him off if he didn't marry Leanne, so he did. But once he found out the baby was a girl, he quit pretending to care about either of them unless his parents were around. Cade turns on the charm when he wants something."

"Ugh. What an utter tool. And his parents were bankrolling him? I thought he worked as a locksmith."

"He was, but you know how expensive it is to live in Seattle. Plus, Cade has champagne tastes. Back then he drove a Camaro."

"Like a true douchebag."

Dustin chuckled. "Yeah. I tried to talk Leanne out of getting married so soon. She and Cade barely knew each other."

"I don't understand the rush."

"Exactly. We said we'd help care for the baby, and she could see how her relationship with Cade went before she made any major decisions. But Leanne was in love. She's always had a blind spot where Cade's concerned. Still, I don't think Cade would have gone through with it, even with his parents pressuring him, if it weren't for the settlement money."

"But Leanne was eighteen. She didn't have access to her trust money."

"She was eighteen when she met him and nineteen by the time Kendal was born. No, she didn't have access to her trust, but Cade must have somehow found out about it. I for sure didn't tell him, but he knew."

Andrea gently bit her lower lip for a few seconds. "The settlement was written about in the *Seattle Times* back in the day. He could have googled it."

"Yeah." Dustin rubbed his chin. "Maybe. Or perhaps Leanne told him. She would have said anything to keep him with her—that's how strongly she felt. She wanted Kendal to have both of her parents in her life from the very start."

Andrea nodded. "So Leanne and Cade get married, Leanne drops out of college and has Kendal, and Cade moves to Port Inez." She tightened her seat belt. "I take it your friendship with him had soured at that point?"

"You could say that. Only now he was my brother-in-law, so instead of kicking his ass for taking advantage of my little sister, I had to welcome him as part of our family. We helped get him set up as a locksmith in Port Inez, but the town never has enough business for him. That's how come Heidi and I started giving him odd jobs with Karlsson Construction."

"When did you find out Cade had a gambling problem?"

"Not until Kendal was a toddler." Dustin thought back to that first time he had realized something was seriously amiss. "It was Thanksgiving, and Heidi and I had finished a flip. She cooked the sides while I smoked a turkey. Nathan closed the pizzeria early, and we all gathered in the new house for dinner. Since Leanne and Cade had a toddler, all they had to do was show up."

Andrea smiled warmly. "That was nice of you guys."

"Getting from point A to point B with a toddler is harder than it sounds," said Dustin, who, having spent a vast amount of time shuttling his nieces around, spoke from experience. "Anyhow, dinner went wrong as soon as they arrived. Cade saw the real estate agent's sign at the front of the driveway and declared he wanted to be our listing agent. He said selling houses wasn't that hard to do and that he could save us a ton of money by selling it himself. Heidi and I both told him no way. I think Heidi was actually a bit nicer than me about it. She said that maybe if he got his real estate license, we could consider him as our future agent, but definitely not until then."

"Yeah, that would be a hard pass for me too. Selling homes is difficult work, even in a hot market."

"Exactly. But Cade always thinks he's smarter than everyone, especially us. He told us that we were stupid and shortsighted and that we never listened to his opinions on anything."

"Sounds like a fun Thanksgiving."

"And that was *before* he threw a glob of mashed potatoes at Nathan."

"He did what?"

"Straight at his head. If Cade had thrown it at Heidi, I would have decked him. But you know how mild mannered my brother is; Nathan just laughed it off."

"Yikes. But what does this have to do with gambling?"

"As soon as we finished eating dinner, Cade took off. Heidi hadn't even served the pies yet. He said he had important business to do, and we all thought that meant a locksmith call. But later that night, around midnight, Leanne called Heidi and asked her to come over and watch Kendal. Leanne needed to rush over to the Point Casino because Cade had been caught stealing chips and was in lockup until she bailed him out."

"Whoa."

"Yeah. Gambling and thieving on Thanksgiving. What a guy. Did I tell you he lets Kendal sit in the front seat even though that's illegal?" Once Dustin started venting about Cade, he couldn't stop.

"This isn't the 1950s," said Andrea. "The airbag could kill her!"

"I know, right?" The anger that had built up over the past seven years oozed out like lava. "When the girls were smaller, Cade bragged about never changing diapers, saying it was 'women's work.'"

"Ugh!"

"He's pretty much trashed the house we rent to them." Dustin thought about the three-bedroom rambler that Karlsson Construction had lovingly refurbished, and he seethed. "He didn't pay the gas bill one winter, and so they heated the house by leaving the oven open and—"

"Wait, with small kids in the house?" Andrea's mouth gaped open. "The girls could have burned themselves."

"Yeah, can you believe it? And the heat from the oven caused the cabinets to warp. Brand-new maple cabinets, completely ruined. I mean, Leanne shares some of the blame in this, too, but she's young, so I give her a break."

"How does the front yard look?"

"Like a junkyard because they won't pay for trash pickup." Dustin squeezed the steering wheel with a death grip. "The gutters would be overflowing with leaves and the roof choked by moss if I didn't clean them myself three times a year. I can't let our investment be ruined by neglect."

"It's good that you take care of the roof stuff instead of Cade," said Andrea. "He'd probably pretend to fall off a ladder and sue you for a million dollars."

"True." Dustin grunted. It felt good to unload his frustrations. He didn't mean to dump them on Andrea, but she was definitely a sympathetic listener.

"I bet it's especially difficult for you to watch what's happening between Cade and Leanne considering how important family is to you." Andrea tilted her head toward him.

Dustin's shoulders tensed. Every time he looked back on the situation, he wished he had done things differently. "I feel like I failed her," he admitted. "If I had given Leanne better guidance, she might have made different choices."

"That's being unfair to yourself." Andrea rested her hand on his knee. "Leanne's a grown woman capable of making her own decisions."

"Yeah, but her childhood was so messed up. She didn't have—"

"She had you, Heidi, and Nathan taking care of her," Andrea interrupted. "Give yourself some credit."

"But—"

Andrea's phone rang, and she looked at the screen. "It's the coin shop," she said. "I need to take this." She accepted the call. "Hi. This is Andrea Wint."

Dustin kept his eyes on the road as he listened to the one-sided conversation. The coin dealer wasn't nearly as loud as Heidi, so he could hear only snippets of what the man said.

"That's right," Andrea gushed. "I'm passionate about double eagles, especially ones in higher grades." She winked at Dustin. "Do you have any in stock?"

It still seemed weird to Dustin that Andrea wasn't being direct with the dealer. Why not be blunt and tell him what the situation was? But maybe it was like dealing with stonework vendors. Dustin never shared his true budget because they'd always try to upsell him from quartz to marble and then pad the price some more when he asked for beveled edges.

"You have one that's uncirculated?" Andrea asked, her eyes widening. "It just came into the shop this morning?" She leaned forward in her seat. "We'll be there in an hour. Hello? Hello?" Andrea yanked her phone away from her ear and stared at the screen. She tapped it madly, trying to reconnect the call. "I lost him!" she cried.

"It's these trees," said Dustin. "Reception's a crapshoot out here."

"Damn!"

"I'm sorry. And I hate to burst your bubble, but we're not an hour away from Port Angeles. We still have at least two to go."

"Don't tell me that," Andrea groaned. "Even if we hurry, we might not make it before he closes."

"Maybe he'll stay late knowing he has a high-end buyer coming?"

"Let's hope so." She frowned. "I bet that double eagle is one of my coins. The dealer said he had acquired it this morning."

"Will you be able to identify it?"

"Maybe. I'll definitely know if it's the right grade and date, but I won't be able to prove definitively if it's mine or not. The best we can hope for is more information." She squeezed her eyes shut. "Oh no. This means I'll miss my visit with my dad this afternoon." She opened her eyes again. "And he probably won't notice," she added in a quiet voice.

"Maybe that's a good thing in this instance."

"Yeah, maybe."

"Did I ever tell you what your dad said to me after that Halloween party?"

"No." Andrea's expression softened, and she looked at him expectantly.

Dustin hadn't intended on sharing this story with her, but he wanted to cheer her up, and it was the first thing that floated into his head. "I was dressed like two strips of bacon, if you might recall."

"How could I forget? I sewed them onto the black turtleneck myself."

"Which meant I couldn't take the bacon off unless I also removed my shirt. So I kept it on—even though I hate turtlenecks, by the way—because I didn't want to sleep in your living room half-naked and have your mom walk in on me."

"I'm sure my mom would have loved to see you without your shirt on." She grinned mischievously.

"I'm going to pretend you didn't say that. Anyhow, your dad walked into the living room the next morning, and there I was snoring away. He got about three inches from my face and said: 'Morning, son. Rise and shine.' It scared the crap out of me. I jumped up, not knowing where I was or what was going on. Then I saw him and realized that I was in my lawyer's living room and that I'd brought his daughter home forty-five minutes past her curfew."

"*And* that you were dressed like a pork product."

"Exactly. It didn't matter what I was dressed like. I knew I was toast."

Andrea chuckled. "What did my dad say after that? Do you remember?"

"I sure do. He handed me a glass of orange juice and said: 'I always told my daughter to grow up into a woman who could bring home the bacon. I guess I should have been more specific with my instructions.'"

Andrea's chuckles turned into full-fledged laughter. "My dad! He always had a droll sense of humor."

"I expected him to ream me out for bringing you home late, but instead he asked me what happened. I explained that a friend of yours had double-parked and blocked in my truck. Your dad told me that if that happened in the future, I should find a pay phone and call him."

"Pay phone." Andrea snorted. "That makes me feel old." Her smile melted away. "I'd call my dad now and tell him I was safe, but that would just confuse him. Thanks for sharing this story with me."

"You're welcome."

"What was your father like? You never talked about him when we were dating, and I didn't want to hurt you by asking. Did he love reading, too, like you do?"

"Yes." Dustin nodded. "My dad would listen to the radio while he worked. But at home he'd read one nonfiction book after another. He wasn't cerebral like your dad, but he sure did love books about World War II." It felt good talking about Josh. Dustin never talked about him to anyone, not even Heidi. Nineteen years later, the pain of losing his parents was still raw.

"And he was a furniture craftsman, right? I can't quite remember."

Dustin rubbed tension out of the back of his neck before returning his hand to the steering wheel. "He was a cabinetmaker, which is how I got my start in construction. My mom ran an at-home day care out of our house."

"Crystal's Kids," said Andrea. "I remember Heidi mentioning that she felt bad for those day care families left in the lurch after the accident."

Dustin nodded. "Yeah. Our mom would have hated that. She loved those kids."

"So your father made cabinets?"

"Custom cabinets. He'd take orders from Seattle all the time. He was expensive, but nobody could beat his craftsmanship."

"Like the window seat in my dining room." Andrea twisted a lock of hair around her finger. "You built that, didn't you?"

Dustin felt a rush of pride. "I did. My dad taught me a trick or two. But most importantly he gave me opinions."

"About what?"

"About houses and how important it was to be true to design. He thought form should follow function and that the fewer frivolous details there were, the better. He also thought that homes should honor their era whenever possible. My dad would have hated what home design has become. Farmhouse sinks without farms. People putting up fake shiplap over perfectly good walls."

"What's shiplap?"

"Shiplap in its true form means horizontal wood boards used in construction for housing or shedding. But what it's become is a design trend where people put up boards over perfectly good plastered walls because they're trying to copy what they see on a home-design show."

"Oh. So they're faking it to get the look."

"Yeah, it's annoying. Other trends bug me too. Tearing down cabinets to install open shelves for dishes that will just get dusty. Crown molding—what the hell is that for? Painting brick. Stuffing fireplaces so full of perfectly cut wood that you couldn't actually start a fire if the furnace was out. My dad would have thought that was ridiculous."

"It sounds like you think some of that's ridiculous too." Andrea poked him gently in the shoulder.

"Those things don't bother me as much as the other things I see in the business, like people cutting down one-hundred-twenty-year-old cedars to get a better view. People abusing their septic system and risking environmental damage. Homeowners who take down popcorn ceilings on their own without hiring asbestos-abatement teams. Developers who want to build too close to the water. And don't get me started on front-loader washing machines."

"Front-loader washing machines?" Andrea raised her eyebrows. "Where did that angst come from?"

"You can't close them all the way without them stinking." Dustin shook his head in disgust. "All the real estate agents say they're a selling point that buyers expect. But are front loaders really such a great deal if you have to leave the door cracked open all the time?"

"I guess not. I never thought about it before." She leaned on the center console and rested her chin in her hand, staring at him. "You're full of surprises today. I never knew you had so many pet peeves."

"I'm not surprising. I'm the same guy I ever was."

"Maybe you are. Because I didn't ask you about pet peeves; I asked about your father. You told me some of his opinions about home design, but you didn't tell me what he was really like."

"What do you mean? I just told you all about him."

"Did you?"

"Sure I did. I said he taught me that form should follow function."

"But what about other things? What type of music did he like? Did he follow politics? What did you do together on the weekends? Did he prefer burritos or tacos?"

A tiny rip began at the center of his heart and tore all the way down. Dustin knew the answers to only *some* of her questions. "My dad listened to John Mellencamp and Bruce Springsteen," he said. "And on the weekends he worked or watched football." But as for politics, he didn't know how Josh had voted, and he could no longer remember what his father liked to order when they drove to Bremerton and ate at a Mexican restaurant.

Fear flooded the space in his heart where he kept memories of his father. He had only a limited amount. It wasn't like he could go to the store and make new ones. The memories stockpiled in his soul were fading. He remembered Josh's opinions about what type of sandpaper to use on oak, but he couldn't recall the cadence of his father's laughter. The harder he tried to recall specific details about his dad, the more his mind blanked out. The sound of Josh's voice—gone. The scent of his aftershave—missing. They had old home movies—sure. But Josh was always the one holding the camera. It was easier to picture his mom and siblings than it was to remember his dad.

"Dustin?" Andrea touched his sleeve. "Are you okay?"

"I'm fine." He dug deep. There had to be something else he could tell her about his father. But all he could come up with was the yellow Ford truck. It was a three on the tree with a sticky clutch. Sometimes the bed was full of cabinets to deliver, wrapped up in old blankets and a blue tarp. Dustin could visualize sitting in the passenger seat, but he could no longer see Josh's hands on the steering wheel. "My dad wore a red coat," he said, borrowing Leanne's memory. "It was buffalo plaid wool. My mom sewed it from a kit."

"What was your mom like?" Andrea asked gently.

Crystal, at least, was easier to remember. "She was a lot like my sisters but more like Heidi than Leanne. My mom talked a lot and was really social. She would have loved Facebook. Heidi's always tagging me in pictures I don't remember her taking of me. Then, when I eventually go onto Facebook, there will be a dozen comments from people I barely know. My mom would have loved that. She kept up with everyone in town, sometimes to an extreme. When I was little, I pitched a huge fit in the fabric store because we were there for hours gossiping with the owner."

"I didn't know Port Inez had a fabric store."

"It doesn't now. But it did back then. My mom would make cushions for the day care and a lot of our clothes. Now it's cheaper to buy stuff in stores, but then it wasn't."

"What would she think of the business you've built?"

"She'd be proud of us." Dustin's chest swelled. "She'd want to help with the flips. Sew curtains or something, even though we don't usually do window coverings."

"Don't I know it. I spent three thousand dollars on blinds." Andrea reached forward and adjusted the heating vent.

"My mom would be sad that I was—" Dustin stopped himself before he said *lonely*. He wasn't ready to admit that to Andrea—or to himself. "Still single," he said instead. "She probably would have given me a subscription to that dating app that's so popular."

"Good Catch?"

Dustin nodded. "That's the one. Heidi was on it for a while."

"I know. She wouldn't shut up about it. She wanted me to sign up for it too."

"Did you?"

Andrea shook her head. "No. It was right when my dad was moving to the memory unit."

"That must have been stressful."

"It was. But I didn't mean to sidetrack you. Tell me more about your mom and how she'd hate that you were single."

"She wouldn't *hate* me being single, but she would be sad that I hadn't given her grandkids. My mom kept a big box of our childhood toys in the attic that she wouldn't let the day care kids play with." He choked up thinking about it. What a stupid thing to be emotional about. A box of old toys? He was stronger than that. He wondered if his toy tool bench was still there.

"Why'd she keep them in the attic? Were they antiques?"

"No." Dustin shook his head. "They were the toys we had when we were little. Wooden blocks and stuff like that. She was saving them for her grandchildren."

"Do Kendal and Jane get to play with them?"

"I don't know." Tension crept up his neck again. "I'm not sure where those boxes went. Maybe they're still in the attic. Sorry," he added. "That was a dumb thing to share."

"It's not dumb." Andrea rested her palm on his shoulder. "It's a sweet thing to remember about your mom and how much she dreamed for your future."

Dustin blinked back tears. "Yeah, maybe," he said in a gruff voice. "Let's listen to the audiobook." He turned on the sound system without waiting for her answer.

As the narrator's deep voice filled the small space, Dustin let the familiarity of the story wash over him. He concentrated on the words and pushed away his emotions. But then the book mentioned the growing unrest before World War II, and that made him think of his father and Josh's love of history books.

What the hell had happened? Why couldn't he remember more details about his father? Trying to think about them left him feeling spent and vulnerable. Emotions were like water, and when they weren't contained, they could do a lot of damage.

There, he thought with relief. *That was a memory about Josh to cherish.* At long last he could finally picture his dad sitting in the Ford truck. Josh was wearing his red coat and giving him that exact piece of advice: "Emotions are like water and can do a lot of damage if you're not careful," he had said.

Dustin had been thirteen years old at the time. It was spring break, and he was home from school helping Josh install custom cabinets at a jobsite in Harper Landing in the exclusive neighborhood of Burke Woods. It was a big deal because Dustin had wanted to go on a beach hike with his friends. Their Boy Scout troop was trekking the South Coast Trail from Third Beach to the Oil City Trailhead and had invited Dustin to come along. The troop would have provided the wilderness permit, tents, and bear canisters. All Dustin would have needed were his hand-me-down hiking boots from Nathan. But Dustin couldn't go because his dad needed his help.

The cabinets were works of art, but Dustin couldn't have cared less. When he looked at them, he didn't appreciate that they were solid oak with slide-out drawers. He ignored the corner cabinets with lazy Susans. And the spice rack that gracefully emerged from a hidden space above the sink? That pissed Dustin off the most because Josh had made him attach it. It had been a lesson in properly adhering hinges that thirteen-year-old Dustin hadn't wanted to learn, not with his friends camping on the beach without him.

Josh had spent five weeks building the cabinets, and Crystal had suggested small improvements to make them even better, like glass doors to display fancy dishes. "I'll build cabinets like these for you someday," Josh had told her, although everyone knew that was unlikely to happen. His cabinetry business kept him too busy, yet not busy enough to hire extra help. That's why Dustin's spring break was ruined. He was free labor. Still, Dustin remembered the pride he had felt as he'd helped his father load them onto the truck. By present standards the oak cabinets would be considered out of style, but at the time they were stunning.

But when they reached the jobsite, they encountered a disaster. Overnight a pipe had burst in an upstairs bathroom, flooding the partially assembled kitchen with water. The brand-new wood floor was warped beyond repair, and the newly plastered walls were destroyed. The builder had arrived ten minutes before and was swearing at a subcontractor responsible for the mistake.

Dustin's father remained calm, even when the builder told him he wouldn't issue the final payment for the cabinets. "This will bankrupt me," the builder said. "You might as well take those cabinets to the junk pile, because I can't afford them anymore."

"We have a contract," Josh said in a clear voice.

"Take me to court, then." The builder spat on the ground. "You'll be out attorney's fees, and you'll still never see a dime. I'm ruined!"

Dustin and his dad drove the whole ride back to Port Inez in silence. Josh didn't speak until he rolled down the window to pay the ferry toll. Finally, Dustin couldn't take it anymore. "My spring break was wasted for nothing," he exploded.

"Not for nothing," said Josh. "You learned new skills."

"Who cares? The only reason I stayed home was because you needed help. Now that guy totally ripped you off. Why didn't you punch him in the face?"

"Because violence wouldn't have solved anything," Josh said. "Losing my temper wouldn't have helped either. Did you see how the builder reacted to the burst pipe? Stamping his foot and spitting on the ground like an animal? Instead of seeking a solution to his problem, he's throwing a tantrum. Look, I'm sorry you couldn't go on that trip. I wish things were different. But emotions are like water. They can do a lot of damage if you're not careful."

One look into his father's eyes, and Dustin knew that the conversation was over. When they arrived home, Josh left the cabinets in the truck for three whole days. Dustin sulked around and barely spoke to him. On the fourth day, Josh and Nathan brought half of the cabinets into the house and installed them in the family kitchen. The other half went into the dining room. Dustin was relieved that Josh didn't ask for *his* help because he never wanted to be bothered by the cabinets again.

That summer the Karlsson family had eaten peanut-butter-and-jelly sandwiches every day for lunch and macaroni and cheese for dinner. They'd visited the food pantry on Monday nights and grown vegetables in their garden to supplement their meager rations. But nobody had said a word about the lost income. In the mornings, Crystal would pop open the hidden spice rack to get cinnamon for their oatmeal and say, "These cabinets look like a million bucks. Thanks, babe."

Josh would kiss her on the top of her head. "You're worth every penny," he'd say. "One of these days I'll refinish the dining room table to match."

Back on the road to Port Angeles, Andrea turned off the audiobook. "Earth to Dustin," she said. "You look like you're on another planet."

"Oh." He snapped to attention. "Sorry."

"What were you thinking about?"

"Nothing. Just construction stuff." Dustin kept his eyes fixed firmly on the road; then he flicked the audiobook back on and retreated into silence.

CHAPTER ELEVEN

Don't tell my brother but I have bad news, read the text from Heidi. Andrea angled her screen away from Dustin so he couldn't see. They were almost at the Port Angeles Coin Shop and had turned off the audiobook so they could focus on the navigational instructions squawking from Dustin's phone. Cade has drained the joint bank account he shares with Leanne, Heidi texted. She doesn't even have money left to buy groceries!

Damn. Andrea let out the breath she was holding in a whoosh of air.

"Is something wrong?" Dustin asked.

"Heidi texted. I guess Leanne must have unblocked her number." Andrea wasn't sure if she agreed with Heidi that it was a good idea to keep this information from Dustin. Why can't I tell him? she typed.

Because there's nothing he can do about it. Except freak out.

Andrea agreed that Dustin would freak out, but she thought he had the right to know.

"What's going on?" Dustin asked.

"Hang on," said Andrea. "Let me text her back." Her thumbs hovered over the screen as she thought about how to reply. Is Leanne okay?

She's coming around. After her ATM card was declined at the grocery store she called me. I've talked her into canceling her credit cards.

That's good, Andrea replied. I think we should tell Dustin. He can handle it.

It'll make him so mad he'll give you the silent treatment all the way home, even though it's not your fault.

He'll still talk to me, Andrea typed, but she wasn't sure that was true. The ride from Ocean Shores to Port Angeles had started out so promising. But then Dustin had clamped shut like a razor clam. He had barely spoken two words to her since she'd asked him about his parents. For the past hour all they'd done was listen to the audiobook.

I can tell him when you get home, Heidi offered.

No, I'll do it. Andrea looked up from the screen in time to see Dustin pull up to the curb in front of the coin store. Text you later, she wrote. She slipped her phone into her purse and looked at Dustin. "Heidi has convinced Leanne to cancel her credit cards," she said, starting with the good news first.

"That's great." Dustin parked the truck and turned off the ignition. "Maybe Leanne's finally listening to reason."

"There's more." Andrea unclicked her seat belt. "Cade drained their joint bank account."

"He did what?" Dustin's voice dropped so low that it was practically a growl.

"The money's gone." Andrea touched his shoulder. "Heidi didn't say how much was in the account, so I don't know."

Dustin squeezed his eyes shut. "Hopefully Leanne kept her trust fund safe." When he didn't open his eyes or respond to the touch of her hand, she pulled away, realizing that Heidi might be right. Maybe Dustin would process this information by retreating into silence.

Andrea climbed out of the truck and slung her purse over her shoulder. Her heart beat hard. Perhaps kissing Dustin back at the Quinault had been a mistake after all. She shouldn't have rushed into things because now her feelings were hurt. Steeling herself, she resolved to focus on the task at hand. At least they had arrived at the shop with ten minutes to spare before it closed.

Dustin slammed the door to his truck. He pressed his lips into a thin white line and clenched his fists. His eyes flashed fury.

"Let me do the talking," she said. "You look like you might bite someone's head off."

"I'm fine."

"You don't look fine."

"I'm *fine*." Dustin folded his arms. "But sure, you take the lead on this one. The only thing I know about coins is that the national park quarters are cool."

"They're the gateway drug to coin collecting." Andrea lifted her chin. "Those and the state quarters."

Dustin's jawline softened. "What about the ones with drummers on the back?"

"You mean the bicentennials? I used to sort through rolls from the bank when I was little to spot them." She led him across the sidewalk to the coin shop. It was a small business wedged between a gastropub and a bookstore. A couple of shops down was an impressive mural depicting Port Angeles's history as a logging town.

Dustin tried to open the door. "What the hell?" he asked when the handle wouldn't budge.

"It's locked." Andrea pressed a buzzer to the left of the door. "Most coin stores do that for security." When nothing happened, she tried the button again, this time holding it down longer. Still nothing. "That's odd," she said. "We have nine minutes before the store closes, and the owner knew we were coming." She peered through the window and saw a short, squat man with white hair bent over a glass case. "He knows we're here." She pressed her face up to the glass. "He's choosing to ignore us on purpose." Andrea pulled out her phone and dialed the number for the shop. She knocked on the window with one hand and held on to her phone with the other. After four rings, the call went to voice mail.

"What a jerk," Dustin muttered. "Doesn't he want our business?"

"Maybe not." Andrea frowned. "Coin stores closing early is nothing new, but I spoke to him on the phone an hour ago. His name is Franklin, and he knew I was coming to buy a double eagle. Ignoring me is odd."

"That's one word for it." Dustin rapped his knuckles hard on the glass. That caught the owner's attention. When Franklin looked through the window, Andrea waved at him and made direct eye contact.

The dealer glared at her but came out from behind the counter and walked over to the door. He opened it a crack. "We're closed," Franklin said. "Come back on Tuesday."

Andrea wedged her foot against the doorjamb. "I'm here for the double eagle. We'll be fast."

Franklin's puffy face turned pink. "I said we're closed. You'll have to come back during operating hours."

"But we drove all the way from Ocean Shores." Andrea batted her eyelashes. "Please?" she asked in a sweet voice. "You promised to show me if I got here before three."

"Oh, all right." He opened the door. "But this will have to be quick. I've got things to do."

"Thank you." Andrea scanned the shop and processed what she saw. The beige carpet was old and tattered in spots. Dingy walls showed fingerprints. A bulletin board in the corner advertised coin shows from three years ago. The whole place was run down except for where it mattered—the security features and the inventory. Andrea saw four cameras, one in each corner of the room, monitoring the long glass counters of merchandise. She peeked into the cases as she followed Franklin to the back. Some coins were in labeled cardboard holders with plastic windows, and some were in plastic slabs with grades. There was an entire display case devoted to antique guns and another for gold bullion and estate sale jewelry. The side wall was lined with gun safes. By Andrea's quick estimate, there was over half a million dollars' worth of merchandise in the shop. It didn't matter what the decor looked like; this place was loaded.

"So you're a double eagle collector, are you?" Franklin asked. He wore a long-sleeved button-down shirt yellowed by perspiration stains and a pistol on his hip.

"That's right." Andrea nodded. "Although I love all of Saint-Gaudens' work. I collect double eagles, and ten-dollar eagles have a place in my heart too."

"Well, you're in luck." Franklin jingled his keys and unlocked a case. "I have two you'll want to see."

"Two?" Andrea swept a lock of hair behind her ear. "On the phone you said one."

"That was before I knew you collected the ten-dollar pieces too." He brought out a slabbed coin and put it in front of her.

As soon as she saw the plastic coating and third-party grading cer-tification, Andrea knew the coin didn't belong to her. Her father never kept coins in slabs, no matter how valuable. Part of the fun of collecting for Tom had been popping them out of the slabs and slipping them into his collector books. Later, once Andrea had possession of Tom's coins, she'd kept them in plastic flips in her safe so they were easier to transport one at a time to the Owl's Nest.

Andrea picked up the slab and examined it closely. It was a ten-dol-lar gold piece from 1928. Andrea hadn't lied when she'd told the dealer she admired them. While Tom had specialized in double eagles, she'd once owned three ten-dollar eagles that she'd inherited from her grandmother. Grandma Wint had commissioned a jeweler to fashion three of her husband's coins into a necklace, much to the dismay of Grandpa Wint and Tom. Every time Andrea had seen her grandma wear it, she'd felt disappointed in her grandmother for ruining the coins. Sure, Grandma Wint had probably thought she was participating in her husband and son's hobby by having the necklace made, but it was a crime against numismatics that couldn't be absolved. No self-respecting coin collector would take a valuable coin with historic significance and mar it like that. When Andrea had inherited the necklace after her grandmother had passed away, she'd immediately sold it.

"Mint state," Andrea said, admiring the coin's grade. "Beautiful. But I'm not collecting that year." Technically, that was true. "Can I see the double eagle?"

"You can, but it's for serious collectors only."

"What makes you think she's not serious?" Dustin asked, stepping beside her.

"It's from 1907." The dealer ignored Dustin's question and locked eyes with Andrea, like he was testing her.

Andrea didn't flinch. "Which issue?"

"In high relief."

"Well," said Andrea, "it's a good thing my credit card has a high limit."

The dealer nodded and went into a back room. He came out a minute later holding a velvet-lined tray. The gold coin lay in a sea of navy, sparkling in the fluorescent light. It was loose, unslabbed, and brilliant.

"May I?" Andrea asked before she touched the coin.

"You may." Franklin set the tray down on the counter.

Andrea held the coin gently by the edges and examined the date. There was no way of knowing if the coin was hers or not. None of Tom's collection had distinguishing bag marks, the scratches that came from the coins being transported by the US Mint in canvas bags. Toning couldn't help her identify it either, because gold didn't tone. But based on the date, Andrea knew that the double eagle *could* be hers.

Andrea placed the coin back on the velvet. "How much are you selling it for?"

"Twenty thousand dollars," he said. "Like I said, it's for serious collectors only."

Andrea smiled coolly. "I own a 1907 double eagle that's just like this," she said. "But it's worth over thirty thousand dollars, which makes me wonder why you have yours priced so low."

"Do I?" Franklin scratched his head. "Maybe you were overcharged."

Andrea rolled her shoulders back. "Mine is the most valuable coin in my collection. It was purchased from Green Lake Coin Store eight years ago. I'm sure they kept the records." Andrea vividly pictured the day when her father turned sixty and celebrated by making the coin purchase of his dreams. "Last night my coin was stolen, along with all of the double eagles in my collection."

Franklin's face turned beet red. "What are you implying, young lady?"

"I'm implying that you have acquired stolen goods." Andrea pointed to the four cameras. "And that you have evidence to turn over to the police."

"How dare you," he said, so forcefully that spit flew out of his mouth. "You come into my store and accuse me of thievery?" He jutted out the hip where his pistol hung.

Dustin stepped in front of her and held out his arms. "Nobody's accusing you of anything except for being swindled."

"That's not true." Andrea poked her head out from behind Dustin's broad back. "I'm accusing him of knowingly acquiring stolen goods. Otherwise, why did he try to sell it to me for ten thousand dollars less than it was worth?"

"He's got a gun," Dustin whispered. "Be cool."

"Franklin's not going to shoot me. Are you, Franklin?" Andrea folded her arms across her chest. "That would be bad for business. The last thing you'd want is federal investigators swarming all over the place, poking their nose into things. So let's settle this ourselves."

"No," said Dustin. "Let's call the police and let them sort this out."

"The police?" Franklin grabbed the gold and clenched his fist around it. "There's no need for them to be involved."

"That's my coin!" Andrea shoved her way past Dustin and lurched over the counter, reaching for the dealer's hand.

Franklin yanked his fist away. "Oh no you don't, missy. It's mine now."

"You bought stolen property. Probably by accident." Dustin pulled out his phone and tapped on the screen. "I'm looking up the number for the Port Angeles Police Department."

"Wait!" Franklin shouted. "Stop!" He scurried around the counter and lunged for Dustin's phone, but Dustin held him off with his free hand.

"Too late. It's already dialing. Hello?" Dustin said in his deep voice. "I was calling to request assistance."

"I'll give you the coin!" Franklin threw it on the ground.

"My double eagle!" Andrea shrieked. "You'll scratch it." She dropped to her knees and swiped it off the dirty carpet.

"Hang up! Hang up! Hang up!" Franklin begged.

"Sorry, sir. Could you please hold a sec?" Dustin glared at Franklin.

"Involving the police will slow you down," the dealer pleaded. "You'll lose the trail if you have to stay here and fill out paperwork. He's probably halfway to Oregon by now."

Dustin glanced at Andrea, and she nodded. She had to admit that the coin dealer was right. Every minute that passed meant Cade's trail cooled.

"My apologies, sir. Wrong number." Dustin hung up the phone. "We want details," he said, pointing his finger at Franklin.

"And those videotapes." Andrea rose to her feet.

"There was no need to call the cops." Franklin shifted his weight from foot to foot. "I run a clean business here."

"Not from what I can tell." Andrea prayed there wasn't dirt on her coin. She didn't dare wipe it for fear of adding hairline scratches. "Who knows how many people you've swindled out of their loved one's collections?"

Franklin sneered. "It's not my fault people don't know what things are worth."

"Um . . . yeah, it is." Andrea stared at the sign that read **WE APPRAISE COINS** hanging behind him. "Tell us what you know about the man who sold you this coin."

"He was about your age," said Franklin. "Drove one of those camping vans. And he and his wife were in a big hurry."

"Wife?" Andrea asked.

"Girlfriend, mistress, whatever." Franklin shrugged. "I don't ask questions. Her red hair looked as fake as dime-store rubies."

"Did the seller have more coins with him?" Andrea asked.

"Yes ma'am." Franklin removed a less-than-pristine white handkerchief from his back pocket and wiped his brow. "He brought in several dozen pieces."

"My whole collection," Andrea murmured.

"He wanted a hundred thousand for the lot," said Franklin. "But I told him I didn't keep that much cash on hand. I tried to trade him bullion for it, but his lady friend knew the price of gold."

"You tried to swindle him, did you?" Dustin tilted his head to the side.

"You can't cheat a cheater," the dealer said defensively. "That 1907 was the best in the collection. I thought I should at least get that. Luckily, the woman saw a diamond ring in the jewelry case she wanted. She wouldn't shut up about it until the guy agreed to the trade."

"You traded a diamond ring for my double eagle?" Andrea asked.

"That's right, and the ring was worth two grand, at least." He held out his palm. "So I think that—"

"Oh no you don't," said Dustin. "We're not paying you anything. But you're giving us those videotapes."

"What videotapes?" Franklin asked.

"The digital files." Andrea eyeballed the camera to her right.

"They're dummies," said the dealer. "All of them, fake."

"What?" Dustin asked. "That can't be true."

"Go see for yourself."

Andrea walked over to the corner and tried to reach a camera, but it was too high. Dustin, however, was able to easily retrieve it. He hitched it from its perch, and they looked at it closely. "Damn," Dustin muttered. "He's telling the truth."

"Decoys." Andrea's shoulders sagged. She'd been fooled. But so, she realized, had Cade. She turned around and looked at Franklin. "How much did you have that diamond ring listed for?"

"Why does that matter?" he asked.

"I want to know if the seller knew how much my coins were worth." Andrea held the double eagle close to her torso.

"He knew something." Franklin locked up the open case. "He thought each one was worth two grand."

"Even this one?" Andrea asked, lifting her fist.

"Even that one," Franklin said with a scoff. "I had the ring tagged at forty-five hundred, and he thought he was getting a deal. Told her they'd get married when they reached Ashland."

"Ashland?" Dustin asked. "What's in Ashland?"

"No idea," said Franklin. "Now if you'll excuse me—"

"Not so fast." Andrea marched across the room. "I'll be contacting every coin shop from here to San Diego in the next few days, alerting them to my stolen collection. Not just the brick-and-mortar stores but the online dealers too. If you want me to keep your name out of this, then I expect you to call me if you hear anything or if the seller comes back." She unzipped her purse and took out her business card. "Understand?" she asked, handing it to him.

"You'll never recover your lost coins," he said, not taking the card. "There are unscrupulous collectors everywhere."

"Takes one to know one, I suppose." Andrea dropped the card on the counter, spun on her heel, and walked out of the shop. Her hand was sweating so much she worried it would harm the coin. But it was in her keeping now. She had it safe. *I did that for you, Dad,* her heart whispered. She'd stood up to a man with a gun and argued her way into getting what she wanted, like a true lawyer's daughter. As soon as she was outside, she slipped it into a fresh plastic flip she kept in her purse.

"So," said Dustin. "That went well."

"Yeah, maybe." She whipped around and faced him. "But you heard what Franklin said; I'll probably never get my collection back."

"You got the most valuable piece, though, right? Who spends thirty thousand dollars for a coin, by the way? That could buy a car. That could buy *two* cars."

"It's none of your business what my dad chose to spend his money on." Andrea crossed her purse over her shoulder and shielded the bag with her arm. It felt safer that way, even though there wasn't anyone nearby to steal it. "I don't judge you for driving an eighty-thousand-dol-lar truck."

"How do you know how much my truck is worth?"

"I did the graphics and brochures for a Ford dealership." Andrea tapped her foot on the ground. "Your truck has all the bells and whis-tles, which is why it's so pretty."

"There you go again, calling my truck *pretty*." Dustin walked away from her, charging straight for the truck. "It's not pretty," he hollered. "It's a work truck."

She hustled to keep up with him. "Then why did you get the upgraded rims?" she asked, knowing right where to poke to hurt him. Dustin's frugality was a point of pride for him.

"They came with the Limited package," he said. "Now are we driving home or what?" He swung open her door.

"Well, we're certainly not going back to the hotel room," she said as she climbed inside.

"Didn't think so." He stomped to his side of the cab and got into the driver's seat, then jammed his finger on the ignition button.

Both of them sat in silence as the engine hummed to life. Andrea hadn't put on her seat belt yet because she was hugging her purse. Dustin stared at the steering wheel, wearing a glum expression. Neither of them spoke for a full two minutes.

"I'm sorry," Andrea said, unable to take the silence any longer. "I don't know what just happened."

"No, I'm sorry." Dustin hung his head. "I shouldn't have said anything about your dad's coin."

"Thirty thousand dollars *is* a lot of money." Andrea loosened her grip on her purse. "But it was my dad's sixtieth birthday present. When my mom turned sixty, she got a diamond tennis necklace, and my dad got this double eagle he always wanted. It was the last one he needed for his collection." She fidgeted with the tassel on her purse. "*Need* being a subjective word."

Dustin took out his phone and tapped on the screen. "We should get on the road. I still want to file a police report here in Port Angeles. I'm looking up the directions now."

"Good idea," said Andrea, feeling zero scruples about betraying the shady coin dealer. Some of her favorite childhood memories were of visiting coin shows with her dad and watching him make the sketchy dealers squirm. He'd use his encyclopedic knowledge of coin value to prove they were overcharging him and then mention being personal friends with the King County prosecuting attorney and the news desk chief of the *Seattle Times*. Name-dropping wasn't something Tom usually did—unless it was in defense of numismatics.

Dustin fastened his seat belt. "If we hurry, we can get back home in time for you to see your dad before he eats dinner."

"So we're giving up, then?" Andrea felt weighed down by defeat.

"I'm not driving to Oregon on a wild-goose chase. I have work deadlines and two nieces to take care of."

"Yeah." Andrea stared at the tips of her shoes. "You're probably right." Dustin really did have those duties waiting for him at home—she knew that, but she also felt the nagging worry that maybe this meant Dustin didn't want to spend time with her anymore. He seemed awfully eager to rush home and send her away on the ferry. Perhaps this was an excuse to stop seeing her. "I just hate the thought of giving up." She smoothed the hem of her sweatshirt.

"It doesn't mean we're giving up." Dustin stared through the windshield. "I'll hire a private investigator if I have to."

Andrea put her purse by her feet and reached for her seat belt. "And I'll call every coin shop I can find."

"You can start contacting them right now if your phone will pick up a signal," he said, not looking at her. Dustin was all business now, and his severity stung.

"Okay." The tension between them hung like a dark cloud. "I love your truck," she said, trying to soften the mood. "Almost as much as I loved the Yo-Mobile."

He grinned for half a second before his sober expression returned. "Thanks." He put the truck into gear and drove away from the curb.

Andrea swallowed and dug her phone out of her purse. Dustin's cool demeanor was too much to process right now, but at least she could still pursue the coins. She looked up the number for the shop in Green Lake and called them first. The shopkeeper was horrified when she explained what had happened. He promised to keep his ears open if he heard anything about a double eagles collection for sale. Andrea hung up the call, eager to rehash it with Dustin, but he didn't say one word to her. By then they had reached the police department. Dustin parked, and they went inside. The officer at the front desk took their statement and had them fill out forms explaining what had happened. They got back on the road thirty minutes later, and Andrea began calling coin shops again.

She dialed number after number, working through the list she had found on the internet. Most of the time she reached voice mails and left messages, but occasionally she spoke to a coin dealer on the other end. It was nice when a human picked up because it made her feel less lonely. Dustin had become horrible company. He wore his silence like a shield.

"I'll call you if I hear anything," Andrea said when he parked in front of her blue house at twilight. Part of her hoped that he'd walk her to the front door.

"Same," he said, not bothering to turn off the truck. "I can drop you off at the ferry if you'd rather."

"No thanks." She undid her seat belt. "I'll grab a sandwich before I go see my dad."

"Smart." Dustin nodded.

"Okay then. Bye." Andrea climbed down from the truck and paused when her feet hit the gravel, waiting for Dustin to at least say goodbye. When he didn't, she hurried to her door. She felt the truck's presence as she unlocked the handle. Dustin drove away the moment she crossed the threshold.

"What the hell just happened?" she asked her dark house. "For a minute I thought we had something." She kicked off her shoes and sank onto the floor. "Never mind," she said, leaning against the stairs. "There's no *we* anymore. He's nothing to me, and I had no expectations." But the sound of her voice echoing in the empty foyer made her feel more alone than ever.

CHAPTER TWELVE

Sometimes Dustin wondered which was harder—his hard hat or his head. Ever since driving away from Andrea's house last night, he'd felt like a damn fool. Why had he ruined things? Those kisses back at the Quinault Resort had been spectacular. But everything had unraveled from there, and Dustin blamed himself. The threat of losing people was always on his mind, churning his emotions like dark waters. It was easier to say nothing at all than to speak from the heart.

Now it was Sunday morning, and he was at the jobsite, playing catch-up for missed work yesterday. Karlsson Construction was on a tight deadline, with the goal of listing the house as soon as Kitsap County could pass inspection on the electrical work. Heidi was upstairs painting the master bedroom, and workers were out front replacing the roof on the porch. Kendal and Jane were there in the kitchen, wearing bright-pink hard hats with their names written on them in purple script. It wasn't really a hard hat zone, but the girls loved to dress the part. Leanne had picked up an extra shift deep cleaning the pizza parlor that morning, and Dustin was on day care duty.

He still hadn't told Leanne about Cade cheating on her with Lisa, the redheaded cocktail waitress, and wasn't sure how to bring it up without her completely shutting down. Hopefully Heidi would handle it, because Dustin hated uncomfortable conversations. Plus, his track record of explaining difficult things to Leanne was poor. When she turned sixteen and wanted to get her driver's license, he'd told her, "You're not ready. You might kill someone on the freeway if you don't practice more." She'd scheduled her test anyway and failed it. When she had first started dating Cade, he'd tried to warn her about him, saying, "Cade only dates women who are desperate. You're better than that." Leanne had dated Cade anyway, trying to prove him wrong.

"That's not how you ungroup," Kendal told Dustin from her perch at the kitchen island. "Ms. Nguyen says to ungroup." Her math homework lay in front of her, next to Jane's crayons. The girls sat on a makeshift bench constructed from a plank of wood and two stepladders.

"I don't know what ungrouping is," said Dustin, "but you can't take nine away from seven, so you have to borrow from the six next door."

"That's not a six." Kendal tapped the paper with her pencil. "That's a sixty. It's in the tens place."

"Okay, but you still need to cross it out and give ten to seven." Dustin frowned. When had first-grade math become so confusing? Supervising Kendal's math homework while he tried to paint the mudroom was proving complicated.

"I need help with my homework too," said Jane. She was drawing either a dog or a horse; Dustin couldn't tell.

"You don't have homework," Kendal said in a superior tone. "You're just in kindergarten."

"I do *too* have homework." Jane jutted out her bottom lip. "I'm supposed to bring three different apples to school tomorrow."

"Three different apples?" Dustin raised his eyebrows. "Does your mom know?"

Jane tore the wrapper off the worn-down point of her brown crayon. "She went to the store to get them, but her card wouldn't work."

"Oh," said Dustin. "Well, don't worry. I'll get your apples. Why do you need three types?"

"For science." Jane crumpled up her drawing and threw it on the ground.

"What did you do that for?" Dustin reached down and picked it up. "That was a great . . . er, um . . . animal."

"It was a robot!" Jane went boneless and collapsed on the counter, burying her face in her arms.

"What do I do after I give the ten to the seven?" Kendal asked.

"You add them," said Dustin. He patted Jane's back with one hand and pointed at the subtraction equation on Kendal's homework with the other. "Ten and seven become seventeen, and then you subtract nine from seventeen. Shh, Jane. It'll be okay. You can draw another robot."

"I don't want to draw a robot. I want to buy apples!" she wailed. "If I show up at school without apples, I won't be part of the graph."

"The graph?" Dustin asked.

"Yeah." Jane lifted her head. "We're gonna graph all the apples that people bring to see which one is most popular."

"I can see why you'd want to be part of that." Dustin rested his elbow on the counter and stooped so he'd be at eye level with her. "What color apples do you want to get?"

"Red, pink, and green." Jane sniffed and wiped her nose on her sleeve.

"Let me get you a tissue, and then we'll order those apples on my phone." Dustin stepped over to the powder room and brought back some toilet paper.

"On your phone?" Jane asked.

"How do you do that?" Kendal had a note of skepticism in her voice.

"I use my grocery-delivery app." Dustin swiped his phone to life. "Normally I wouldn't do that for such a small order, but this is a homework emergency." He showed the girls how he could click on the pictures and add things to his cart. "There," he said. "Three different varieties of apples. Should we get anything else while we're at it?"

"Get some Paul Mitchell shampoo and conditioner for Mom," said Kendal. "That'll make her happy."

"She loves that stuff, but Dad says it's too expensive," added Jane.

"Dropping it into my cart." Dustin forced a small smile. Why was Cade chiding Leanne on how much she spent at the grocery store when her settlement allowance had paid out more than enough for them to live on for years? Irritation made him add a pack of Red Vines to the cart. Make that two packs. Stress was getting to him. "There," he said after he had submitted the order. "The apples will be here in an hour. Now you don't have to worry about showing up to school empty handed."

Jane clasped her arms around his neck. "Thank you, Uncle Dusty!"

"Let's get back to *my* homework." Kendal chewed on her eraser. "Ms. Nguyen said to use the box method on the next problem."

"The what?"

"The box method." Kendal rolled her eyes. "Didn't you go to college?"

"I did, but . . . Heidi?" Dustin called in a loud voice so his sister would hear him from upstairs. "Some assistance, please." He turned back to the girls. "I'll let your aunt Heidi help you on this one. I need to finish painting the shoe cabinet."

Heidi trotted down the stairs wearing jeans and a long-sleeved T-shirt. "You bellowed?"

"Uncle Dusty keeps messing up my math homework," said Kendal.

"Tag." Dustin grabbed his paintbrush and shot Heidi a look. "You're it."

"Fine with me." Heidi picked dried paint off her shirt. "I always was better than you at math anyway."

"And you're so humble about it too," he muttered.

"It's not your fault you didn't learn how to do math," said Kendal. "Mom said that college doesn't make people smart."

Dustin winced. "I do *too* know how to do math," he said, unsure of why he felt the need to defend himself to a six-year-old. "And your mom's right that a college degree won't necessarily prevent you from making dumb decisions." He and Heidi exchanged a glance, and Dustin knew she was thinking of Cade as well.

"Have you heard from Andrea?" Heidi asked in a gentle voice.

"No." Dustin shook his head. "Why would I?"

"I don't know," said Heidi. "I just thought—"

"Well, you thought wrong," said Dustin, more sharply than he had intended. He gripped the paint can and walked away to the mudroom.

Dustin got to work painting the cabinets with expert precision. It was meditative, how the brush went back and forth in even strokes. He didn't need to think about anything but the task at hand. At least that was what he told himself. Focus on the now. This moment was what mattered: finishing the house, selling it quickly, buying the next property. Dustin already had his eye on a dilapidated rambler half a mile from the dock. Heidi thought it had potential, too, since it was within walking distance of the fast foot ferry to Seattle.

But even though he tried to settle his mind, dark thoughts kept coming. What did selling this house mean, anyway? *More money.* Did he need more money? *No, not really.* What did he need? Dustin wasn't sure, but he knew that whatever it was would be centered on his family being safe. *Secure. Protected.* That meant getting Leanne and the girls out of a bad situation and bringing Cade to justice so he couldn't hurt them again. As for himself, if he could get eight solid hours of sleep without waking up to a nightmare, that would be enough. The nightmares had started after his parents' accident and came and went in cycles, triggered by stress.

Last night's terror had been the worst. Dustin had dreamed that he and Andrea had been driving in the old Yo-Mobile, and a big-leaf maple had crashed down on them and split the cab in two. Dustin had woken up beating at his pillow, trying to pull Andrea from the wreckage. He shuddered thinking of it now, the images still fresh and raw.

His phone vibrated, and Dustin set down his paintbrush, hoping it was one of the private investigators he had contacted that morning via their websites. Instead, he saw a text from Leanne.

I'll pick the girls up at 12:30. Nathan's sending me home with a pizza so don't feed them lunch.

Okay, Dustin replied. At least she was communicating with him—barely. Have you heard from your in-laws? he asked. That was one of the things that had occurred to him at four o'clock this morning, when he hadn't been able to fall back asleep. Mr. and Mrs. Tolbert might know of Cade's whereabouts.

They haven't seen him either. Not that it's any of your business.

Dustin felt his blood pressure bump. None of his business? Of course it was. But he didn't have the words to defend himself. I love you, he typed instead, trying hard not to screw up. He stared at the screen, anxious for her reply, waiting for his little sister to say that she loved him too.

You don't know what it means to love, she texted instead.

Dustin struggled to connect his thumbs with the proper keys in his haste to type. I know that loving people doesn't mean stealing from them.

Cade didn't steal from me. What's mine is his.

This was a horrible conversation to have over text, but Dustin didn't want to have it over the phone either—or in person, for that matter. Cade's cheating on you, he wrote. He has a girlfriend from Port Angeles named Lisa.

You're lying!

I'm not.

You'll say anything to make me hate Cade.

Dustin swallowed, not wanting to tell Leanne the rest of it, knowing how much it would hurt her. He bought Lisa a diamond ring.

Leanne didn't respond. Dustin stared at the screen, waiting for her to answer, but all he saw was his last text. *Damn.* He'd blown that big time. There must have been a better way to deliver that bad news, but if there was, Dustin didn't know how. His relationship with his baby sister was ripping apart at the seams.

Scowling, Dustin closed out of his messages and opened up his browser, quickly finding the list of private investigators he was considering hiring to find Cade. He'd already submitted two contact forms that morning before the girls had arrived. Sitting on the mudroom floor, he filled out a third form on the spot. Hopefully one of them called him back later today. They needed a professional's help.

After he finished that task, he went back to painting cabinets. Dustin was halfway done when he ran out of paint. That was odd. "Hey, Heidi," he asked, walking into the kitchen. "Where's the second can of paint for the mudroom?"

Heidi stood behind Kendal and Jane at the island. "What do you mean, second can of paint?" she asked. "I only bought one, and it's sitting over there next to the sink."

As soon as he saw the other paint can, Dustin knew he had made a mistake. "Uh-oh. Then what did I just paint half of the mudroom with?"

"I don't know." Heidi raced out of the room. "Matte finish?" she hollered. "That was for the laundry room!"

"Somebody's in trouble." Kendal tapped her pencil on the counter and wiggled.

Jane jumped down from the makeshift bench and hugged him. "It's okay, Uncle Dusty. I still love you."

"Thanks," said Dustin. "I love you too. And everyone makes mistakes."

Jane looked at him. "Even Daddy?"

Dustin nodded. "Everyone. But I believe it's important to fix my mistakes. That's what grown-ups do." He gently disentangled himself from her arms and picked up the correct paint can. "See you guys in a bit." Dustin went back to the laundry room, ready to deliver his mea culpa to Heidi.

"Did you or did you not study my vision board?" she asked.

"I looked at it."

Heidi shook her head. "Not carefully enough, it would appear. The mudroom needs semigloss so it's easier to clean if it gets dirty."

"Okay, okay. Sorry I didn't check with you first." Dustin set down the can of paint.

"I bet this is because you have too much on your mind."

"I'm fine." He picked up a screwdriver to pry off the lid.

"You're not fine; you have multiple stressors hitting you at once."

"So does everyone. There's this house to finish and Cade being a total jackass."

"And all of your unresolved tension with Andrea," Heidi added.

"Don't be ridiculous."

"Maybe you should call her."

"No way."

"Why not?"

Dustin flipped on the fan in the mudroom. "Because I haven't called her in eighteen years."

"What about going over there and talking to her in person?"

"I'm not going to do that either."

"Didn't you promise to replace the locks on her front door?" Heidi put her hand on her hip.

"I did," he admitted.

"Right now her house isn't safe because Cade might have made himself a spare key."

Dustin's stomach clenched. "That's true."

"You should go over there today and replace those locks."

"I'm not sure I'm the right—"

"*I'm* sure." Heidi pointed at him. "And you promised. Why are you so afraid to talk to Andrea?"

"I am not." Dustin began prying open the pan.

"It sure seems like you are. What happened between the two of you on your trip?"

"Nothing happened."

"Nothing happened?"

"Nothing." Dustin opened the lid to the can more forcefully than he meant to, and it almost spilled.

"Maybe that's why you're so annoyed." Heidi tilted her head. "Nothing happened."

"Don't be ridiculous."

"Why didn't you tell me you broke up with Andrea in high school because you thought she liked another guy?"

"How'd you know about that?" Dustin stuck a stick into the mixture and stirred it up. "Andrea told you, didn't she?"

"Yes." Heidi nodded. "And I can't believe I had to wait eighteen years to find out."

"Well, you weren't the one dating her." Dustin dipped his paintbrush into the goop and carefully painted the first stretch of baseboard. He held his hand steady, refusing to let Heidi rattle him.

"Why do you bottle everything up?" Heidi crouched down and sat next to him on the floor. "I could have helped if you had confided in me."

"Yeah, well, it's too late to do anything about it now."

"It's too late for the past eighteen years, but it's not too late for now." Heidi folded her hands on her knees. "I know you still love her."

"What?" He scrunched up his face like the paint fumes bothered him. "I do not."

"You never stopped loving her."

"Do we have to talk about this?" Dustin focused his gaze on the baseboard.

"Yes." Heidi nodded. "We do. After you broke up, you barely said a word to anyone for months."

"I don't remember that."

"It's true. It wasn't until you drove off to college that I finally saw you smile again."

"Yeah, well, that's in the past."

"And this is the present." Heidi touched the sleeve of his flannel shirt. "All you have to do is go over there and knock on her door."

"I wouldn't know what to say."

"Maybe you wouldn't need to say anything," said Heidi. "Maybe you just need to show up."

"You don't understand how badly I screwed up yesterday." Dustin cringed when he remembered how his low mood had ruined the drive.

"You screw up all the time, but I still love you." Heidi pinched his cheek.

"Ouch!"

"I think that—"

Crash! Their conversation was interrupted by a clattering noise from the kitchen. Dustin dropped his paintbrush on the lid and leaped to his feet, following Heidi as they raced to the kitchen. Dustin's heart rate sped out of control. As soon as he saw Kendal and Jane, both still wearing their pink hard hats, safe at the island, he felt better. He embraced them in a hug while he tried to figure out where the noise had come from.

"What happened?" Heidi asked.

"You mean the noise?" Kendal shrugged. "I'm not sure, but one of the roofers said some bad words."

Jane tried to explain further. "He said—"

"No you don't." Kendal covered Jane's mouth with her palm.

"Why can't I say them?" Jane asked despite being muffled. She pulled down Kendal's hand. "Dad says them all the time."

"Well, I'm sorry you had to hear those words here," said Dustin. "I'll go remind the roofers that there are little girls present."

"I'm not little," Jane pouted. "I'm in kindergarten."

"That's practically a baby," said Kendal.

Jane scrunched up her face. "Is not."

"Is too." Kendal glared back at her.

"Okay, you two," said Dustin. "Girls who fight don't get to write secret messages on the walls of the upstairs bathroom before we cover them with fresh wallpaper."

Bam! Another large noise made them all jump and was instantly followed by a string of curse words that could rip bark off of cedar.

"Girls," said Dustin in a quiet voice. "Why don't you go upstairs and help Aunt Heidi with the walls? Bring the crayons with you." Dustin pushed up his sleeves, ready to let the roofers have it. Checking that his hard hat was in place, he eased open the sliding door, stepped out onto the unstained deck, and closed the door behind him. The roofing foreman was unloading a pallet of composite shingles, and two guys were on the old porch roof ripping off shake shingles.

"Jim," Dustin said, his voice growling. "I'm paying you double to work on the weekend because we're on a tight deadline, but I'll fire you today if my nieces hear one more F-bomb."

"Sorry, boss." Jim stood. "We found two rats' nests up there, and one of my guys wigs out around rodents."

"Roof rats?" Dustin asked.

"Damn straight." Jim reddened. "I mean darn straight."

"I'll let the exterminator know."

"Sorry about the language," said Jim. "It won't happen again."

Dustin nodded. "I appreciate that."

"But I don't think kids should be on a construction site, period," said Jim. "It's not safe."

Dustin bristled. "The inside of the house is finished," he said. "And my nieces are wearing hard hats."

"Still." Jim raised his eyebrows. "My boys are that age, and I would never bring them to work with me because it's too dangerous. My wife would have my hide if I suggested it."

"Well, Kendal and Jane's mom is at work," Dustin said. "And their father is missing. Not that it's any of your business."

"You mean Cade Tolbert?" Jim scratched the back of his neck. "I heard he was murdered."

"What? Who told you that?"

"Eileen."

"Who's Eileen?"

Jim rubbed his forehead like Dustin was the one being exasperating. "My wife. She heard it from her sister, whose coworker at the salon is dating Mack."

Mack was dating someone? Oh crap. Did Heidi know? That probably explained why she'd been extra edgy. "Mack shouldn't have blabbed about a case he won't even help figure out," said Dustin. "Cade's not murdered; he stole my money and ran off with it."

"You don't say." Jim opened his eyes wide.

"What's more, I have reason to believe he stole valuable antiques from a friend of mine."

Jim grinned. "Wait until I tell Eileen. I never find things out before her. What sort of antiques?"

"Coins," said Dustin. "Gold coins. He broke into a house and stole them. Now if you'll excuse me, I've got a mudroom to finish." Dustin turned to go back inside but stopped when he saw the grocery-delivery van drive up. Dustin walked down the path so that the carrier wouldn't step on a nail in the middle of the roofing mess. When he saw who was holding his groceries, he froze. It was Kendal's first-grade teacher, whom Dustin had met at the winter carnival a couple of months ago. Donna Nguyen was in her early thirties and single, as Kendal constantly reminded him.

"Ms. Nguyen?" Dustin asked. "What are you doing here?"

Donna's cheeks turned pink. "Kendal's uncle," she sputtered.

"The name's Dustin Karlsson." He held out his hand to shake, but she handed him the bag instead.

"I thought the name on the receipt looked familiar." Donna yanked her hand back. "This is my side job."

"Aren't you still teaching?" Dustin didn't know how much teachers made at Port Inez Elementary School, but he was shocked that Ms. Nguyen needed a part-time job.

"I am." Donna pulled an electronic device out of her vest pocket and typed on the screen. "But my rent has gone up twice since the fast foot ferry to Seattle started running." She put the controller back into her pocket. "I'm trying to save money for a down payment, but I can't keep up with the market."

"It's a hot one," said Dustin, feeling guilty. Seattleites buying property in Port Inez were part of the reason Karlsson Construction made so much money. They couldn't flip houses fast enough to keep up with demand.

"Hot is right." Donna swallowed. "Um . . . Kendal told me that you like to eat."

"Yeah, as much as the next person, I suppose."

166

Donna covered her face with her hand. "I meant eat dinner. Kendal said you like to eat dinner."

"Yep. As well as breakfast and lunch." Dustin didn't understand where this was going. Was Kendal telling people he had a big appetite? Sure, he had a sweet tooth for Girl Scout cookies, but that wasn't something to brag about.

"What I'm trying to say is, would you like to go out to dinner with me?" Donna asked. Only she said it so fast that it came out in a jumble, and Dustin wasn't sure he had heard her right.

"Are you asking me out?" he exclaimed, suddenly noticing Donna's pretty brown eyes and formfitting leggings.

"I am," she said, before holding her breath.

Caught off guard, Dustin didn't know what to say. He had never taken his niece's matchmaking seriously. But now a perfectly lovely, apparently eligible woman stood before him asking him out, and Dustin was speechless. The only thing he was certain of was that the woman he *did* want to take out to dinner lived in a blue house on the bay.

"I would love to say yes," said Dustin. "But I'm involved with someone at the moment." He figured that was partially true.

"Oh." Donna took a step back.

"I'm seeing her later tonight, in fact," Dustin added. He *had* promised to replace Andrea's locks, after all. "Thank you for asking me, though. Kendal thinks the world of you."

"Sure. Yeah. Thanks. She's a great kid too." Donna stuffed her hands into her vest pockets and raced back to the van. "Gotta go. More orders to fulfill."

Dustin waved as she drove off. Then he looked up at the house and saw Heidi, Kendal, and Jane watching from the second-story window. He wondered how much of that conversation they had heard.

All of it, as it turned out. As soon as he entered the house, the girls barreled down the stairs and bombarded him with questions.

"Why'd you say no?" Kendal asked. "Ms. Nguyen is amazing."

"Don't you like dinner, Uncle Dusty?" Jane asked.

Heidi folded her arms across her chest and studied him. "So you're involved with someone, are you? Does this mean you'll see Andrea tonight?"

"I said I'd fix her locks, didn't I?" He dropped the bag of groceries on the kitchen counter, took out a box of Red Vines, and ripped open the package.

Kendal pouted. "I can't believe you told Ms. Nguyen no."

"She plays the ukulele," said Jane. "And you don't."

"Are those Red Vines to share?" Kendal asked.

"Sure." Dustin selected a handful for himself and then gave Kendal the box.

"Not so fast." Heidi not only took the box away from Kendal, but she yanked three pieces of licorice out of Dustin's hands. "We haven't had lunch yet." She gave each girl a vine and kept one for herself. "Your mom will be here any minute with pizza." Heidi glanced sideways at Dustin. "Apparently Uncle Dustin had an interesting conversation with your mom that he didn't tell me about."

A crick in the back of Dustin's neck tightened, and he rubbed away the pain. "Yeah. Sorry about that."

"Are you?" Heidi whipped his shoulder with a Red Vine. "Because it seems to me that you don't like to tell me anything."

"Mom says you shouldn't play with your food," said Jane.

Kendal stuffed the candy in her mouth. "Uncle Dusty," she said, with her mouth full of red goo. "If you date Ms. Nguyen, she could be my aunt."

"You could date my teacher," said Jane. "But Mrs. Jackson is old."

"She's not *that* old," said Heidi. "Ayumi went to high school with Uncle Nathan."

"That's old," Jane said with a shrug.

At this rate, Dustin was never going to finish the mudroom. The paint can was still open and ripe for disaster if someone bumped into it.

"I need to finish painting the cabinets," he said. He looked down at the papers next to the grocery bag. "And Kendal has three more subtraction problems to solve." He slapped Heidi on the back. "Aunt Heidi can help you with the—what is it called? The box method?"

"The box what?" Heidi twisted licorice around her finger.

Dustin shrugged. "Beats me." He slipped away before anyone could stop him.

CHAPTER THIRTEEN

The trick to meal prep was to include the big three: protein, veggies, and carbs. Of course, carbs like potatoes and squash were also vegetables, and that was where it became confusing. Andrea debated that logic with herself as she stood at her kitchen counter with glass containers lined up in a row. It was easier to query the nature of vegetables as carbohydrates than it was to address her wounded pride. Every time she thought of Dustin driving away last night, without so much as a goodbye, her pain deepened. No, it was much better to channel her frustration into a cooking rampage. The rotisserie chicken she was deboning was juicy and would go great with the petite potatoes and onions she had just finished roasting in the oven.

Her phone rang, and she glanced at the screen to see who was calling. When she saw that it was Lydia, she thought about ignoring it, but she knew her mom would fret until she called her back. Andrea hadn't contacted Lydia since her last text the day before. After quickly washing her hands with soap and water, Andrea accepted the call right before it went to voice mail.

"Oh," said Lydia. "You're home. I was just about to leave a message."

"This is a cell phone, Mom. I might be home; I might not be."

"Are you out? I don't want to bother you if you're out on a date."

Andrea frowned. She didn't appreciate her mother's passive-aggressive way of investigating her love life. "No. I'm home and cooking dinner." She grabbed the smoked paprika out of the cabinet and showered it over the potatoes until they turned orangey red.

"Cooking dinner for yourself or someone special?"

"What do you want?" Andrea's question came out rudely, but she was eager for Lydia to get to the point. "Sorry. It's just that I'm right in the middle of something."

"The two-bedroom apartment in Roger's building has already sold."

"I thought you said it was being staged next week."

"That's what the owners told me. But they received an off-market offer and took it. 'Less stress that way,' they said."

"Good for them."

"If we had acted sooner, maybe—"

"Mom, I was never going to buy the apartment."

"But—"

"I'm in the middle of a massive cooking project."

"Okay, I won't keep you. But I did want to know if you had found the coins. Roger said that if you don't recover them within forty-eight hours, they would probably be missing forever."

Andrea grimaced, not wanting to acknowledge that Roger was likely right. "He's a podiatrist. When did he become a stolen-goods expert?"

"Don't you remember me telling you he was robbed when he lived on a houseboat after his divorce?"

Andrea put the paprika away and found the salt. "Vaguely."

"You made that crack about pirates."

"Did I?"

"You said he should have named the boat the *Jolly Roger* so they would have left him alone."

"Oh yeah." Andrea chuckled. "I did say that."

"This isn't a laughing matter. The thieves took everything that wasn't bolted down, including the barbecue."

Andrea bristled. "Are you comparing Dad's coins to a barbecue?"

"Of course not, but that's not the point. Roger could have been killed!"

"Was he onboard at the time?"

"No. He was at a bunion conference."

"That was lucky," Andrea said, grateful her mother couldn't see her smirk.

"It *was* lucky. Roger is an absolute sweetheart who didn't deserve to be robbed, especially after his ex-wife took him to the cleaners."

"About Dad's coins . . . ," Andrea said, hoping to change the subject.

"Have you made any progress?"

"I spent most of today calling coin shops up and down the West Coast, contacting dealers. I also logged on to coin forums and posted about the missing collection."

"What about your homeowner's insurance?"

Andrea looked out the kitchen window at the glowing sunset. "I called them too." When she had left a message with their twenty-four-hour answering service, it had felt like defeat. Sure, the rider on her policy would recover her losses, but in this case, money couldn't replace money. Tom's coins had a sentimental value that was priceless.

"Can't the police help?" Lydia asked.

"You would think." Andrea leaned against the counter. "But the local sheriff won't do anything. I called him today too. He said most property crimes go unsolved unless the goods are located."

"That's what you get with a rinky-dink sheriff's department." Lydia clicked her tongue in disapproval. "I thought you said Heidi's brother-in-law probably did it?"

"Yes, we think so. But the sheriff said that it's not a crime to be a missing person, and until there's proof that it was Cade, then there's nothing he can do to help."

"What a mess." Lydia sighed. "I suppose it's just as well that your father is too out of it to know what happened."

"Yes," Andrea said, irked that her mother was right. "And I have the 1907. I showed it to him this evening."

"Did he recognize it?"

"Of course," Andrea said, even though that was only partially true. When she had visited Tom a couple of hours ago, he had been pleased to examine the double eagle, but she wasn't positive that he could distinguish it from the other dates in the collection.

"Tomorrow morning you should rent a safe-deposit box at the bank, like I've been telling you to do all year."

"Yes, Mom. I'll do that."

"Has Dustin called?"

"No," said Andrea. "Why would he do that?"

"I don't know. I thought maybe he'd have information on the guy who stole them."

"I'm sure he would let me know if he heard anything."

"Or maybe Dustin might want to see you? Is he single?"

"Mom, I've got to go."

"I don't like to say bad things about your father, but—"

"Then don't." Andrea's patience had run out. "The turnips are almost done."

"Okay, well, would you like to come over to the penthouse next weekend for dinner? You never did try that halibut that Roger caught in Alaska. There's one filet left in the freezer."

"Sure. Fine. Sounds great," Andrea said, mainly to get her mother off the phone. "Text me the details."

"Love you," said Lydia.

"Love you too." Andrea hung up the phone, the conversation needling her. As much as the robbery stung, her mother's probing questions about her love life hurt even worse, especially when she had asked about Dustin.

Andrea absolutely, positively, did not want to think about Dustin or the way he had kissed her at the Quinault Resort. She had been actively *not* thinking about it all day. So what if he hadn't called her? She wasn't expecting him to. Her phone's ringtone was set to high in case the Owl's Nest called, not Dustin. What had happened at the hotel was an accident. It obviously didn't mean anything to Dustin, so she wouldn't let it mean anything to her either. In fact, it meant so little to her that she'd filled her day with a bunch of important activities. Not only had she contacted coin forums and visited her father, but she'd also organized her linen cabinet, despammed her email, and wiped down all the hard surfaces in the house, including the baseboards. Now she was finishing off her cooking rampage.

Andrea picked up tongs and pinched them like an angry crab. She filled each glass container one-third full of chicken and then added the potatoes and carrots. A timer buzzed. She put on her hedgehog gloves and pulled a second baking sheet out of the oven. Pale-white turnips and golden rutabagas sizzled in olive oil. After sprinkling them with salt and pepper, she turned the root vegetables over and popped them back into the oven to roast for twenty-five minutes. Andrea stared at the glowing oven light for longer than was necessary as dark thoughts caught up with her. *How stupid could I be?*

For a few hours yesterday, she had thought that Dustin actually still cared for her. Her mind had raced from kissing in the hotel room, to picking out wedding invitations, to painting a nursery in the blink of an eye. Sure, she had a history of rushing into doomed relationships, but yesterday had been different. Andrea hadn't just rushed; she had crashed. Reality had shattered her. Dustin didn't want her, and she was an idiot for thinking otherwise.

Except she wasn't an idiot. Standing upright, Andrea walked back to the counter and chopped fresh herbs. Cooking dinner was her routine every Sunday night. Her life had become procedural. She filled her days with work, walks with Heidi, and her late-afternoon visits to her father. Busyness was a gauze she wrapped around her broken heart to keep it from crumbling further. You couldn't be lonely if you were busy. You might turn into a woman who collected hedgehog décor, but was that really so awful? No, what was awful was knowing that she had been so close to the fantasy—so close to *believing* the fantasy.

Andrea drizzled homemade aioli sauce across the onions and added a dash of garlic salt. "My name is Andrea Wint," she said out loud. The best way to banish a nightmare was to stick to a script. "I am an accomplished, successful, thoughtful person who is worthy of love." Tears splashed against her cheeks, and she wiped them away with her sleeve. Instead of making her feel confident, her affirmation made her feel worse. That was wrong, because there was no shame in being single. No, the shame came from being tricked. She needed to stop being so gullible.

Andrea ran the garbage disposal, and when it stopped, clogged with potato peels, the doorbell buzzed insistently, like this wasn't the first time it had been rung. "Now what?" Andrea asked herself, wondering who could be at the front door. Heidi always called before she came over, and there was nobody else in Port Inez who visited her on a regular basis. Maybe there was a package she needed to sign for?

Wiping her hands on a towel, Andrea briefly thought about removing her hedgehog apron but decided to leave it on. If the visitor was a solicitor, her apron could be part of her "Can't talk now—I'm cooking dinner" story to get rid of them.

"Coming," she called as she walked through the hallway to the front door. As soon as she looked through the peephole, she wished she had ditched her dorky apron, but it was too late. Dustin stood on her porch wearing a down jacket over his flannel shirt.

This was the moment to put her resolve into action. She wasn't going to fall for it if he feigned interest in her again. Andrea squared her shoulders and opened the door, wearing a blank expression. "Hi, Dustin," she said. "I'm surprised to see you here."

"I would have used the hedgehog knocker," he said in his deep voice that even now turned her knees into butter, "but I wasn't sure if it was decorative or not."

She narrowed her eyes. "It knocks fine, thank you. Is there something you needed? I'm in the middle of cooking dinner." Cooking ten dinners, actually, but Andrea didn't brag.

His eyes twitched, and he took a sharp breath. Andrea felt good knowing her boundaries were making an impact. Dustin held up a plastic bag from the hardware store. "I'm here to replace your locks and to add this to your sliding glass door." Dustin showed her a broom.

"I don't understand. Why would my slider need to be swept?"

"I'll cut the bristles off and use the handle as a physical barrier to keep the door from sliding open." Dustin reached into the bag and pulled out hardware. "Then these are for the windows—to lock them manually."

"You've thought of everything," said Andrea. "Now, after it's too late," she added, hoping the barb cut. She watched his eyes fill with a hurt that reflected her own. But instead of feeling like victory, it bruised her further. "Well," she said, holding the door open wider. "You better come in." She tried to ignore the jolt of electricity that flickered inside her when he walked past. There was that old zing of attraction again, unbidden and begging for attention. Andrea refused to fall into its trap.

"I'll get right to work." He set down the bag and his toolbox. "Wow, something smells good. I'm sorry to interrupt your dinner."

"You didn't." Andrea tightened her ponytail. "I hadn't started eating yet." She spun on the toe of her wool sock. "Call me if you need anything."

Her heart didn't stop pounding double time until she reached the privacy of the powder room and shut the door behind her. She turned on the faucet and slowly washed her hands with foaming soap, concentrating on the lather, refusing to acknowledge what had just happened. *Dustin was in her house. He'd come to make good on a promise.* But the truth was, it was too little, too late. Andrea turned off the faucet and dried her hands. The root vegetables still had another twenty minutes to go in the oven, so she used this as an opportunity to load the dishwasher and clean up her mess. Then, as an afterthought, she slid two containers of chicken and potatoes onto the bottom rack of the oven to warm. Dustin was here at dinnertime, after all, and it would be impolite to not offer him food.

Over in the entryway, Dustin was making a racket. Andrea heard what sounded like a drill or perhaps an electric screwdriver. She didn't stop to investigate, but she did set the dining room table with two places and poured two glasses of water. She adjusted the blinds so she could see out across the bay. The sun had already set, but twilight lingered. The Harper Landing–Port Inez ferry sailed off into the horizon, its lights glittering across the water. Andrea took off her apron and sat on the window seat.

"Okay then." Dustin cleared his throat, and Andrea turned around. He stood in the hallway between the kitchen and dining room, his expression unreadable. "The front door's fixed," he said, "and I added a chain lock as well. Now I'll go work on the side door to the garage."

"Thanks." Andrea nodded. She thought about inviting him to stay for dinner but lost her nerve. Just because there were two plates didn't mean that one of them was for him. When he turned away, she thought she recognized something in his green eyes that she felt herself: disappointment. Andrea waited until she heard the front door close and then looked back at the view. She thought about her options. Could she invite him for dinner without making a fool of herself? Perhaps. Or maybe she'd turn into a quivering bowl of Jell-O if he gave her one granule of hope.

Andrea didn't want to be Jell-O. She knew she was stronger than that. She'd built up a successful business on her own, hadn't she? Maybe that was the way to deal with Dustin—as a business associate. She still needed to find out if he'd discovered more information about Cade.

The timer buzzed, and Andrea made her decision. By the time Dustin returned to the house from rekeying the door to the detached garage, she had two plates of food on the dining room table.

"This is for the slider," said Dustin, holding a sawed-off broom handle.

"Thanks."

He walked across the room and dropped it into the slot by the sliding glass door. "Now you have a manual barrier to prevent entry."

"Great." She pointed to the table. "Have you eaten? I have extra."

His eyes met hers. "Really?" he asked, with a hopeful tone that caught her off guard.

She shrugged and sat down. "Like I said, I have plenty, and I want to hear if you've found out more information about Cade."

"Of course." Dustin frowned and turned away. "I'll wash my hands and join you."

A few minutes later they both sat at the table with their reflections staring back at them from the windows. The inky-black sky had become a mirror. "This smells delicious," Dustin said as he sliced into a potato, preparing to take a bite. "Roasted potatoes are my favorite."

"Glad you like them." Andrea allowed herself a small bit of pride and then pushed the feeling away and focused on business. "I've called every coin shop or online dealership I can think of as well as my home-owner's insurance."

"That's good. Leanne still refuses to believe that Cade is in the wrong about anything. But I've contacted several private investigators. One sounded like a scam artist, one wasn't taking new clients, and the third hasn't called me back yet. Based on my research I like the third agency best because they operate out of an RV, so they can hit the trail at a moment's notice. Hopefully that one will work out."

"Luck seems to be in short supply around here. At least I got the 1907 back."

Dustin finished chewing his bite of potato. "Yeah, and . . ." He took a deep breath, and then another. Dustin blinked quickly, his eyes watering. "Did you put chili powder on these potatoes?" He picked up his glass of water and pounded it down. Then he drank hers as well, without asking.

"It's paprika," said Andrea. "Smoked paprika."

"It's definitely not paprika." Dustin—panting—jumped from his seat and ran to the kitchen to refill his water glass.

"Paprika," Andrea said again, suddenly unsure. She nibbled a tiny bite of the crimson-colored potatoes and immediately spit it out. "Bleh!" She reached for her water glass, but it was empty. "I'm so sorry," she shrieked, hurrying into the kitchen. "I don't know what happened."

Dustin flung open the refrigerator and grabbed the milk. "My eyes won't stop watering," he said, drinking straight from the carton. "I look like I'm crying." He wiped his face and hollered. "Ah! Now it's in my eyes!"

"How did *that* happen?" Andrea asked. "You weren't eating with your hands." She took the first mug she could find from its hook by her coffee maker and grabbed the carton of milk from him.

"I don't know." Dustin turned on the faucet and held his face underneath the spray. Water coursed down his face and dampened his red flannel shirt. "I eat chili all the time, and this never happens to me."

Andrea gulped down her milk. "It wasn't chili powder!" She opened the spice cabinet to prove it. "See?" she said, grabbing the paprika. Only when she looked at the bottle, she noticed it was completely full. When she unscrewed the cap, she saw the seal was still intact. "Wait a sec," she muttered as she stared at the unopened paprika. "If I didn't use smoked paprika, what did I use?"

"Did you do this to me on purpose? Was this your way of getting back at me for being a total ass yesterday?"

"What? No. Of course not." Andrea rifled through the cupboard, looking for a red spice. "Although I'm glad we're in agreement that you were a jerk." Finally, she spotted a familiar jar. "There. This is the paprika I used." As soon as she read the label, she realized she'd made a horrible mistake. "Oh, crap." She bit her bottom lip and turned to Dustin. "Whoops?" She handed him the bottle.

"Ghost pepper paprika," he read through teary eyes. "World's hottest. Guaranteed to make your mouth burn alive." He dried his face with a hedgehog towel.

"I didn't do it on purpose. They must have given me the wrong thing in my grocery order."

"Yeah, right. Or you wanted to teach me a lesson."

"Teach you a lesson?" Andrea marched over to her refrigerator and flung open the freezer. "There are eight more dinners just like this one in my meal-prep arsenal. Do you really think I did this to you on purpose?"

"Oh." Dustin hung up the dish towel. "Sorry. I—"

"You're a jackass—that's what you are." Andrea slammed the freezer door shut. "I can't believe I was in love with you." She pointed her finger at him. "I can't believe I fell for you *again* either. Or that I got all broken up over your umpteenth rejection."

"Andrea, wait." Dustin held up his hands.

"Well, let me tell you something, mister." Andrea pushed up the sleeves of her sweater. "I don't torture people at my dining room table. How dare you accuse me of stooping to something that low?"

"I'm sorry." Dustin stepped backward. "I did this all wrong."

Andrea snorted derisively. "You think?"

"I was coming here to apologize. To tell you that I screwed up."

"You're damn right you screwed up." Andrea dumped the spicy paprika into the sink and tossed the jar into the recycling. "But if you think you can just waltz in here with your toolbox and fix things, you've got another think coming."

"Andrea, I—"

She flicked on the garbage disposal to drown out his half-assed apology. Only instead of churning to action, the disposal ground to a halt. It was then that Andrea remembered the potato peels, which her plumber had told her to never, ever run down the drain. Water pooled in the sink, a crimson tide of spice, potato peels, and turnip tops.

"Uh, Andrea?" Dustin pointed at the sludge. "It looks like your garbage disposal is clogged. Would you like me to fix that for you?"

"No," she snapped. She flicked off the switch. "I mean yes, and send me a bill." Andrea hung her head and stomped away, but he was two steps behind. "Why are you following me to the living room?" she asked.

"I'm not following you." Dustin raked his fingers through his damp brown hair. "I'm getting my toolbox."

"Oh." Andrea flopped down on the couch and watched him walk back to the kitchen. Her stomach growled. Pizza sounded good, but probably Dustin was sick of pizza since his brother owned the parlor. *Wait, why do I care?* He could starve as far as she was concerned.

Although he *did* say he was coming over to apologize . . . Andrea sat with that thought for a moment while she opened up the food-delivery app on her phone. Choices in Port Inez were limited, and Sunday night meant a long wait. When her tummy rumbled a second time, Andrea's willpower failed her. She went back into the kitchen and took out a spoon and a pint of Ben & Jerry's ice cream. "How's it coming?" she asked.

Dustin lay on the ground with his head underneath the sink and the disposal next to him. He had put her stockpot underneath the pipes. "It was clogged with potato peels, but I've cleared that now, and I'm putting everything back together."

"Thanks." Andrea jammed her spoon into the ice cream. It was somehow easier talking to Dustin when she couldn't see his face. Not that the rest of him wasn't equally attractive. His legs were so long they spread from one end of her wood floor to another.

"I meant what I said about coming over here to apologize," Dustin mumbled from inside the sink cabinet. "I know I screwed up."

"Go on." Andrea licked her spoon.

"I shouldn't have been in such a foul mood on the road home from Port Angeles. That was me and my issues—nothing to do with you."

"You could've fooled me."

Dustin's foot kicked out as he reached his hand for the dismembered garbage disposal, his face still concealed. "I was angry at Cade, worried about Leanne, and, most importantly, disappointed with myself for not being able to stop any of it. Heidi says that I bottle things up until I implode."

"Or accuse people of poisoning you?" Andrea's spoon scraped the bottom of her ice cream carton. She'd eaten the Chunky Monkey faster than intended.

"I'm sorry about that too. I know you're not the vengeful type."

"What type am I?" Andrea asked, genuinely curious to hear what Dustin would say.

"The kind type. The friendly type. The type of person who would convince her mom and dad to invite my family over for dinner for our first Christmas without our parents and then give each of us matching scarves."

Andrea had forgotten about that. She'd been into a knitting phase in high school until she'd realized that she sucked at it.

"I mean, my scarf unraveled the third time I wore it," said Dustin, "but it was the thought that counted."

"I never did master casting off." Andrea set down her spoon.

"But that doesn't mean you aren't smart. You're the only person I know who likes to read the display signs on museum exhibits as much as me." He scooted out from underneath the sink and looked at her sheepishly before standing and focusing his attention on the faucet. First he turned on the water and then the garbage disposal. It roared to life without incident. "Fixed now." Dustin flicked off the switch and washed his hands.

Andrea stared into her empty ice cream tub. While she wasn't entirely mollified, her feelings had definitely softened. Still, the hurt lingered. "I can't believe you thought I'd poisoned you."

"Not poisoned." Dustin dried off his hands. "Taught me a lesson, maybe. Heidi used to do that type of stuff to me all the time. Still does, in fact." He hung up the dish towel. "A couple of weeks ago she taped dozens of magazine pages onto the windshield of my truck to prove her point that we should buy Shaker cabinets for the kitchen. It took me an hour to scrape off the tape."

Andrea grinned for a half second before forcing the smile to disappear. She knew about that particular prank because she'd helped Heidi search through home-decorating magazines, looking for the right images. But Andrea would never consider doing something like that herself. "Do I look like Heidi to you?"

"No." Dustin stepped forward, his eyes clear and full of hope. "You look like the person who helped me cram for my AP Calculus test. Who stood next to me when I opened my acceptance letter to Washington State University. And who introduced me to sushi, which I have never grown to like, by the way, despite your insistence that I would."

"Your loss." Andrea didn't want to admit it, but she could vividly picture those things too. It was like every moment she had shared with Dustin was encased in a plastic coin holder. Preserved forever—she could examine them one at a time until her heartbreak stung. "But all of those things were a long time ago."

Dustin took another step forward. "Then why are they so clear in my mind that they could have happened yesterday?"

"Memories are funny that way, I guess."

"Not all memories. Just the ones we work hard to remember." Dustin sat on the barstool next to her and rested his hands on the counter. "I came here to apologize for being a jerk yesterday and ask if you could forgive me. I wish we could rewind time and go back to that hotel room and start over."

"And I would forget about you icing me out and then accusing me of"—Andrea lifted her hands to make air quotes—"teaching you a lesson?"

"Yes." Dustin nodded and then studied his hands. "I realize that's a lot to ask."

"It is." Andrea nodded. No matter how hard she fought it, she was still a hopeless romantic. Her heart longed to fling herself into Dustin's arms and tell him all was forgiven. But her head told her not to—or maybe it was her backbone. "I'm not in a position where I can afford to be jerked around. My dad is counting on me. *I'm* counting on me. A part of me will always love you, but another part can't trust you."

"What?" Dustin raised his eyebrows. "I'm completely trustworthy. I'm the most trustworthy person I know."

Andrea pointed at the sink with her thumb. "To fix a garbage disposal or remodel a house, yes, but I can't trust you to confide in me or protect my feelings."

"That's not true," he sputtered. "I've told you things I've never told anyone else."

"Yeah, maybe, but you still won't tell me what made you so upset yesterday."

"I did tell you." A tiny vein in Dustin's jaw twitched. "Cade annoyed me and—"

"No, it was something more than that, something deeper. You were angry with Cade Friday night, too, but you still talked to me. And then today, you were so quick to believe the worst in me, just like at prom."

Dustin started to say something, but then his mouth gaped open. "I . . ."

She had rendered him speechless, and that made her sad, because it was so easy to do. Heidi was right; Dustin couldn't talk about his emotions. Andrea had thought she was the exception to that rule, but now she realized the truth: Dustin couldn't share his heart with anyone.

"Look," she said as she pushed away her ice cream carton. "My dad wasn't wrong all those years ago when he told you I feel things intensely." She slid her hand into her pocket and touched the steel penny for support. "I love you. Now, then, and maybe always. But I refuse to let you break my heart again."

"I wouldn't," Dustin whispered.

"Can you honestly promise me that?" Andrea searched his face for an answer and saw hesitancy. "That's what I thought." She stood up. It wasn't lost on her that he hadn't said that he loved her back, and that was gut wrenching. "Thanks for the help around the house. I'll install the window locks after you leave."

"Good idea," he said, his voice shaky. His phone buzzed, and he pulled it out of his pocket to look at the notification. "That's the private investigator. I better take this."

Andrea nodded, her hand still clenched around the penny.

"Hello?" Dustin asked as he collected his wrench from the sink and headed into the entryway.

Andrea took the coin out of her pocket and stared at it. She knew she had done the right thing in standing up for herself, but that didn't ease the burn.

CHAPTER FOURTEEN

Mellow Yellow was the name of the paint Dustin was applying to the living room walls of the remodel, but he didn't feel mellow at all. It was Monday morning, and he was still wound up about what Andrea had said to him the night before. She'd all but come out and asked him if he could make a commitment to her, and he hadn't known what to say. Would he ruin things again if they got back together? He wished he could have said absolutely not, but the truth was, he wasn't sure. Maybe she was right and he was untrustworthy—not about life in general but where relationships were concerned.

"This color looks like baby poop," said Nathan, who was painting beside him. Port Pizza was his life. In the last stages of a house flip, though, it was all hands on deck. Dustin and Heidi didn't have Nathan on payroll, and their brother never asked for financial compensation, but helping each other out was something the Karlsson siblings did. Under normal circumstances, Leanne would be here, too, since the girls were at school, but she wasn't speaking to any of them.

"I didn't pick the color, obviously." Dustin studied it with a critical eye. "I think it will fade once it dries."

"Let's hope." Nathan squinted at the plaster and shook his golden-blond head—the same shade as Leanne's. Nathan was shorter than Dustin and had a wiry build.

"How do you know what baby poop looks like anyway?" Dustin asked. Unlike him, Nathan had been hands off when Kendal and Jane were little. Nathan loved his nieces but wasn't much of a kid person. He said that he'd gone to enough parent-teacher conferences for Leanne to last him his whole life.

"The one time I babysat Kendal, she had a blowout all over me."

"Oh." Dustin chuckled. "I'd forgotten about that. It was Leanne and Cade's first anniversary, right? Heidi and I were signing escrow papers or something." He dipped his roller into the paint and went back to work.

The brothers kept painting, not saying anything else for the next half an hour. It was easy for Dustin to be with his brother. Unlike Heidi, Nathan never pressed him to confide. Sometimes they went an entire workday without saying one word. Their father had been like that, too, Dustin realized. Josh had never spoken unless he'd had something important to say. Crystal had claimed it was because she did enough talking for both of them. Thinking about his father helped another memory resurface. Dustin continued to paint as the memory washed over him.

He had just turned sixteen and gotten his license. Dustin had borrowed the yellow Ford truck without asking, picked up a couple of friends, and driven to the drive-in theater in Bremerton. After the movie was over, Dustin had tried to back out of the parking lot but had put the engine into drive instead of reverse and accidentally rear-ended the person in front of him. Luckily nobody had been hurt.

Crystal made a huge fuss when she saw the broken headlight and checked him for signs of whiplash. She said she wouldn't be a good mother unless she worried and then railed at him for taking the truck without permission. But Josh didn't say one word about the incident until the next day, when he slipped a piece of paper in front of Dustin's nose with *$200 a month* written on it. "This is how much our insurance is going up due to your accident," he had said. "Starting this Saturday, you're my new part-time employee." Dustin had never taken the truck without permission again.

"I hear you saw Mary," Nathan said, pulling Dustin back to the present.

"Your old girlfriend? Yeah." Dustin swept the paint roller in a W formation. "I did, when Andrea and I were at the Clearwater."

"Did she seem okay?" Nathan paused, midstroke, and looked at Dustin.

"Yup. Gorgeous as ever."

"That's good." Nathan went back to painting.

"Uh-huh." Dustin stepped back to examine their progress. The first coat was almost done.

The brothers painted for another thirty minutes in complete silence until Heidi entered the room. "Don't let me interrupt your scintillating conversation," she said, "but have you seen the blue masking tape?"

"It's over there." Nathan pointed. "By the window."

"Thanks." Heidi walked across the room and picked up the roll of blue tape. Then she gazed at the walls. "I love this color. It'll go great with the refinished wood floor."

Dustin, who had spent enormous effort bringing the original fir boards back to life, hoped that Heidi was right. To him, the color looked like mustard, but he could see that the drier parts at the edges had softened to a pale butter. "How's the upstairs bathroom coming?" he asked. "Do you need help?"

"Nope." Heidi threaded her arm through the roll of tape like it was a bracelet. "All that's left is the baseboard. So, um, anything you want to tell me about?"

"No." Dustin froze. "Everything's fine down here." He went back to painting.

But Heidi wasn't done with him. "I went for a walk with Andrea this morning."

"Good for you." Dustin clenched his jaw. He knew where this train was headed, and he wanted to switch tracks. "This is supposed to be satin finish, right? Not semigloss?" Maybe if he could change the topic, she'd stop bugging him about Andrea.

Heidi read the paint can. "Satin. That's right. So anyway, Andrea and I walked to the coffee stand and back and—"

"Hunter's Fuel?" Nathan asked, interrupting her. He looked sideways at Dustin for a split second and winked. Dustin felt good knowing that his brother was on his side.

"That's right," said Heidi. "And Andrea said—"

"Why did you pay for coffee when you could brew it at home?" Dustin asked.

"Yeah," said Nathan. "What happened to that fancy machine that grinds the beans that you wouldn't shut up about six months ago?"

"I still have it." Heidi slipped the ring of tape from one wrist to the other. "But now I wish I had bought a Nespresso machine like Andrea has. Speaking of Andrea," she continued, undeterred by her brothers' attempts to sidetrack her, "she told me that—"

"You never answered the question about why you were buying coffee at a drive-through espresso stand." Nathan's mouth twitched like he was struggling not to smile.

"Yeah," said Dustin. "Especially since you were on foot."

"It's a good destination to walk to. Okay?" Heidi blew a puff of bangs out of her eyes. "They sell chai lattes there. But that's not the point. Andrea told me that you went over to her house last night and changed her locks."

"*I* didn't go over there," said Nathan. "Why would I do that?"

"Not you, doofus." Heidi swatted Nathan's shoulder. "Dustin." She punched Dustin in the arm for good measure. "Why didn't you tell me that you went to Andrea's?"

"Why should I?"

"Because it was my idea!" Heidi said in an exasperated tone. "I want to help you."

"Some help you are." Dustin's forehead furrowed. "Going over there was a horrible idea. Andrea pretty much told me that she never wanted to see me again."

Heidi rolled her eyes. "That's not what she said."

"How would you know? You weren't there."

"Because unlike you, Andrea tells me things. She said she told you that she can't risk dating someone who won't share his feelings. Something that Karlsson men are horrible at."

Dustin thought about his father, the broken headlight, and the terse note. Had his dad been too angry to talk? Maybe. But at the time, Dustin had appreciated not being lectured. And what about those damn oak cabinets? Josh had never said one word about how angry he must have been over the lost income.

"Hey," said Nathan as he poured paint into the pan. "I can talk about my feelings just fine. Don't drag me into this."

"Why shouldn't I?" Heidi asked. "How are things going three months post-Mary? Do you still think breaking up with her was a wise decision?"

Nathan grimaced. "That's none of your business!"

"What about you, Heidi?" Dustin pointed his roller at her. "How do you feel about Mack dating some chick who works at the salon?"

"What?" Heidi's eyes became as round as saucers. "Mack's dating someone?"

The annoyance Dustin had felt a second earlier softened when he saw the pain in his sister's eyes. "You didn't know?"

"No." Heidi shook her head. "I didn't." She sat on the drop cloth protecting the floor. "When did this happen? How did you find out?"

"Oh boy." Dustin set down his roller and crouched next to her. "One of the roofers told me. I thought you knew."

"I didn't, and it makes me feel awful." Heidi hugged her knees. "See how I did that? I said exactly what I felt. I feel sad knowing that Mack's dating someone else. I should feel happy for him because we're supposedly friends, but I don't. I'm mad, sad, jealous, and conflicted, all rolled up into one."

Nathan whistled. "I'm not sure it's possible for a person to feel all those emotions at the same time."

"It *is* possible," said Heidi, "and you shouldn't make jokes when people share how they feel." She squeezed Dustin's hand. "Now you try."

"Try what? Whistling? I've never been able to whistle like Nathan."

"Not funny." She whacked his hand and flung it away. "You're impossible. If I didn't love you so much, I would have given up on you ages ago."

Dustin sighed. He was just about to open his mouth and say something—anything—that might appease Heidi when Nathan came to his rescue.

"You do realize that you're my sister, Heidi Karlsson, and not Oprah Winfrey, right?" Nathan asked. "Dad never told people what he was feeling, and he was the strongest man I knew."

"Yeah," said Dustin, feeling vindicated. "Exactly."

"Don't be ridiculous!" Heidi said, her voice rising. "Dad's a horrible example to follow on this one."

"What do you mean?" Dustin scratched his head. He'd never in the nineteen years since the accident heard her say one negative thing about their father.

Heidi rested her hands on the cloth. "First of all, Dad might not have told us what he was feeling, but he for sure told Mom. Don't you remember how they would go out to the truck when they argued? They thought we couldn't hear them, but we could."

Dustin swallowed hard. He realized that Heidi was right. He'd forgotten about it, but his parents had totally done that. "Mom did most of the talking," he said. "That doesn't prove your point."

"Actually, it does," said Heidi. "One of the things they used to argue about was how she never knew what he was thinking. When she became pregnant with Leanne, she worried a lot about money, and Dad wouldn't say one word about how broke they were."

"How do you know that?" Nathan asked, sitting down next to her.

"Because I was going into middle school at the time and wanted money for new clothes." Heidi brushed lint off her jeans. "Mom caved and told me they were broke. Then she offered to sew me a new outfit from anything I could find in the remnants section at the fabric store."

"I don't remember her sewing you anything," said Nathan.

Dustin didn't either, but he'd been in elementary school at the time.

Heidi gazed up at the ceiling and let out a deep breath. "I told her I wouldn't be caught dead in homemade clothes." She shut her eyes for a few seconds, and when she opened them, they were wet. "I still feel guilty about hurting her feelings."

"It wasn't your fault," Nathan said brusquely. "You were just a kid."

"I was old enough to know I had wounded her pride." Heidi let go of the masking tape and rolled it across the floor.

"Dad's business always struggled," said Nathan. "Port Inez was quieter back then, and there wasn't much demand for carpentry."

"Really?" Dustin asked. "Are you sure about that? I remember him working six days a week."

"Because he had a side hustle refinishing furniture he found at thrift stores," said Nathan. "Don't you remember?"

Dustin shook his head. "No."

"He stopped doing that when I was in second grade," said Heidi, "which explains why Dustin doesn't remember. That's where that crappy dining room table came from. Dad was going to refinish it but never had time."

"It was originally from Ethan Allen," said Nathan. "There's a maker's mark underneath that says so."

"I didn't know that." Heidi smiled. "No wonder Mom and Dad wanted to keep it."

"Why did Dad stop the side hustle with the furniture?" Dustin asked.

"Because business picked up slightly when new homes were built in Harper Landing," Nathan explained.

"Like that big job with the custom cabinets in Burke Woods?" Dustin scratched his elbow.

"Yes." Heidi's shoulders slumped. "And then that job fell through, and Dad's company suffered a huge financial loss, which again, he never talked about."

"Emotions are like water," Dustin whispered before he could stop himself.

"What was that?" Heidi asked.

Dustin looked off into the distance. "It's something Dad said to me when we were driving back from the jobsite. He said, 'Emotions are like water. They can do a lot of damage if you're not careful.'"

"But that doesn't mean that you can't talk about them." Heidi pushed up the sleeves of her sweatshirt. "Instead, Mom and Dad had us eat mac and cheese for dinner all summer because we were too poor for anything else. But nobody said why."

"We knew why," said Nathan. "There was no need to talk about it."

"But you're wrong." Heidi stretched out her legs. "Mom needed to talk about it. She told me how proud she was of the hard work Dad had done. She admired his craftsmanship. She was angry that the contractor had taken advantage of him and wanted to take the guy to small claims court, but Dad wouldn't do it."

"Why didn't he?" Dustin asked. "That would have been a good idea."

"Dad couldn't handle the confrontation," said Heidi. "He was so angry he couldn't speak about it."

"What does this have to do with me?" Dustin asked. When he saw lightning bolts shoot out of Heidi's eyes, he grinned. "I'm kidding, Oprah. Calm down."

"I miss Mary," Nathan blurted out. "There, I said it. Maybe I should have proposed or something. Hell if I know."

"Obviously you should have proposed." Heidi threw her arm around him and gave him a side hug. "She was perfect for you."

"Except that she wanted kids, and I don't," said Nathan. "That was a deal breaker. I kept hoping she'd change her mind, but every time she'd pass a family pushing a stroller, she'd get all teary eyed, and I'd feel guilty."

"Are you sure you don't want kids?" Dustin asked. "You were great with Leanne when she was little."

"Because I had to be." Nathan leaned back on his hands. "I went from being a twenty-one-year-old culinary-school graduate working the graveyard shift at one of the best restaurants in Seattle to being a full-time single dad to two teenagers and a first grader. Plus all that financial pressure before the settlement came through? I don't think you fully understand how close we came to losing the house. Kids are expensive. I did what I had to do, but I don't want to go through that again."

Dustin felt guilt burn in his stomach like coal. "Then I went off to college and left you here with all that responsibility."

"It wasn't your fault," said Nathan.

"At least by that time Tom had won the lawsuit, and bills weren't an issue," said Heidi.

Nathan nodded. "The money helped, and so did the free labor when you came home from college on breaks. I wouldn't have been able to open Port Pizza without your man power, Dustin."

"And my fabulous decorating advice," Heidi added.

Dustin poked her in the ribs. "Your humility is truly your greatest feature."

"Your turn," said Nathan.

"To be humble?" Dustin asked. "I'm trying to but—"

"No, idiot," said Nathan. "Tell us what's on your mind."

"Shit," Dustin muttered, staring out the living room window.

"I always knew you had poop for brains," said Heidi, "but you can tell us more than that."

"No, I mean, shit." Dustin stood. "Andrea just drove up."

"That doesn't mean you're off the hook," said Heidi as she jumped up too. "Spill it, mister."

"I went over there to tell her I loved her, and then I accidentally accused her of poisoning me," Dustin said in a rush. "Then she kicked me out. Are you happy now?" He watched as Andrea opened the door to her Nissan Leaf and stepped onto the driveway.

Heidi rolled her eyes dramatically. "Only you, Dustin." She tugged his sleeve, pulling him away from the window. "But those are things that happened. Not how you feel about them."

"Give him a break, Heidi," said Nathan. "He already told us how he felt. Didn't you hear him say *shit*?"

"Yeah." Dustin nodded. "That's how I feel. I feel like shit." There was a knock at the front door, and he lurched back.

"Be right there!" Heidi hollered.

"You look awful, Dustin," said Nathan. "There's paint on the back of your shirt."

"There is not." Dustin twisted to see. "I never spill paint on myself."

"Maybe you brushed up against the wall or something." Heidi pushed him toward the bathroom. "Go do a quick cleanup while I answer the door."

"Thanks," said Dustin.

"You're not welcome." She frowned. "I seem to recall you sending me off to meet Mack with wallpaper paste in my hair."

"Sorry about that." Dustin scooted into the bathroom and closed the door behind him. He stared at his reflection in the mirror. Nathan was right. He did look like crap. His brown hair stuck up in every which way, and there was a streak of paint—which looked like baby poop—on his ancient blue flannel. Dustin shrugged out of it, grateful that he had on a gray T-shirt underneath. It was tighter than he liked it but clean. He washed his hands in the sink and swished his mouth out with water—just in case he got close enough to Andrea that she could smell his coffee breath. Then, after raking damp fingers through his hair to tame it, he took a steadying breath and opened the door.

Andrea stood next to Heidi and Nathan wearing tight jeans, a white blouse, and a long flowing red sweater. Her hair was swept to the side, and sparkling gold earrings hung from each earlobe. The way her neck was exposed made Dustin long to nibble it, but he knew that feeling was futile. Especially when he saw her cool glare.

"Uh, hi." He shoved his hands in his pockets. "Happy Monday."

"Yes," said Nathan in an unusually loud voice. "Happy Monday, everyone." He whistled a cheery tune and went back to painting.

"Hi," said Andrea.

Dustin stood there, unsure what to do.

Heidi grabbed his arm and pulled him closer. "Now that the greetings are out of the way," she said with a smile, "Andrea has something to tell you."

Dustin felt ten pounds lighter. Andrea was here to talk to him? Maybe he hadn't screwed up as badly last night as he'd thought.

Andrea lifted her chin. "It's about the case," she said.

Dustin felt the weight press down upon him again—only this time the load was even heavier. "New information?" he asked.

"Yes. Maybe . . . the owner of Green Lake Coin Store called me, and he has something he wants to tell me in person. He said it was too sensitive to go into over the phone."

"That sounds promising," said Dustin.

Andrea nodded. "I know, right? I shouldn't get my hopes up, but at least it's a lead. I'm headed there right now and wondered if you'd like to come with me?"

"Yes," Dustin said without hesitation. "Absolutely." He forgot about the construction deadline and focused on the opportunity to spend one more afternoon with Andrea. "I'll grab my keys."

"Hang on," she said. "I'll drive. Your truck will be too hard to park in the city."

"It'll be fine," he said. "I can park it anywhere."

"No," Andrea said, her eyebrows knitting together. "It'll limit our options and slow us down. I need to get to the coin shop and back in time to visit my dad tonight. *I'm* driving."

Dustin pictured the last time he'd been Andrea's copilot, eighteen years ago. The time when she'd sped through a yellow light that had turned red on Aurora Avenue and almost gotten them both killed. He wasn't planning on dying tonight, so he hoped her skills had improved since then. "Fine," he said. "I'll get my coat." Three minutes later they were on the road.

The inside of Andrea's Nissan Leaf smelled strongly of lavender. It was much smaller than his truck, and Dustin had to fold himself like a pretzel to fit in the passenger seat. He buckled up and remained quiet as she backed out of the driveway and onto the two-lane country road. The radio was off, and they drove in silence. Looking into the back seat, he saw a dozen reusable grocery bags strewed across the upholstery, plus a laundry basket full of neatly folded clothes. That explained the lavender scent but not why Andrea had a collection of men's sweatpants, socks, and boxers in the car with her.

As if she knew what he was wondering, Andrea answered his question. "That laundry is for my dad. The Owl's Nest will wash it for him, but their machines are industrial strength and tear everything to shreds after a few months. So I usually do his laundry myself." She frowned. "Sometimes I end up doing other people's clothes, too, by accident. Things get lost in the memory unit really fast since nobody can remember what belongs to them."

"That must be rough. Tom's lucky to have you looking out for him."

"It is what it is," she said, and her stoicism left a pang in his heart. "How did things go with the private investigator? Did you hire them?"

Dustin nodded. "I did. I sent in the retainer fee and signed the contract this morning. The PI said it'll take a few hours to run the background checks and there might be news for me as early as tonight."

"That's good. At least it's something." Andrea clicked on her blinker and prepared to turn into the ferry line. Since it was approaching eleven on a Monday, traffic was light, but there was still a five-minute backup to get through the tollbooth.

The silence between them felt oppressive, and Dustin knew he should say something—anything—to lighten the mood. But what could he say? Maybe he should listen to Heidi's advice and tell Andrea what he was feeling. "I keep thinking about last night," Dustin said. "I wish—"

"It's over," said Andrea. "How about some music?" She turned on the sound system without waiting for a reply. Only instead of the radio, an audiobook came to life.

"The Scottish Highlands rolled out like an ocean of purple heather," said a narrator with a thick brogue.

"Oh, sorry." Andrea reached back to turn it off, but Dustin touched her hand and stopped her.

"I love audiobooks," he said. "You know that."

"A herd of sheep, without a shepherd, huddled together for warmth, against the brisk, icy wind."

"No, I know." Andrea blushed a rosy pink. "It's just that—"

"But Lady Violet didn't notice the dropping temperatures," said the narrator. *"Not with Craig Sinclare's hand clamped across her buttocks and the hot pressure of his—"*

Andrea pounded her hand on the media console, desperately trying to turn it off, but she accidentally pressed the wrong button. Instead of switching from the audiobook to the radio, she increased the volume.

"With his kilt stretched out beneath them, part blanket, part shelter from the storm, Lady Violet—"

Dustin watched as Andrea's cheeks turned from pink to crimson red. He struggled to keep a straight face even though he wanted to laugh—not at what she was reading but over her mortification of being discovered.

Andrea lurched the car forward and then to a stop in front of the tollbooth. She turned the car completely off and then tried to roll down the window. Flustered that it wouldn't work, she turned the car back on again to make the window descend.

"Put her hands on his hot chest, tugging at the homespun cloth and—"

Jabbing her finger against the console, Andrea finally managed to turn off the audiobook. She rolled down the window and looked at the tollbooth operator.

"What's going on?" the ferry worker asked.

"What?" Andrea gasped.

"How many are in your car?"

"It's just the two of us." Andrea flashed her prepaid pass, and the operator waved them through.

Andrea drove into the ferry waiting area a wee bit too fast and slammed on the brakes inches before hitting the person in front of her. Dustin's seat belt bit into his shoulder, but he didn't say a word. He wished he knew something about crash-test ratings on a Nissan Leaf that would reassure him, but he was completely ignorant.

"That sounds like it was a good book," he said, trying to make small talk. "Real lively."

"You wouldn't understand what was going on," Andrea said as she adjusted the visor. "Too much of the plot has already passed."

"Yeah. From the bit I heard, it definitely sounded plot driven. Historical too." Seeing her embarrassment, he decided to move on to safer topics. "The ferry's already unloading."

"Yeah. We'll probably board in ten minutes."

"This coin shop we're visiting . . . is it the same one that sold your dad the 1907?"

"It is." Andrea relaxed back into her seat. "I think that's why the owner wants to help me. He knew my dad because he was such a frequent customer."

"Speaking of fathers, I need to tell you something." Dustin didn't know if this was the right approach or not, but he knew he had to try.

"What?" Andrea took her eyes off the dashboard and looked at him. Dustin hoped that was a sign that she would be willing to listen to what he had to say.

"The other day when we were driving back from Ocean Shores and you asked me about my parents . . ." Dustin's palms began to sweat, and he brushed them across his jeans. "I never talk about them, not to anyone. Not unless Heidi, Nathan, or Leanne bring them up, and they hardly ever do."

"Really? Why not?"

"I can't speak for my siblings." Dustin tugged at his collar. "Leanne hardly remembers them at all, and Nathan's not a big talker to begin with. But for me, it's because it brings up emotions that are hard for me to express. That's what Heidi would say, at least, and maybe she's right. On Saturday, when you asked me about my parents, I tried to talk about them and got wrecked. I was a jerk to you, and I'm sorry. Then last night when I tried to apologize, I made things worse because I was so nervous. In the course of forty-eight hours, I went from being furious, to tired, to elated, to hopeful, to sad, to nervous, and then ashamed." He looked at his lap for a moment before meeting her eyes again. There, he had done it. He'd told her exactly how he had felt. He almost wished Heidi were here to clap for him because he knew his big sister would be proud.

Andrea, on the other hand, looked at him skeptically like she didn't trust what he was saying. "Why are you telling me this now when it's too late?"

"Is it too late?" Dread crept over him. "Does it have to be?"

She turned away and looked out her window. "I can't risk another heartbreak. I need to focus on taking care of my dad and managing my business."

"I won't break your heart," he said firmly. He'd been too flummoxed to say that the night before, but he was sure of himself now. "I promise."

She twisted in her seat so she could stare at him directly. "Why should I believe you?"

Dustin held out his hand, palm up. "There are six people I care about more than anyone in the world." He extended his fingers one by one. "Nathan, Heidi, Leanne, Kendal, Jane . . ." Dustin closed his hand and pointed to Andrea. "And you."

This was the moment. He was finally doing it. His emotions were like water, and they were flowing out of him, rushing out with a force that gave him the strength to speak his truth. Maybe they'd cause damage, or maybe they'd cut through the impasse that had trapped him all these years.

"Your dad was right about us, but he was also wrong. Yes, I'm as intense as you, but that's not a bad thing. Andrea Jessica Wint, you've been on my heart forever." Dustin stared into her blue eyes that were the same color as the house he had restored for her. "I love you. I always have, and I always will."

CHAPTER FIFTEEN

Andrea's focus scattered. Dustin was declaring his love for her *now*, when they were about to board the ferry? Andrea had been terrified of driving onto the ferry her whole life. She didn't need to look at her fitness tracker to know that her heart rate had spiked. Dustin watching her made her even more nervous. Even Lady Violet wouldn't be able to put up with this type of pressure, and she'd fought off Vikings.

"Did you hear what I said?" he asked.

Andrea blinked. "Yes. You said you loved me." Her attention flipped from one distraction to another. A drug-sniffing beagle and its handler walked around the Subaru in front of her. In the row to the right, a Westfalia camping van had the engine running. That meant that the ferry was about to board.

"With all my heart," said Dustin. "And I was hoping you felt the same way."

"I already told you that I love you." Her foot tensed on the brake. "Yesterday, when you *didn't* say it back."

"I know. I was an ass."

"And a poor listener." The Subaru parked in front of her flashed its lights. "If you'd have been paying attention, you'd know that I can't stop falling in love with you. As a teenager, as an adult, in a Halloween costume, or on a coin hunt around the peninsula. Boom." Andrea took a deep breath, filling her lungs with oxygen. "I'm hooked." The car behind her honked. Andrea scrambled to turn on her Leaf. "Can we not talk about this right exactly at this moment?" she pleaded. "I don't want to crash into the side of the giant metal boat I'm about to drive onto over a flimsy ramp."

"Sure." Dustin grinned and rested his elbow on the armrest of his door. "We have a whole lifetime to talk about your affection for me."

His smile melted Andrea like butter, but she couldn't think about it now. "Don't you remember how much I hate driving onto the ferry?"

His grin disappeared and was replaced by a concerned look. "But that was years ago."

"Some things don't change," she said in a panic.

"You're doing great."

"Because I'm still on the dock." Andrea inched the car forward. "Hopefully we're in the lane that parks in the center row of the ferry."

"Why?"

"Because the side rows are harder but not as bad as the side ramps. Those are the worst." Andrea shivered. "They make me feel like I'm going to roll into the water."

"Do you want to trade seats? I could drive."

"It's too late for that." Andrea's fists clenched over her steering wheel as she drove onto the pier and across the gate onto the ferry. A ferry worker waved his arms, indicating that she should go right, even though the Subaru had been sent to the left. Now she was behind the Westfalia, which was stopping on the side ramp. "Crap," Andrea muttered as she was forced to park on the incline. She turned off her ignition, set the emergency brake, and prayed it would hold. Looking over her shoulder, she saw the ferry worker bend down to insert blocks underneath her rear tires as a safety precaution. The wind whipped up whitecaps on the waters of Puget Sound.

"Well done," said Dustin. "You did fine." He said it kindly and not in the patronizing tone her father had always used when he had taught her to drive.

"I don't know about that."

"Really." Dustin unclicked his seat belt. "I couldn't have done it better myself." He reached for her hand. "I'm sorry I distracted you."

"Poor timing is kind of our thing." Andrea was grateful it was too cold for her palms to be sweaty.

"It is." Dustin squeezed her hand reassuringly. "So what was that you were saying about not being able to help falling in love with me?"

"You heard me the first time. And the second." Her heart felt fragile, like a broken eggshell pieced back together with glitter glue. She gazed into his green eyes and prayed a thousand prayers that he was speaking the truth and that he wouldn't break her heart.

"Maybe I need to hear it a third time."

"Oh no you don't." Andrea shook her head. "If anyone's overdue for pouring out their emotions, it's you." She tapped him on the chest. She believed him when he said that he loved her. Dustin was the most loving man she knew, next to her father. But was he strong enough to stick with her on rocky days?

"I've loved you from the first moment I saw you open up that suitcase of old toys." Dustin cupped her face with his hands and held her steady.

"Lincoln Logs are classics. I wouldn't call them old." She wanted to trust him, but what if he let his doubt or fear hurt her again?

"I've loved you with every scrap of information I could glean from Heidi about what you were doing over the past two decades."

"Now you sound like a stalker."

"You didn't keep tabs on me through my sister?"

Andrea scrunched up her face. "Maybe," she admitted.

"Then we were both honed in on each other. Like bald eagles that bond for life."

"Or barred owls."

"Or owls," he agreed. "I've loved you every time I've driven by your house and pictured you reading a book on your window seat."

"That seems oddly specific." Andrea grinned. "You didn't know for sure I'd be reading in the window seat."

"I knew." He traced her cheek with his thumb and leaned forward so that their lips were centimeters apart. "Just like I knew that every other woman I've met in the past eighteen years couldn't compete with you."

When his lips crushed against hers, Andrea decided, then and there, that Dustin Karlsson was worth the risk. Not just because he was such a good kisser that zaps of energy pulsed all the way to her toes but because if she didn't take this chance, it would be the biggest regret of her life.

Andrea undid her seat belt and slinked out of the webbing. Dustin's hands scooped behind her back and pulled her against his firm chest. Her fingers slid across his tight gray T-shirt and linked around his neck. When their tongues touched, Andrea was flooded with a feeling she hadn't known in a long time: hope. Hope that this time, things would be different. Hope that Dustin meant what he said about loving her. Hope that the boy of her adolescent dreams had become the man who would embrace her future.

Andrea kissed Dustin back with the intensity of a woman who could do nothing halfway. It was her curse and her superpower. Her glittery, eggshell heart was in his hands now, and she prayed with all her soul that he would protect it.

Moments became minutes, and minutes stretched out longer than she had realized.

"Why are those windows foggy?" a squeaky voice asked outside the driver's side.

Andrea froze, Dustin chuckled, and they pulled away from each other. She looked sheepishly through the foggy windows at a small boy staring back at her.

"There was a problem with their defroster," said the boy's mother. "Move along so we can go up on deck."

"Maybe we should do that too," said Andrea, looking back at Dustin. "Go on deck, I mean. Before the car becomes too humid."

He grinned and leaned forward so that his lips were inches from hers. "It's like we're back in the Yo-Mobile," he whispered in a husky voice. Dustin drew a heart in her fogged-up window and wrote DK + AW in the center. Before she could say anything, he opened his door and got out of the car. Andrea grabbed her purse and climbed out too.

Icy wind blew in through the open ferry windows, but Andrea's blood was so hot she didn't notice. She followed Dustin up the long staircases that went to the top decks. When they reached the passenger deck, they found an empty booth looking out at Mount Rainier and sat down. Dustin put his arm around her shoulders, and Andrea snuggled next to him on the vinyl bench.

"This brings back memories." He kissed her neck. "Riding the ferry together."

"It sure does." She rested her head against his chest and closed her eyes, enjoying the moment.

"I won't screw up this time."

"I know."

"I meant what I said about the bald eagles."

"Or barred owls," she added. "Don't forget them."

"I'll tell you everything I'm feeling, from now on, even if it's hard."

"Everything?" She opened her eyes and looked up at him. "What about tough things, like if one of us wanted kids and the other didn't?"

"You don't want kids?"

"What? No, of course I want kids."

"Phew." He hugged her tighter. "Because I want at least a couple."

"At least." Here she went again, planning eternity after one steamy makeout session in a car. But maybe this time it would be all right.

"Give me another tough question," said Dustin. "Let me show you that I can do it."

"Would you visit my dad with me?"

"Yes. Of course. That's not a hard question."

"But it is." Andrea turned her face toward Dustin's chest so that she could block out the world. "It's impossible to visit him without crying. I don't know if you'll be able to handle it."

"I'll cry with you," he said. "It'll be good for me. Plus, I'd like to visit Tom."

Andrea nodded. "Maybe we can go this afternoon on our way home."

"I'd like that."

Andrea's phone vibrated in her purse, catching her attention. "I need to take this," she said, pulling the zipper. "It might be the Owl's Nest." But when she looked at the screen, she saw it was from out of state. "No, wait," Andrea added. "It's San Carlos Coin Market in California. Hello?" She sat up straight. Dustin removed his arm from around her shoulders and rested his elbows on the table.

"Hi, is this Andrea Wint?"

"Yes, this is she. I left a message on your answering machine yesterday about my father's stolen double eagle collection."

"That's what I'm calling about," the man said. "I'm Henry Farlston, the owner of San Carlos Coin Market. Yesterday I was at an estate sale, so I wasn't here when this incident happened or else I would have alerted the authorities."

"What incident?" Andrea asked.

"Last night, right before closing, a man came into the shop with a large collection of double eagles for sale," said Henry. "My assistant was managing the shop, and he doesn't have authority to make purchases over five thousand dollars. By his estimate, this collection was valued at over one hundred thousand dollars."

"And that was without my 1907." Andrea shook her head.

"A 1907? My assistant didn't mention that date."

"That's the only coin that's been recovered so far," Andrea explained. "The rest are still missing."

"Well, this could very well have been your collection," said Henry. "Unfortunately, my assistant hadn't checked our voice mail messages or he would have called the police. Instead, he told the man to come back the following day—that would be today—so that I could assist with the transaction."

"Is he coming?" Andrea's whole body tensed. This could be the break they needed.

"No," said Henry. "The man insisted that the sale happen yesterday and then became belligerent when my assistant said that wouldn't be possible. Something about the interaction seemed off to my employee, so after closing, he went back over the security footage and made a separate file for it."

"You have video?" Andrea's hopes soared. Dustin shot his fist in the air.

"Yes," said Henry. "It's black and white and a bit grainy, but I can send it to you if you would like."

"That would be great," said Andrea. "Thank you."

"What's your email address? I'll send it to you now."

Andrea rattled off her email and then gave him Dustin's as well so she wouldn't have to hang up to see the video. When it came through on Dustin's phone and she saw Cade's familiar light curls and Hollywood smile beaming back at her, Andrea didn't know whether to be happy or furious.

"That's him," said Andrea. "His name is Cade Tolbert, and he stole the safe in my house where my coins were kept."

"I'm sorry this happened to you," said Henry. "I'll make a report to our local police department in case that helps."

"Thank you," said Andrea. "I appreciate that."

"My assistant said it was the collection of a lifetime."

"It was." Andrea's eyes dampened with tears. "It *is*, and I'm going to get it back."

"That's the spirit," said Henry. "I have friends on the board of the ANA. I'll let them know what happened."

"The American Numismatics Association? Thank you so much."

"I'm not sure there will be anything they can do," said Henry. "But this is a story they'll want to know about."

"My father has Alzheimer's now, but he would have loved knowing that his collection had the attention of the ANA."

"It will be famous," said Henry. "One way or another."

By the time she had hung up the phone, the ferry was approaching Harper Landing. Andrea used the restroom, and then she and Dustin headed back to her car. As they buckled up, they discussed what to do next.

"This evidence changes things," said Dustin. "I mean, not for us but in terms of what my PI can do."

"And the sheriff too, right?"

"Absolutely. Do you need my help navigating, or can I call Mack right now?"

"I'm horrible with ferries but great with city traffic."

"That's right. You've lived here your whole life."

"Almost my whole life." She squeezed his hand. Seattle-phobia had been Dustin's Achilles' heel for as long as she had known him. She knew that traveling to the city made him vulnerable, yet he was doing it once again for her sake. "You make the calls, and I'll get us to Green Lake." Andrea spoke with more confidence than she felt. Sure, navigating the streets of Seattle was easy for her, but disembarking the ferry scared her, especially since she was parked on the ramp in such a precarious position. Cars didn't belong over water, and the ramp that connected the ferry to the dock made a *clankety-clank* noise that was unnerving. It was like driving down the tongue of a giant steel monster. But once it was her turn to enter the cute town of Harper Landing, Andrea let her shoulders relax. She drove up Main Street and headed for Interstate 5, then picked up speed as she merged into the carpool lane.

Andrea listened as Dustin spoke with Mack on the phone and convinced him not only to update the police report with new information but to seek a warrant for Cade's arrest. Dustin's next call was to the private investigator he had hired. The picture was a huge help. Andrea realized that as soon as she was able, she should go back onto the coin forums and post Cade's photo and an update about her missing coins.

"Well, that went well," he said after hanging up with the PI. "Cade's credit card records are interesting. He bought gas in Ashland yesterday morning and booked a hotel last night in San Francisco."

"I thought Leanne canceled their credit cards?"

"She did," said Dustin. "At least she told us she did. But apparently Cade has a card in his own name that I'm not sure if she knew about."

"How did the PI get the credit card records?"

Dustin shrugged. "No idea. I figure the less I know about that, the better."

Andrea exited the freeway, and as she approached the Woodland Park Zoo, she merged into the left lane on instinct. In this part of Seattle cars could park in the right-hand lane at certain times of the day, which blocked traffic. "I had an idea about the coin forums," Andrea said right as her phone rang. Bluetooth transferred the call to the media console.

"Hi, Andrea," said her mother. "I'm so glad I caught you."

"I'm driving right now," said Andrea. "Can I call you back later?"

"This will only take a second." Lydia spoke faster. "I'm at the store buying ingredients for éclair cake to make this Friday when you come to dinner. That was Dustin's favorite, wasn't it? Has he called? Have you heard any more news about the coins?"

Dustin coughed loudly into his fist. Andrea didn't know if he had a tickle in his throat or was trying to let Lydia know of his presence.

"Mom," Andrea snapped. "I'm in the car with Dustin right now. This isn't a good time to talk."

"Oh hello, Dustin!" Lydia spoke in a dreamy voice. "What a funny coincidence that I was just thinking of you."

"Hi, Lydia," said Dustin as he fought back laughter. "And you're right; I do love your éclair cake."

"Well then, you absolutely must join us for dinner Friday night," said Lydia. "I insist."

"Mom!"

"That would be great," said Dustin. "I look forward to it." He grinned at Andrea.

She didn't know whether to be annoyed with her mother or grateful that she not only would get to spend more time with Dustin but now wouldn't have to face a meal with Lydia and Roger alone.

"We're having halibut," said Lydia. "Freshly caught in Alaska."

"It's from your freezer, Mom."

"I mean it *was* fresh," Lydia clarified. "Originally."

"That's how fish works," said Andrea. Traffic slowed as they drove by Green Lake. "We've got to go." She said goodbye to her mother and hung up the phone before Lydia could get one more word in. "Well, some things haven't changed," she said to Dustin as she flicked on her blinker to park.

"What?"

"You can't say no to my mother's cooking."

"Her éclair cake, Andrea. Think of her éclair cake. Who could say no to that?"

"It's actually not that good." Andrea zipped into a tight spot against the curb and parked her car like a champ, grateful they weren't driving Dustin's truck. "It has graham crackers in it." She pretended to retch. "Yuck."

"I love graham crackers. I keep them on hand for Kendal and Jane, but sometimes I get into them if I'm out of ice cream."

"How did I not know that about you?"

"You don't know all my secrets." Dustin tucked a strand of hair behind her ear. He leaned forward and brushed their noses together. "And it's been a while."

Her lips found his a second later, and she became lost in rediscovering the familiarity of his kisses. She tiptoed her fingers across his neck and caused him to sigh. Andrea felt like a magician. It took exceptional powers to make a guy as stalwart as Dustin sigh. When he did it again, she giggled.

"What's so funny?" he asked as he brushed kisses across her jawline.

"You," she said. "You're both the same and different."

"What's different about me?" He cupped her face in his hands and waited for her response.

"Well, for one thing, you let me drive, although maybe you shouldn't have."

"You didn't give me much choice," he said with a grin.

"And for another, your cheeks don't have peach fuzz anymore." She ran her knuckles lightly across his thick stubble. He had been cleanly shaved the night before but already had a shadow. She rested her hands on his thick deltoids. "And I don't remember your shoulders feeling like this."

"Hazard of growing up, I guess." Dustin ran his fingers through her hair. "You've changed a bit yourself over the years."

"I have?"

His smile faded, and his eyebrows knit together with concern. "You seem sadder. Not now but in general."

Andrea nodded and tightened her grip on his shoulders, allowing his strength to bolster her. She rested her forehead against Dustin's. "That's true," she whispered. She didn't like to admit it, not to Dustin, Heidi, her mother, or even herself, but she had been sad. The move to Port Inez had been a positive one, but even a fresh start wasn't enough to make up for the grief. "I've had a lot of things to deal with the past couple of years. I haven't been depressed, and if I was, I'd see a therapist, but my father's illness has been a lot to manage. Then there's my mom and Roger, and me getting older too."

"You deserve happiness." Dustin smoothed her hair. "You deserve joy." He kissed her once more, and when they pulled away, he stared into her eyes. "I can't promise that we'll get your coins back, but I can promise you happier times ahead, starting with tomorrow night. Will you go out to dinner with me?"

"You mean on a date?" Her heart beat ridiculously fast, like she was a teenager again and they were making plans together for the first time.

"Yes. A real date. No bacon and egg costumes required."

"Oh, come on." She laughed. "That Halloween party was certainly memorable."

"Agreed." He unclicked his seat belt. "But this time I was thinking about something with tablecloths."

"Tablecloths?" Andrea double-checked that her key fob was in her purse. "I had no idea you could be so fancy."

"I'm not," he said as he opened his door. "But it's not often you get a second opportunity like this, and I intend to make the most of it."

"In that case, I'll wear heels." She opened an app on her phone to pay the parking meter.

A couple of minutes later, she and Dustin were walking hand in hand to the Green Lake Coin Store, and there was a definite spring in both of their steps. Andrea wondered where Dustin was planning on taking her tomorrow night. Port Inez had only three restaurants: Port Pizza, which didn't have tablecloths; the BBQ Trough, known for its all-you-can-eat buffet; and the Sub Shack, which was roughly what it sounded like. But Andrea didn't have time to wonder further, because they had arrived at the entrance to the coin store, and Dustin was ringing the bell to wait for entry like a numismatic pro. When the buzzer sounded, he opened the door and let her go first.

Walking into the Green Lake Coin Store was like stepping into her childhood. It had the same parquet floors, painted yellow walls, and showcase of international flags along the left wall where the world coins were displayed. The opposing wall had framed pictures of the Colosseum and Parthenon, right behind the case with ancient coins. But at the back, where customers would see it first, was the artwork that Andrea loved the most, a full-size poster of Lady Liberty from Saint-Gaudens's original design. Standing next to the poster was a man she recognized but hadn't seen for several years: Gordon Mackle, the shop's owner.

Andrea waved and walked up to him. "Hi, Mr. Mackle," she said. "Thanks for calling me."

"Please," he said. "Call me Gordon." He held out his hand to shake.

"It's good to see you again," said Andrea as she shook Gordon's hand. "This is my—" She froze, unsure of how to describe Dustin.

"Boyfriend, Dustin Karlsson." Dustin extended his hand. "Nice to meet you."

The glitter glue that patched up Andrea's heart became a little bit stronger when she heard Dustin describe himself as her boyfriend. She stood straight and looked Gordon in the eye, eager for answers. "What did you have to tell me about my stolen collection that couldn't be said over the phone?"

Gordon scanned the shop, as if verifying that there weren't any customers present to overhear what he had to say. "I needed to tell you this face to face." He paused.

"What?" Andrea asked.

Gordon tugged down the sleeve of his black sweater. "It's about the 1907 I sold your father."

"What about it?"

"I intentionally misgraded it," Gordon said, adjusting his collar. "With your father's approval," he added hastily. "I didn't cheat him."

"I don't understand." Andrea removed the coin from her purse. She had it with her so she could rent a safe-deposit box for it in Harper

Landing later that day. She unfolded the plastic flip and laid it on the counter. "Why would you misgrade it?"

Gordon swallowed. "A Mint State 63 1907 double eagle would be worth between twenty to thirty thousand." Gordon picked up the coin holder. "But this isn't an MS 63; it's an MS 66+ and valued at over a hundred thousand."

"A hundred thousand dollars?" Dustin repeated.

"No," said Andrea. "That can't be right. My mom got a diamond tennis necklace when she turned sixty that cost thirty thousand, and my dad used the same amount to buy a coin for his birthday."

Gordon cringed. "I wasn't privy to the whole story, but I knew that Tom wanted to keep the true value of the coin secret from your mother." He gave the coin to Andrea. "Let me show you the paperwork from the auction house. I've kept it in my safe all these years." Gordon hurried away and returned a minute later with a manila envelope. He removed thick parchment paper with a shiny silver seal and passed it to Andrea. "The agreement was that I would give this to you after your father passed. I believe he wrote that as an addendum to his will. But in light of current circumstances and your father's declining health, I believe he would want you to have this information now, in case it helps your investigation."

Andrea read the parchment paper as quickly as possible, her lips moving as she absorbed every word. "It's true," she said when she reached the end. "He paid thirty thousand dollars on his Amex and the other seventy-two thousand with a cashier's check."

"But wait," said Dustin. "The dealer in Port Angeles didn't say it was worth that much."

"Franklin the gun nut? He's an idiot." Gordon frowned. "He's also not used to evaluating the same caliber of coins that come through my shop. You can imagine what would happen to my reputation if word got out about this. People wouldn't be able to trust me."

"I wouldn't worry about that," said Andrea. "Discretion is a dealer's best asset." She closed her hand around the plastic holder. "Your secret is safe with me. I know that's what my father would have wanted. Thank you for being a good friend to him."

Gordon leaned his weight on the counter. "I always enjoyed visiting with him every time he came into the store."

"I know he felt the same way about you too," said Andrea. She slid the paperwork back in the envelope and put the coin in her purse. "My dad doesn't remember much these days, but he often reminds me that Green Lake Coins is the best place to shop."

"I appreciate that," said Gordon. The doorbell rang, and he looked up. "I better get that."

"We need to go too," said Dustin. "Thanks for your time." He put his hand on Andrea's back, and the gentle pressure comforted her. She was still processing the news of her father's lie. It hadn't quite sunk in yet. When they walked out of the store and into the bright day-light, Andrea blinked, and her eyes struggled to focus. Twenty minutes ago there had been clouds. Now there was blinding sunlight. Andrea couldn't keep up with any of it. First she'd found out that her father had interfered in her and Dustin's relationship back in high school. Now she'd discovered that he'd lied to her mom about a major purchase. Tom had been sneaky—that was the word for it—but she couldn't confront him over past mistakes because he wouldn't remember any of them.

Andrea turned to Dustin and let his strong arms wrap around her in a firm embrace. "How do I do this?" she mumbled.

"Do what?" Dustin asked as he rubbed her back in circles.

"Know that my dad lied."

"He was a lawyer," said Dustin. "Of course he lied."

She lifted her head off his shoulder and shot him a look. "A lawyer joke? Really?"

"What?" Dustin shrugged. "I was trying to lighten the mood." He kissed her forehead. "Your dad was the smartest, kindest, most generous man I knew. He took on our case against one of the biggest construction companies in Seattle, without us paying him one dime in retainer fees because we couldn't afford it. Don't you think he deserved a special gift to himself?"

"That he lied to my mom about? No, I don't." Andrea couldn't believe that she was taking Lydia's side on this one, but she was. "My mom worked hard too. She might not have earned a paycheck, but she was every bit as smart and generous as my father."

"*Is*, not was."

"Yes." Andrea bit her lip. "*Is*. I can't believe my dad did this to her." She pictured the coin in her purse. "Crap!" Spinning away from Dustin, she charged toward her car.

"What?" he asked, taking long strides to keep pace with her.

"I'll tell you when we get to the car." She walked faster. It wasn't until they were both safely inside her Nissan Leaf, with the doors shut and locked, that she shared her revelation. "I just realized I'm walking around Seattle with a hundred grand in my purse."

"Oh." Dustin chuckled. "That's not good."

"No, it isn't." Andrea turned on the car. "Bringing you to visit my dad today will have to wait. I need to rent a safe-deposit box stat."

CHAPTER SIXTEEN

Nathan was right: the bottom of the dining room table *did* have a maker's mark from Ethan Allen. Crouched on the carpet and staring up at the scratched wood, Dustin couldn't believe he'd never noticed it before. How many times had he transformed this table into a blanket fort as a child? Hundreds, and yet he'd never seen the stamp. Upon standing up, Dustin inspected the marred surface. The walnut would never match the oak cabinets his mom had used as a china hutch, but he could see why his parents had brought this piece home. The heft and interlocking leaves spoke of quality you couldn't find in stores today, not unless you were willing to pay thousands of dollars. A skilled refurbisher could bring the finish back to life. "Hmm . . . ," Dustin grunted, thinking about that possibility. But he didn't have time for that now. Instead, he shook out the yellowed tablecloth and covered the walnut.

When Dustin had promised Andrea a fine-dining experience, he'd pictured exactly this: the hand-embroidered tablecloth he remembered his mom creating over countless evenings watching TV together as a child and the Spode dishes that had graced every holiday dinner that Dustin could remember. Dustin thought that the best way he could show Andrea the depth of his love was by inviting her here, into the heart of his childhood home. But now that he surveyed the results, he felt nervous. Maybe he should have made reservations at the Western Cedar in Harper

Landing or someplace expensive like that. Andrea was probably expecting a restaurant experience, not a time warp. If only he'd had more time to plan this better. Dustin had spent all day at the jobsite, had raced home to shower, and was due to pick Andrea up in twenty minutes.

Dustin approached the oak cabinets and flinched. For a moment, when he spotted his reflection in the glass, he caught a glimpse of his father. That surprised him because Nathan was the one who took after Josh, both in height and hair color. All Dustin had gotten from his dad were Josh's green eyes. Dustin stared at his reflection, searching for what had brought the familiarity to mind. There it was, in the lines around his eyes and the way his jaw jutted out at the corner. Dustin had seen Josh wear that same determined expression.

It was too much for Dustin to handle right now. He looked away from the glass. But when he put his palm on the wood to open the door, he remembered Josh's tutelage that spring break when he was thirteen years old. "I prefer traditional hinges, not the European ones," his father had told him. "You've got to spend extra time getting the hardware installation right because these doors will open and close for years to come." It was advice Dustin adhered to every time he remodeled a kitchen.

He took a deep breath. So what if he'd missed out on a backpacking trip? His friends from middle school were long gone. If Dustin really wanted to, he could track them down and plan another vacation to the beach. But that week with his father . . . that was everything. He could never get that time back again.

Dustin opened the door all the way and breathed in the stale air that vaguely reminded him of Thanksgiving. He selected two plates, two teacups and saucers, and the smaller plates for bread that likely had a special name he couldn't remember. Then he laid out two place settings like his mom had taught him. Crystal had always taken pride in her wedding china and brought it out for important dinners. It didn't matter how tight their budget was; she could always make birthdays special by taking out her Spode. Like that summer when they were so broke. Every Sunday night they had eaten leftovers in the dining room instead of at the kitchen table.

If Dustin had time, he would go into the backyard and pick ferns for a centerpiece. That was one of the ways that Crystal had dressed things up too. The daffodils were up and would make a beautiful bouquet. But after glancing at his phone, Dustin knew he was out of time. He sent a quick text to Nathan. Are you sure you got this?

Don't worry, Nathan replied a minute later. I was first in my class at culinary school.

Thx. I owe you.

Duh.

Dustin grabbed his key and wallet and opened the front door. Then he shut it and ran back to the kitchen with daffodils on his brain. He couldn't show up empty handed. After taking the kitchen shears from the knife block, Dustin charged out to the backyard and hacked away at the daffodils growing underneath a big-leaf maple. When he had a decent-size bunch, he jogged back to the house, wrapped the stems in a damp paper towel, and flew out the door.

He couldn't believe how nervous he was. This was Andrea, after all, and he'd known her half his life. Longed for her half his life was more like it. She had been the unattainable gold standard for life partners. His dream prom date had grown into the woman who made him feel wistful every time he passed her blue house on the bay. Now he was preparing to bring her back to the Karlsson homestead.

Dustin had inherited his parents' house by default. At first, all of the Karlssons had lived there. But when Heidi had returned from college, she had rented a cottage with a friend and then eventually purchased her own house after Karlsson Construction had gotten off the ground. Nathan had stayed until Leanne had gone off to college, and

then he'd moved into the apartment above Port Pizza. Finally, it was only Dustin left.

He knew he should gut the place—he was in the business of restoration, after all—but he couldn't bear to change one thing, not even the furniture. Heidi complained about the sagging couch springs every time she visited, but when Dustin sat on the ancient microsuede, he remembered jumping up and down on the cushions when he was little. His dad's recliner, patched with duct tape, was a memorial to the hardest-working man he knew. Josh's and Crystal's fingerprints were all over the house, and Dustin wouldn't consider sanding them away. But now that he was minutes away from seeing what his house looked like through Andrea's eyes, he was nervous. She hadn't been there in eons, and yet almost nothing had changed.

The shirt and tie he wore worried him too. He was definitely overdressed for eating dinner in his own house, but Andrea had mentioned wearing heels, so he didn't want to show up in jeans. No, he wanted tonight to be spectacular. The problem was that he was woefully out of practice when it came to dating. It had been eighteen years since he'd gone out with a woman he had truly loved.

Dustin parked his truck in Andrea's driveway and walked up to her front porch with flowers in hand. He took a deep breath and lifted the hedgehog knocker. Damn, that thing was prickly. It was like he was holding a hedgehog's rear end. But at least it made a satisfying clank.

Andrea opened the door a few seconds later wearing a short blue dress the same color as her eyes and sparkly silver shoes. Dustin hadn't seen her bare legs since last summer when he'd sold her the house, and he marveled at how long they looked in high heels. "You're beautiful," he said as his eyes roamed over her from head to toe. "These are for you." He handed her the daffodils.

"Are these from your yard?"

Dustin nodded. "I didn't have the chance to go to the store."

"I love them." She gazed at them tenderly. "Let me put them in a vase, and I'll be ready to go. Would you like to come in?"

Jennifer Bardsley

Dustin looked down at his muddy shoes. "I'll wait here on the porch so I don't track dirt inside." As the person who had refinished her floors, he was in the habit of protecting them.

"I'll be fast." She darted away, and Dustin realized he'd missed his chance to kiss her hello.

Damn, he was out of practice. No wonder he kept screwing things up. When Andrea came back wearing a long black raincoat, he waited for her to shut the door and lock it behind her before taking his chance. "I'm excited for tonight," he admitted, staring into her blue eyes.

"Me too." She stepped closer.

Dustin closed his eyes and kissed her on instinct, his nervous anticipation disappearing now that she was near. Holding her in his arms was grounding, but feeling her lips give way to his tongue sent him shooting toward the sky. Joy flooded through him. Twilight had fallen, the stars were popping out one by one, and Dustin could feel Andrea's heartbeat against his in the moonlight. He wished he could turn that moment into eternity, but he knew he had a schedule to keep. "Come on," he said, taking her hand. "We better hurry, or we'll be late."

"For our reservations?"

"Something like that." Dustin held her hand, and they walked to his truck. When he opened her door, his eyes lingered on her legs as she climbed into the cab.

"So where are we going?" Andrea asked. "You're full of mystery."

"Am I?" Dustin adjusted the volume on the classical radio station he'd turned on. "I'm the same guy I always was."

"High school Dustin took me on picnics or to the BBQ Trough but never to a place with tablecloths."

Uh-oh . . . Dustin's nerves returned full force. Andrea was expecting a restaurant. He'd completely screwed up. Was it too late to board the ferry to Harper Landing? He quickly did the math. Yes, it was. By the time they sat down at Western Cedar, they'd be starving.

"Like I said, I haven't changed a bit." He turned away from the ferry and headed for home. "Picnics are still my favorite, but it's too cold for one tonight. I love barbecue, but not when I'm wearing a tie."

"I noticed your tie." She walked her fingers up his arm, making him quiver. "You look quite handsome."

"This is the only tie I own," he admitted. "Heidi insists I wear it whenever we meet with our finance guy."

"I can see why." She patted his leg. "You look like a *GQ* model."

He laughed. "You might not be so complimentary after you see where I'm taking you. But I guarantee the food will be five stars."

"You have me intrigued."

He picked up her hand and kissed her knuckles. "You've been intriguing me for decades."

"Messing with your head is more like it."

"That too." His shoulders tensed when he turned off the main road and drove up the long windy driveway that led to his house. It was dark, but surely she recognized where they were by now. He parked in front of his house and held his breath as he looked to see what her reaction would be. When he saw her smile, he relaxed. "I promised you a table-cloth, and I know the perfect one."

"Can't wait to see it." She scampered out of the truck before he'd opened his door. "I've only been here three times," she said as they walked up to the front porch. "The first was when Dad brought me to babysit Leanne while he spoke with you, Heidi, and Nathan."

"I remember that." Dustin stuck his key in the lock. "You and that suitcase full of Lincoln Logs."

"That's right. The other two times were when I visited Heidi before you and I started dating."

Dustin grinned. "I remember asking Heidi questions about the washing machine so I could check you out." He opened the door and waved her inside.

"You thought you were so sly," she said as she crossed the threshold. "But no teenage boy is that desperate to do laundry."

Dustin flicked on the light and revealed the ancient interior. "Um . . . I've been so busy remodeling other people's houses that I haven't gotten around to my own yet."

She walked across the threadbare carpet into the living room and spun around, her arms out wide. "It's perfect. What a time capsule."

"That's one way to put it." He walked to the dining room and lit the candles with a match.

"I love all the family portraits."

Dustin looked over his shoulder and saw her standing in front of the fireplace, staring at old family photos.

"My mom was obsessed with portrait studios," he explained. "Especially if she had a coupon."

"And what's this?" Andrea walked away from the mantel to the door leading to the backyard. On the wall next to it were lines and squiggles.

"Oh, that's nothing." Dustin raked his fingers through his hair. "It's silly, really. I should paint over it."

Andrea ran the tip of her index finger down the list of names and dates. "Is this a height chart?"

"Yeah." Dustin flicked on a light so she could see it better. "My mom made it. I don't know why she put it here where everyone could see it instead of the basement." Reading his mother's loopy happy handwriting made him smile. "Notice how she dotted the *i* with a heart on my name."

Andrea tapped her finger against one of the hearts. "No wonder you haven't repainted. It would be difficult to erase this history."

Dustin shrugged.

"Nobody ever tracked *my* growth on a wall like this. My mom only cares about how things look. She never even hung my school artwork or report cards up on the refrigerator because she said it ruined the aesthetic."

"Your home was beautiful. I always admired it."

Andrea grimaced. "It was a regular Pottery Barn catalog. My mom kept the house so clean that there was never a safe place to play, not even the playroom. If my dollhouse wasn't arranged just so, my mom would stay up late to fix it before she went to sleep."

"Maybe she was bored and needed something to do?"

"Why are you defending her?" Andrea stood.

"Labradoodles are loyal, I guess." Dustin placed his hands lightly on her arms. "Your mom not only fed me, but she showed me all the scrapbooks she'd made of your art classes over the years. What did she do again? Take a picture of each project and then glue them in her photo album? They were film pictures, too, not digital. She had to take them to be developed."

"Oh, well, yeah. That's true that she did that. But did you know she threw my artwork away after she took the pictures?"

"How much artwork would there be if she'd kept it all?"

Andrea looked sideways. "I don't know. A lot."

"My mom had to throw stuff away, too, because with four kids, there was a lot of it. I appreciate that your mom had a system, but I'm sorry it was at the expense of your feelings." He massaged her shoulders with a light touch. "Would you like a glass of wine?"

"I'd love one, thanks," she said, relaxing.

"Take a seat, and I'll be right back." But when he saw her move toward the decrepit couch, he touched her elbow and guided her to the dining room. "In here would be better."

"It's so pretty with the candles."

"They really 'class the joint up,' as my dad used to say."

There, his heart whispered. *Another memory about my father.* He hadn't even needed to dig to find this one. Josh's words had resurfaced on their own. The more Dustin talked about the past, the easier it was to remember things. He went into the kitchen and uncorked a bottle of wine, thinking about his dad's commentary about candles. Crystal had loved them, but candles had been a luxury they could rarely afford. She'd bring them out for holidays, though. Dustin could picture his dad's face in the candlelight, looking so much like Nathan's. "These really class the joint up," he'd say, with a twinkle in his eye.

When Dustin came back into the dining room holding two glasses of merlot, he found Andrea looking inside the oak cabinets. "Oops," she said, closing the glass door. "You caught me admiring the china."

"I've got nothing to hide." He grinned.

"No pirate treasure hidden somewhere?" she asked as she sat at the table.

"Nope." Dustin handed her a glass and sat beside her. "I'm boring. But I do have something special I wanted to show you." He pointed at the cross-stitch handiwork at the center of the tablecloth.

"What a cute squirrel," said Andrea. "Where'd you get this?"

"My mom made it. But forget the squirrel; look at that little guy over there." He directed her focus to a critter on the left.

Andrea squealed. "A hedgehog! Oh my goodness! Your mom made this?"

Dustin nodded. "She worked on it for months. I must have been in middle school at the time."

"I can't believe it! Did your mom like hedgehogs?"

"I have no idea. I think maybe this was from a kit. She was always searching the fabric store for kits on clearance. Embroidery, cross-stitch, needlepoint—anything but quilting because she said the corners were too hard."

"Wow. I had no idea you were so well versed in the fabric arts."

"I'm not." Dustin chuckled. "But I can tell the difference between stitches that make an X and ones that go all over the place. Unfortunately, this tablecloth has a tragic history that I feel compelled to tell you." *A history besides it being one of the few things Leanne remembers about our mother,* he thought with a pang of sadness.

"You know I love history. Do tell."

226

"Like I said, Mom worked on this pattern for months. She'd bring it out every night when we watched TV. But we only used it a few times because *someone*—I don't like to name names, but . . ." He coughed. "*Nathan* spilled cranberry sauce all over it on Thanksgiving." Dustin pointed out the red stain next to the brass candlesticks.

"That poor raccoon." Andrea shook her head. "He never had a chance."

"Nope, not with Nathan around. But I can't say anything too bad about Nathan because—" The doorbell rang, interrupting him. "Speak of the devil." Dustin stood. "I'll be right back."

"Who's here?"

"You'll see." Nathan had promised to deliver the food himself, not trusting one of the normal delivery guys to bring the extraordinary, not-on-the-Port-Pizza-menu creation he'd been cooking all day: beef Wellington and spring risotto, paired with a fresh spinach salad. But when Dustin opened the door, he saw his little sister holding a red pizza-delivery bag. Dustin's stomach clenched. What was Nathan up to? Was this his brother's way of interfering and trying to patch things up between him and Leanne?

"Hey," he said. "I'm surprised it's you. Come on inside where it's warm."

Leanne wore black jeans and an official Port Pizza hoodie. Her blonde hair was held back by a clip, and she wore gold stud earrings. "I can't believe I got suckered into this. I could be earning tips right now." She crossed the threshold and closed the door behind her.

"I'll give you a tip." Dustin took out his wallet.

"Don't bother," she said with an icy glare.

"I hope that's not pizza."

"I love pizza," said Andrea, entering the space. "Hi, Leanne. It's nice to see you again."

"Hi." Leanne unzipped the bag and pulled out three foil-covered dishes. "It's not pizza. Here's your beef Wellington, risotto, and salad."

"Yum." Andrea smiled. "Sounds fancy."

"It is." Leanne's expression thawed. "Nathan taught me how to make risotto once, and I've never cooked it again because it's a pain in the butt." She handed Dustin the containers. "I need to tell you something."

"What?" Dustin's brain went to high alert.

"Cade's on his way home." Leanne lifted her chin. "You were completely wrong about him. He loves me and the girls and wants to do right by us."

Dustin didn't know what to say. He looked quickly at Andrea to gauge what she was thinking, but she raised her eyebrows like she was shocked too. "What makes you think Cade's coming home?" Dustin asked, saying each word slowly and in as calm of a voice as possible.

"I don't *think* he's coming home; I *know* it," said Leanne. "He called me this morning and said he'd been knocked out and drugged during the robbery and then woke up in San Francisco."

"That's not—" Dustin started to argue, but Andrea caught his eye and shook her head.

"Setting aside the fact that he had no reason to be at my house, he also has a girlfriend," said Andrea. "A redhead named Lisa who lives in Port Angeles."

Leanne whipped her gaze to Andrea. "Since when is it a crime to have a friend of the opposite sex? They're acquaintances, nothing more."

"We have video of him in Northern California trying to sell Andrea's coins," said Dustin. "I'm sorry that's difficult to hear, but it's the truth."

"No, this is the truth." Leanne's expression was fierce. "Cade is driving home right now. He tried hitchhiking for a while, but that was slow going, so I sent him money to rent a car. He'll be here by morning."

"You sent him money?" Dustin felt sick to his stomach. The hurt from watching his baby sister be taken advantage of was making him physically ill.

"I thought he took money from your joint account?" Andrea asked.

"How do you know that?" Leanne scowled. "My personal finances are none of your business."

"They are her business when your husband robbed her," said Dustin. "And Andrea brought up a good point. Why would you need to send Cade money after he siphoned off everything in your joint account?"

"The robbers did that, not Cade." Leanne shook her head like she was arguing with a toddler. "Cade would never steal from me. Besides, it wouldn't have been stealing since both our names were on the account."

"How much did you send him?" Dustin asked.

"I need to go." Leanne reached into her pocket and took out her keys. "I'm on the clock at Port Pizza for two more hours."

"How much money did Cade get out of you?" Dustin asked again.

"Not that much." Leanne turned her back and began walking away.

"How much?" Dustin asked in a voice so low it was practically a growl.

She looked over her shoulder at him and chewed on her fingernail. "There was a ransom," she said. "He had to pay the kidnappers so they would let him go."

"I thought you said Cade was hitchhiking," said Dustin. "That implies that he was already free from his supposed kidnappers. Why would he need ransom money?"

"I don't know, okay? Maybe they were tracking him down or something. Cade didn't have time to explain. But sending him that money was worth it. He's my husband."

"Blood money," Dustin rasped out.

"What?" Leanne asked.

"You gave him blood money, from our parents' death."

"You're being dramatic." Leanne zipped up her hoodie. "I don't have to answer you."

"You don't want to tell me because he's made you feel ashamed," said Dustin. Anger crashed through him in waves. "How much did Cade get out of you this time?"

"All of it." Leanne squared her shoulders and looked him in the eye. "I made the transfer this morning, and now he's coming home."

"Leanne, you didn't," Dustin whispered.

"I did, and I regret nothing." She raced out the front door and slammed it shut behind her.

Dustin felt like he was trapped in a riptide of emotions that threatened to carry him out to sea. He leaned against the wall to steady himself and almost toppled the coatrack next to it. His raincoat fell to the ground, but he ignored it. "Tell me I misheard that," he begged.

Andrea shook her head sadly. "I wish I could." She wrapped her arms around him. "I'm sorry," she said, hugging him tight.

"Blood money," he whispered again. Dustin's eyes focused on the container of beef Wellington he held that he knew Nathan had carved time out of his busy day to prepare for him and Andrea. Steam seeped from the lid. "What do I do now? How can I help her listen to reason?"

"I don't know that you can. Leanne's a grown woman, and it's her money to do whatever she wants with."

"Was her money," said Dustin. "Now it belongs to Cade, who— let's face it—is never coming home, no matter what foolish lie Leanne clings to."

"But that doesn't mean we can't bring Cade to justice. Maybe now that he has ready access to cash, he'll be less likely to sell my coins."

"Or maybe he's already sold them."

"Don't say that. I'm not giving up, and you shouldn't either."

"No. You're right." Dustin filled his lungs to the bursting point and exhaled in a rush. "We need to stay positive." Leanne was broke. Cade was a cheat. The coins were still missing. But Andrea's arms were around him, and dinner smelled wonderful. He would concentrate on that.

CHAPTER SEVENTEEN

"I think you should call the PI," said Andrea, anger coursing through her. She sat at the dining room table next to the oak cabinets. How many times could Cade lie and get away with it? If he *did* come back to town, she sure as hell wanted him booked and charged. If Mack wouldn't do anything, Andrea would call the local news. Leanne's admission shocked her. It was as if the young woman had allowed love to kill her brain cells. Andrea knew that her own history didn't make her a love expert, but at least she had never lost her backbone. "Perhaps there's something the investigator can do with this new information."

"Good idea." Dustin reached for his phone but then put it back in his pocket. "Wait. Cade's caused enough trouble. I don't want him to ruin our dinner."

Andrea didn't want that either. She hadn't double-shaved her legs and shimmied into a tight dress for nothing. But when it came to recovering her coins, she knew this tip might be important. "Dinner won't be ruined. I can plate the food while you call the investigator." She stood. "I'll get a knife for the beef Wellington."

"Okay. Thanks. I'll be fast." Dustin tapped his phone.

Andrea walked away from the dining room and into the tiny kitchen. The oak cabinets were worn, and the tile countertops had dark grout that was chipped in places. Andrea gazed at Dustin's black refrigerator. It was littered with drawings from Kendal and Jane, plus pictures from the Little League team Karlsson Construction sponsored. In the upper corner, right where people could see it, was a family picture of Dustin, Nathan, Heidi, Leanne, and their parents. The whole family was suntanned, and Leanne squinted because she was the only one not wearing sunglasses. The edges of the photo curled up, and the paper had yellowed, but the picture held a place of honor on the fridge.

"Oh, Leanne," she whispered. "I wish you'd protect yourself. You're too good for a scumbag like Cade."

Andrea reached for the steelie in her pocket, but when her fingers hit the tight fabric along her hips, she realized it wasn't there. This dress didn't have pockets. The steel penny was in a plastic coin holder in her purse, back in the dining room. For the first time ever, Andrea had sympathy for Grandmother Wint turning those ten-dollar coins into a necklace. It might have been a crime against numismatics, but she wished she hadn't sold it and was wearing it tonight. Now, almost all her family treasures were gone. Her foolishness in thinking a safe would protect her father's precious memories had ruined everything.

No, not everything. Andrea scanned the refrigerator and landed on Dustin's picture. She was here, wasn't she? Banking on a second chance with the love of her life. Andrea selected a knife from the block on the counter, found salad tongs and a serving spoon in a drawer, and returned to the dining room.

"Thank you," Dustin was saying to the private investigator. "I hadn't thought of that."

Andrea served the salad first, still thinking about her father. Her betrayal of Tom was twofold. Not only had she lost his double eagles; she was also ignoring his advice all those years ago that she and Dustin were too intense for each other.

"Ashland, San Francisco, San Carlos, and then where?" Dustin asked over the phone. "Leanne thinks he's on his way home." Dustin's tone dripped with incredulity. "Yeah," he said. "That seems unlikely, but I'm glad you're on the road visiting those places in person so I don't have to."

Andrea removed the foil from the entrée and sliced the beef Wellington. She put a large helping onto Dustin's plate and a smaller portion on her own. Tom didn't know everything. As much as Andrea looked up to him, she knew he wasn't infallible. He'd lied to her mom about the price of that 1907, after all. That had been a scummy thing to do. So had telling Dustin that they should break up. Thinking on that now, Andrea realized she should be furious, except she couldn't be. Not with Tom living with Alzheimer's disease.

"Okay," said Dustin. "I'll tell her. That's a good idea."

After sitting down in her chair next to Dustin, Andrea put her napkin across her lap. Dinner smelled wonderful, but she wasn't thinking about food. The coins and her father's memories were both gone. Her relationship with her mother had fractured. What did she have to offer Dustin but a broken human being full of so much anguish that she missed the feeling of a steel penny in her hand?

"Thanks. I'll talk with you soon." Dustin hung up. "Sorry it took me longer than I'd thought."

"Don't apologize. It's okay."

"It's not okay. But—hey? What's the matter? You seem sad."

Andrea let out a deep breath, her posture slumping in a way that made the strapless bra she wore pinch her skin. "If my father hadn't told you back in high school that we were wrong for each other, if he hadn't stuck his nose into something that was none of his business, do you think we would have stayed together?"

"I don't know." Dustin sipped his wine. "You can't predict the future, and you can't rewrite the past."

"That's not an answer."

"I don't have answers. And Washington State was my dream school—or my dad's dream school for me, at least. I wouldn't have wanted to transfer to Central, even though it's a fine college."

"I know. But I might have transferred."

"Or I might have burned out the clutch in the Yo-Mobile driving back and forth to Ellensburg to visit you every weekend. I can't rewrite the past, but your dad was right about us being intense. I would have stuck with you until you were through with me."

Andrea stared into his green eyes. "I don't think I would have ever been through with you."

He picked up her hand and kissed it. "Then do me a favor, even though it's a big ask. Let's not think about Cade's cockamamie story about being kidnapped or Leanne's naivete for believing it. Ignore the fact that I just got off the phone with a private investigator or that a lot of awful things have happened to us over the years. Let's be two people sitting at a candlelit table eating off these fancy dishes. Stop thinking about what your dad thought about us, and consider what my mom would have wanted if she had been gifted with the opportunity to meet you."

"And what would that be?"

"She would have wanted to love you forever, just like me."

Andrea closed her eyes, and tears misted her lashes.

"No crying," Dustin murmured as he kissed them away. "Dinner's getting cold."

"You're right." Andrea squeezed his hand. "Let's eat." She breathed deeply. "Your brother has outdone himself. This smells incredible."

"Wait until you taste it. The salad should be good, too, but only if you like filberts."

"What are filberts?" Andrea looked at the salad. A bed of spinach was topped with dried cranberries, blue cheese, and roasted hazelnuts. "Oh," she said. "You mean hazelnuts."

Dustin chuckled. "City girl. You're in Port Inez now. Time to start speaking like the locals. We call them filberts here."

"Yay for filberts." Andrea popped one in her mouth and finished chewing. "Nuts are supposed to help prevent Alzheimer's. Leafy greens and berries too." She didn't know why she brought that up; it just slipped out.

"How about wine? Is that a preventative as well?" Dustin held up a bottle of merlot from Chateau Ste. Michelle.

Andrea nodded. "Red wine is on the list. There's an eating plan my dad's doctor recommended called the MIND diet. It's basically the Mediterranean plan but with more berries." She cut a small bite of beef Wellington. Red meat and pastry were *not* recommended on the plan, but she wouldn't worry about that now. No, Andrea intended to savor every morsel. "Oh my gosh," she moaned. "I didn't know meat could taste this good."

"Nathan used to work for Tom Douglas," said Dustin, naming one of the most famous chefs in Seattle. He topped off her wineglass. "But that was before our parents' accident."

"Well, he didn't overdo it with the paprika—that's for sure." Andrea waited for Dustin to refill his own glass and then proposed a toast. "To Nathan, for cooking this wonderful meal, and to Leanne, for inadvertently bringing us back together."

"And to Heidi, who would be the first to say that she's right about everything and, in this case, actually was."

"What do you mean?"

"She told me I needed to stop bottling up what I was feeling and share the truth about how much I loved you."

"I knew Heidi was my best friend for a reason. She's smart."

"She'd be the first to tell you that too." Dustin grinned. "Listen, I know I said we wouldn't talk about Cade again tonight, but before I forget, the PI had an idea to share with you. How about going at this from a different angle? Instead of letting every coin shop from here to Mexico know that you've been robbed, perhaps do the opposite. Set up an account where you pretend to be a buyer looking for a good deal on double eagles."

"Hmm . . . that would assume that Cade was online poking around coin forums. Do we think he's that sophisticated?"

"No, but maybe the coin dealers are. It would just take one unscrupulous person to connect you with Cade."

"It's worth a shot. I could set up a fake account. But you're right. We shouldn't let him ruin our night." Underneath the table, Andrea wiggled out of her high heels because her arches were cramping. Her bare toes sank into the shag carpet. She picked up a teacup and admired the Victorian pattern. "I can tell that family dinners were important to your mom," Andrea said, changing the subject. "She put a lot of care into this room."

"She did." Dustin held up his knife and frowned at the tarnish. "None of it's worth much—this is silver plated, not sterling—but it was valuable to her, and so it's valuable to me."

"It's strange how when people leave us, either in body or mind, their possessions remain just as normal as ever." A lump formed in Andrea's throat. She thought of the 1907 in her safe deposit box, as bright and shiny as the day her father had purchased it.

"Yeah, that's why I haven't gotten around to remodeling this place. I know parts of it are ugly, and all of it is outdated, but my mom picked out this carpet. My dad built these cabinets."

"It must be like living in a hug."

"Exactly."

Andrea traced the cross-stitched hedgehog with her fingertip. It was hard knowing that she would never meet Dustin's parents, but she felt like a little bit of Crystal's spirit was embroidered with every thread. "Can I tell you something that'll make me sound stupid?"

"You can tell me anything, and I'll never think it's dumb."

"I don't know about that." Andrea sipped from her wineglass and set it down carefully. "It's about home-renovation shows. I know viewers love them, but I hate the parts when the hosts say horrible things about how outdated the interiors are. Because you know what? At some point in time those houses were someone's dream home. There was a person, probably a woman, who picked out the pink bathroom tile or brick fireplace. You can acknowledge that something is old without making fun of it." Andrea was surprised at her own emotions as she said this.

"Pink tiles are usually from the 1950s. The color has a special name: Mamie Eisenhower pink. It was the First Lady's favorite color."

"That's right! I can't believe you know that. She used so much pink in the White House that reporters started calling it—"

"The Pink Palace," said Dustin before she could finish. "Fellow history lover here."

"Takes one to know one." Andrea leaned forward and kissed him. She felt a buzz when their lips touched, like she was an Edison light bulb illuminating shadows. Dustin's hand cupped the back of her head and kept her steady as they banished darkness together. When they pulled apart, her pulse raced.

"My whole career is built on respecting the past," said Dustin in a husky voice. "I know exactly what you mean about how much it hurts when people ridicule old homes."

"You do?"

He nodded. "I always try to remain true to the original architecture and blend modern amenities with what the house wants. Like your house, for example, had those bay windows in the dining room that cried out for window seats."

"I bet they did."

"And the upstairs bathroom needed a skylight to counter gray days."

"Now it's flooded with light."

"But can I ask you a question without you being offended?"

"That depends on the question." Andrea tilted her head to the side, feeling intrigued. "Go for it."

"I was surprised that you haven't filled your house with antiques. I thought for sure you'd outfit it with old relics."

"I thought about it, and I do have a few pieces, but most of my furniture is from IKEA. Otherwise I get too attached to things, and they become difficult to get rid of. I'm still mad at my mom for selling my dad's desk."

"Ouch. That must have stung."

"It did. It was a rolltop too. When I asked her why she didn't offer it to me first, she said I wouldn't have had room in my condo."

"Would you have had room?"

"I would have made room. Even if I had to put it smack in the middle of my living room, I would have found the space."

"Maybe that's why she didn't tell you about it."

"Huh?" Andrea asked.

"Because she knew you would have felt obligated to—"

"Not obligated. I would have wanted it."

"Wanted, then. You would have wanted something that would have made your life difficult."

"Maybe . . . ," she admitted. "It would have been difficult in my condo in Seattle, but my house in Port Inez has plenty of room. My mom doesn't care, though. As soon as she met Roger, she got rid of everything that belonged to my dad, even though he's still alive." Andrea burned with indignation as she remembered her mother packing up Tom's Brooks Brothers suits for donation.

"That must hurt." Dustin rubbed her back.

Andrea nodded. "All she cares about is erasing the past and moving forward with Roger. She's unfeeling."

"Your mom must have changed a lot, because that's not the Lydia I remember."

"You're a well-fed labradoodle. You have to say that."

"It wasn't just food. She made me feel welcome every time I came over. She set a place for me at the dinner table just in case I could stay the evening. Hell, she even bought a spare charging cord for my flip phone so that I could recharge the battery before driving home."

"That was my mom being a good hostess. I never said she wasn't good at entertaining."

Dustin leaned back in his chair. "There's entertaining, and then there's sending an orphaned teenage boy home with frozen casseroles to feed his siblings. Your mom did that, too, multiple times."

"Don't think you're special," said Andrea. "I mean to my *mom*. Of course you were special to *me*." She didn't care if she hurt her mother's image by saying this. "My mom was the queen of frozen casseroles. Meal trains were her hobby."

"What's a meal train?"

"You know, like, when someone has a new baby and everyone in the neighborhood brings them meals. I'd come home with news that a classmate's dad had colon cancer, and my mom would immediately start making lasagna, even if she didn't know them."

"And you think she's unfeeling?" Dustin scratched his head. "I've never brought food to a stranger."

"Yeah, well, you're not my mom. She loves to cook. When I came home from college on winter break one year, she signed us up for a bunch of cooking classes together without asking. It was a global-cuisines course for two whole weeks when all I wanted to do was relax."

"But now you can cook," said Dustin. "I mean, I'm assuming. I won't taste anything you make in the future without double-checking the spice drawer."

"Very funny." Andrea rolled her eyes. "Yes, I can cook." She loaded the last bite of beef Wellington onto her fork but didn't eat it. "I could probably even manage a fancy meal like this if I practiced. That doesn't mean I can forgive my mom for turning her back on my dad." Andrea fought unbidden tears. "She shipped him off to the Owl's Nest and never looked back. She'll write checks and sign medical forms, but that's it."

"That's difficult to comprehend. I'm sorry."

Andrea let out a deep breath. "It feels like as soon as he couldn't fit into her storybook-perfect world, she cut him out of the picture. Me, too, because a thirty-six-year-old daughter with a string of failed relationships isn't something she can brag about to her friends."

Dustin locked eyes with her. "There is plenty to brag about when it comes to you. I might even have to recover my long-lost Facebook account password to do just that. You own your own business. You care for your father. You're well read. And—" Dustin's gaze roamed over her. "I don't mean to sound shallow, but you look smokin' hot in that dress."

"Smokin' hot, huh?"

"Damn right. The only way you could be hotter is if we rolled you in spicy paprika."

She laughed. Dustin's warm praise was the confidence boost she needed.

"I forgot to add courageous," he continued. "It's not everyone who could pack up and move to a new place like you did, especially to a small town like Port Inez that's so different from Seattle."

"I feel like I stick out," Andrea admitted. "Every time I go to the IGA to pick up groceries, the cashier looks at me weird for bringing my own bags."

"Which cashier?"

"Gwendolyn. The one with the rose tattoo on her forearm."

"Gwen looks at me weird when I *don't* bring reusable bags. Plus she gives me a lecture on how plastic bags are bad for sea life."

"So what's her problem with me, then?"

Dustin shrugged. "Probably because you're new to town. Or . . ." He looked down at his plate and scraped the gravy.

"Or what?"

"Or it could be because Gwen and I went to homecoming together our junior year."

"She's *that* Gwen? As in Gwennifer?"

"Yeah. She changes her name about every five years. In elementary school she went by Gwennie."

Andrea was shocked. It had never occurred to her that she might be shopping with Dustin's old girlfriend. "How long did you go out? I'm not sure you ever told me."

"For three months, and it was a long time ago. But . . ."

"But what?"

He loosened his tie. "Well, it's about the Yo-Mobile."

"Uh-huh." Andrea didn't like where this was going. She couldn't believe how jealous she felt knowing that Dustin might have driven someone else around in his old truck besides her.

"I don't have proof, but I think it might have been Gwen who painted off the other letters."

"Why would she do that?"

"Because she thought it would be funny, and I always said no. My truck wasn't new, but it was new to me, and I wanted to keep it in as pristine a condition as possible. But then a couple of weeks after homecoming, we broke up. The next morning when I went out to the driveway, I saw that the *T*, *O*, *T*, and *A* were gone."

"At least she matched the paint pretty well," said Andrea.

"Yeah." Dustin chuckled. "At least there's that."

"So are there any other ex-girlfriends wandering around Port Inez that I should know about?"

"No." He flushed. "I told you I haven't dated much."

"Oh, come on. There's having a long-term relationship, and then there's dating someone a few times. You haven't gone out with anyone in the decade since you and your old girlfriend Samantha broke up?"

Dustin scratched the back of his neck. "Well, I have gone out a few times. I went on a double date with Heidi, Mack, and the hostess at the BBQ Trough a couple of times, but we didn't have anything in common beyond a mutual love of smoked pork."

Andrea made a mental note to avoid the BBQ Trough in the future. "Anyone else?"

"The children's librarian, Vivian, who is actually really great, and you two would probably get along well—only she was hung up on her old boyfriend." Dustin slung his elbow over the back of his chair and smiled. "Which I immediately recognized since I was hung up on you."

"Keep going. I want to know all of your ex-girlfriends to avoid."

"But not Vivian, because you two could be friends."

"Maybe . . ."

"Are you jealous?"

"No!"

Dustin grinned, and a look of pure satisfaction crossed his face. "You *are*. And it's adorable."

"There's nothing about this that's adorable," said Andrea in a prim tone.

"Speaking of adorable, Kendal's first-grade teacher asked me out on Sunday, and I said no."

"Of course she asked you out." Andrea's hand slapped the table. "You're the perfect package! Handsome, unmarried men who like kids are a rare find."

"You think I'm handsome?"

"Of course I think you're handsome."

"On a scale from one to ten, how handsome do you think I am?"

"Why, Dustin Karlsson, are you fishing for compliments?"

"Maybe," he said with a boyish smirk. He leaned forward. "Or maybe I'm just rusty at flirting . . . among other things."

"Other things like . . . ?" She tilted her head.

Dustin took her hand in his and kissed her fingertips. "I can think of quite a few things I'm rusty at, actually." His lips traced up her bare arm, one kiss after another. He paused, right above her elbow.

"I look forward to freshening up your skills with you," Andrea whispered in his ear. He turned toward her, and their lips met with a yearning that took her breath away. "You don't seem rusty to me," she said when they parted.

"That's because you're a good teacher and—" His phone interrupted him. "Sorry." Dustin fumbled with the screen. "I'll turn it off." He hung it up. "That's—"

But then Andrea's phone rang too. "Uh-oh." She dove for her purse, fearful that it might be the Owl's Nest calling. If her father got a second strike . . . thankfully it wasn't the memory-care unit; it was Heidi.

"Andrea," her best friend said in a tense voice. "I'm so glad you answered. Is Dustin there?"

"Yes, he's here, but can it—"

"I've got a disaster on my hands!" Heidi shrieked.

"Oh no. Hang on." Andrea handed Dustin the phone. "It's your sister."

"Now?" Dustin grimaced. "Hi, Heidi. What's the matter?"

"The toilet!" Heidi shouted, loud enough that Andrea could hear. "It's overflowing and broken, and oh my gosh, Dustin, you have to come. I can't handle another crisis!"

"And you think I can?" Dustin brushed hair off his forehead. "I mean, of course I can. You're not in this alone. Did you turn off the water?"

"I did, but it's too late." Heidi sounded frantic. "You know Leanne only has the one bathroom. I've got to put the girls to bed, and there's water flowing down the stairs. No, Jane! Don't splash in it!"

"Oh jeez." Dustin rested his elbow on the table and sighed heavily. "I'll be right over." He hung up and gave the phone back to Andrea. "I am *so* sorry."

"Are you a plumber? Why not call a plumber?" As soon as she said it, Andrea realized the answer. An after-business-hours call like that would probably be expensive, and Leanne had given all her money to Cade. "Never mind," she said. "Let's go see if we can help." She shoveled the last bite of beef Wellington in her mouth and gulped down her wine.

"Easy there, killer. No need to choke."

"Sorry." Andrea sensed her cheeks turning red.

Dustin chuckled. "I appreciate your enthusiasm for wanting to help, but if Kendal and Jane have to pee in the woods until we get there, it'll be natural consequences. This isn't the first time they've clogged the toilet."

"It's not?" Andrea didn't have much experience with children beyond babysitting in high school, but she wondered how much damage two little girls could do.

"Nope." Dustin scooped hazelnuts and dried cranberries onto his fork. "Two Decembers ago Kendal flushed all of the lip balm Santa had left her down the toilet. It took me four hours to fish out. Then last summer, Jane stuck a broken CD down the pipes."

"Where'd she get a CD?"

"From the library." Dustin shook his head. "I wasn't able to retrieve it, and we ended up replacing the entire toilet because it was wedged in there so tight."

"Whoa!"

"Whoa is right." He folded his napkin and dropped it on the table-cloth. "I'm sorry to end our dinner like this, but it's true what Heidi said about them only having one bathroom." He hung his head dejectedly. "This wasn't how I wanted this night to go."

"Me either." Andrea slid her shoes on and stood. The three-inch heels put her lips closer in line with Dustin's. "I liked where it was headed too." She slid her hands over his shoulders and kissed him.

Dustin wrapped his arms around her and held her tight. "You are everything I dreamed about and more." He closed his eyes and pressed his forehead to hers. "Thank you for being so understanding."

She sighed. "We'll have lots more nights like tonight, won't we?"

"You mean when my circus of a family ruins our plans? Probably."

"No, I meant . . ."

"Yes." Dustin nodded. "A lifetime."

As they left the house, Andrea glanced over her shoulder when they passed the kitchen and looked at the cluttered refrigerator one more time. Someday her picture would be on that fridge, or one just like it, and Dustin would be in the photograph, smiling beside her.

CHAPTER EIGHTEEN

It had been forty-five hours and eleven minutes since he'd last seen Andrea. Every nerve in his body reached for her, like they were two magnets pulled far apart. Their interrupted date two nights ago still aggravated him. But the biggest stress weighing on Dustin was Leanne. She hadn't uttered a peep since Tuesday night when she had told him that Cade was on his way home. There was still no sign of Cade, even though the drive from California would have taken only fourteen hours. Dustin worried about his sister getting her heart broken and her bank account drained. He'd called the private investigator this afternoon, but Kelly hadn't turned up anything new, even after driving all the way to San Carlos to speak to the owner of the Coin Market in person. The Google alert Dustin had set up on his phone for "Cade Tolbert Kidnapping" hadn't unearthed clues either. Dustin didn't think there was a chance in hell that Cade's ransom-note story was true, but he'd set that alert up just in case.

Now it was late Thursday afternoon, and his week was about to get a whole bunch better. He parked a few blocks up the street from the ferry terminal. Any second now Andrea would walk off the ferry after her evening visit to the Owl's Nest, and he intended to surprise her. He hadn't seen her since he'd dropped her off at her house Tuesday night before heading off to discover that Kendal had flushed her report card and homework folder down the toilet. "It wasn't a report card," she had told him and Heidi with tears streaming down her face. "It was a progress report." Dustin still didn't know what could be so bad about a first grader's progress report that would warrant deploying a toilet auger, but that was Leanne's problem, not his, and Leanne still wasn't speaking to him.

When Dustin parted with Andrea, the plan had been to see her the next day. Breakfast, lunch, dinner—Dustin hadn't been specific, but he'd assumed they'd share a meal at the very least and hopefully something more. His arms ached to hold her. His lips yearned to feel hers pressed against them. But more than that, Dustin wanted to simply be. Be next to her. Be with her. Be in her presence and feel the peacefulness of her nearness wash over him and settle his soul.

But yesterday at the jobsite, right when he'd thought he could sneak away and visit Andrea for a cup of coffee, the insurance company had called about Leanne and Cade's rental. The moisture mitigators were on site examining the flooded hallway carpet next to the bathroom. Should they replace it or just dry it out and hopefully get another two years out of the carpet? Dustin had gone over there to inspect the damage himself and decided that installing brand-new laminate was the best choice. He'd been about to leave to see Andrea for dinner when she'd called with a work crisis of her own. The advertising campaign she'd designed for a private school in Seattle needed to be overhauled before it went to the printers. They wouldn't be able to see each other until Thursday.

Tonight his plan was KISS: Keep It Simple, Stupid. Not that Andrea was stupid, obviously. She was one of the smartest women he knew. After an easy meal at Port Pizza, he would suggest they head back to his place and watch the new Ken Burns documentary. Andrea wouldn't be able to resist Ken Burns. She had a PBS bumper sticker on her Leaf. When Dustin pictured Andrea snuggled up next to him on the couch, a fire in the hearth and grainy archival photos flashing across the television, his heart raced. It would be just like high school, only this time there would be nobody to interrupt them when snuggles turned into scorching-hot kisses.

Cars were streaming out of the ferry now, and Dustin spied a tiny train of people walking off the top deck. Finally, he saw her slim figure and golden-brown curls—she was walking up the hill with her head bent down. She held something in her hands, and he couldn't tell what it was for a minute, until she came closer, and he saw that it was a book. Andrea was so engrossed by what she was reading that she didn't see him, even after he'd stepped out to the curb and waved. "Hey, good looking," he called. "What are you reading?"

She snapped her head up, startled at first, but then a smile warmed her face as they locked eyes. "*Boys in the Boat*," she said, waving the paperback. "What are you doing here?"

"Picking you up." Dustin crossed the sidewalk and swooped her up in his arms, spinning her around in a circle.

She laughed. "Literally or figuratively?"

"Hopefully both." He set Andrea on her feet and kissed her. Her hair smelled like sunshine, and her lips were as soft as the petals of the wild roses growing next to the sidewalk. "Did you miss me?" he asked.

"Like you wouldn't believe," she said, entwining her arms around him.

Feeling Andrea's heartbeat next to his own steadied him. That dysregulated feeling he'd had just a while earlier disappeared. He stroked her hair, his fingers lost in her tresses. He slid his palms down her back and held her firmly by the waist. Her lips parted, and his tongue explored her mouth, hungry for the taste of her. It wasn't until a passing motorist honked that Dustin remembered where they were—on the sidewalk of the main road out of town. The entire ferry load of cars from Harper Landing was driving past them, witnessing their extremely public display of affection. The sooner it was just Andrea, Ken Burns, and him, the better.

"I guess this means you missed me too," Andrea teased.

"Desperately."

"Desperately? You've never struck me as being desperate."

He growled and nibbled at her earlobe. "I'm starving for you and not ashamed to admit it."

"Look at you, freely sharing your emotions." Andrea raced her fingers up his arm. "I'm impressed. Want to come to my house, and I'll make you dinner?"

"Sounds delicious." Dustin's plans were already regrouping. The Ken Burns DVD sitting on his coffee table would have been great, but there were some interesting history documentaries streaming on Netflix too. They would be the perfect excuse to stretch out on the couch next to Andrea, hopefully with the lights dimmed low.

"No paprika," she said. "I promise."

He opened the door to his truck, and she climbed inside.

"How was your dad?" he asked once he was behind the steering wheel.

"Exhausted from a field trip. They drove to a diner in Skagiton today."

"Is that safe?" Dustin turned on the blinker, preparing to merge into the road. Right now it was flooded with traffic unloading from the ferry. "I mean, is it not too confusing for them?"

"Not everyone gets to go." Andrea turned on the seat warmers. "Only the verbal residents. When they get to Skagiton, Carol's Diner is reserved just for them. Dad said he ate meatloaf and apple pie. I wasn't sure if that was true or not, but I checked with a caregiver, and she said yes, that's what was on the menu."

"That's good that he gets out."

Andrea nodded. "Yes. I used to try to take him places on my own, but it's too hard now. I can't send him into public restrooms by himself, and I can't accompany him to the men's room."

"That's something I could help with if you ever wanted to take him someplace."

"Really?" Andrea's blue eyes sparkled like sapphires. "You would do that for me?"

"I'd do it for you and for him." The traffic slowed, and Dustin merged onto the road. When his phone rang, Bluetooth picked up the call on his stereo.

"Hey, Dustin, it's me," said Nathan.

"Hi, Nate. Can I call you back later?"

"Sure, but I don't really need a callback; I just need you to stop by the Pizza Parlor and drop off the booster seats. Hopefully in the next hour. Leanne and the girls are going to stay with me at my apartment for a few days since the dehumidifiers are making so much noise. Kendal and Jane are here already."

"Sorry about that. The moisture mitigators have to dry out the floorboards before I can put down the new laminate." Dustin hated laminate, but it seemed like a more durable option than laying down new carpet in a home with small children.

"I understand. Leanne and the girls can take my room, and I'll sleep on the couch. This way it'll be easier for Leanne to pick up hours after they go to bed. Since they'll just be upstairs, I can keep tabs on them with a baby monitor while they sleep."

"Where'd you get a baby monitor?" Dustin asked.

"Um . . . it was Mary's idea."

"From the casino?" Andrea blurted. She covered her mouth with her hands a second later.

"Is someone in the truck with you?" Nathan asked.

"Yeah. Andrea is here." Dustin pulled into a parking space. "Look, we just arrived. I'll see you with the boosters in two minutes."

"Sounds good." Nathan hung up.

"Sorry about this," said Dustin.

"No worries."

"I'll be fast."

"I'll come with you." Andrea unbuckled her seat belt.

"You don't have to do that. I can carry both boosters myself."

"I know you can, but I feel like I should put in an appearance and say hi to Nathan in person so he doesn't think I was intentionally eavesdropping."

"Nathan knows that." Dustin opened the back door and grabbed both booster seats. "He always gives people the benefit of the doubt."

"I know he does." Andrea stuffed her hands in her pockets. "But I also want to officially meet these famous nieces of yours. I've only seen them that one time at the Owl's Nest, and I've never been properly introduced."

"Oh." Dustin grinned. "In that case, brace yourself. They're the two sweetest—and sometimes naughtiest—girls in all of Washington State."

Andrea opened the door for him, and the rich scent of oregano and simmering marinara sauce greeted them. A line had formed in front of the hostess station, and people waiting to be seated lounged on the leatherette banquette seating by the front door that Heidi had designed herself.

"Follow me," Dustin told Andrea as he sidestepped the crowd and walked past the hostess, straight to the back, where the kitchen was located. They entered the kitchen and kept going to the end of the room, where a scratched wooden table stood behind the wood-burning pizza oven. The table was out of the way from the hustle and bustle of the workers yet in a position of full visibility. Kendal sat at one end, nibbling her fingernails and staring at a worksheet in front of her. Jane was at the other, gluing dried macaroni to purple construction paper.

"As I was saying," Dustin said, wearing a huge smile. "Here are the two sweetest girls in Washington State. Andrea, please meet my nieces, Kendal and Jane Tolbert." He set the boosters on the empty bench seat.

"Hi, girls." Andrea waved. "I've heard so much about you."

Jane looked up from her art project and smiled. "I like the flowers on your raincoat."

"Thank you." Andrea knelt down so she was eye level with Jane. "What are you working on?"

"The *ur* sound." Jane held up the paper so Andrea and Dustin could see. The letter *u* was completely formed with macaroni, and the *r* was halfway done. "*Ur* like *purple*," Jane explained. "That's why it's purple paper." She chewed on her bottom lip and stared at Andrea's floral-print raincoat. "The *ur* sound is in flowers too. Right?"

"The flour in pizza but not the flowers in gardens." Andrea shrugged. "It's confusing. The flowers on my raincoat are spelled with an e-r."

"Duh," said Kendal. "Everyone knows that."

"Be nice to your sister," Dustin said in a warning tone.

"I wasn't talking to her." Kendal folded her arms across her chest. "I was talking to your girlfriend, who thinks she's so good at spelling." The hate radiating from Kendal's stare was entirely directed at Andrea and so hot it could have lit the pizza oven.

"That was rude," Dustin sputtered. He didn't know what to do. Kendal was always well mannered. Jane, not so much. Jane could get into trouble faster than you could ask, *Does it smell like nail polish?* Kendal, on the other hand, was dependable unless she was really out of sorts. The only time Dustin had ever witnessed her throw a tantrum was when she had stayed up too late on Halloween and had been a total crab the next morning.

"What are you working on?" Andrea asked, still smiling bravely against the scorch of Kendal's glare.

"The box method, not that it's any of your business."

"For subtraction or multiplication?" Andrea asked.

"Subtraction."

"I love the box method for subtraction. It's my favorite party trick." Andrea sat on the remaining bench and scooted closer to Kendal.

"Really?" Kendal asked. "My mom and Aunt Heidi and Uncle Dustin don't know what it is."

"Maybe they don't know as many cool party tricks as I do." Andrea inched a little bit closer and looked down at Kendal's paper.

"Ms. Nguyen said it's not a trick; it's just another strategy for solving equations that good mathematicians should know."

"She sounds like a wise person. Your teacher is right, and I shouldn't have called it a trick."

"Ms. Nguyen is always right," said Kendal. "And she would have made a much better girlfriend than you."

Aha. "Okay, Kendal, that's enough." Dustin didn't like to reprimand the girls. It wasn't his place. He preferred his role as Mr. Fun. But he couldn't allow Kendal to be rude to Andrea just because he'd chosen Andrea over Donna. "Is this how you'd like me to treat your friends?" he asked her. "By being rude to them?"

Kendal scowled. "I'm not being rude; I'm telling the truth."

"There you are." Nathan dashed through the entrance to the kitchen and rushed over to them. "Sorry about that. I had an unhappy customer to deal with. They insisted that the Genoa sausage was actually overpriced pepperoni. How's your math homework coming, Kendal?"

Kendal's face turned beet red. "Horrible," she whispered. A few seconds later, she burst into tears. "And I got a one on my progress report for math."

"What's a one mean?" Dustin asked.

Nathan shrugged. "No idea."

"It means *emerging.*" Andrea unzipped her purse and took out a package of tissues. She offered one to Kendal. "There's nothing wrong with being an emerging learner, but I can help you with your homework if you want. Would you like to work on the box method together?"

Kendal looked at Andrea suspiciously before taking the tissue and honking her nose. "Sure," she muttered. "Thanks."

"You know what the box method is?" Dustin asked.

"Yeah," said Andrea.

"How?"

"I donated some graphic design work to an auction for the MoPop a few years ago, and the winning bid was a PTA president from Capitol Hill." Andrea put away the tissue package and took out a pen from her purse. "My assignment was to put together a resource guide explaining the new math methods to parents because they were so confused." Andrea closed the gap between her and Kendal and tapped on the paper. "You did a great job drawing the box. Now, instead of saying four hundreds and zero tens, we'll say that the box is forty. What comes next?"

"Um . . ." Kendal stared at the paper. "Can I cross out the forty and make it a thirty-nine?"

"Yes." Andrea nodded. "That's right. Then you take that one—which is really a ten—and give it to the three in the ones place, making thirteen."

"And thirteen take away four is . . ." Kendal squeezed her eyes shut and wiggled her fingers. "Eight?"

"That's close," Andrea said in a patient voice. "Try again. We can draw a picture if you want."

"It looks like you've got this covered," said Nathan. "Dustin? Could I talk to you a sec?"

"Sure, but we weren't intending to stay. This was supposed to be a quick pit stop. Andrea's cooking me dinner."

Nathan slapped Dustin on the back. "I'll feed you. You know that. Salad and pizza are already coming for the girls; I'll have them add extra." Nathan grabbed his elbow and pulled him away but not before Dustin heard Jane say to Andrea, "Will you help me next? I've got glue in my hair." He shot Andrea an apologetic look, but she was so focused on the girls that she didn't notice.

Nathan opened the back door and pushed Dustin out into the cold. "Look," Nathan said, shutting the door behind them, "I didn't want to say anything in front of Kendal and Jane, but Leanne's really messed up.

There was no customer emergency with pepperoni. I was upstairs in my apartment checking on Leanne. She's crying her eyes out."

"Do you think she's finally realized the truth about Cade?"

"I think she's starting to. She told Jane this morning that her dad would be home soon. But when Kendal asked if he would be here in time for dinner, Leanne said she didn't know."

"If she had a definitive time frame, she would have told them."

Nathan nodded. "That's what I thought too. And then Jane offered her a bag of apples to make her feel better, and Leanne freaked out."

"Over apples?" Dustin leaned against the building. "Why?"

"Because Jane stole them."

"What?" Dustin stood straight.

"From school." Nathan covered his face for a moment before dropping his hand. "Apparently the teacher emailed all the parents last night. The kids were only supposed to take home three apples, but a whole bag went missing, and nobody knew who had taken it. So when Leanne saw the apples, she realized that Jane was the thief."

"Just like her father." Dustin rubbed his jawline.

"Yeah, exactly. Jane's such a charmer that nobody realized she had stuffed it in her backpack."

"What did Leanne do about that?"

"I'm not sure. But she took the bag of apples with her when she drove the girls to school, so I'm hoping she dealt with it."

"Good," said Dustin. "At least there's that. Was Leanne supposed to work today?"

"The afternoon shift and the evening shift." Nathan gripped his forehead. "That's part of why it's such a mess up front. I had to send one of my waiters out on delivery since Leanne bailed on me."

"Sorry, bud, but I'm not delivering pizzas. If that's what this is about, the answer is no."

"I wouldn't ask you to." Nathan chuckled. "I imagine you and Andrea have better things to do tonight than drive in circles for tips."

"I certainly hope so."

"But you should stay for dinner. Kendal really does need help with math. I think that's why she flushed her progress report down the toilet. It seems like Andrea might be the only one who can figure this stuff out."

"She's a math hero, all right." Dustin hitched his thumb in his pocket. "Do you think Leanne will ever get her money back?"

"I don't know. I talked to a friend of a friend who's a divorce lawyer, and she said that Leanne's settlement money would have originally been considered separate property, but once she put it in the joint account, which they use to pay bills, Cade has a legal right to spend it. If they divorce, he'll have a claim to half of it."

"*If* the money is still there," Dustin said, unable to keep the ominous tone from his voice. "But if there *is* money left, Leanne might be able to get half of it back. The sooner we can get her to consult a divorce attorney and freeze their assets, the better. Has Leanne let you look at her bank balance?"

Nathan shook his head and opened the back door to the pizzeria kitchen. "No, but there's nothing we can do about that now. Let's go have dinner."

Dustin followed Nathan inside. "Okay, maybe. I'm not sure Andrea wants to stay. Kendal and Jane might have scared her away by now." But when he paused at the doorway for a moment, watching her interact with the girls, Dustin was pleased to see that Andrea was laughing. Jane stood on her chair and wiggled, dancing to an unknown tune. Kendal was smiling, too, bent over her paper and looking up at Andrea for affirmation every few seconds. Andrea somehow managed to keep tabs on both of them, answering Kendal's questions while at the same time admiring Jane's dance moves.

"Order's up, boss," someone called from the pizza oven.

"Thanks," said Nathan. "Go take a seat," he told Dustin. "Heidi should be here soon, too, and Leanne promised me she'd come downstairs for dinner."

Ten minutes later his entire family, including Leanne, was squeezed around the table, passing the salad dressing and extra napkins. The dark circles under Leanne's eyes were so pronounced that they looked like bruises, but she was no longer crying. Instead, she wore a steely expression like the next words out of her mouth would be sharp. Kendal and Jane flanked her, cozied up to their mom as close as they could sit. When Leanne didn't help herself to pizza, Kendal put a slice of it on her plate. Small talk around the table was forced as everyone tried to avoid the elephant in the room: Cade wasn't there.

"So then," Heidi said, continuing the story of how she had sweet-talked the code enforcement office into giving them an earlier appointment for the electrical inspection, "I asked the scheduler where she went to high school because her name reminded me of someone I knew at Port Inez High."

"Did it?" Andrea asked. "Or were you bluffing?"

"I was totally bluffing. Her name was Jennifer. There are, like, a gazillion Jennifers out there. Talk about a common name. How was I supposed to remember her? Anyhow, Jennifer says yes, she did graduate from Port Inez High School, and was I perhaps related to Nathan Karlsson?"

"Wait." Nathan looked up. "What do I have to do with this?"

Heidi helped herself to another slice of pizza. "Jennifer Leary. Do you remember her? She certainly seemed to remember you."

"No." Nathan shrugged. "Her name doesn't ring a bell."

"Are you sure? Jennifer went on and on about senior year's honors English class and how she knew you'd be a chef after you brought home-made pretzels to the holiday buffet."

"Oh." Nathan's forehead crinkled. "*That* Jennifer. I remember the pretzels, but I barely remember her."

"The pretzels, on the other hand . . ." Dustin elbowed Nathan in the ribs. "Those were unforgettable. Why don't you make them anymore?"

"With the Gouda cheese sauce." Heidi licked her lips. "That was the best part." She looked at Leanne. "You remember them too, right?"

Leanne stared back blankly. "No. I don't."

"You were two or three," said Dustin. "It would be weird if you did remember."

"Mom got so mad at me," said Nathan. "I burnt the sauce in her favorite pot, and the whole house stunk right as the day care parents arrived to pick up their kids. She was really embarrassed." He chuckled. "She didn't punish me because it was an honest mistake, but I spent over an hour scrubbing the bottom of the pot with a Brillo pad."

Heidi clapped. "Good job."

"Good job for washing a pot?" Nathan asked.

"No, doofus. Good job for sharing a story about Mom." Heidi looked over to Kendal and Jane. "Grandma Crystal had a day care at what's now Uncle Dustin's house. Did you know that?" The girls shook their heads, and Heidi continued. "Our basement was full of toys, and there were even cots she'd drag out for nap time. Kids loved her."

"They sure did," Dustin added. "She sewed cushions for them to sit on during circle time. Our whole downstairs smelled like graham crackers and applesauce because that's what she served for snack."

"That's not all she served for snack," said Nathan. "She'd also make ants on a log with peanut butter and celery sticks."

"Peanut butter?" Kendal slapped her hand on the table. "That's dangerous."

"It wasn't dangerous," said Dustin, coming to his mom's defense.

"What if someone was allergic?" Kendal asked.

"Oh." Dustin dabbed grease off his pizza. "Well, times were different back then. There weren't so many kids with food allergies."

"That was true in Seattle too," said Andrea. "I only knew one boy growing up who was allergic to peanuts, and he was the brother of a friend in my Girl Scout troop."

"Yeah," said Heidi. "This was a long time ago. Grandma Crystal took really good care of her day care kids, I promise."

"That's right; she did." Dustin knew that Kendal and Jane learning about their grandma was important. "Grandma was so patient that she reminded me of the mom from that TV show with the bald toddler. What was it called?" He looked at Leanne since she was the one who had watched it when she was little.

"*Caillou*?" she supplied.

"That's it," said Dustin. "Caillou's mom was a saint."

"I never liked *Caillou*, but I love *Gravity Falls*," said Kendal. "I wish they'd make another season."

"Yeah," said Jane. "Mabel is my favorite."

"I haven't seen *Gravity Falls*, but I love Joanna Gaines's new show," said Heidi.

Dustin rolled his eyes. "You know how I feel about Joanna Gaines and her love of shiplap."

"Just because you don't appreciate modern country," said Heidi, "doesn't mean that—"

"I don't have time to watch TV," said Nathan, interrupting her tirade.

"Neither do I," Leanne said bitterly. "I don't have time for anything."

"And who's fault is that?" Dustin asked, the words slipping out of his mouth.

"Nobody's." Leanne frowned. "I make my own decisions. Always have. Always will."

The sadness in her eyes made Dustin want to jump in and save her. If there was something he could say . . . try . . . offer . . . that would dissolve that vacant look, he would do it. But everything he'd done up to that point had backfired. He'd warned Leanne away from Cade, and she had married him anyway. He'd supported her through nursing school, and she had dropped out. He'd helped her with childcare for Kendal when she was twenty years old and probably too immature for parenting, and she'd immediately had another baby. He'd provided her a house, and she had trashed it. It was almost like he was an enabler.

Oh hell, that was it. Hot shame washed over him as Dustin realized his role in all of this. He *was* an enabler—Nathan and Heidi too. Cade's parents, Mr. and Mrs. Tolbert, were probably guilty of enabling Cade and Leanne as well. They'd offered so much assistance to the couple over the years that the two of them had become helpless. Cade was a crook, a cheat, and a louse, but Leanne was something sadder. She was a mess. The worst part was that Dustin didn't know what to do about it now. If this was just about Leanne, he'd take a major step back and let her learn from her mistakes the hard way. But there were Kendal and Jane to consider. He couldn't let them suffer. His nieces deserved a safe, nurturing childhood, and he'd do anything to make sure they got it.

"Uncle Dusty," said Jane. "You haven't told us what your favorite show is yet."

"Yeah, Uncle Dusty." Andrea smirked. "Let's hear it." Dustin knew that Andrea knew that he hated when people shortened his name to Dusty. That, too, was something he'd let Leanne get away with. She'd trained the girls to call him Uncle Dusty from the very beginning because she knew it annoyed him. How had he not seen until now that she took the love he offered her and threw it back in his face?

"History documentaries are my favorite," he said. "History has so much to teach us. If we pay attention, we won't repeat our past mistakes." Boy, wasn't that the truth. He didn't know what the way forward was for Leanne in the future, but that was her problem to figure out, not his. All he had to do was continue to be a good uncle, and he was great at that. When the time came, he could help the girls with college, too, since Leanne had probably ignored his advice about opening them up 529 accounts.

Dustin reached for Andrea's hand underneath the table and squeezed it. Right now, his future meant spending time with Andrea, and he intended to enjoy every minute. "Speaking of television, I was hoping that you might watch a documentary with me tonight. I'm sure Netflix has something good."

"That's an idea." Andrea rested their hands on his leg. "Or we could watch the new Ken Burns documentary that just came out. I got the DVD for free after contributing to a PBS fund drive."

"Ken Burns, you say?" Dustin gave Andrea a sly smile. "You've just described my ideal date." He kissed her cheek. "So long as you're sitting on the couch next to me."

"Always," she murmured, making his heart go wild.

CHAPTER NINETEEN

When Andrea's alarm buzzed at six thirty in the morning, she ignored it and drifted back to glorious sleep. But when her phone rang an hour and a half later, she picked it up in case it was regarding her father. "Hello?"

"Well, look who's finally awake," said Heidi.

Heidi, whom Andrea was supposed to meet an hour ago for their Friday-morning walk. Andrea glanced at the clock. It was eight already. "Shoot. I'm so sorry. I should have called."

"Yes, you should have, instead of standing me up."

"That was bad." Andrea wedged her phone under her ear, pulled on flannel pajama pants, and stuffed her feet into her hedgehog slippers. She really needed to buy some cuter sleepwear. Even she could see that the hedgehog theme was getting out of control.

"I waited for you for ten minutes. When you didn't come, I walked over to your house."

"Oh. You did?" Andrea raced to her bathroom and brushed her hair with a furious intensity that made it frizz instead of taming it.

"Yeah, and it wasn't until I saw who was parked in your driveway that I gave up."

"Um . . . yeah." Still holding the phone under her ear, Andrea opened the bottle of mouthwash. "Can we talk later? I gotta go."

"Not so fast. I need to talk to Dustin. I've been calling him all morning, and his phone is going straight to voice mail."

"You know I love you, but can't this wait?"

"It's about the flip. The code inspector will arrive in thirty minutes, and Dustin has to be here. I can't explain the electrical stuff—that's his job."

Andrea poured mouthwash into a cup. "Okay, I'll tell him."

"No, I should tell him. Let me be the bad guy."

"That sounds like a good idea to me." Ignoring Heidi's chortle, she put on her bathrobe and belted it at the waist. "Hang on; I'll hand him the phone." Andrea gargled mouthwash as she hurried downstairs. She spit it out in the powder room before walking into the kitchen.

Dustin stood at the stove, frying bacon and eggs. His thick brown hair was rumpled in a dashing way, like he'd just stepped out of the wind—or rolled out of bed. "Well, hello there," he said in a husky voice. "Hungry?"

"Yes." Andrea felt her cheeks redden. "Famished." But first things first. She handed him the phone. "It's your sister."

"Go away, Heidi. I'm busy," Dustin said loudly, without taking it.

Andrea chuckled but didn't hang up. "It's something about an inspection?"

"Oh, shoot." Dustin turned off the stove and took the phone.

Heidi was a loud talker, so it was impossible for Andrea not to hear both sides of the conversation. "Okay, okay," he told her. "I'll leave here in ten minutes."

Ten minutes? Andrea felt like a piece of Velcro being slowly ripped apart. She wasn't ready for Dustin to go yet. They had too much to talk about. *And so many things to do while not talking.* She sighed and tried to quell her disappointment. At least they had plans for dinner tonight, even if it was with her mom and Roger.

"Yeah, okay, see you soon. Bye." Dustin hung up, placed the phone on the counter, and groaned. "So much for our romantic breakfast. I wonder how many meals my family can ruin for us in one week?"

"I love your family." Andrea stepped close and entwined her hands around his neck. "And I love you."

"The feeling is mutual." Dustin pulled her closer, and she breathed in the fresh scent of soap that clung to him like the morning chill. His green eyes were the same color as the fir trees outside. But snuggled against his chest was a warm place to be, and when their lips crushed together, Andrea felt a blissfulness she'd never experienced before. The sky was gray, the weather rainy, yet Dustin infused her with a sunshine that burst forth, filling her kitchen with a coziness that bathed everything in a warm glow. He steadied her, sheltered her, held her upright like the century-old trees in her front yard. "I am so honored you gave me a second chance," he murmured as his lips traced her jawline.

"Me too." His lips kissed a path to the top of her neckline, making her giggle. "Speaking of second chances, maybe you would let me cook you dinner tomorrow night? I promise not to poison you."

He looked up. "Sounds delicious. But Sunday night I'll cook," he said, hugging her tighter.

"I didn't know you cook."

"I'm more of an indoor griller," he admitted. "But you can do a lot with those things: meat, veggies, peaches. Microwave some rice, and boom, there's dinner."

"Well, that's good to know."

"That you can grill veggies?"

"No." She laughed. "That you can cook. That means—" She stopped herself just in time. Andrea had been about to say *that I won't be stuck with the cooking for the rest of our lives*, but that seemed presumptuous. "That we'll have dinner plans three nights in a row," she said instead, rubbing her thumb against his prickly stubble.

"At the very least." He picked her up, making her giggle, and set her down again. "I'm not sure three nights in a row will be enough. Forever, on the other hand . . ." Dustin sealed her mouth against his, and when their tongues touched, she felt tingles all the way down to her toes.

Andrea closed her eyes, lost in the feeling of Dustin's hands on her back holding them together. She wouldn't come undone. Not with him here. Not knowing that he was coming back tonight and the day after that and the next day too. Their future spread out in front of her with unlimited possibilities. When her eyes fluttered, her gaze landed on the refrigerator, devoid of adornment. Maybe by this time next year it would be covered with pictures of her and Dustin.

"I like the sound of forever," Andrea said when they stopped for breath. "But first, coffee. Have you had some?" Looking around for evidence, Andrea didn't see any signs that he'd already had a cup.

"No, but I can grab some at work. I couldn't figure out your fancy machine."

"My Nespresso machine?" Andrea laughed. "It's not that complicated." Wiggling out of his grasp, she opened a cabinet and removed a travel mug. "If you eat fast, you'll have time for those bacon and eggs."

"If I inhale them, you mean?"

Andrea popped in a pod and turned on the machine. "I don't want you to show up to your important meeting on an empty stomach."

"Good point. Where are the plates?"

Andrea got two plates and a couple of forks while Dustin's coffee brewed. She would add the used pod to the recycling bag later so it wouldn't go into the landfill.

Dustin ate on his feet. "Sorry to eat and run."

"Just so long as you come back and return my mug." Andrea secured the lid and handed him the coffee. "It's my favorite. I wouldn't loan it to you unless I trusted you completely."

"This looks like Spike."

"It *is* Spike. I scanned an old photo of him and made a custom mug one day when I was bored."

Dustin took her hand and pecked her cheek. "I'll take good care of it," he promised.

Andrea's phone buzzed with a text from Heidi. Has Dustin left yet? He's going to be late.

She frowned. "I finally see what you mean about my best friend being annoying."

"You don't know the half of it." Dustin chuckled. His parting kiss was so hot it promised to keep her warm until suppertime.

An hour later, Andrea was showered, dressed, and cozied up on her window seat with her computer on her lap. She had work to do on the private school campaign that had gotten screwed up. The head of school had originally provided her with a bevy of student photos to use on the website and advertising campaign, but it turned out that the photo-release forms they had acquired from the parents had expired. Andrea had to cut and paste throughout the entire campaign, keeping the photos from students who had quickly submitted the new form and replacing the ones who hadn't. It was time consuming but important, especially since she was dealing with minors.

Before she finished her work, though, she checked the coin forums where she had created a phony profile. Gus McHenderson from Nashville, Tennessee, was a highly motivated buyer looking for double eagles, willing to PayPal sellers money right now, no questions asked, if they had what he was looking for. For a profile picture, Andrea had used an old photo of Tom wearing an ugly sweater she had knit him in high school. *Tried* to knit him, that is. It had fallen apart the second time Lydia had washed it. In retrospect, Andrea would have been more successful if she'd learned to knit in the era of YouTube videos instead of books she'd borrowed from the library.

After logging in as Gus, Andrea scrolled through the message boards of the first forum on her list. She saw the post she had made as Andrea Wint last Sunday about her stolen collection and was pleased to see there were a few more comments of support. Gus's post had a couple of responses as well.

266

One was a spam post. "WE BUY AND SELL USED COINS" in all caps with a website attached from an online dealer in Florida. Even though it was probably pointless, Andrea clicked on the website and filled out the inquiry form on the off chance they had bought from Cade. The next comment was from a frequent poster alerting her to "Andrea Wint's stolen collection." When she saw what the person had written, it made her misty eyed. There were scoundrels in the numismatic world, but most collectors were honorable.

"Be careful what you buy," the poster had written. "There's a valuable collection of double eagles that was recently stolen from Seattle."

"Thanks," Andrea wrote. She tapped her chin. Was Gus an honest person, or was he a shady collector? This was her chance to recover her coins, not establish a second identity with the same values she held dear. She needed people to see that Gus was willing to buy stolen coins. "But I don't need your advice," Andrea added. "This is America, and I can buy whatever I want." Submitting the response felt weird, but so had being robbed. Andrea clicked over to the other forum where Gus had an account.

The Andrea Wint thread over there was completely dead, but the Gus McHenderson thread was hot. Lots of people responded with double eagles for sale. Andrea spent the next forty-five minutes responding to them one by one, hoping that one of the sellers had multiple double eagles listed. If they lived along the West Coast, that would be even better. Cade could have sold a portion of her collection anywhere from here to the last place they knew he had visited, which was San Carlos Coin Market near San Francisco.

Thinking about Cade's itinerary made Andrea remember something Franklin from Port Angeles had mentioned. He'd said something about Lisa saying they were going to Ashland. At the time, Andrea had made a mental note of it, but then she'd never followed up. She wasn't sure if Dustin had either or if he'd passed that information along to the private investigator he had hired. She'd text Dustin and ask him right now but didn't want to interrupt his meeting with the code inspector.

Scratching her head, Andrea began an open-ended search for the keywords *Ashland, Oregon.* It brought up lots of results, but as she scrolled down the page, one thing in particular caught her attention: the Oregon Shakespeare Festival. Thespians from all over congregated in Ashland each summer to celebrate the theater.

Hamlet . . . hadn't Dustin said that Cade had played a minor role in *Hamlet* back when he and Leanne had first met? Although Cade had never struck her as the cerebral type who appreciated Shakespeare, he was definitely clever enough to memorize lines. He was an actor—or at least wanted to be. Maybe he had friends who were still in that world, friends who lived in Ashland and were part of the Shakespeare festival?

Andrea looked for coin stores in Ashland and found one that she'd already called on Sunday. She couldn't recall if she'd left a voice mail or spoken to a live person, so she called again.

"Hello," said the voice on the other end. "Ashland Gold and Coins."

"Hi." Andrea launched into her spiel about her stolen collection. "I know I called on Sunday, but I was double-checking if you might have any information for me."

"You called on Sunday?" the guy asked. "I'm closed on Sunday."

"I probably left a message, then."

"Sorry about that. I never check my voice mail. I don't want the government to track me."

"Er . . . um."

"They keep a tally of all the places you've called. Back when answering machines were on tape, it was different, but these digital files—that's how they get you."

"Right. So . . . I'll keep that in mind for the future. Back to my stolen coins, has anyone come into your shop with a large collection of double eagles?"

"Yes, actually. This Monday a guy banged on my door to open up, even though I'm closed on Mondays, and convinced me to let him and his girlfriend in."

"Really? Was she a redhead?" Andrea's nerves rushed with excitement.

"Yeah, and a real looker too. She wanted to do a trade for a pair of ruby earrings in my estate case, but the boyfriend said no. He wanted cash only."

"Did you buy them?" Andrea's voice was barely above a whisper, she was so nervous.

"No, I didn't. I don't keep that much cash on hand, and the guy didn't want gold. I asked if he'd be willing to come with me to the bank for a cashier's check, and he wigged out on me."

"Wigged out on you? How?"

"Started talking about video surveillance and not wanting to be tracked, which I totally understand, but in this instance, that raised suspicion, so I sent him on his way."

Andrea sighed. "That was the right decision," she said. "Otherwise you would have acquired stolen property."

"Yeah, something seemed off about the guy. I have his picture if you want it."

"Yes!" Andrea squeaked.

"Ashland Gold and Coins has a security system that rivals Fort Knox. Gotta stay one step ahead of the government so they don't screw you over."

"Um . . . yeah. Can I give you my email for the video?"

"Sure can."

"Did he happen to mention where he might be headed next?" Andrea asked after she'd given him her email.

"Kind of. The guy asked for shops I would recommend in California. That was before I got a bad feeling about him."

"Did you give him some recommendations?"

Jennifer Bardsley

"I'm ashamed to say I did. The San Carlos Coin Market near San Francisco and Brentwood Rare Coins in LA."

Brentwood. Andrea felt the hairs on her arm stand up. That was right next to Hollywood. The perfect place for an actor to visit. What if Cade's ultimate goal was to try his luck at acting again? Headshots were expensive. So were personal trainers, high-end hairdressers, and the other accoutrements actors needed to compete. Between her coins, Leanne's money, and that new sprinter van Cade had purchased, he could live off the grid for a long time while he pursued his ambition. Cade might have even changed his name by now.

"Thank you so much for your help." Andrea hung up and called the Brentwood shop right away.

The phone rang five times before going to voice mail. Listening to the automated message, Andrea was annoyed to discover that the shop was open only three days a week: Tuesday, Wednesday, and Thursday. It must be nice being a coin dealer in one of the richest parts of America. Probably most of the dealer's business was in private sales. Andrea left a message, typed up her notes, and emailed them to Dustin so he could forward them to the PI. By that point there was a message waiting for her from the Ashland dealer with the security footage of Cade and Lisa. She gritted her teeth when she saw it, annoyed that they were still at large. After watching it three times, she forwarded that email to Dustin as well. Hopefully this would help the PI nab him.

With that out of the way, Andrea focused on work. The sooner she could finish the private school campaign, the better. If she hurried, she'd have time to drive to Bremerton and buy new clothes. Andrea wiggled her toes inside her slippers. These hedgehogs had had a good life, but it was time for them to go.

270

CHAPTER TWENTY

From the outside, the Owl's Nest looked like a typical retirement home or perhaps a tony condominium. Dustin had never been to a memory-care facility before, and it was nicer than he would have guessed, especially after hearing Andrea's angst over Tom living here. Then again, Dustin had zero experience with Alzheimer's or dementia, so he wasn't sure what to expect. They had timed it so that they could visit Tom before they drove down to Seattle for dinner with Lydia and Roger.

"Okay, so . . ." Andrea paused before she opened the door. "He's probably not going to remember who you are, but don't take it personally. Although he might, because sometimes he remembers things from the past easier than the present. And the smell—I should warn you. The whole place smells like lemons. I think it's the disinfectant they use. I know that sounds bad, me telling you that it smells, but it's an acceptable scent, unlike some of the other places we considered, which smelled horrible." Andrea shuddered. "Also, don't use the bathroom here. It's not that they don't clean it, because they do, every day, just . . ." Andrea winced. "Sometimes—"

"Relax." Dustin placed his hands on her shoulders to steady her. Telling his sister Heidi to relax never worked, so he didn't know why he had said that to Andrea, but it was the first thing that popped out of his mouth. Apparently, they were both nervous. "I will follow your lead on everything, okay? Don't worry about me. I want to be here with you and help any way I can. Okay?"

Andrea nodded, gulping for air. "Okay."

He hugged her tightly, as if encircling her in his arms would offer protection against the sadness she faced. "I'm excited to see your dad again. I wish it were under different circumstances, but I'm still glad."

"Thanks for coming with me." Andrea opened the front door, and they entered an antechamber. She held her palm under a hand-sanitizer dispenser and rubbed her fingers together. Dustin did the same. Next, Andrea rang a doorbell by the second door and waited to be buzzed through.

When they entered the lobby, Dustin didn't detect the lemon scent Andrea had warned him about. The first thing he noticed was the architecture. The common space had been designed to look like a small town. False fronts at the back of the room were painted like an idealized version of Main Street, USA. There was a post office, a barbershop with a red-and-white-striped pole, and even a fruit stand. In the center of the room were tables and chairs and a baby grand piano.

"This is the town center," Andrea explained. "It's where they bring everyone for group events." She walked over to the receptionist at the front desk. "Hi, Marie, I'm a bit early tonight."

"I can see that." The woman put down the paperback she was reading. "Who's Mr. Handsome?"

"This is my boyfriend, Dustin Karlsson from Port Inez."

"Nice to meet you, Dustin. You've picked a winner."

"I sure have." Dustin squeezed Andrea's hand.

"Where can I find my father?" Andrea asked.

Marie looked at a chart on her desk. "He's in the music room."

"Great. Thanks."

"Wait a sec." Marie handed her an envelope. "There's a message for you."

"Maybe it's an update about my dad's shower schedule." Andrea ripped it open. A few seconds later she gasped.

"What does it say?" Dustin asked, feeling concerned.

Marie, too, appeared curious, although she quickly looked back to her book when Andrea lifted her head.

"It's from the general manager," said Andrea. "They've expunged the strike against my dad from his record."

"That's wonderful news." Dustin put his arm around her in a side hug. "Does it say why?"

Andrea shook her head. "No. It barely says anything." She passed the paper to Dustin.

"Dear Mrs. Lydia Wint and Ms. Andrea Wint," he read out loud. "This letter is to notify you that the strike against Thomas 'Tom' Wint has been expunged from his file. The safety and security of our residents is our highest priority."

Andrea looked at Marie. "Do you know anything about this?"

Marie put down her novel. "No. Sorry. Since I've been working the reception desk, I miss out on everything. I adore your father, and I can't imagine him having a strike against him in the first place."

"Thanks, Marie. I guess we'll go visit him now. Could you please buzz us in?"

"Sure. Here you go."

Dustin followed Andrea through another set of doors that Marie unlocked for them. Despite the cheery atmosphere, he got the sense that they were entering a prison. Dustin pushed the thought away, but it lingered. The security was there to keep residents safe. He'd seen enough Silver Alerts in Washington State to know that dementia patients wandering off and becoming lost was a serious issue. Still, it was unnerving knowing they were locked inside.

"These are the bedrooms," Andrea explained as they walked down the hallway. Some doors were open, and he could see beds, dressers, and chairs. "Most of the rooms are doubles, but my dad has a single."

She pointed to a shadowbox by an open door. "They put each resident's name and a little bit about them in these shadowboxes. My dad has a box too. I'll show you."

They walked farther down the hall until they found Tom's room. His shadowbox had pictures of Tom through the years as well, including a cute one of Tom and Andrea when she was a little girl, standing next to the Mariner Moose. "This is great," said Dustin. "Who made it?"

"My mom did."

"She did a really good job."

"Yep. The shadowboxes help the residents find their rooms. This hallway is a circle, so people can walk laps and not get lost. All they have to do is keep going, and they'll eventually find the room with their shadowbox right at the front of it." Andrea checked her watch. "We'd better hurry. We don't have much time, considering we'll be fighting work traffic."

Dustin heard the music room before he saw it. Someone was singing "Yankee Doodle" into a microphone, and there was a clamor of tambourines. They came upon a space decorated like a family room, with couches and recliners. A couple dozen people were there, in various stages of engagement. Tom was one of the tambourine shakers. He not only shook the instrument to the beat; he also looked at the instructor while she sang into the microphone.

"Stay here while I get him," said Andrea. She crept discreetly into the room and crouched in front of her father. When Tom saw Andrea, he put down the tambourine and smiled. She took his hand and brought him to Dustin, and all three of them walked down the hall to the dining room. They were greeted by the rich aroma of freshly baked bread.

"Hi, Dad. How are you doing?" Andrea said after they had sat down.

"Oh, I'm doing fine. How about you?"

"Good." Andrea nodded. "Dad, this is Dustin Karlsson, my boyfriend."

"Hi, Tom. It's good to see you again."

"Hi." Tom smiled back but didn't converse further. He had aged considerably since the last time Dustin had seen him. His sparse hair and wrinkles were to be expected, but the elastic-waist pants and gray sweatshirt caught Dustin by surprise. Tom used to be such a classy dresser.

"It's been a while since we last saw each other," said Dustin. "You were the lawyer who represented my family against a construction company."

"Oh," said Tom. "Well, what do you know?"

"There was a crane that collapsed and killed my parents."

"That's horrible." Tom gripped the edge of the table. "Do they live here?"

"No." Dustin's muscles tensed. He'd been here only a few minutes, and he'd already said the wrong thing. "This was a long time ago."

"Music class sounded like fun," said Andrea, changing the subject. "You're great with the tambourine."

Tom lifted his hand and shook it. "You have to rumble them. That's the trick."

"The music was lovely," said Andrea. "I'm sorry I needed to take you out of your class for our visit."

"Oh, don't worry about that," Tom said affably. "A lot of those people there are, you know . . ." He raised his eyebrows. "I don't think they're all there. I keep telling Lydia that we should go home. This place has been fine for a while, but it's time to go home." Tom scratched his shoulder.

Dustin watched as the expression on Andrea's face froze into a vacant smile. A few seconds later, she recovered and changed the subject yet again. "The menu says you had turkey sandwiches for lunch. Were they good?"

"If you say so." Tom shrugged.

Dustin tried to think of something he could contribute to the conversation, but he was out of his element. The decor, perhaps? "I like the wood paneling." He pointed to the walls. "It makes me think of a cabin."

"That's by design," said Andrea. "They want people to feel at home in an era they remember." She looked at Tom. "Dad, the menu says there will be beef stroganoff for dinner. You love beef stroganoff."

"Good." Tom nodded.

"These little flower arrangements at the center of each table are nice." Dustin picked one up and turned it around so he could examine all angles. He wasn't a botanist, but he did have experience with landscaping and was good at identifying flowers. "Lemon balm and mint are a nice mixture, especially with the yellow roses." He held the arrangement to his nose and breathed deeply. "Are you sure this isn't the lemon scent you mentioned?" Dustin asked as he passed the vase to Andrea.

She closed her eyes and sniffed. "That's part of it. The rest is Lysol." Andrea reached into her pocket and pulled out a silver coin. "Dad, I've brought something to show you." She placed it in his hand.

"A steelie," Tom exclaimed. "Well, this is a surprise."

"What's a steelie?" Dustin asked, genuinely curious.

"A steel penny from 1943." Tom inspected both sides. "This one's from Denver. See that *D*?"

Dustin squinted. "Barely. I think I might need to get my eyes checked."

Tom showed the coin to Andrea. "Have I ever told you about steelies before?"

"A few times." She pressed her lips together in a tight line. "Tell me again."

"It was World War II, and there wasn't enough copper," Tom began, launching into a full explanation of the numismatic history of the coin. For a moment, Dustin caught a glimpse of the man he remembered. Smart, educated, articulate. Here was the hero who had challenged one of the biggest construction companies in the Pacific Northwest on behalf of four orphans who had lost everything. "Keep this in a safe place," said Tom as he passed the steelie back to his daughter. "It's not worth much, but it does have history."

"Yes, Tom," said Dustin. "It sure does."

Fifteen minutes later, when he and Andrea were walking briskly toward her car, Dustin had no idea what to say. Andrea didn't look to the left or the right; she stared straight ahead with a grim expression on her face. Dustin worried that he'd screwed up more than he'd realized. He had tried his best back there, but attempting to remind Tom about the Karlsson lawsuit had been a bad idea.

When they reached the Nissan Leaf, Andrea lifted her hair at its roots, like she would yank it out if she weren't careful. "Gah!" she burst out. "I hate that."

"I'm sorry. I shouldn't have tried to remind your dad about who I was. I thought—"

"No. Don't apologize. I'm not upset with you." Andrea spun around. "I'm angry at all of it. I hate the dread I feel when I approach the complex, and I hate the relief I feel when I leave. I hate that he needs to be there, and I hate that being there is a luxury that most dementia patients can't afford." She turned around and pounded her fist on the roof of the car. "I hate all of it." Tears streamed down her cheeks.

"Shh," Dustin said, wrapping her in his arms. "I'm here." He didn't know what to do except hold her.

"Do you know how hard this is? To see the person you love not be the person you love anymore?"

"No." Dustin shook his head. "I don't."

"People think Alzheimer's is just about forgetting, but it's not." Andrea looked at him. "My dad's disappearing, right before my eyes, and there's nothing I can do about it."

"That's awful." He squeezed her tighter.

"He's not himself anymore. And I'm still me, and I need him." She crushed her face against Dustin's chest. "I need my dad, but he's gone."

"I'm sorry."

"Sometimes I can make it through the visits just fine, but other times I can barely keep the tears inside."

"You can let them out now; I'm here."

"And it's only going to get worse."

"I'll be with you when it does."

"Dustin, I'm scared." Andrea stared up at him again. "What if I get Alzheimer's too?"

"I'm going to feed you so many nuts and berries and leafy green vegetables that they could put you on a poster for the Mindful diet, so don't worry about that."

She laughed, despite her tears. "It's called the *MIND* diet, not the Mindful diet."

"See?" He kissed her nose. "It's already working. You're sharp as a tack."

He kept her in his arms, stroking her hair and hugging her, until she quieted. When they climbed in the car, Dustin offered to drive, but Andrea declined. The drive to Seattle wasn't as bad as expected, thanks to the carpool lane. Dustin used the time to help Andrea decompress, peppering her with jokes and funny stories about Port Inez, like how the BBQ Trough refused to serve salad because the owners thought lettuce was bad for your health.

"What?" Andrea asked. "How?"

"Salmonella outbreaks from romaine lettuce. The only vegetables you'll find at the BBQ Trough come from cans or the fryer."

"That's some creative thinking. French fries as a health food." Andrea chuckled.

It was good to hear her laugh. Dustin studied her as she kept her eyes on the road. Tears dried and with a smile on her face, you'd never know the storm of emotions she had so recently endured. Her devotion to her father was commendable, but he worried about the toll it took on her. He vowed, then and there, to lighten her load. Comfort her when she was sad, cheer her when she felt defeated, and be there by her side as her dad's condition worsened.

At the moment, that meant lively conversation and searching through the radio stations until they found one that played songs popular when they'd been in high school. By the time they arrived at Roger and Lydia's condo overlooking Lake Washington, they were both in high spirits.

"Wow." Dustin's mouth gaped open as he stared at the complex. "Brutalism at its best—or worst, depending on your opinion."

"What's brutalism?"

"It's a building style from the 1950s known for concrete and austerity."

Andrea scrunched up her nose as they walked to the front door. "So you're telling me that Roger's building looks like a prison on purpose?"

Dustin nodded. He didn't mention prisons had crossed his mind an hour ago when they'd visited her father. "Does the condo have a killer view?"

"Yes," Andrea said begrudgingly. "It's spectacular." She pressed a call button and waited.

"You're here!" Lydia said in a delighted tone. "Come on up."

The door buzzed, and Andrea opened it. They stepped into the elevator a moment later, and Andrea hit the button for the penthouse.

"You seem thrilled to be here," said Dustin, trying to lighten the mood with sarcasm. "Your enthusiasm is contagious."

"It's not too late to go home."

"Tell you what." Dustin slid his arms around her waist and pulled them together. "Let's put in an appearance, enjoy your mother's delicious cooking, and then go home. You know I've been dreaming of her éclair cake for eighteen years."

"Éclair cake, huh? Is that *all* you've been dreaming about?" She walked her fingertips up his chest and slid her hands down his shoulder blades.

"Yes," he joked. "That's the only reason I'm here." The elevator parted, and they entered a hallway with two doors: one for Roger and Lydia's apartment and one for the stairs. When he took Andrea's hand, it was sweaty. It killed him to see her so nervous.

He wasn't a big talker in social situations, but he would make an effort tonight to keep the conversation going and ease Andrea's discomfort any way he could.

Lydia opened her front door almost as soon as they stepped off the elevator. "You made it," she said, wearing light-blue slacks and a crisp white blouse. Shorter than Andrea, but with similar coloring, Lydia had more wrinkles than the last time Dustin had seen her. But her blue eyes held the same friendliness that he remembered. "How was traffic?" she asked.

"Not that bad." Andrea gave her mother a quick hug. "Mom, you remember Dustin, right?"

"Of course!" Lydia swooped in with a hug and caught Dustin by surprise.

"I'm so glad to be here," he replied, hugging her back.

"So is this the famous Dustin I've heard so much about?" A small man stood behind Lydia. He was two inches shorter than her and wore thick glasses.

The frozen smile on Andrea's face threatened to crack. "Hi, Roger."

"Dustin Karlsson, nice to meet you." Dustin held out his hand and pumped vigorously when Roger shook it.

Idle small talk filled the next ten minutes. Since Dustin had never been there before, Lydia was eager to show off the apartment. Dustin oohed and aahed at the view of Lake Washington. It was impossible not to, even at night, when all you could see was twinkling lights. He asked Roger questions about the history of the building. Roger didn't know much about it, but he did identify it as having been constructed in 1953.

"Roger, why don't you pour drinks while I pop the halibut in the air fryer?" Lydia grinned. "It's my new toy, and I love it. Wait until you taste how crispy the fish turns out."

"She bought two," Roger added. "One for fish and one for french fries."

"Chips, honey." Lydia winked. "Tonight we're calling them chips."

"Where do you have room to store two air fryers?" Andrea asked. "Roger's kitchen is half the size of your old one."

Lydia's cheeks turned pink. "It's my kitchen now, too, and perfectly adequate." She spun on her foot and left the living room.

Roger, who was pouring glasses of white wine, explained. "I keep the second air fryer in my half of the closet, where my shoes used to be."

"Where do your shoes go now?" Dustin asked.

"In the coat closet, where I used to keep my guitar."

Andrea picked up a glass of wine. "Where's your guitar?"

"Right over there." Roger pointed to a Fender hanging on the wall. "I hadn't played it in years because my ex-wife said I was horrible at it. I was in a garage band with other podiatrists called the Shoe Finders, and my ex ridiculed us so bad on Facebook that I felt compelled to drop out. For the sake of the band, you know. Luckily it was in my car when my houseboat was robbed, or it would have been stolen too." He poured the last drops of wine into the fourth glass. "When your mom was redecorating our apartment and found the guitar, she asked me to play. The Fender was so out of tune that I had to get it professionally restrung. But now I play a few times a week."

"Are you talking about your guitar?" Lydia asked, floating back into the room. "You should hear him. Roger's excellent. Like Seattle's version of Eric Clapton."

"I don't know about that." Roger shrugged. "But it's relaxing and a fun thing for me to do while you work on your flower arrangements."

"Which are stunning, by the way," said Dustin, without embellishment. "I'm not a decorator—that's my sister Heidi's job when we redesign a house—but the arrangement on your coffee table could be from a professional stager."

"Thank you." Lydia folded her hands in her lap and smiled. "I pick up flowers from the market a couple of times a week and go for it."

Dustin looked at the arrangement more closely. Something about it seemed familiar. Interspersed between the daffodils and tulips, he spotted foliage with a unique scent. "Is that lemon balm?"

Lydia nodded. "It is. Good eye."

"Or nose." Dustin leaned forward to smell it. "And I smell mint too."

"And yellow roses." Andrea's face went white. "Lemon balm, mint, and yellow roses—just like at the Owl's Nest."

Lydia sat up straight but didn't say anything. Roger sat next to her on the couch and put his arm around her shoulder. "Your mom brings flowers to five different memory-care units every week, including your father's."

"What?" Andrea asked. "Since when?"

"Since forever," Roger said. "And I couldn't be prouder of her."

"Not forever." Lydia twisted her hands in her lap. "Just a couple of years. The hardest part has been sourcing edible plants."

"Edible plants?" Dustin asked.

"In case someone accidentally thinks they're food," Lydia explained.

"Mom, why didn't you tell me you were doing this?" Andrea asked.

Lydia sniffed. "It's too hard."

"Do you visit Dad when you drop off the flowers?"

"Sometimes. But usually not. I have too many deliveries to make. The last time I saw him, he kept asking me when his wife would come to take him home." Tears flooded Lydia's eyes, and Roger gave her his handkerchief.

"It messes her up for days when she visits Tom and he doesn't recognize her." Roger patted her knee. "I hate to see her so unhappy."

Tears rolled down Andrea's cheeks, too, and Dustin wished he, like Roger, had a handkerchief to offer. But he'd never owned a handkerchief in his life. He did know something about grief, though, and moving forward. He had learned that wisdom from Tom.

"When my parents died, Tom gave me good advice," said Dustin. Andrea, Lydia, and Roger looked at him. Dustin picked up Andrea's hand and covered it with his own. "Andrea's already heard this story, but maybe it bears repeating. Tom told me that although he had never met my parents, he knew that they would want me to go forward and live my life with happiness. Every single day I was to find a new reason to be happy."

"That's wonderful advice and sounds so much like the Tom I used to know." Lydia looked at Andrea directly. "Your father's in a safe place. If visiting him every day makes you happy, you should do it. But it tears me to shreds, and your dad wouldn't want that." She leaned her head against Roger's shoulder.

Andrea took a deep breath and exhaled loudly. "No," she said. "He wouldn't." Dustin watched as Andrea looked around the apartment, almost like she was seeing it for the first time. "Dad would want you to be right here. He'd want you to be happy, and so do I."

"Oh, sweet pea. I'm so glad to hear you say that." Lydia jumped from the couch and gave her daughter a hug. "Roger, be a dear, and get another handkerchief." As soon as he left, she spoke quickly. "I'm glad Tom gave good advice on that occasion, and, Andrea, I don't like to speak ill of your father, but—"

"Then don't," Andrea interrupted.

"No," Lydia said in a firm voice. "I have to tell you. Darling, I'm not sure you know, but your father purposefully interfered in your relationship with Dustin all those years ago. He told me all about how he broke you up by telling Dustin that you were wrong for each other. I argued with him, but he wouldn't listen. I was going to tell you, but your father talked me out of it."

"I know what happened," said Andrea. "I mean now, eighteen years later, I know."

"I've come to the conclusion that as wise as Tom was, he wasn't right about everything," said Dustin.

"No." Lydia shook her head. "He wasn't, and I want to apologize for my role in that mess. I should have done more to help."

"Here you go." Roger reentered the room and gave Andrea a folded square of fabric. "It's bleached, I promise."

"Thanks." Andrea wiped her eyes.

"We were just talking about Dustin and Andrea dating in high school." Lydia tapped her toes on the ground. "The thing is, you two *were* really intense with each other. I shared your dad's concern that all of those late-night phone calls were ruining your sleep schedule. Why, even the commute to visit each other cut into your study time. You had all those AP tests to prepare for, and so I could see your father's point. Hitting the pause button could be viewed as a good idea."

"But, Mom," said Andrea, "it turned into an eighteen-year pause."

"And that's truly unfortunate." Lydia bit her lip for a second. "Like I said, I wish things had gone differently. I'm sorry."

Dustin let out a deep breath. "Well, what is it we've been talking about, Andrea? You can't rewrite the past, and you can't predict the future. All you can do is make sure that today is great." He kissed her hand.

"I'll drink to that." Roger lifted his glass, and the others followed.

"Oh, wait." Andrea reached for her purse. "I forgot to tell you the good news. I got the best letter from the general manager of the Owl's Nest today." She handed Lydia the envelope.

Lydia read the letter quickly and sniffed. "I already knew about this. They emailed me a copy."

"I don't understand how it happened," said Andrea. Dustin wondered that too.

Lydia smiled sheepishly. "It's because I dusted off my legal letterhead and sent them a certified letter."

"You did what?" Andrea gasped.

"I told them that the Department of Social and Health Services would want to know about unsafe happenings at a memory-care facility under their oversight. Certainly a stranger waltzing into your father's room in the middle of the night with no repercussions qualifies."

"Tom should be allowed to defend himself," said Roger. "I would have punched an intruder too."

Lydia nodded. "It's outrageous that they filed a police report. I didn't accuse the Owl's Nest of neglect, per se, but I let it be known that I'd contact the DSHS if necessary."

"Go Mom," Andrea exclaimed. "You're a badass."

"That's what I said." Roger grinned. "She's cute as a button, especially in those clogs, but better not get on her bad side. I consider myself warned."

"Oh, Roger." Lydia giggled.

"I just have one question for you," said Dustin after he put down his glass. "Back to those incredible flower arrangements you've been designing—where do you source all of this lemon balm? That's not something you usually find at the store."

"That's a great question." Lydia leaned back in her seat. "There's a gardener in Burke Woods named Luke Holter who grows it for me. He plants a special plot of edible plants just for my memory-care bouquets."

"You're amazing, Mom," said Andrea. "I love you."

"I love you too, sweet pea."

Emotions are like water, Josh had said. *They can do a lot of damage if you're not careful.* But sometimes, Dustin realized, emotions could heal, and the best thing was to let those feelings flow.

CHAPTER
TWENTY-ONE

On the way home from Lydia and Roger's apartment, Dustin received a phone call from the private investigator that changed everything. Andrea had just passed Northgate when the call came through. She turned off the radio so Dustin could hear better and kept her eyes on the road.

"Wow," he said after exchanging greetings. "Cade has an appointment at Brentwood Rare Coins?"

Andrea gripped the steering wheel tighter as excitement raced through her. "I left two voice mails for that shop, but they never called back," she whispered.

Dustin conveyed that information to the PI and then paused while he listened. Andrea wished she could hear what the investigator was saying. Thankfully, Dustin repeated some of the information. "Cade has a private showing tomorrow afternoon at one p.m. Yes. That's definitely a lead."

"Is the shop cooperating with the police?" Andrea asked.

Dustin nodded.

Andrea's skin tingled with anticipation. She was driving them up Interstate 5 but itched to take the next exit and turn them around so they could drive south toward Sea-Tac Airport.

"Yes, we can fly to LA," Dustin said into the phone. "We'll be there by tomorrow morning." He looked at Andrea. "Right?"

Andrea switched on her blinker. "Yes. Absolutely." She checked her blind spot before merging into the right-hand lane.

The night passed by in a blur of activity. Dustin booked them plane tickets on the way to the airport. They stopped by Target to pick up a change of clothes and toiletries before checking in to a hotel right next to the airport so they could catch their six o'clock flight. By the time they were in the air on the way to LAX Saturday morning, they were exhausted but also keyed up. Andrea's hand shook as she brushed her teeth in the tiny bathroom. She struggled to rip open the package of mascara and lipstick she'd purchased at Target the night before but did manage to apply it in a way that made her look more human than zombie. Nobody would know that she'd hardly slept a wink, unless you counted her napping on Dustin's shoulder as they flew down the West Coast. She returned to her seat and caught a few more Zs before they touched down.

Any updates? said a text from Heidi when Andrea was able to switch her phone out of airplane mode.

Not yet. We just landed. We're renting a car and driving over to Brentwood in a bit.

Keep me posted. I wish I was there so I could punch Cade in the face when they finally nab him.

Don't give Dustin any ideas, Andrea texted. Ha ha, she added to show she was joking. She didn't think Dustin would punch Cade. Not unless Cade had physically hurt Leanne or one of the girls. Dustin was strong, but he was also steady. She looked into his green eyes as they prepared to deboard the plane and smiled. His steadiness would hopefully be a source of comfort for the rest of her life. It would be like growing old next to the shelter of a Douglas fir tree.

"I'll drive," said Dustin when they picked up the rental car. Andrea was so tired she didn't object, although she figured she'd do better in the city traffic.

"I assume you mean to drive with your hands instead of your knees," she said as he crammed his long legs into the compact car. He pushed the seat back as far as it would go, but his knees still brushed against the steering wheel.

"Very funny." He grinned and turned on the car.

Andrea plugged in the directions for the Starbucks across the street from the coin store, where they were meeting the private investigator. They didn't talk for a while so that Dustin could concentrate on following the directions and getting them safely out of the airport snarl.

"Do you think we'll get the chance to talk to Cade?" she asked once they were safely en route.

"I'm not sure. Kelly—that's the PI—said that the police would be cued into the shop's surveillance and, as soon as Cade had made the sale and money changed hands, that they would bust in and arrest him. At that point we would ID him and the stolen items."

"What about Lisa? Will she be there too?"

"Kelly didn't mention her on the phone."

"I wonder what will happen to Cade after he's caught?" Andrea pulled down the sun visor and wished she had thought of purchasing sunglasses at Target.

"He'll be charged with a class B felony, which in Washington State means up to ten years in prison and a fine of as much as twenty thousand dollars."

"Ten years in prison. Wow."

"But he probably won't serve that much time."

"Yeah." Andrea swallowed the lump in her throat. She felt bad knowing that Kendal and Jane's father might be locked up. Her own father was locked away for a different reason, and it was horrible. Andrea pushed that comparison away. It was too painful to deal with right now. At least Tom's prison wasn't one of his own making. He was a victim, just like her, and the one thing that could help him was the thing Cade had stolen.

Andrea's phone buzzed, and she read the message. What's going on now? Heidi wanted to know.

"It's your sister again," Andrea said. We're in the car, she texted. Nothing new to report.

I have news. Tell Dustin I met with the realtor this morning and he has four offers on the flip.

Andrea looked at Dustin, trying not to squint in the bright sunlight. "You didn't tell me you had listed the flip."

"We haven't. Hopefully next week, though, if all goes well."

"Heidi says you have four offers already."

"Sweet. That's two more than we had last week."

"How is that possible? No, wait, don't answer that. Real estate is nuts—I get it. But if Port Inez becomes the new Seattle, then let's consider moving."

"I hear you on that one. But I don't think it will happen. Port Inez can only build up so far. We have geographic barriers that prevent us from urban sprawl."

"You mean like the water?"

Dustin nodded. "It's good to be on a peninsula."

Andrea texted Heidi back. Dustin is happy about the 4 offers. Talk to you soon.

Her phone yapped, barking a new direction to follow. Andrea turned the sound up so Dustin could hear it better. The LA traffic was on par with Seattle. Even though the coin shop was only twelve miles from the airport, it took them over forty minutes to survive the gauntlet.

When they finally arrived, they found an ordinary-looking strip mall across the street from a tiny cottage with **BRENTWOOD RARE COINS** spelled out in elegant font.

"This is it." Dustin turned off the ignition and prepared to open the door.

"Wait."

"Why?"

"What if Cade sees us?"

"He's not here yet."

"How do you know?"

"It's only eleven thirty. Cade's appointment isn't until one. He's not the type to show up early for anything."

"Oh." Andrea picked up her purse but then paused.

"What if he stops in at the Starbucks before the appointment and sees us?"

"Then I'll tackle him, and to hell with the consequences."

Andrea shot him a look. "Don't joke."

"Who says I'm joking? After what he's put my sister and nieces through, I'd love to sock him."

"But—"

"I wouldn't." Dustin tilted his head to the side. "I could never look Kendal and Jane in the eyes again knowing I'd beat up their dad."

Andrea felt her shoulders relax. "Good. I don't know what I'd do if you were charged with assault."

"Call your mom? I hear she's a good lawyer."

"Very funny. I don't think she's licensed to practice in California."

"Well?" Dustin unlocked the doors. "Shall we?"

"Let's." Andrea hopped out of the car and followed Dustin into the coffee shop. She looked around but didn't see anything out of the ordinary, which made her feel slightly better. "I guess we should order something," she said. "Something expensive, since we'll be here a while."

"By *something expensive*, do you mean whipped cream, chocolate, and bad decisions?"

Andrea grabbed Dustin's belt loop and tugged him closer. "That sounds like a fun date with my boyfriend. Too bad we have a crime to solve."

"Indeed." Their lips brushed together, and heat crested off them in waves until Dustin's phone buzzed. He ended the kiss reluctantly to read the message. "It's from Kelly. She's parking now."

"She?" Andrea's eyebrows shot up. "You never told me that the PI was a woman."

"How sexist of you to assume otherwise," Dustin said with a sly grin.

Andrea would have retorted with something clever, but she was too tired to be witty. Besides, they were at the front of the line now, and it was time to order. A few minutes later, when she was picking up her venti Frappuccino with extra whip, a woman wearing jeans, cowboy boots, a country western shirt, and a blazer walked in. She was in her late fifties or early sixties; Andrea couldn't tell for certain. When the woman saw Dustin, she walked straight to him.

"Kelly Webster," she said, holding out her hand. "We talked over the phone."

"Thanks for taking the case." Dustin shook her hand and then introduced Andrea. "My girlfriend, Andrea Wint."

"Andrea Wint of the lost coins," said Kelly.

Andrea felt a smile tugging at the corners of her mouth. The way Kelly said that made her feel like she was the heroine of a historical romance novel. Maybe something with Scottish lairds or Vikings. She decided right there that she liked Kelly.

They sat down at a table with a good view across the street and waited.

CHAPTER
TWENTY-TWO

This was it. They were so close Dustin was sure he'd be able to see the smirk on Cade's face when he arrived. Dustin tried to pay attention as Kelly reviewed the dossier of information she'd collected that had already been shared with the police. There was the receipt from the appliance store showing the cash refund for the returned refrigerators. The credit card bill for the copper pipe Cade had stolen as well as pictures from the jobsite. The insurance appraisals for Andrea's coins, including the new accurate one for the 1907. But most damning of all was the video evidence from the shops in Ashland and San Carlos showing Cade attempting to sell stolen goods.

"What about Lisa?" Andrea asked. "Where does she fit into this?"

"She's a potential accomplice," said Kelly. "But right now, we don't have evidence of her actively trying to make the sale."

"How could she not be guilty?" Andrea pointed to a picture printed out from the San Carlos Coin Market video. "She's right there."

"We don't have proof that she knew the coins were stolen." Kelly's phone beeped, and she looked at the screen and frowned.

"Is that the police?" Dustin's muscles tensed.

"No, it's the RV park in Santa Monica where my fifth wheel is parked. They have to close the pool because of a health-and-safety issue. That usually means a kid pooped in the water."

"Yuck." Andrea wrinkled her nose.

"I hitched up my truck and started driving south as soon as I got the case," Kelly explained. "Being able to visit locations is important in my job because oftentimes informants will confide things in person that they won't tell you over the phone. But in this situation, that didn't necessarily give us the advantage. It was you, Andrea, and all that legwork you did calling coin shops and posting on forums pretending to be Gus McHenderson. All I had to do was connect the dots."

"You've worked hard on this." Dustin kissed Andrea's hand. "I'm glad you're on my team."

"Forever." She squeezed his fingertips.

"Back to Lisa," Dustin said, turning toward Kelly. "You don't think the police will charge her?"

"I'm not sure what they'll do." Kelly collected her papers. "It depends on if Cade rats her out or not. My guess is that she did know the coins were stolen, but she could say she didn't. We *think* she picked Cade up after the robbery in Port Inez and drove him to Port Angeles, but we don't know that for sure. That's for the prosecutor to unravel."

"Makes sense." Dustin grunted.

"What was that noise for?" Andrea asked.

Dustin shrugged. "I don't really care what happens to Lisa. As far as I'm concerned, she's another woman Cade screwed over."

"There!" Kelly pointed through the window. "That looks like him now."

Dustin watched a man with blond hair walk up to the front of the coin shop and ring the doorbell. The man glanced around nervously, then pulled something small out of his pocket and twirled it around. "Bingo," he growled. "He even has his lucky rabbit's foot with him."

The shop's door opened just wide enough for Cade to slide through, disappearing inside the store.

"Here we go," Andrea murmured. Underneath the table, she put her hand on Dustin's knee.

This was what they'd worked so hard to accomplish. Finally they had the opportunity to bring Cade to justice.

Kelly's phone rang, and she answered it. "Red van. Yes. I see it. That's you?"

Dustin could hear only Kelly's part of the conversation.

"Tell us when you're ready," said Kelly. "Yes, I'll stay on the line."

Minutes dragged by like hours. Seconds felt like eternity. Andrea's palm resting on his knee was the only thing keeping his legs from shaking. So much energy coursed through him that he could have run a marathon.

When a black-and-white police car showed up, sirens blaring, and parked in front of the coin shop, Dustin tasted victory. Two officers hopped out of the car, and a third emerged from the red van.

"Wonderful," said Kelly. "My clients will be right over to make the ID." She put down her phone. "They caught him. A plainclothes officer at the back of the shop is already making the arrest."

Dustin jumped up from the table without bothering to push in his chair. They flew out of the coffee shop and to the curb at record speed, then waited impatiently for the traffic signal to change in their favor. They were buzzed into the coin shop in time to hear an officer read Cade the tail end of his Miranda rights.

"Dustin?" Cade gasped, ignoring his right to be silent. "*You're* here?" A sneer spread across his lips.

"I wouldn't miss this for the world." Dustin's anger was a hot fire. His rage at what Cade had done consumed him.

Cade tried to jerk forward, but the officer tugging on his handcuffs held him back. "This is all a big misunderstanding," Cade babbled.

"Tell them, Dustin. Tell them I'm your brother-in-law and this is all a big mistake."

Dustin glared at him. "Like staging your own kidnapping was a mistake?"

"Or ripping my safe out of the wall and stealing my inheritance was a mistake?" Andrea asked.

"You've got this all wrong." Cade's gaze bounced from Dustin, to Andrea, and to the police officers like a Ping-Pong ball. "This is just a big misunderstanding."

"You asshole," Dustin said. "Do you know what you've put us through? What you've put my whole family through?" Dustin widened his stance. He was about to tell Cade he was a worthless piece of shit until he caught a glimpse of Kendal staring right back at him. She was there in Cade's face. Looking at Cade was like staring at a grown-up version of his niece. The fear in his eyes and the way his chin trembled made him look like he could crumple into tears at any second, just like Kendal had after Dustin had fished her homework folder out of the toilet. They both had the same bone structure too. Jane was in him as well, especially the way he pouted right now. If it weren't for the handcuffs, Cade might pitch forward like Jane did during one of her tantrums.

"Do you recognize this man?" the officer holding the tablet asked.

"Yes." Dustin nodded. "This is my brother-in-law, Cade Tolbert, who stole seven thousand two hundred dollars from an appliance store by claiming he worked for my sister's and my home-renovation business."

"And I recognize him as the handyman from the Harper Landing memory-care facility who overheard my dad talk about my hidden safe and coin collection," said Andrea.

Cade opened his mouth to say something but then closed it. Maybe he was finally realizing the gravity of his situation and had decided to shut up until he had a lawyer. The glare Cade shot Dustin was so searing it could have grilled steak.

"We need you to identify the coins as well," said the officer standing next to an old man wearing a bow tie behind the coin case.

Andrea walked up to the glass and examined the gold pieces one by one. "Yes. I believe these are mine. There seem to be five missing."

"Those might have already been sold," said Kelly. She opened up her dossier and pulled out a stapled packet. "Do you need a copy of the appraisal forms?" she asked the officer.

"No ma'am, we already have them."

"Can I have my coins back now?" Andrea asked.

"Sorry." The officer shook his head. "We'll need to take these away as evidence to establish chain of custody. If they are yours, and that seems highly likely, then you'll get them back eventually."

"You're Gus McHenderson," said the coin dealer. "Gus is you."

"That's right." Andrea grinned. "How'd you know?"

"Well, I didn't really, but you just admitted it," the dealer said in a voice that seemed like he was very pleased with himself. He slipped his fingers into the pocket of his dress shirt and handed her his business card. "Harold's my name. Rare coins are my game. I'm also a contributor to *The Numismatist*, and I think readers would like to hear about the recovery of your family collection. Can I write about it?"

"Yes. Absolutely." Andrea looked at the card and put it in her purse. "My father would love to know that his collection became famous."

"Because I made it famous," Cade blurted out. "Me! Cade Tolbert."

Harold removed his glasses and polished them with a cloth. "Oh, I don't think we need to mention your name in the article, Mr. Tolbert." He looked at Andrea and grinned. "I just thought of a title: 'Wint's Mint.' Catchy, am I right?"

Dustin, who had never in his wildest dreams imagined he would read a coin magazine someday, grinned. "It's brilliant."

EPILOGUE

Their home lit up like a gingerbread house with over three thousand twinkling white lights. It had taken Dustin all day to accomplish but was worth the effort when he saw Andrea's smile. She said he had gone overboard, but he pointed out that she hadn't exactly gone for minimalism inside either. That was true, but it wasn't her fault. Now completing the second trimester of pregnancy, she was in full-on nesting mode. She'd even gone so far as to ask Lydia for decorating tips, which was why their living room looked like it was straight from the holiday edition of the Pottery Barn catalog. The six-foot Douglas fir standing in the corner had a velvet tree skirt at the bottom embroidered with their last name: Karlsson.

Their summer wedding had been an intimate affair. Dustin hadn't cared where they held the ceremony, but when Andrea had said she wanted a backyard wedding at his childhood home so that Crystal and Josh could be there in spirit, he'd choked up. Andrea had wanted Tom to be there, too, but hadn't thought it would be possible. Escorting Tom away from the memory-care unit required a caregiver who was trustworthy, flexible, and willing to help Tom in the restroom. They'd both known they couldn't manage those things on their wedding day. But then Roger had volunteered to shepherd Tom, and Andrea had accepted with gratitude. When she and Dustin had stood under the tree canopy of century-old cedars, firs, and hemlocks, the people they loved most in the world had encircled them, watching them wed. Kendal's and Jane's flower girl dresses had matched Andrea's sundress.

"How long until dinner?" Dustin asked. "That roast has been tempting me all day."

"Let me check." Andrea took a quick peek at the thermometer in the prime rib. She'd purchased the biggest rib roast Costco sold and told Dustin to close his eyes and plug his ears when they got to the register so that he wouldn't know how much it cost.

"Need any help?" Nathan asked. He'd been wandering in and out of the kitchen all day like a lost puppy.

"No." Andrea took off her oven mitts. "I told you—this is your day off from cooking. Pour yourself a drink, and try to relax."

"Yeah," said Heidi, who was halfway into a glass of wine. "Stop being such a workaholic."

"Look who's talking," Nathan shot back. "Didn't you and Dustin sign papers for a new flip three days ago?"

"That doesn't count." Heidi grabbed a shrimp from the appetizer buffet on the counter. "I've always wanted to renovate a farmhouse, so this is more like a grand opportunity."

Dustin grinned. "It'll be a fun one all right. This is your chance to design with your favorite aesthetic while also remaining true to the bones of the house."

"Wait until you see my vision board." Heidi had a mischievous glint in her eyes. "I finally get my farmhouse sink and shiplap."

"Don't talk to me about shiplap." Dustin groaned. "It's Christmas. At least give me this one day."

"It's going to look like Joanna Gaines exploded in there when I'm done." Heidi pinched his arm.

"Ouch!" Dustin yelped.

"You're going to love it." Heidi laughed.

"Do you see what I have to put up with?" Dustin asked Andrea. "Why is she your best friend?"

"Because she's always right." Andrea checked the timer on the pressure cooker with the green beans. "You know that."

Dustin slid up behind her and gently wrapped his arms around her, laying his hands on her stomach. "How are you feeling?" he asked softly. "Are you sure you shouldn't sit down? You've been on your feet all day."

She looked over her shoulder and up into his green eyes. "I feel fine right now, but I promise I will claim exhaustion when it's time to do the dishes."

"That's fair." He kissed the sensitive spot behind her ear, making her giggle. "Thank you for this," he whispered.

"For what?"

"For all your hard work making Christmas so special for my family."

"Thank you for sharing your family with me." Andrea turned around and hugged him the best she could with her growing baby bump between them. "I love you so much," she said.

"I love you too." Dustin's lips met hers with a kiss so delicious that it would put a holiday feast to shame.

"Ahem," said Heidi. "Don't be gross."

"Sorry," Andrea said, blushing.

"I'm not." Dustin kissed her again, but this time it was a chaste peck on the cheek.

"We're out of sparkling cider," said Leanne, entering the kitchen. "Kendal drank a whole bottle when I wasn't looking. Sorry about that."

"No problem," said Andrea. "We have more in the garage. Why don't you help your brother bring some in, along with the Jell-O that's chilling out there?"

"Sure," Leanne said with a shrug.

"That would be perfect." Dustin shot Andrea a grateful look. His relationship with Leanne had improved slightly now that Cade had filed for divorce. Nobody had seen that one coming. It had nearly broken Leanne when she'd found out, but she'd moved forward with a gritty strength that was pure Karlsson. After finally acknowledging that he had robbed and betrayed her, Leanne had hired a lawyer and filed a court order to freeze their remaining assets. Cade was tangled in the criminal justice system and had not yet gone to trial. He'd already siphoned off three million dollars to places unknown, but there was still a million of the settlement money at stake, and Leanne's lawyer was hopeful she'd get half of it back someday. Until then, Leanne had reopened Crystal's Kids so she could earn a living and stay home with her daughters at the same time. It made Dustin nervous that it was an unlicensed day care at the moment, but Leanne would finish her online schooling soon, and the business would be officially certified.

Dustin led Leanne through the house and out to the garage. He flipped on the lights so they wouldn't trip. His Ford truck and Andrea's Nissan Leaf took up most of the space, but there was room for the row of oak cabinets against the back wall. He'd moved them from his old house before he and Heidi had renovated that kitchen. The Karlsson home had become a rental for now. Nobody could bear selling it.

"Brrr . . ." Leanne rubbed her arms. "It's cold in here."

"Sorry about that." Dustin walked to the cabinets where the bottles of sparkling cider and three crudely wrapped packages sat waiting on the counter. "Maybe this will help." He picked up the first present and handed it to her. "I wanted to give this to you in private before things got too hectic in there." He couldn't wait to see her open it.

"What is it?" she asked. "And who wrapped this thing, my day care kids?"

"I did," he said indignantly. "And I even curled the ribbon."

"Kind of," she said, laughing. "At least you curled part of it."

"Everyone's a critic. Go on; open it." His heart stopped as she tore back the paper.

"Wow, Dustin. An old wool sweater." She unfolded it. "With only two moth holes. Um . . . thanks."

"Yeah." Crestfallen that she obviously hated it, Dustin scratched the back of his head. "Maybe someone can fix those for you. Not Andrea—she's horrible with yarn—but someone else."

"It's a nice shade of green."

"It's the same color as Dad's eyes. That's why Mom bought it for him."

"What?" Leanne looked up.

"Yeah. I wish I could have given you his red buffalo flannel coat, the one you said you remembered, but he was wearing it the day he died."

"This sweater was *Dad's*?"

"You mean you didn't know? We have a picture of him wearing it that you've probably seen."

"A lot of those pictures are faded, and you can't see the colors."

Dustin nodded. "Good point. I found this in the attic when I was searching for that box of toys I gave to the girls. It's the only item of Dad's clothing that we have left." He took it from her and held it up to her shoulders. "When you wear this, it'll be like Dad's giving you a hug."

"Dustin." Leanne dabbed tears away from her cheeks. "I don't know what to say. Thank you." She embraced the sweater and held it tight.

"Do you like it?"

"I *love* it."

"Good," said Dustin, feeling relieved. "Now for the second present."

"Wait. I have something to say."

"What?"

"I've been meaning to tell you this for a while, ever since you gave Kendal and Jane that box of toys." Leanne hugged the sweater tighter. "Now that it's just the girls and I, um . . ."

"Go on."

Leanne stared at a moth hole in the sweater. "I can see how Kendal and Jane were picking up some bad habits from Cade. Kendal thinks she knows better than everyone, and Jane has a loose definition of property ownership. We're working on that with our family therapist." Leanne looked up at him. "But so often in therapy the good things that come out of their mouths are things *you* taught them. 'Don't call people names. Protect your sister. Women deserve to be treated well.'" Leanne rolled her shoulders back. "They even remind me to put on my seat belt before I've had the chance to close my car door."

"That one's from Heidi," Dustin said, his voice hoarse with emotion. "And I'm proud to be a positive influence in their lives. Thanks for sharing that with me. You're teaching them good life skills too."

Leanne nodded. "I'm trying. It's a process." She smiled. "Okay, enough of that. I want to open another present."

Dustin grinned. "Good. But I should warn you, by this point in the wrapping process, I'd totally given up on curling the ribbon. It's a huge waste of resources, if you ask me." He handed her the parcel.

"Only you would say that." Leanne blew her nose on a tissue before opening the next gift. "Is this what I think it is?" she asked as the white fabric spilled over.

"Yes, it is." Dustin gazed lovingly at his mother's tablecloth. "I really wanted to keep it for myself mainly because of the hedgehog on it but—"

"There's a hedgehog?"

"Yeah. Isn't that something? But anyhow, I know Mom would want you to have it. I have other ways of remembering her. Just promise you'll keep it away from cranberry sauce."

"Will do." Leanne folded it carefully and clutched it with the sweater. "What's in the third package?"

"Oh, uh . . . that one's for my baby girl. I'm going to let Andrea open it later."

"And? What's in it?"

Dustin smiled sheepishly. "My old toy tool bench. I found that in the attic too. Hopefully my daughter loves it someday."

"I'm sure she will." Leanne hugged him. "Especially with such good parents to play with her."

The door opened, and Kendal poked her head inside. "Mom? Are you in there? Jane spilled the bowl of olives when she was trying to put them on her fingers."

302

"Oh boy." Leanne pulled away. "I'm coming."

"Grab a bottle of cider, will you? I'll be right there," said Dustin.

After Leanne left, Dustin pressed his palm on the oak cabinets like he could feel two heartbeats pulsing through the wood. "You're not here with me for Christmas, but these cabinets still look like a million bucks," he whispered. "Way to go on that. All of us are together, and we're about to eat a feast like you wouldn't believe. Just don't ask how much it cost because my own wife won't tell me. Yeah. I know. But you'd love Andrea even though she's not frugal. She's already corrupted me, because guess what we're doing tomorrow? All of us—the whole Karlsson crew—are going to a Seahawks game. I used some of the settlement money to pay for it, so thanks for the amazing Christmas gift. Kickoff's at 1:05 p.m., and don't be late. Okay? I'll be looking for you in the stands. I know you'll be there somehow."

A moment—or maybe a lifetime—later, Dustin wedged a bottle of sparkling cider under his arm so that he could use both hands to carry his mom's Spode bowl of Jell-O into the house. When he came inside, he set them down on the refinished dining room table. It had taken just the right type of sandpaper and stain to make it shine, but Ethan Allen himself couldn't have done better.

"You sure were gone a long time," said Nathan, who was nursing his drink in the kitchen.

"Is everything okay?" Andrea asked.

"It's great. I just need a glass of water." Dustin held a cup by the water dispenser on the fridge and stared at the burgeoning collection of photos. Their wedding day, feeding each other cake. Their honeymoon on Orcas Island in the Airbnb they'd rented. The article from *The Numismatist* with Tom's 1907 double eagle front and center. A picture Jane had drawn that was supposed to be a hedgehog but looked more like a small pig with a skin condition—that one was Andrea's favorite.

"We should take a photo," Andrea said. "Oh! Right as I said that, the baby kicked."

"Can I feel?"

Andrea nodded and placed Dustin's hands on the spot where they both could feel the flutter.

Dustin grinned. "She'll be ready for soccer soon."

"Or a chorus line." The pressure cooker sputtered, catching Andrea's attention. "The countdown to serving dinner is on. We'll have to act fast if we want that group photo before we eat."

"Good point." Dustin looked at Nathan. "How about a whistle to rally the troops? You said you wanted something to do."

"On it." Nathan circled his fingers and blew.

A couple of minutes later the whole family assembled in the dining room. Andrea, Heidi, Lydia, and Leanne sat on the window seat with Dustin and Nathan at their feet holding Kendal and Jane. Roger stood a few steps beyond holding the camera.

"You should get in the picture too," Andrea told Roger. "Use the timer."

"I'll get in the next one," he offered. "Let's get one of the Karlssons first."

Lydia attempted to stand. "In that case—"

"Oh no you don't," said Dustin, sitting loyally at her feet. "You definitely belong in the picture."

"Okay," Lydia said. "But are you sure this window seat is strong enough to hold so many people?"

"It'll hold," said Dustin. "I built it myself."

Andrea put her hand on Dustin's shoulder. He leaned against her knees like they were both rooted together in the center of the picture.

"Say cheese, Karlsson family," Roger said as he lifted up the camera.

When the flash went off, Dustin smiled with an intensity that never faded. History had made them, and the future was full of promise. But right now, in this moment, the present was glorious, and Dustin intended to enjoy every minute of it.

AUTHOR'S NOTE

This book is about history: the personal histories of the characters, the history of the Kitsap and Olympic peninsulas, and the numismatic history of coins. My family went on a road trip to explore the locations, and even though I'm not a gambler, I won $184 playing the slots! That's not the only way I'm lucky. I was lucky enough to fall in love with my husband, Doug Bardsley, over twenty years ago and listen to him when he suggested we move to his home state of Washington.

When tourists travel to Washington, they usually visit Seattle and perhaps Mount Rainier. But Washington is so much more than the Space Needle. If you ever come to Washington State, consider visiting the Kitsap and Olympic peninsulas. You could rent a car at Sea-Tac Airport and complete an entire loop, just like Dustin and Andrea did.

Olympic National Park is one of the most beautiful places in the entire country and features majestic mountains, rainforests, hot springs, beaches, and lakes. The camping is spectacular, but there are also lodges and motels to accommodate you. Bring layers and a raincoat because the weather can be unpredictable, but the old-growth trees are worth it.

Ocean Shores is a fun place to rent a house for the weekend, or perhaps stay at the Quinault Beach Resort and Casino like Dustin and Andrea do in the book. Yes, it's smoke-free and family friendly. Make sure to get a room with an ocean view. You could ride horses on the beach, fly kites, and rent electric bicycles. Fishing expeditions and whale-watching excursions leave from Grays Harbor.

If you're traveling with teenagers, Forks is worth a pit stop so you can take a picture with Bella Swan's two red trucks from the *Twilight* franchise. In Aberdeen, you can pay tribute to Kurt Cobain. Sequim is the place to tour lavender farms, and Port Angeles has beautiful murals that depict the history of the Lower Elwha Klallam Tribe as well as pioneers and logging.

The Kitsap Peninsula is where you could book a stay at the Suquamish Clearwater Casino Resort and visit the Suquamish Museum. There is an incredible park right next to the museum that is the perfect place for kids to blow off steam. A short drive away is the town of Poulsbo, which will make you think you're in Norway. Bainbridge Island is also close and home to the Japanese Exclusion Memorial and the Haleets boulder, inscribed with ancient petroglyphs. If your heart yearns to see a town like Port Inez, be sure to visit Kingston, Port Angeles, or Port Orchard. Have I convinced you to book a trip yet? Doug jokes that I should get a job with the Washington State Tourism Board.

I share this with you because traveling with my family is important to me, and I learned that lesson from my grandma, Darlene Woodson, who died after living with Alzheimer's disease. Before she had dementia, my grandma took me on trips all around the world. We visited Italy after I graduated from college and Tahiti when my son was three years old. We cruised the Bahamas and the Caribbean, snorkeled in Hawaii, and explored the pyramids of Mexico. My grandma didn't buy gold coins. Instead, she gifted her family with a treasure trove of travel memories. I think about my grandma every time I walk past her china cabinet, which now graces my living room. Sometimes, when I open the doors and take a deep breath next to the dishes, I can still smell Thanksgiving.

ACKNOWLEDGMENTS

This book would not be possible without the help of an entire team of people bringing it to your bookshelf or Kindle. Huge thanks to my agent, Liza Fleissig of the Liza Royce Agency. Thanks to my editors at Montlake: Alison Dasho, for your enthusiasm, expertise, and hedgehog wisdom; Krista Stroever, for pointing out ways I could deepen the book in ways I never saw; and to Mindi Machart and Stephanie Chou for your keen copyediting and proofreading skills. Writers who read early versions of my manuscript and offered valuable feedback include Sharman Badgett-Young, Maan Gabriel, and Laura Moe. My critique partner, Penelope Wright, helped in an enormous way by reading it multiple times and providing expert notes. My son, Bryce Bardsley, fine-tuned critical scenes as well.

Writing can be a solitary endeavor, but I've been blessed by friends in the writing community who are always ready to listen, commiserate, and cheer me on. Thank you to the 2021 Debuts, the Nine Livers, the Sweet Sixteens, my agency sibs, and so many more.

In April of 2021, while in the middle of writing my first draft, I was struck with transient global amnesia and landed in the hospital. For about forty-eight hours, I couldn't remember the previous six months. The irony of writing a book about memories and losing my memory is not lost on me. My family and friends were extremely patient, and I made a full recovery. When I went back to my manuscript, I was able to understand the Wint family in new ways—not just as a person who had cared for a family member with memory loss but as someone who had experienced it herself. Every time I write a book, I put a piece of my heart into it. This book has a piece of my brain as well.

Finally, thank you to my readers. I appreciate you tremendously. If you enjoyed your visit to Port Inez, I hope you'll consider hopping on the ferry and taking a jaunt over to my Harper Landing books as well. There's a delicious cup of frozen yogurt at Sweet Bliss with your name on it.

ABOUT THE AUTHOR

Photo © 2021 Rachel Breakey

Jennifer Bardsley believes in friendship, true love, and the everlasting power of books. A graduate of Stanford University, she lives in Edmonds, Washington, with her husband and two children. Bardsley's column I Brake for Moms has appeared in the *Everett Herald* every week since 2012. She also writes young adult paranormal romance under the pen name Louise Cypress. When Bardsley is not writing books or camping with her Girl Scout troop, you can find her walking from her house to the beach every chance she gets. To find out more, visit www.jenniferbardsley.com or join her Facebook reader group, "Jennifer Bardsley's Book Sneakers."